"And are you glad you took the job?"

"So far," Vanessa replied. "What about you? Do you wish you'd offered it to someone else?"

"Giving you the job was one of the smartest decisions I've ever made." Conall gently smoothed her hair away from her cheek. "And coming on this trip with you was even smarter."

By now her breathing was coming in shallow sips and she had to swallow before she could finally form one word. "Why?"

"Because it's opened my eyes. And I'm beginning to see all the things I've been missing."

"Conall." His name passed her lips as she hesitantly pressed a hand against his chest. "This... You... I don't understand."

"That makes two of us."

"But we—"

"Don't talk," he whispered. "Talking won't change the fact that I want to kiss you."

Lessons in Baby Wrangling

USA TODAY BESTSELLING AUTHOR

STELLA BAGWELL

&

NEW YORK TIMES BESTSELLING AUTHOR

TINA LEONARD

Previously published as *Daddy's Double Duty*
and *The Rebel Cowboy's Quadruplets*

 HARLEQUIN®

ISBN-13: 978-1-335-47371-4

Recycling programs
for this product may
not exist in your area.

Lessons in Baby Wrangling

Copyright © 2022 by Harlequin Enterprises ULC

Daddy's Double Duty
First published in 2011. This edition published in 2022.
Copyright © 2011 by Stella Bagwell

The Rebel Cowboy's Quadruplets
First published in 2014. This edition published in 2022.
Copyright © 2014 by Tina Leonard

For questions and comments about the quality of this book,
please contact us at CustomerService@Harlequin.com.

Harlequin Enterprises ULC
22 Adelaide St. West, 41st Floor
Toronto, Ontario M5H 4E3, Canada
www.Harlequin.com

Printed in U.S.A.

CONTENTS

After writing more than one hundred books for Harlequin, **Stella Bagwell** still finds it exciting to create new stories and bring her characters to life. She loves all things Western and has been married to her own real cowboy for forty-four years. Living on the south Texas coast, she also enjoys being outdoors and helping her husband care for the horses, cats and dog that call their small ranch home. The couple has one son, who teaches high school mathematics and is also an athletic director. Stella loves hearing from readers. Contact her at stellabagwell@gmail.com.

Books by Stella Bagwell

Harlequin Special Edition

Men of the West

Her Kind of Doctor
The Arizona Lawman
Her Man on Three Rivers Ranch
A Ranger for Christmas
His Texas Runaway
Home to Blue Stallion Ranch
The Rancher's Best Gift
Her Man Behind the Badge
His Forever Texas Rose
The Baby That Binds Them

The Fortunes of Texas: The Lost Fortunes

Guarding His Fortune

Montana Mavericks: The Lonelyhearts Ranch

The Little Maverick Matchmaker

Visit the Author Profile page at Harlequin.com for more titles.

Daddy's Double Duty

STELLA BAGWELL

To my late father,
Louis Copeland Cook,
who always said don't do anything
unless you intend to do it right.
I hope he thinks I have.

Chapter 1

His secretary was crying!

Conall Donovan stared at the woman behind the cherrywood desk. Vanessa Valdez had been in his employ for more than two months and during that time she'd been nothing but cool and professional. He could hardly imagine what had brought about these waterworks. In the past hour, he hadn't even yelled once! And even if he had, it wouldn't have been directed at her. She was the epitome of a perfect, professional secretary.

Cautiously, he approached the desk. "Vanessa? Is something wrong?"

With one slender hand dabbing a tissue to her cheek, the petite brunette glanced at him. At thirty-five, she looked more like twenty-five, Conall thought. And though he wouldn't describe her as gorgeous, she was an attractive woman with honey-brown hair brushing the tops of her shoulders and curling in pretty wisps around her head. Usually, her large brown eyes were soft and luminous but presently her eyes were full of tears.

"I'm sorry," she said in a strained voice. "It's… I… Something has happened."

"Your father? Has he taken ill?" he demanded.

Vanessa paused and he could see her throat working as she tried to swallow. The sight of her discomposure struck him unexpectedly hard. In spite of her being an old family acquaintance, they hardly shared a close bond. For the most part, the woman kept to herself. The only reason he knew she'd lost her mother two years ago, and that her aging father now resided in a nursing home, was because he happened to attend the same small church where her parents had been regular members. Still, these past months, Vanessa had become a quiet and dependable fixture in his life and he'd come to respect her dedication to this job and the subtle finesse she used with clients in order to make his life easier.

"No," she answered. "It's not my father."

When she failed to elaborate, Conall fought back an impatient sigh. He hardly had time to play mind reader.

"Do you need to take the rest of the afternoon off?" he asked bluntly. There was still a hell of a lot of work that he needed finished by the end of the day, but if necessary he'd somehow manage without her. Even if it meant calling on his mother, Fiona, to fill in for the remainder of the afternoon.

Shaking her head, his secretary sniffed and tried to straighten her shoulders. Even so, Conall could see tears sparkling upon her smooth cheeks and he was shocked at the sudden urge he felt to round the desk and wipe them away.

Hell, Conall, you've never been good at consoling women. Just ask your ex-wife. Besides, women and tears don't affect your iron heart. Not anymore.

While he shoved that unbidden thought away, she finally answered in a ragged voice, "I—I'll be all right, Conall. Just give me a few moments to…get over the shock."

Shock? As usual, the phone had been ringing all afternoon. The Diamond D Ranch was a huge conglomerate, with business connections all over the world. With it being the middle of summer, they were in the busy height of Thoroughbred racing season. His office was only one of several set in a modern brick building situated north of the ranch yard and west of the main ranch house. His younger brother Liam, the ranch's horse trainer, also had his own office along with a secretary, and then there was the general accounting for the ranch, which took up several rooms. As for Conall's job, he rarely saw a quiet moment during working hours and the overflow of correspondence kept his secretary extremely busy. Especially now that he'd also assumed the job of keeping the Golden Spur Mine operations running smoothly.

"Look, Vanessa, I realize I'm asking you to handle an undue amount of work for one human being. But it won't always be like this. I have plans to hire an assistant for you, just as soon as I have a chance to go over a few résumés."

Her brown eyes widened even more. "Oh, no, Conall, it's not the work!" She gestured toward the piles of correspondence lying about on her desk. "I can easily handle this. I just received a call from Las Vegas," she attempted to explain. "It was…horrible news. A dear friend has passed away. And I…well, I just can't believe she's gone. She was—"

Suddenly sobs overtook the remainder of her words and Conall could no longer stop himself from skirting the desk and taking a steadying hold on her trembling shoulders.

"I'm very sorry, Vanessa."

Averting her face from him, she whispered, "I'm okay. Really, I am."

Whether she was trying to reassure him or herself, or the both of them, Conall didn't know. In any case, she was clearly an emotional wreck and he had to do something to help her, even if it was wrong.

"No, you're hardly okay," he said gruffly. "You're shaking. Let me help you over to the couch."

With firm hands, he drew her up from the rolling desk chair and with an arm at her waist, guided her to a long leather couch positioned along the far wall.

"Just sit and try to relax," he ordered as he eased her small frame down. "I'll be back in a minute."

Once she was safely settled, Conall hurriedly crossed the room and stepped into his private office, where he kept an assortment of drinks to offer visiting businessmen. After pouring a mug half-full of coffee, he splashed in a hefty amount of brandy and carried it out to her.

"Here," he told her. "Drink this. All of it."

With trembling hands wrapped around the heavy cup, she tilted the contents to her lips. After a few careful sips that made her gasp and cough, she lowered it and cast him an accusing glance.

"That has alcohol in it!"

"Not nearly enough," he said dryly.

"It's more than enough for me." Straightening her shoulders, she offered the cup back to him. "Thank you. I can talk now."

Relieved to see a faint bit of color returning to her face, Conall took the cup and after placing it on the floor, he eased down beside her. "All right," he said gently. "Tell me what happened to your friend."

Closing her eyes, she pressed slender fingers against her forehead. Conall couldn't help but notice the long sweep of her lashes as they settled against her damp cheeks. Her complexion reminded him of a pink pearl bathed in golden sunlight and not for the first time he thought how her skin was the most fetching thing about her. Smooth and kissable.

Now why the hell was he thinking that sort of thing, especially at a time like this? Kissing a woman's soft skin was all in his past. And that was where it was going to stay.

With her eyes still closed, she began to speak. "I became friends with Hope Benson not long after I arrived in Las Vegas. We both worked as cocktail waitresses in the Lucky Treasure casino."

Conall was stunned. He'd not known that Vanessa had ever worked as a cocktail waitress. Not that it mattered. Everyone had to start somewhere. And she'd obviously climbed the ladder. A few months ago, when she'd left Nevada, she'd been a private secretary to a casino executive.

"I didn't realize you ever worked as a waitress," he mused, speaking his thoughts out loud.

The guttural sound in her throat was self-deprecating. "What did you expect, Conall? I left Hondo Valley with nothing. It took lots of long, hard hours to put myself through college."

Of course he'd known that Vanessa was from a poor family. She was the same age as his sister Maura, and the two women had been good friends ever since elementary school. During those years, Vanessa had often visited the ranch. Being two years older, Conall hadn't paid much attention to her. With the house full of six Donovan kids, there were always plenty of friends hanging around and Vanessa had simply been one more. The main thing he recalled about her was that she'd been very quiet, almost to the point of being a wallflower.

After Conall had gone away to college, he'd heard in passing that Vanessa had moved to Nevada. That had been fifteen years ago and since then he'd not heard anything else about his sister's old friend. In fact, she'd completely slipped his mind until two months ago, when she'd called him about the secretarial job.

She'd moved back to Hondo Valley to stay, she'd told him, and she was looking for a job. He was secretly ashamed to admit that he'd not expected Vanessa to be qualified. As a teenager, she'd seemed like the shy, homemaker sort, who'd want to devote her life to raising a house full of kids and keeping a husband happy. He couldn't imagine her as a career woman. But out of courtesy to his sister, he'd invited her to come out to the ranch for an interview. When she'd walked into his office, Conall had been stunned to see a very professional young woman presenting him with an equally impressive résumé. He'd hired her on the spot and since that time had not once regretted his decision.

The soft sigh escaping her lips caught his attention and he watched her eyes open, then level on his face. For the moment her tears had disappeared, but in their place he saw something that amounted to panic. A strange emotion to be experiencing over a friend's demise, he couldn't help thinking.

"Sorry," she said. "I didn't mean to sound defensive. God knows how He's blessed me. And now...I just don't know what to think, Conall. You see, Hope was pregnant. Something happened after she went into labor—I'm not exactly sure what. The lawyer didn't go into details. Except that she had to have an emergency C-section. Shortly afterward, she died from some sort of complications. I assume it had something to do with her heart condition—a genetic childhood thing. But she always appeared healthy and I thought the doctors were keeping everything under control. In fact, each time I'd talked with her, she'd assured me that she and the babies were doing fine."

Conall's attention latched on to one word. "Babies? Are you talking plural?"

Vanessa nodded. "Twins. A boy and a girl. They were born three days ago and Hope's lawyer has just now had a chance to go over the legalities of her will and wishes."

"And what does this have to do with you?" Conall asked.

Across the room the telephone on Vanessa's desk began to ring. She started to rise to answer it, but Conall caught her shoulder with a firm hand. "Forget the phone," he ordered. "Whoever it is will call back or leave a message. I want to hear the rest of this."

Groaning, Vanessa dropped her head and shook it

back and forth as though she was in a dream. "It's un-believable, Conall! Hope wanted me to have custody of her babies. I—I'm to be their mother."

"Mother?" The word burst from Conall's mouth be-fore he could stop it. "Are you…serious?"

Her head shot up and for a brief moment she scowled at him. "Very serious. Why? Do you think I'm inca-pable of being a mother?"

A grimace tightened his lips. Leave it to a woman to misread his words, he thought. "I don't doubt your abilities, Vanessa. I'm sure you have…great motherly instincts. I was questioning the validity of your friend's wishes. Isn't the father around?"

Her shoulders slumped as she thrust a shaky hand through her hair. "The father was only in Hope's life for a brief period before they went their separate ways. When she learned that she was pregnant, she contacted him with the news, but he wanted nothing to do with her or the babies. Seems as though he was already pay-ing a hefty amount of child support to his ex-wife and he wasn't keen on adding more to his responsibilities. By then Hope had already come to the conclusion that he wasn't the sort of man she'd ever want back in her life. And she certainly didn't want him to have any claims to the babies. When she confronted him with legal documents, he was only too glad to sign away his parental rights."

"What a bastard," Conall muttered.

Vanessa sighed. "I knew she was making a mistake when she first got involved with the creep. But she re-ally fell hard for him. Poor thing, she believed he loved her and she desperately wanted a big family. You see, she was adopted and didn't have many relatives."

"What about her parents?"

"If you mean her real parents, she never looked for them. She considered the Bensons to be her true parents. But when Hope was still very young, they were killed in the Loma Prieta earthquake in California," she said ruefully. "Luckily, Hope escaped being physically injured, but I don't think she ever got over the emotional loss of her parents."

"Damn. Sounds like your friend didn't have an easy life."

"No. Life is never easy for some," she sadly agreed. "Hope was forty-two. She figured this would be her last and only chance to have children. That's why she risked carrying the babies. Even though doctors had warned her about being pregnant with her type of heart condition, she wanted them desperately."

"Had you discussed any of this with your friend?" Conall asked. "I mean, about you becoming their mother if something happened to her?"

Vanessa nodded glumly. "At the very beginning of her pregnancy Hope asked me to be their godmother. I agreed. How could I not? The two of us had been good friends for a long time. We…went through some tough times together. And I wanted to reassure her that no matter what, I'd see that the babies would be well cared for. But I also kept telling her that she was going to be okay—that everything with her and the babies would be fine. I wanted her to concentrate on the future she was going to have with her children." Tears once again filled her eyes. "Oh, Conall, I didn't think… I refused to believe that Hope might die."

Conall hated himself for not knowing the right words to ease the grief that was clearly ripping her apart. But he'd learned with Nancy that he wasn't good at dealing with women's problems.

"None of us ever wants to consider losing someone we're close to, Vanessa. But we can't go around thinking the worst. Where would that get us?"

Where indeed, Vanessa wondered dazedly. Swallowing at the painful lump in her throat, she rose to her feet and wandered aimlessly across the room.

For years now, she'd desperately wanted children. But as she'd struggled to obtain a degree in business management, she'd set aside having a family. Then when she'd finally achieved that goal, she'd slowly begun to work her way off the casino floor and into the business offices. First as a simple file clerk, then on to secretarial assistant, then a jump to office manager, and finally a great leap to personal secretary to the CEO of Lucky Treasures. During that climb, she'd met her now ex-husband, and she'd believed her dreams of having a family of her own were finally going to become a reality. But Jeff had turned out to be nothing but a hanger-on, a man only too happy to let his wife support him while he went his free and fancy way.

Vanessa supposed it was a good thing that children had never come from their short marriage. But since the divorce, she'd grieved long and hard for what hadn't been and prayed that someday her fate would change. Still, she'd never expected to become a mother in this shocking fashion and the news was almost too much for her to absorb.

"I suppose you're right, Conall. We can't dwell on what might go wrong. But I—" She stopped in front of the huge picture window that framed a view of the mountain ridge that ran along the north edge of the massive horse ranch. "Right now I'm...stunned. In the next few days, the lawyer expects me to be in Vegas to pick up the babies! There's so much I'm going to have to do! I live in my parents' house. Do you remember it?"

Vaguely, Conall thought. It had been a long time since he'd driven through that mountainous area northeast of the Diamond D, but he did recall the tiny stucco home where the Valdez family had resided for so many years. The place had always needed work. And to give him credit, Mr. Valdez had done the best he could on a carpenter's salary. But his four sons had been the worthless sort, never lifting a hand to help their parents or themselves. As far as Conall knew, Vanessa's brothers were all gone from the area now and all he could think was good riddance. She didn't need any of them trying to mooch her hard-earned money.

"Yes, I remember," Conall told her. "Are you living there by yourself? I mean, do you have enough extra room to accommodate the babies?"

"It's just me living there," she replied, "so there's enough room. But the place isn't equipped to handle two infants! You see, I came back to Hondo Valley, so that I'd be around to see after my father's needs. I know he has great medical care in the nursing home, but he needs my emotional support—especially now that Mama is gone. And since I'm divorced now I never dreamed about raising a family there! Dear heaven, there are so many things I'll have to change—buy—to make a nursery for the babies!"

She jerked with surprise when she felt his hands fold over the back of her shoulders. She'd not heard him walk up behind her, but even if she'd been warned of his approach, his touch would have been just as jolting to her senses. Conall Donovan was like no man she'd ever known. For a time, when she'd been a sophomore in high school and he a senior, she'd had an enormous crush on him. He'd been one of those rare guys who'd possessed brains and brawn. He'd also been a perfect gentleman, who'd been nothing but nice and polite to his sister's poor friend. Now after all these years, he was her employer, and she'd done her best to forget about the crush. Until a few minutes ago, when he'd touched her for the very first time.

"Tell me, Vanessa, do you want these babies in your life?"

The question caused her to whirl around to face him and just as quickly she wished she'd kept her back to him. The man's presence was always overwhelming, but up close like this, it was downright rattling her already ragged senses.

Nearly black hair lay in undisciplined waves about his head, while one errant hank teased a cool gray eye that peered at her beneath a heavy black brow. His features were large, rough and edged with a haggardness that could only come from working long, hard hours without enough rest. His clothes, which ranged from faded jeans to designer suits, always fit his tall, well-honed body as though they'd been tailored for him. And probably had been, she thought wryly. He was certainly rich enough to afford such an extravagance.

As far as Vanessa was concerned, she always thought of Conall Donovan as dark, dangerous and delicious. And something totally beyond her reach. And standing only inches away from him like this only reinforced those descriptions of the man.

Nervously licking her lips, she attempted to answer

his question. "Of course I want the babies! There's nothing I want more." She didn't tell him that during her short marriage she'd wanted children, but her husband had insisted he loved her too much to want to share her with a child. Now Vanessa very nearly gagged when she thought of how phony those words had been. Jeff hadn't loved her. He'd only loved himself. But Conall didn't want to hear about the personal mistakes she'd made. Besides, they were far too humiliating to share with a man like him.

"I've always wanted children. And I want Hope's twins to be loved. I'm positive that I can give them that love and raise them as if I gave birth to them myself. But I'm not sure how I can handle all the changes I need to make right now. I have very little time and—"

"Whoa! Slow down, Vanessa. Let's take one thing at a time," he said. "What do you need to do first?"

Behind her, the phone began to ring again, but the subtle change in his expression was telling her to, once again, forget the telephone.

Turning her palms upward, she tried to breathe normally and assure herself that this man's sexual aura wasn't going to suffocate her. "I suppose the first thing is to go to Vegas and collect the babies. They've already been released from the hospital and placed in temporary care at a Catholic orphanage."

With a dour frown, he turned away from her and began to pace back and forth in front of her desk. Momentarily relieved by the space between them, Vanessa drew in a much-needed breath.

"I'm sure they're being well cared for," he said suddenly. "But I'm certain you'll feel better once we fetch the children back here as soon as possible."

We? Where had that come from? This was her problem. Not his. But that wasn't entirely true, she reminded herself. Conall was depending on her to keep his office running smoothly. Bringing two infants all the way from Vegas and getting them settled was going to chop into her work time. Naturally, this whole thing was going to affect him, too, she thought sickly. And what was that going to do to her job? A job that she'd quickly come to love, and now, more than ever, desperately needed.

"I'm sorry, Conall. I suppose I'll have to ask for time off while I make arrangements to fly out and collect the twins. If you feel you need to let me go permanently," she added ruefully, "then I'll understand."

Stopping in his tracks, he scowled at her. "Let you go? What the hell, Vanessa? Do you think Donovans fire our employees whenever they need help?"

Seeing she'd offended him, she drew in a deep breath and blew it out. "I didn't mean it like that. You obviously have tons of work to deal with. You can't do it alone and you put your trust in me to be here every day. I can't expect you to suffer just because I have a problem."

He waved a dismissive hand through the air. "This isn't like you're asking for time off to go on a shopping binge or some other frivolous excursion," he barked, then resumed pacing. "I'll deal with the problems here in the office. Mother will step in your place for the time being. As for me, I suppose I could ask Dad to deal with my most pressing obligations. He doesn't know anything about the mining business. But he can always call me with questions," he went on, more to himself than to her. "I'll discuss this with my parents tonight. In the meantime, you get on the phone and buy plane tickets for tomorrow. You can be ready by then, can't you?"

Vanessa was accustomed to his rapid-fire orders. Some days he rattled them off as though she were a tape recorder. But this afternoon, she'd been knocked off-kilter and the sudden personal attention Conall was giving her wasn't helping her brain snap into action. She stared at him with confusion.

"Tickets? Pardon me, Conall, but I only need one round-trip ticket."

Walking back to her, he held up two fingers. "You need to purchase two tickets. I'm going with you."

She gasped and he smiled.

"What's wrong?" he asked. "Afraid you'll fall asleep on the plane and I'll see you with your mouth open?"

Was he saying something about her mouth? she wondered fuzzily. And had something gone wrong with the room's thermostat? Sweat was popping out on her forehead and upper lip. Her legs felt oddly weak and there was a loud rushing noise in her ears.

"Conall— I—"

The remainder of her words were never uttered as she slumped forward and straight into his arms.

Chapter 2

"Poor little thing. The shock must have gotten to her."

From somewhere above her, Vanessa could hear Fiona Donovan's concerned voice, but try as she might, she couldn't open her eyes or form one word.

"Her pulse is getting stronger. She's coming around."

This statement came from Bridget Donovan, the doctor of the family. Vanessa could feel the pressure of the young woman's fingers wrapped around her wrist.

"Well, if the truth be known, Conall probably forced her to work through lunch," Fiona continued in an accusing tone. "She probably hasn't had a bite to eat all day."

"Mom, I don't force Vanessa to do anything," Conall said brusquely. "She probably stopped long enough to eat a sandwich or some of that gooey stuff from a carton that she seems to favor."

"You don't know whether she ate or not?" Fiona shot back at her son.

"Hell, no! I've been in my office since before daylight and didn't come out until a few minutes ago when I found her crying. I don't know about her lunch! But you can see she's not starving. She has plenty of meat on her bones."

His last remark was enough to spike Vanessa's blood pressure and with a weak groan, she slowly opened her eyes to see she was lying on the couch in her office. Bridget was kneeling over her, while Conall and his mother stood just behind the young doctor.

"Hello, pretty lady," Bridget said with a bright smile. "Glad to see you're back with the living."

Vanessa's fuzzy eyesight darted over the redheaded doctor and then slowly progressed up to Conall's dour face. Next to him, Fiona was smiling with happy relief.

"What...happened?" Vanessa asked weakly. "I was talking to Conall and the next thing I knew there was a strange rushing noise in my ears."

"You fainted," Bridget explained. "Thankfully Conall caught you before you hit your head on the desk or the floor. When he called over to the house for help, I happened to be home on a break from the clinic. How are you feeling now?"

"Weak and groggy," Vanessa admitted. "But better."

"Good. Your color is returning," she said. "Conall tells me you received a bit of a shock about your friend."

"Yes. I was feeling a bit shaky, but I never dreamed I'd do anything like...faint! This is so embarrassing." She glanced back at Conall to see his expression was still grim and she figured he had to be terribly annoyed for all this interference in his work schedule. Over the past couple of months, she'd learned his work was his life and he didn't appreciate anything or anyone intervening. "I'm sorry, Conall. I've disrupted the whole office and your family."

"Nonsense!" Fiona blurted out before her son had a chance to utter a word. "You had every right to have a little fainting spell. Most women have nine months to prepare to be a mother. From what Conall tells us, you didn't have nine minutes."

"I'm just glad I happened to be home," Bridget quickly added. "Conall feared you were having a heart attack." She clamped a strong hand on Vanessa's shoulder. "Sit up for me and let's see how you do now."

With the young woman's help, Vanessa rose to a sitting position. "I'm fine. Really," she told the doctor. "I feel much stronger now and my head isn't whirling."

"Well, from what I can see, you had a simple, garden-variety faint. It happens to the best of us sometimes," Bridget assured her. "But if you have any more trouble—weakness, dizziness or anything like that—please get to your doctor for a checkup. Okay?"

"Yes. I promise. Thank you, Bridget."

"No problem," she said, then with a broad smile, she rose to a standing position and pointed a direct look at her brother. "I've got to get back to the clinic, so I'm leaving the patient in your hands, Conall. You might go lightly on her the remainder of the day."

"Vanna is going to get the rest of the afternoon off," Fiona spoke up, using the shortened name that Maura had given Vanessa many years ago when the two had been teenagers. "In fact, Conall is going to drive her home."

Vanessa opened her mouth to argue, but quickly

decided not to make the effort. Fiona could be just as formidable as her son and with Bridget agreeing that Vanessa could clearly use some rest, she had no choice but to go along with the family's wishes.

Once Bridget had departed the small office, Conall said to Vanessa, "I'll get your things and we'll be on our way."

While Conall collected her sweater and handbag from a tiny closet located in the short hallway separating her office from his, Fiona was already taking a seat at Vanessa's desk.

"While you two are gone," she said to Conall, "I'll take care of the plane tickets and see to organizing anything else you might need for the trip to Vegas. If there are still empty seats, do you want the first flight out?"

"That would be great, Mom. See what you can do."

With her things thrown over his arm, he walked over to the couch and slipped a hand beneath Vanessa's elbow.

"Think you can stand okay now?" he asked gently.

Since she'd gone to work for this tall, dark powerhouse of a man, he'd been polite enough to her, but mostly he was all business. It felt more than strange to have him addressing her about personal things and even more unsettling to have him touching her.

"Yes," she assured him, then feeling her cheeks warm with an embarrassed flush, added, "I don't think you need worry about having to catch me again."

Not bothering to make a reply, he began to guide her toward the door. Across the room, Fiona flung a parting question at her son.

"Conall, the hotel rooms. How many nights do you need reserved? Or do you have any idea about that?"

"No idea," he said. "Better leave that open."

"Right," she replied, then tossed a reassuring smile at Vanessa. "Don't worry, Vanna. Everything is going to be just fine. Why, in no time you'll have those little babies of yours home and in your arms."

Vanessa thanked the woman for her kind thoughts and then Conall ushered her out to a shiny black pickup truck with the Diamond D brand emblazoned on the doors.

After he'd helped her into the cab and they were barreling past a fenced paddock filled with a row of busy mechanical horse walkers, he said, "You gave me a fright back there when you fainted. Are you sure you're okay?"

He was staring straight ahead and Vanessa could read little from his granite-etched profile. For the most part, she'd always thought of him as an unfeeling man, but maybe that was because he didn't allow his feelings to show on his face. He was certainly going out of his way to help her. Which created an even bigger question in her mind. Why? Even if she was his one and only secretary, her personal problems were none of his responsibility.

"I'm okay, Conall. Really. I just feel…silly for causing you and your family so much trouble." Her gaze turned toward the passenger window as they curved away from the Donovan ranch house. The structure's stalwart appearance hadn't changed since she'd left the Hondo Valley more than fifteen years ago. And she liked to think the big Irish family that lived inside hadn't changed, either—that if she stepped inside, she'd still feel like Cinderella visiting the castle.

"Forget it," he practically snapped.

She looked at him. "But you—"

He interrupted before she could say more. "Let it rest, Vanessa."

Sighing, she smoothed the hem of her skirt over her knees and stared ahead. One minute everything had been going along fine. As fine as it could be for a divorced woman with her family split in all directions and an aging father too debilitated from a stroke to leave the nursing home. Yet those problems seemed small in comparison to what she was facing now.

Still, Vanessa realized she couldn't give in to the overwhelming shock. She had to straighten her shoulders and take up the reins of her life again. But taking them out of Conall's hands was not going to be an easy task. He was a man who was all about using his power to bend operations to his liking. And she was all about independence. She didn't want to be beholden to anyone and that included her boss. Yet this was one time that agreeing to a little help might be the sensible thing for her to do. Especially for the babies' sake.

"You don't like accepting help from anyone, do you?" he asked as he steered the truck off Diamond D ranch land and onto the main highway.

The man must be a mind reader, she thought. "I like taking care of myself," she answered truthfully, then realizing how ungrateful that probably sounded to him, she glanced over and added, "But this is one time I can't take care of things entirely on my own. And I am grateful to you, Conall. Please know that."

He didn't say anything for a while and she was wondering if she'd offended him, when he said, "You can tell me if I'm getting too personal, Vanessa, but what about your brothers? If I remember right, you had four of them. Are any of them close enough to help you with the babies?"

Vanessa choked back a mocking laugh. Her brothers couldn't care for themselves, much less two needy babies. "My brothers all moved far away from here. They conveniently forgot their parents and only sister. And that's fine with me, 'cause I wouldn't ask them for the time of day," she said flatly.

"That's too bad."

She heaved out a heavy breath. "It's probably for the best, Conall. None of them have ever made much effort to become responsible men. The only one who comes close to it is Michael—the one your age. And he's hardly in the running for sainthood," she added.

He didn't make any sort of reply to that and Vanessa figured he was thinking badly of her. The Donovan family had always been a strong unit. They lived together, worked and played together, and stuck close even when life's problems crashed in unexpectedly. He probably couldn't understand why she and her brothers lacked the love and devotion it took to keep the Valdez family bonded. But then, she'd never understood it herself.

"Sorry," she said quietly. "I didn't mean to sound so…judgmental. But believe me when I say there are no relatives around to help. Not with the babies, my father, the home place, anything."

In other words, she had her hands full, Conall thought grimly. As he'd suspected, the Valdez brothers had left Lincoln County. He'd not seen any of them in years and even when they had still been around, Conall hadn't associated with any of them. He'd never been into strutting around in black leather and begging for scrapes with the law. Some time back, he'd heard the eldest son had served time for distributing drugs over in El Paso, but as far as he knew, no gossip had ever surfaced about the remaining three.

Conall cast a brief glance at her. What had her life been like these past years she'd been away from the valley? She'd certainly climbed the workforce ladder. But in spite of her having more financial security, she was more or less alone in life. Like him.

Which only proved that riches didn't always come in the form of money, he thought.

Ten minutes later, on a five-acre tract of land near the tiny settlement of Tinnie, Conall pulled the truck to a stop in front of a rickety picket fence. Beyond the whitewashed barrier was a small stucco house of faded turquoise. One mesquite tree shaded the front entrance, while a short rock walkway crossed a bare dirt yard. A brown-and-white nanny goat stood on the porch as she reared on her hind legs and nipped at a hanging pot of red geraniums.

Even though he'd not been by the homestead recently, the Valdez home looked pretty much as it always had. Seeing the family's modest existence normally wouldn't have affected Conall one way or the other. Rich and poor was a fact of life. Not just in the New Mexico mountains, but everywhere. Yet now that he was beginning to know Vanessa, he was struck by the stark simplicity of the place. She'd left a very high-paying job to return to this, he thought incredibly. All because her father had needed her. How many women would do such a thing?

As she collected her handbag and jacket, Conall

walked around to the passenger door to help her to the ground.

"I'll walk with you to the door," he told her. "Just in case your knees get spongy."

With his hand at her back, they walked through a sagging gate and down the rough walkway. To the east, far beyond the house, clouds had gathered over the Capitan Mountains, blotting out the sun and hinting at an oncoming rainstorm.

When they reached the porch, the goat ignored them as they stepped up to the door. "Would you like to come in?" she asked.

He smiled. "Some other time," he assured her. "If we're going to leave in the morning, I have a hundred things to tend to before we go. Richardson is coming about the pool at three. I need to be there to see what sort of ideas he has. And to get his estimates for the cost."

The idea of discussing plans to enlarge the swimming pool for Diamond D racehorses, while Vanessa was worrying how she was going to house two needy infants, made him feel rather small and out of touch. But it was hardly his fault that their worlds were so different.

"Sure," she said, then suddenly looked up at him. Her features were taut with stress. "Could you let me know about our flight time? Since my vehicle is still at the ranch, I suppose I'll need someone to pick me up and take me to the airport."

Placing his forefinger beneath her chin, he passed the pad of his thumb slowly along her jaw line. "Relax," he said softly. "I'll take care of everything, Vanessa. Just pack your bags and let me do the rest."

She nodded and then her gaze skittered shyly away from his and on to the closed door behind her shoulder. Conall told himself it was time to drop his hand and back away. But something about the tender line of her cheek, the warm scent emanating from her hair, made him bend his head and press a kiss to her temple.

For one moment her small hand fluttered to a stop against the middle of his chest, and then just as quickly she was pushing herself away and hurrying into the house.

Conall stared after her for long moments before he finally moved off the porch and walked back to his truck.

Later that evening, as Vanessa attempted to pack what things she needed for the trip to Vegas, the phone rang.

Praying it wasn't another call from Hope's lawyer, she picked up the phone located on the nightstand by her bed and was surprised to hear Maura's voice on the other end of the line.

Even though the two women had been longtime friends, Maura had a husband and two young children to care for, along with her part-time job at Bridget's medical clinic in Ruidoso. She was too busy to make a habit of calling.

Without preamble, Conall's sister exclaimed, "Bridget just told me about your friend—and the babies! Dear God, I can't imagine what you must be feeling right now!"

Swiping a weary hand through her hair, Vanessa said, "I feel like every ounce of energy has been drained from my body, Maura."

"Bridget told me about you fainting. Thank God Conall was there with you. How are you feeling now?"

"Physically, better. I'm packing for the trip right now. But my mind is racing around in all directions. How can a person feel grief and happy excitement at the same time? I feel like I'm being pulled in all directions." She eased down on the edge of the bed. "But mostly, Maura, I'm scared."

"Scared? You?" Maura scoffed. "You're one of the strongest and bravest women I've ever known. What do you have to be scared about, anyway?"

Brave? Strong? Maybe at one time, years ago when she'd first headed out to Las Vegas on her own, she'd been brave and determined to make a better life for herself. But her mistakes with Jeff had wiped away much of her confidence.

"Two little infants, that's what! You've got to remember I've never had a baby. I don't know the first thing about taking care of one."

Maura's soft laugh was meant to reassure her friend. "Trust me, dear friend, giving birth doesn't give you an inside corner on taking care of babies. It's a learn-as-you-go thing. Believe me, you'll be fine. And isn't it wonderful, Vanna? You with children! You've wanted some of your own for so long now."

As tears stung, Vanessa squeezed her eyes shut. "That's true. But I didn't want them this way—with my friend dying. She was…well, I've talked about her to you before. She was such a generous person and so fun and full of life. She was planning to…come back here for a visit later this summer to show me the babies and see where I grew up. Now—" her throat tightened to an aching knot, forcing her to pause "—I'll be bringing the babies back without her."

Vanessa could hear Maura sniffing back a tear of her own. "Yes, it's so tragic, Vanna. I would have loved to meet her. But it wasn't meant to be and you can't dwell on her death now. You have to concentrate on the babies and remember how much your friend wanted them to be loved and cared for."

"You're right, Maura," Vanessa said as she tried to gather her ragged emotions. "I have to move forward now."

Maura cleared her throat. "Well, Bridget says that our brother is traveling with you to Vegas. Frankly, I'm shocked about this, Vanna. The rare times he leaves the ranch are only for business reasons."

Surely Maura could see that Conall considered Vanessa a business reason and nothing more. "I tried to tell him it wasn't necessary."

"Oh. I thought you might have asked him to go."

Vanessa drew in a sharp breath. "Are you serious? I would never ask Conall to do anything personal for me! He just made all these decisions on his own. And I have no idea why."

"Hmm. Well, his last secretary was a real bitch," Maura said bluntly. "And everyone in the family has heard him singing praises about your work. I'm sure he wants to keep you happy."

Vanessa released a short, dry laugh. "I've been told that good secretaries are hard to find." But earlier this afternoon, when he placed that brief kiss on the top of her head, she'd definitely not felt like his employee, she thought. She'd felt like a woman with something worthwhile to offer a man.

Dear God, the shock of losing Hope and becoming a mother all at once had numbed her brain. Conall Donovan would never look at her as anything more than his employee. Socially, he was several tiers above her. And even though he wasn't a snob, he was still a Donovan.

"Doesn't matter why he's going," Maura said. "I'm just glad he is. You need someone to support you at a time like this. And Conall has a strong arm to lean on."

Vanessa had no intentions of leaning on Conall. Certainly not in a physical way. But she kept those thoughts to herself. "Yes. Your brother is a rock."

"I wouldn't exactly call him that. Yes, he can be hard. But there's a soft side to him. You just have to know where to look for it," Maura explained. "There was a time—" She broke off, then after a long pause, added in a rueful voice, "Let's just say Conall wasn't always the man he is now."

Shying far away from that loaded comment, Vanessa said, "Well, I'm hoping we can wrap up everything in Vegas quickly."

"And I'd better let you go so that you can finish your packing," Maura replied. "Is there anything I can help you with while you're gone? Check on your father? Your house?"

"It's kind of you to offer, but I'll keep in touch with the nursing home. And I think the house will be okay for a couple of days. But just in case, you know where I leave an extra key so that you can get inside."

"Yes, I remember. In the little crack behind the window shutter."

"Right," Vanessa replied. "But I doubt we'll be gone for that long. Besides, the best thing you can do for me is share your experienced mothering skills. I'm definitely going to need advice."

Maura laughed. "Just wait, Vanna. You're going to see that a woman can never learn all there is to know about mothering. You just have to go by instinct and you happen to have a good one."

"I can only hope you're right," Vanessa murmured.

The next afternoon, after the short flight to Las Vegas, Conall dealt with their luggage, then picked up their rental car and headed to their hotel. Thankfully Fiona hadn't booked them into one of the resort monstrosities that lined the busy strip, but a nice peaceful villa on the desert outskirts of the city.

After checking in and sending their bags to adjoining rooms, they drove straight to the lawyer's office to deal with the legalities of claiming the twins and arranging to store Hope's ashes.

By the time they finally arrived at the orphanage, an old, ivy-covered Spanish-style building located on the outskirts of town, Vanessa's exhaustion must have been clearly showing. As they followed a silent Sister down a wide, empty corridor, Conall brought a steadying hand beneath her elbow.

"I'm thinking we should have waited until tomorrow to see the babies," he said in a low voice. "I'm not sure you're up to this."

Vanessa straightened her shoulders as best she could. For the life of her, she wasn't about to let this granite piece of man think she was made of anything less than grit and determination.

"I'll be fine. And seeing the babies is the best part of this trip," she assured him.

Conall studied her pale face and wondered what his secretary could possibly be thinking. Even for the strongest of women, she was receiving a heavy load to carry. Especially without a man to help her.

He didn't know anything about Vanessa's marriage or divorce. In fact, he'd only known she was divorced because she'd stated it on her résumé. Of course he could have questioned Maura about her friend and most likely his sister would have given him an honest account of what had occurred. But Conall had never been one to pry into another person's private life, unless he believed there was a good reason to. He liked his privacy and tried his best to respect everyone else's. And even if she was his employee, he didn't consider Vanessa an exception to that rule. Except there were times, he had to admit to himself, that he was curious about her.

He gave her a wry smile. "To be honest, I'm looking forward to seeing them, too."

At the end of the corridor, the kindly nun ushered them into a sunny nursery filled with rows of cradles and cribs, all of them occupied with babies ranging from infancy to twelve months old. Three more nuns were moving quietly around the room, tending to the needy children, some of whom were crying boisterously.

"The twins are over here in the corner," the Sister said, motioning for the two of them to follow.

When she finally stopped near a pair of wooden cradles made of dark wood, she gestured toward the sleeping babies. Since the newborns were yet to be named, the two were differentiated with blue and pink blankets, while paper tags were attached to the end of each cradle, one reading Boy Valdez and the other Girl Valdez.

"Here they are," she announced. "Take as much time with them as you'd like. And if you need anything, please let me know. I'll be just down the hall in Mother Superior's office."

Conall and Vanessa both thanked the woman as she left and then they turned their entire attention to the sleeping twins.

Both babies had red-gold hair with the boy's being a slightly darker shade than his sister's. To Conall, they appeared extremely tiny, even though the Sister had told them earlier that each baby weighed over five pounds, a fair amount for newborn twins.

"Oh. Oh, my. How…incredible," Vanessa whispered in awe as she stared down at the babies. "How perfectly beautiful!"

She bent over the cradles for a closer look and Conall watched as she touched a finger to the top of each velvety head. And then suddenly without warning, she covered her face with one hand and he could see her shoulders began to shake with silent sobs.

Quickly, he moved forward and wrapped an arm around her waist. "Vanessa." He said her name softly, just to remind her that she wasn't alone.

She glanced up at him, her brown eyes full of tears. "I'm sorry, Conall. I thought I could do this without breaking down. But…I—" Her gaze swung back to the babies. "I can't believe that I've been blessed with two beautiful babies. And yet I look at them and…can't help thinking of Hope."

His hand slipped to her slender shoulder and squeezed. "Your friend had the perfect name. Through you, she's given her children hope for the future. Remember that and smile."

She let out a ragged sigh. "You're right, Conall. I have to put my tears for Hope behind me and smile for the babies." Glancing up at him, she gave him a wobbly smile. "I've chosen names for them. Rose Marie and Richard Madison. What do you think?"

"Very nice. I'll call them Rose and Rick, if that's all right with you."

Her smile grew stronger. "That's my plan, too. Shall we pick them up?"

He stared at her, amazed that she wanted to include him. "We? You go ahead. I'm just an onlooker."

She looked a bit disappointed and Conall realized he felt a tad deflated himself. But whether that was because he actually wanted to hold the babies and was stupidly pretending indifference or because he was disheartening her at this special time, he didn't know.

Frowning, she asked, "You don't like babies or something?"

"Of course I do. I have baby nieces and nephews. But I didn't hold them when they were this small. Come to think of it…none of them were ever this small." He gestured toward the twins. "I might do it all wrong."

"I might do it all wrong, too," she suggested. "So we might as well try together."

Realizing it would look strange if he kept protesting, he said, "All right. I'll watch you first."

She bent over Rose's cradle and after carefully placing a hand beneath the baby's head, lifted her out of the bed and into her arms. After a moment, Conall moved up to the other cradle and, in the same cautious manner, reached for the boy.

Once he had the child safely positioned in the crook of his arm, he adjusted the thin blue blanket beneath little Rick's chin so that he could get a better look at his face. It was perfectly formed with a little pug nose and bow-shaped lips. Faint golden brows framed a set of blue eyes that were now wide open and appeared to be searching to see who or what was holding him.

Vulnerable. Needy. Precious. As he held the child, memories carried him back to when he and Nancy had first married. In the beginning, he'd had so many dreams and plans. All of them surrounding a house full of children to carry on the Donovan name and inherit the hard-earned rewards of the Diamond D. But those dreams had slowly and surely come crashing down.

Now as Conall experienced the special warmth and scent of the baby boy lying so helplessly in the crook of his arm, Conall wasn't sure that Vanessa yet realized what a treasure she'd been handed. But he did. Oh, how he did.

"Conall?"

Reining in his thoughts, he pulled his gaze away from the baby to find her staring at him with a faintly puzzled look on her face. Had she been reading his mind? Conall wondered. Surely not. Down through the years he'd perfected the art of shuttering his emotions. Baby Rick wasn't strong enough to make him change the longtime habit.

"Am I doing something wrong?" he asked.

For the first time Conall could remember, his secretary actually smiled at him with those big brown eyes of hers.

"No. You look like you were tailor-made for the job of Daddy."

Her observation struck him hard, but he did his best to keep the pain hidden, as though there was no wide, empty hole inside him.

"Not hardly," he said gruffly. "I'm not…daddy material."

One delicate brow arched skeptically upward. "Oh? You don't ever plan to have children of your own?"

For some reason her question made him pull the baby boy even closer to his chest. "That's one thing I'm absolutely certain I'll never have."

Clearly taken aback by his response, her gaze slipped away from his and dropped to the baby in her arms. "Well, everyone has their own ideas about having children," she said a bit stiffly. "I just happen to think you're making a sad mistake."

A sad mistake. Oh, yes, it was a sad mistake that she was misjudging him, Conall thought. And sad, too, that he couldn't find the courage to tell this woman that at one time he'd planned to have at least a half-dozen children.

But if he let her in on that dream, then he'd have to explain why he'd been forced to set it aside. And why he planned to live the rest of his life a lone bachelor.

Hardening himself to that certain reality had changed him, he knew. Even his family often considered him unapproachable. But none of them actually understood the loss he felt to see his siblings having children of their own, while knowing he would always be cheated out of one of life's most blessed gifts.

"You have a right to your opinion, Vanessa. Just like I have a right to live my life the way I see fit."

She cast him a pained look, then turned her back to him and walked a few steps away as though she'd just seen him for the first time and didn't like what she was seeing.

Well, that was okay, Conall thought. What his secretary thought about him didn't matter. It wasn't as if they were romantically linked, or even close friends.

He looked down at the baby in his arms and felt something raw and sweet swell in his chest. Vanessa would no doubt provide the twins with love. But they needed a father. And at some point in the future she would probably provide them with one. Then her family circle would be complete and that was only right.

Yet strangely, the idea left Conall with a regretful ache.

Chapter 3

Later that evening, long after their visit to the orphanage had ended, Vanessa sat in a quiet courtyard behind their villa-style hotel, and tried to relax from the hectic pace of the day. Along with the busy schedule of flying, meeting with lawyers and visiting the babies, her cell phone had rung continually all afternoon. Most of the calls were from people here in Vegas who'd been mutual friends of her and Hope and were just now hearing about the tragedy. Vanessa appreciated their concern and interest, but she was exhausted from explaining about the twins and sharing her grief over Hope's death.

Finally, in desperation, she'd left the phone in her room and walked outside to enjoy the cooling desert air. Now as she sat on an iron bench beneath a huge Joshua tree and watched darkness fall on the distant mountains, she wished she could turn off thoughts of Conall as easily as she'd turned off the phone.

The man was an enigma. After weeks of working with him, she still didn't understand what made Conall tick or what drove him to work long, trying hours for the ranch. Clearly he was ambitious. Every morning he arrived at the office at least two hours ahead of her, which meant he went to work before daylight. And when she left in the evenings, even after working overtime herself, he remained at his desk making calls or meeting with horse-racing connections. Running the Diamond D was clearly more than a job to him. It was the entire sum of his life. Did he invest so much of himself because the ranch was family owned and operated?

She could only guess at the answer to that question. But there was no doubt that Conall was a man of striking looks with plenty of money to match. The ranch could easily afford to hire an assistant in order to free Conall from his grueling schedule. With part of his workload eased, he'd be able to travel the world and indulge in all sorts of lavish recreations, with a trail of willing women trotting behind him. Yet none of those things appeared to interest him in the least. She seriously doubted he would accept the help of an assistant, even if the person volunteered to work for free. He was a man who wanted things done his way and refused to trust just anyone to carry out his orders.

Vanessa often wondered if he was still bitter over his divorce, or perhaps he was still in love with his ex-wife and wanted her back. Maura had never mentioned the cause of her brother's divorce and Vanessa wasn't about to question her childhood friend about him. The hopes and dreams and feelings going on inside Conall weren't her business. Or so she kept telling herself. But ever since she'd looked up in the orphanage and seen him standing there with her baby son in his arms, she'd been consumed with unexpected emotions and questions.

The fact that he didn't want or expect to ever have children had shaken her deeply. Of all the men she'd met through the years, Conall had always seemed like a man who would love and welcome children into his life. True, he had a dark and dangerous appearance but it belied the responsible man beneath. He wasn't a roamer or playboy with a wild lifestyle. Why would he not want children? Because there was no room in his heart for them? No. Vanessa couldn't believe he was that cold or stingy with himself. Not after seeing the way he interacted with the twins.

"Vanessa?"

The unexpected sound of Conall's voice had her glancing over her shoulder to see him walking a narrow brick pathway toward her. Figuring something had to be wrong for him to come all the way out here to find her, she rose from the bench and met him on the footpath.

"I'm sorry," she quickly apologized. "I left my phone in the room. Has the lawyer or orphanage been trying to reach me?"

Impatience creased his forehead. "You need to quit all this worrying, Vanessa. No one has tried to reach you through me. The lawyer seemed very competent. I'm sure he'll have the last of the papers for us to sign before we catch our flight out tomorrow afternoon. And from what Mother Superior told us, the babies are perfectly healthy and able to travel."

Shaking her head, Vanessa forced the tenseness in

her shoulders to relax. "I am a bit on edge," she admitted. "My phone has been ringing all evening and—"

Before she could finish, the cell in his shirt pocket went off and after a quick glance at the caller ID he said, "Sorry, Vanessa, I've been having the same problem. This won't take but a minute or two."

With a quick nod, she turned her back and took a few steps away to where water trickled over a three-tiered fountain and into a small pool. As she watched colorful koi swim in and out of water plants, she heard him say, "No. That won't do.…I understand you mean well. But nothing used.…Everything new.…Yes, classic.…No. Something like cherry and antique.…Got it?… Yeah. And anything else you can think of that will be needed." There was a long pause as he listened to the caller and then he replied. "Yeah. Thanks, sis.…Good night."

His sister? That could be Maura, Dallas or Bridget, she thought. Apparently they were planning something together and the notion sent a sad pang through Vanessa. She'd never had a sister to conspire with and share experiences, only older brothers who'd mostly caused great agony for her parents. Now with Esther, her mother, gone and her father, Alonzo, still having trouble communicating with his halting speech, she couldn't look for family support. Unlike Conall, who'd always been surrounded by loving siblings, parents and grandmother.

"Well, now that I have that out of the way," Conall announced behind her, "I came out here to see if you'd like to go to dinner somewhere? We've not eaten in hours."

Vanessa glanced down at herself. She was still wearing the simple pink sheathe she'd started out with this morning, minus the matching bolero sweater, but it was wrinkled and even without the aid of a mirror she knew her hair was blown to a tumbled mess. "I really don't feel like dressing up for dinner, Conall. You go on without me."

He chuckled and the sound took her by surprise. He was a man who rarely laughed and when he did it was usually about something that she didn't find amusing. Now as she looked at him, she was jarred by his jovial attitude.

"Have you taken a look at me?" he asked. "I'm wearing jeans."

Dragging her gaze away from the charming grin on his lips, she slowly inspected the blue denim encasing his muscled thighs and the pair of brown alligator boots he wore. He was one of those few men who looked comfortable dressed up or down, which meant he would probably look even better without any clothes at all.

Dear, God, what was she doing? Now wasn't the time for those sorts of indecent thoughts, she scolded herself. As far as Conall went, there would never be a time for them. And she had more important issues to focus on. Like two little tots with golden-red hair and blue eyes.

"I am hungry," she admitted. For food. Not for a man like him, she mentally added.

"Great. There's a little restaurant right across the street that looks good."

"Just give me a moment to fetch my purse and sweater from the room," she told him.

A few minutes later, they were seated at a small table in a family-type restaurant that featured Italian dishes.

Vanessa ordered ravioli while Conall chose steak and pasta. As they waited for their salads and drinks to be served, Conall glanced around the long room decorated with early dated photos of Las Vegas and simple, home-style tables covered in brightly striped cloths.

Seated directly across from him, Vanessa asked, "Is this place not to your liking? We can always find another restaurant."

Surprised by her suggestion, he turned his gaze on her. "I'm perfectly satisfied. Why do you ask?"

One of her slender shoulders lifted and fell in a negligible way. "I don't know. The way you were looking around and frowning."

"I frown all the time." A wry smile touched one corner of his mouth. "At least, that's what my mother tells me."

"Mothers don't like to see their children frown," she reasoned. "Mine never did. She always told me to smile and count my blessings."

As Conall's gaze dwelled on his secretary's face, he was surprised at how easy and pleasurable it was to look at her and be in her company. He'd not expected to enjoy any part of this trip. He'd only done it because she was a woman alone and in need, and she was a dedicated employee. But he was quickly discovering that Vanessa was more than an efficient secretary, she was a lovely woman and, like it or not, desire was beginning to stir in him for the first time in a long, long time.

"You must miss your mother terribly," he said. "I was surprised when I heard about her passing. The last time I'd seen her in church she seemed very spry."

Her gaze suddenly dropped to the tabletop, but Conall didn't miss the sadness on her face. The image bothered him almost as much as her tears had yesterday. And for some reason he felt guilty for not attending Mrs. Valdez's funeral services. Even though he'd not known the woman personally, he should have made the effort for Vanessa's sake. But at that time, she'd not been working as his secretary; she'd merely been a past acquaintance, who'd left the valley years ago.

"Yes. Mama appeared to be a picture of health. That made her sudden heart attack even harder to take," she said quietly, then lifted her gaze back to him. "Her death was one of the main reasons I left Las Vegas and returned to Tinnie. I missed the end of my mother's life. I want to be around for my father as much as I can before…he leaves me."

Other than the twins, she certainly didn't have much in the way of family. The idea troubled Conall, although he wasn't sure why. Plenty of people he knew had lost their parents or were lacking family of any kind and they didn't necessarily garner his sympathy. At least, not the deep sort of regret he felt for Vanessa.

"You gave up a very good job to return to your family home and your father," he commented. "I have to admire you for that, Vanessa."

Her eyes were full of doubt as they connected with his.

"I'm not sure that I made the most sensible decision, Conall. I did have a good job and a little house in a nice part of town. Materially speaking, I had much more here in Vegas than I ever had in the valley. But…" Pausing, she let out a long sigh. "Money isn't a cure-all."

No one knew that any better than Conall. Money couldn't change the fact that a childhood fever had killed his chances to ever father a child of his own. Nor had money been able to fix his shattered marriage. In fact, being rich had only compounded the problems he'd endured with Nancy. But since his divorce he'd tried his best to bury those painful personal details. They certainly weren't matters he wanted to discuss with a woman, and that included Vanessa.

"You're not worried about the twins' financial future, are you?" he asked. "Hope's life insurance appears to have left them set up nicely for college."

"I'm not worried about the financial part of this," she replied. "My parents raised six children. Surely I can manage two."

"But you're not married," he pointed out.

From the stiff line of her shoulders to the purse of her lips, everything about her looked offended by his comment.

"You think having a man around would be a help?"

The bitterness in her short laugh was something he'd never heard from her before. The idea that this gentle woman might hold any sort of hard streak inside her took him by surprise. "I'm a man," he answered. "I like to think we're a helpful gender."

Frowning, her gaze left his to travel to an insignificant spot across the room. "Look, Conall, I've already had one husband I had to support, I don't want another. I can do just fine without that added burden."

So she'd ended up marrying a man just like her parasitic brothers. No wonder there was bitterness on her tongue. But how and why had she made such a mistake in judgment? He would have thought she'd seen enough freeloading men to spot one at first glance.

Yeah. Just like you'd been able to spot Nancy's twisted character. You didn't use good judgment with her, either. You allowed love to lead you around. And around. Until you were walking down a path of destruction.

Clearing his throat, he tried to ignore the mocking voice going off inside him. "I wasn't trying to suggest—"

Shaking her head, she interrupted, "Forget it, please. I…didn't mean to sound so catty. It's just that after Jeff… Well, I resent the idea of being told I need a man."

Like he resented his family telling him he needed another woman in his life, Conall thought. Hell, getting hooked up with another woman like Nancy would finish him. And finding a nice, family-oriented woman that he could love wasn't as simple as it sounded. Oh, he'd tried. Once the initial blow of his divorce was over, he'd returned to the dating scene and attempted to put his heart into starting his life over with another woman. But as soon as he made it clear that he couldn't father children, all his dates had backed away from him. Sure, for the most part they'd all been kind and empathetic to his problem, but in the end none of them had wanted to start out their lives with a man that couldn't give them a family of their own. After a while, Conall had grown so weary of being rejected over and over that he'd finally given up on finding love, marriage and anything in between. And for the past few years he'd pretty much convinced himself that he was better off being alone and focusing all his attention to his job.

Vanessa's cynical remark was still dangling in the air between them when the waitress arrived with their drinks and salads. After the young woman served them and went on her way, he could feel Vanessa's gaze on him and he paused from the task of stirring sugar into his tea to glance at her. Clearly, from the expression on her face, she wanted to speak her mind about something.

"What?" he prompted.

She hesitated before giving her head a slight shake. The gentle waves of hair lying on her shoulders shook with the movement as did the blue teardrops dangling from her earlobes. Suddenly Conall was wondering how it would feel to thrust his fingers into her silky hair, to nibble on the perfect little shell of her ear.

"I don't know how to say this, Conall, without making you angry."

Trying to concentrate on her words instead of the erotic images in his mind, he asked, "What makes you think I'll be angry? I've not gotten angry with you yet, have I?"

He would admit that he often got frustrated with business dealings and the roadblocks he encountered while dealing with the multitudes of details that went into managing a ranch the size of the Diamond D. But he'd never gotten upset with Vanessa. She'd always given more than a hundred percent to her job and he appreciated her effort.

She reached for the pepper shaker and shook it vigorously over her salad. "Because you're going to think I'm ungrateful. And I'm not. I'm actually very indebted to you for making this trip with me and…everything else you've taken care of. But I—"

A faint smile curled up one corner of his mouth.

"You don't want me telling you how to take care of the twins or what you might need in your personal life. Is that it?"

She studied him for a long moment and then laughed softly under her breath. Conall likened the sound to sweet music.

"That's about it," she answered.

Amused by her streak of independence, he finished stirring his tea. "In other words, while we're on this trip I need to forget that I'm your boss and you're my secretary."

The tip of her tongue came out to moisten her lips and Conall found himself gazing at the damp sheen it left behind. What would she taste like? he wondered. Honey? Wine? Or simply all woman? He certainly didn't need to know. But he sure as hell wouldn't mind making the effort to find out.

She said, "Uh, well, I suppose that's a way of putting it."

The smile on his face deepened and he realized with a start that he was flirting. Something he'd not done in years or, for that matter, even wanted to do.

"Good," he said.

One of her winged brows shot upward. "Good? I thought you were a man who always wanted to be the boss."

Chuckling softly, he reached across the table and enfolded her small hand with his. "Not tonight. I'd rather just be a man having dinner with a beautiful woman. What do you think about that?"

She grimaced, but he could see a faint swathe of pink rushing over her cheeks and her breasts rising and falling with each quick intake of breath. The notion that he was affecting her, even in this small way, was like a heady drink of wine to him, and in the far back of his mind, he wondered what was coming over him. Clearly he wasn't himself. He'd not been himself since yesterday when he'd walked through the office and found Vanessa with tears on her cheeks.

"I think there's something about this town that makes people forget who and what they are. But I never thought you'd be the type to fall prey to its lure," she said dryly. "The next thing I know you'll be saying we should take a stroll down the strip and take in the lights."

"Hmm. That's a great idea. We'll go as soon as we finish eating."

Less than an hour later, after the two of them found a parking space and made their way to the busy sidewalks lining the city's most famous boulevard, Vanessa was still wishing she'd kept her mouth shut. Spending time with Conall away from the office was something she'd often dreamed about, but she was smart enough to realize it was risky business.

In spite of what he'd said back at the restaurant, he was her boss and she depended on him for her livelihood. Allowing herself to think of him as anything more than the man who signed her paychecks would be like inviting trouble right through the front door. Yet here she was walking close to his side and enjoying every second of it.

"Is this the first time you've ever visited Las Vegas?" Vanessa asked as they slowly made their way southward along the busy sidewalk running adjacent to the congested street.

"No. Believe it or not, I was here once with my parents. We'd gone out to Santa Anita to watch one of our horses run in a graded stakes race. On the way back

Mom wanted to stop off and play the slots. So Dad and I endured while she had fun."

The night had cooled to a balmy temperature and as the light wind caressed her face, Vanessa realized this was the first time she'd relaxed since she'd gotten the call from Hope's lawyer.

"You don't like to gamble?" she asked.

"Not that much."

She smiled with amused disbelief. "How can you say that, Conall? You're in the racehorse business. That's a big, big gamble."

He chuckled. "That's true. But in my business I pretty much know what I'm investing in. At least I can see my venture and put my hands on it." He gestured to one of the massive casinos to their right. "In there you're placing your money on pure chance."

"Like the stock market," she joked.

"Exactly," he said with another short laugh, then added, "I didn't realize you could be a funny girl."

"I have my moments."

She was thinking what a nice deep laugh he had and how much she enjoyed hearing it when his arm suddenly slid around the back of her waist and drew her even closer to his side. The sudden contact nearly took her breath, yet she did her best to hide the havoc he was causing inside her. After all, she wasn't that same teenager who'd had such a crush on him so many years ago. She'd grown up, dated, married and divorced. Men weren't a big deal to her anymore. Or so she'd believed. Until tonight. When Conall had suddenly started to treat her like a woman instead of a secretary.

"Even though it's not my cup of tea, I have to admit there's something magical about this town. Do you miss all this?" he asked, as he gestured toward the elaborately designed buildings, the endless lights and the bumper-to-bumper traffic on the strip.

"No. I never was into the bright lights and glamour of this place. I only saw it as a town of opportunities. And I took them. Before I ever left the valley, I decided if I had to work my way through college waitressing, I might as well do it where I could make the most money."

"I certainly don't blame you for that."

No. He wouldn't, Vanessa thought. He was the sort of person who never looked down on anyone because they had less than him. And he admired any person who worked hard for a living.

Conall gestured to an area several feet away where a low curved wall contained a shallow pool with spraying spouts of water. "Let's take a rest over there by the pool," he suggested.

"Sounds good to me," she agreed.

Beneath a huge palm tree they took seats on the wide concrete wall. As the two of them made themselves comfortable, he dropped his arm from her waist and Vanessa was trying to decide if she was relieved or disappointed at the loss of contact, when he reached for her hand and folded it casually within his.

Staring out at the street of heavy traffic and gawking pedestrians, Conall grunted with dismay. "After working in this town, the Diamond D must seem mundane."

"The Diamond D is a busy place, too," she disagreed. "Only in a different way."

The idea that his thigh was pressed slightly against hers and that the heat from his hand was radiating all the way up to her shoulder was making every nerve inside Vanessa tighten to the screaming point. Why was he getting this close to her? She'd worked for the man for more than two months and he'd never touched her in any form or fashion until yesterday when she'd fainted straight into his arms. Now he was behaving as though he had every right to put his arm around her or hold her hand.

If she had any sense at all, she'd put a stop to it, Vanessa argued with herself. She'd tell him to keep his hands to himself and remember that she was his secretary and nothing more. But she'd already made the foolish mistake of telling him to forget about being her boss while they were here in Vegas. And she'd be lying to herself, and to him, if she tried to say she wasn't enjoying the feel of his warm fingers wrapped so snugly around hers.

Clearing her throat, she said, "I have to confess that when I first returned to Lincoln County, I did so with intentions of getting a job at the Billy the Kid Casino. I have a friend there who works in the business office and he would have given me a glowing reference. But I'd already worked in that industry for so long that I thought a complete change might be good for me. And then I read about your job opening and I…" She paused long enough to give him a wry smile. "I almost didn't call you."

One of his black brows lifted slightly and as her gaze wandered over his cool gray eyes and dark profile, she felt her heart thud into a rhythm that actually scared her. The man wasn't supposed to be making her feel light-headed. He wasn't supposed to be making her forget they were hundreds of miles away from the office or reminding her they were in a town that urged people to be a little reckless.

"Why?" he asked. "You didn't think you'd like working for me?"

"That wasn't the reason. I didn't want you giving me the job just because I was Maura's old friend. But I should have known you were the type of man who'd never put sentimentality over business. You'd never be that easy with…anyone."

Suddenly his expression turned solemn and Vanessa felt her heart kick to an even faster rate.

"If it makes you feel any better, Vanessa, I can assure you that you got the job on your own merit. Not through a friendship with my sister."

She nervously licked her lips and wondered why she couldn't tear her eyes away from his rugged face. All around her there were fabulous sights that should be monopolizing her attention. But none of them, she realized, could compete with Conall.

"I'm glad you told me," she said, her voice dropping to a husky note.

"And are you glad you took the job?"

How could she answer that without incriminating herself? This man had no idea that he was the thing that fueled her, pushed her out of bed in the morning and made her want to hope and dream again, even after she'd thought her future had died.

"So far," she said lowly. "What about you? Do you wish you'd offered it to someone else?"

A sexy grin suddenly exposed his white teeth and Vanessa was mesmerized by the sight. She'd never seen this side of him before and the notion that he was showing it to her was almost more than she could take in.

"Giving you the job was one of the smartest decisions I've ever made." Leaning closer, he gently pushed his fingers into her windblown hair and smoothed it away from her cheek. "And coming on this trip with you was even smarter."

By now her breathing was coming in shallow sips and she had to swallow before she could finally form one word. "Why?"

His head drew so close to hers that she could see little more than his mouth and nose.

"Because it's opened my eyes. And I'm beginning to see all the things I've been missing."

"Conall." His name passed her lips as she hesitantly pressed a hand against his chest. "This…you… I don't understand."

"That makes two of us."

"But we—"

"Don't talk," he whispered. "Talking won't change the fact that I want to kiss you."

Even if she could have said another word, she doubted it would have stopped what he was about to do. What *she* was about to do.

His thumb and forefinger closed around her chin and then his lips settled over hers. Vanessa closed her eyes and for the first time in a long time, she stopped thinking and simply let herself feel.

Chapter 4

The desert wind teased her hair and brushed her skin, but it did little to ease the heat building inside Vanessa. Conall's mouth was like a flame licking, consuming, turning her whole body to liquid fire.

Beyond them she could hear the movement of the crawling traffic and among the nearby pedestrians, the occasional burst of conversation punctuated with laughter. Above their heads, the fans of the palm trees whipped noisily in the wind. Yet none of these distractions were enough to jerk Vanessa back to sanity.

Instead, she simply wanted to sit there forever, tasting his mouth, feeling his hands move against her skin. This wasn't the same as the fantasies she'd had of Conall while they'd been teenagers. This was very, very real and so was the effect it was having on her body.

She was melting into him, her senses totally absorbed with his kiss when somewhere behind them voices called out loudly. The interruption broke the connection of their lips and Conall finally lifted his head to gaze down at her.

What could she possibly say to him now? she wondered. Or should she even try?

He cleared his throat and she suddenly realized his hand was cupped against the side of her face. The skin of his palm was rough and raspy, yet his touch was as gentle as a dove's. She wanted to rub her cheek against the masculine texture, experience the erotic friction.

"I guess we'd better be moving along," he said huskily. "Or I…might start forgetting we're in a public place."

Start forgetting? Vanessa had forgotten their whereabouts a long time ago. Like the first moment his lips had touched hers! The idea that she'd become so lost and reckless in his arms was downright terrifying. She couldn't afford to get entangled in an affair with this man. He had the power to hurt her emotionally, not to mention the right to terminate her job whenever the whim hit him.

Trying to put her focus on her new babies, rather than the growing need in her hungry body, she turned and scooted several generous inches away from him.

"I think you're right." Her voice was raw and awkward, but that was better than appearing totally speechless, she thought with a bit of desperation. "And it's getting late. I think we should head back to the hotel."

Apparently he agreed, because he took her by the arm and helped her up from the low concrete wall. Without exchanging any more words, he guided her back onto the busy sidewalk and in the general direction of their rental car.

Close to ten minutes passed before he finally spoke and by then Vanessa had decided he was going to totally ignore what had happened. No doubt he was regretting giving in to the impulse of kissing his secretary. Especially kissing her as though he was enjoying every moment their lips had been locked together.

Oh, God, what had she done? What was he thinking now? That she was easy and gullible and helpless? That she was so stupid she'd allowed his kiss to go to her head and her heart?

"I hope you're not angry with me, Vanessa."

Stunned by this statement, she glanced his way. "I'm not angry. Why should I be?"

He stared up ahead of them and she could see they had reached the parking area where they'd left the car.

He answered, "Because I wasn't behaving like myself back there. Because I shouldn't have taken advantage of the moment like that. You've been through a lot these past couple of days."

So it hadn't really been him kissing her back there, she thought dismally, just a part of him that had succumbed to impulse. Well, that shouldn't surprise her. Conall was normally a calculated man and under normal circumstances he would never plan to make a pass at her. The notion bothered her far more than it should have.

"I'm a big girl. I could have pushed you away."

"Yeah, but—"

She groaned. "Let's forget the kiss, Conall."

"I don't want to forget it. I want to repeat it."

That was enough to stop her in her tracks and she looked at him with faint amazement.

She mumbled, "That's not going to happen."

He moved closer and when his hand came to rest on her shoulder, she felt herself melting all over again.

"Why?" he asked. "Because you liked it?"

Deciding now was the perfect time to be totally honest, she answered, "Yes. And to let anything start brewing between us now would be a big mistake."

A deep furrow appeared between his black brows. "Maybe you're right," he murmured, then before she could make any sort of reply, he placed a hand at her back and ushered her on toward the car. "But I'm not totally convinced that you are. Yet."

A shiver of uncertain anticipation rolled down Vanessa's spine. From now on she was going to have to stay on guard whenever she was with this man. Otherwise, she might wake up and find herself in his bed.

The next morning as Vanessa stepped out of the shower and slipped into a satin robe, a knock sounded on the door. Knowing it was far too early for housekeeping, she glanced through the peephole to see Conall standing on the opposite side of the door.

The sight of him surprised her. It wasn't quite seven yet. Last night when they'd returned to the hotel and parted ways, he'd not mentioned anything about meeting this early.

"It's me, Vanessa."

Drawing in a bracing breath, she opened the door and stared at him. He was already dressed in a pair of dark, Western-cut slacks and a crisp white shirt. His deep brown hair was combed back from his face and there was a faint smile on his lips, a soft sort of expression that she'd never seen on him before.

Her heart beating fast and hard, she blurted, "I'm not dressed yet."

His gray gaze slowly left her face to slide all the way to her bare toes. Vanessa had never felt so exposed in her life.

"I wasn't planning on us going out just yet," he explained. "I wanted to talk with you. Before we left the hotel."

Knowing she would look childish and prudish to send him away, she pulled the door wider and gestured for him to enter her room.

As he stepped past her, she clutched the front of her robe to her breasts and hoped he didn't notice the naked shape of them beneath the clinging fabric.

"Is something wrong?" she asked as she shut the door after him.

"No. And why do you always suspect something is wrong whenever I show up? You act like I'm some sort of bearer of bad news."

Her cheeks warmed with color as she joined him in the middle of the room. "I just…wasn't expecting you to be out so early. That's all. And all this legal stuff with the babies is not like anything I've dealt with before. I'll be glad when I sign the final documents this morning, before anything can go wrong."

"Nothing is going to go wrong," he said gently, "and the babies are what I'm here to talk to you about."

She stared at him, her brows lifted in question. "What else is there to talk about?"

Vanessa saw his eyes slide to the king-sized bed. The covers were rumpled and she'd left a set of black lacy lingerie lying atop the white sheet. She wondered what he was thinking. Was he remembering the kiss they'd shared last night or the intimate times he'd shared with his ex-wife?

"A few things," he said pensively, then focused his gaze back on her face. "I'll call room service for breakfast and we can eat out on the patio while we talk."

It was a statement, not a question, and for a moment she bristled at his authoritative attitude. She wanted to remind him that they were in a hotel room—her room to be exact—and he was supposed to be behaving as a supportive friend, not a boss. But she kept the thoughts to herself. Asking him to forget he was her boss while they were here in Vegas had already caused problems. Now wasn't the time or place to take that risk again.

"All right," she told him. "While you call I'll get dressed."

Crossing to the bed, she snatched up her lingerie, then walked to the closet to take down her dress. Behind her, she heard him picking up the phone.

"What would you like?" he called to her. "Fresh fruit and yogurt?"

Frowning, she turned to look at him. "You mean I get to order for myself?"

A sheepish smile settled over his face and that was all it took to turn her insides to mushy oatmeal.

"Sorry, Vanessa. I don't mean to be bossy but it—"

"Just comes natural to you," she finished with an understanding smile. "I'll bet you always tried to tell your younger siblings what to do and how to do it."

He laughed. "Somebody had to."

This was not the Conall she'd been working for the past two months, Vanessa thought. This man was far more approachable and endearing. He was also far more dangerous.

"Well, I do like fresh fruit and yogurt, but I need something more substantial this morning. Make it bacon and eggs and wheat toast."

"A woman who likes to eat in the morning. I like that," he said.

She was afraid to ask what he meant by that remark, so she simply excused herself and hurried to the bathroom to dress.

By the time she'd finished pulling on her clothes, swiping on a bit of makeup and combing her hair into casual waves around her face, she heard room service arriving.

She stepped from the bathroom just as Conall was handing the server a hefty tip. As the young man headed out the door, he turned to Vanessa.

"Everything is waiting out on the patio," he announced.

"Great. I'm starving."

Outside the morning was perfect with a blue, blue sky and a warm, gentle breeze. The table holding their breakfast was situated on a red brick patio edged by a row of palm trees. Thick blooming shrubs and tall agave plants acted as a privacy fence between the rooms. As Conall helped her into one of the rattan chairs, Vanessa couldn't help thinking the villa would be a perfect place for a honeymoon.

A honeymoon, she thought wryly. That kiss Conall had given her last night had messed up her thinking and had her dreaming about things she had no business dreaming about. She'd had her chance at love and marriage. It hadn't worked. And now she seriously doubted she'd ever find a man who would truly love her. A man she could trust with all her heart.

"I'm sure you've been wondering what I wanted to speak with you about," he said as the two of them began to eat.

Vanessa fortified herself with a long sip of strong coffee as she watched him slather a piece of toast with apricot jam.

"I am curious," she admitted.

"I've been thinking about your housing situation," he said before he bit into the toast.

"What is there to think about? I have my parents' home."

"Yes. But there's a house on the ranch that was vacated only a few days ago. It was just remodeled only last year with new flooring and up-to-date appliances. You'd have plenty of room for yourself and a nursery. And you'd be on the ranch—close by—in case you needed help."

Stunned and just a little vexed, Vanessa looked at him. "You know what my salary is, Conall. I couldn't afford to lease the house."

"Why not? It wouldn't cost you a penny."

All she could do was stare at him. "It's obvious you don't know me, Conall. Otherwise, you'd know that I don't go around looking for, or expecting, handouts."

He leveled a frustrated frown at her. "If you think I'm making you a *special* offer because you're my secretary, then you're in for a surprise. Not all of our employees are housed on the ranch and that's fine, too. But the housing we do supply for our ranch hands and house staff is considered a part of their salary, one of the benefits for working for the Diamond D. As I see it, you are an employee and the house is there—empty for now—but I can assure you, not for long."

Vanessa felt more than a little embarrassed. She'd quickly jumped to the conclusion that he was offering her an exclusive deal. All because he'd made this trip with her and given her that one long, mind-shattering kiss. How foolish could she be? He was a man who liked to help people whenever the opportunity arose. And he'd apparently enjoyed that kiss he'd given her. He'd said he wanted to repeat it. But in spite of that pleasant physical exchange, Conall Donovan didn't view her as anything special. She was simply his secretary.

"I'm sorry, Conall. Since the general-managing office handles that sort of thing I wasn't aware that the Diamond D offered housing to its employees free of charge."

A faint smile touched his lips as his gaze slid curiously over her face and Vanessa wondered how a pair of gray eyes could look so warm or how their gaze could feel even hotter to her skin.

"I see. So does that change your mind about moving to the ranch? I'd certainly feel a lot better about you and babies knowing you had close neighbors."

Up to a point, she could understand his thinking. Her parents' home was fairly isolated, with the nearest neighbor being a good five miles away. And even though the Valdezes' had raised five children in the tiny stucco structure, the rooms were small and limited to what she could do with them.

Still, the home was hers now and she was proud of it. She didn't need the best of things to be happy and that's the way she wanted her twins to be raised—with-

out the need for material trappings. He ought to understand that. He ought to know that for him to merely
imply she needed to find some place "better" was of-
fensive and hurtful to her. Besides, after dealing with
Jeff, she wanted her independence. Needed it, in fact.
But she didn't want to go into that now with Conall.

Reaching for the insulated coffeepot, she added a
splash of the hot liquid to her cooling cup. "I thank
you for the offer. But, no. It doesn't change my mind.
Until I get the hang of it, taking care of two newborns
is going to be…well, challenging. I need to be in a place
where I feel comfortable and at home. And that's at my
own place." Her gaze met his. "I hope you understand."

Conall dropped his attention to his plate as he shov-
eled up a forkful of egg and wondered why he felt so
disappointed. It wasn't as if he was a green teenager
and she'd turned him down for a date. Last night, after
he'd left her at the door of her room, the idea of offering her housing had entered his mind and once he'd
gone to bed, he'd lain awake for some time imagining
how it would be to have her and her new little family
close by. He'd liked the idea so much that he'd rushed
over here early to tell her about it. Now, seeing how
she didn't want his help, he felt deflated and foolish.

"I understand that you women have your own ideas
about things," he said. "I can accept that."

Even though her sigh was barely discernible, he
heard it. The sound put a faint frown between his brows
as he wondered why anything she was thinking and
feeling about him should matter. Hell, she was just his
secretary. Just because she'd become the sudden mother
of twin infants didn't make her any different than the

woman who'd worked in his office for the past two months, he reasoned with himself.

Yet this whole thing with the babies had forced Conall to see Vanessa in a more personal way. And last night, when he'd succumbed to his urges and kissed her, something had clicked inside him. Suddenly he'd been feeling, wanting, needing. All at once he'd felt the dead parts of him waking and bursting to life again.

Conall realized it was stupid of him to hang so much importance on one kiss. But he couldn't put it or her out of his mind.

"I'm glad," she said, "because I don't want to appear ungrateful."

He smiled at her. "Good. Because I have another offer for you. Especially since you turned the last one down," he added.

Her brows lifted with faint curiosity and Conall couldn't help but notice how the early morning sun was kissing her pearly skin and bathing it with a golden sheen. Last night, when he'd touched her face and laid his cheek against hers, he'd been overwhelmed at the softness and even now a part of him longed to reach across the table and trail his fingers across her skin, her lips.

"Don't you think you've already offered me enough?" she asked dryly.

Reaching for his coffee, he tried to sound like he was discussing business with a client. "Not yet. This is something essential to you and to me. I don't want to lose you as a secretary, so while you're at work you're going to need child care services. I insist that the ranch provide you with a nanny. Two, if need be."

She fell back against her chair and Conall could

see he'd shocked her. Clearly, she'd not been expecting him to offer her any sort of amenities simply because she was a Diamond D employee. In fact, she acted as though it would be wrong for her to accept anything from him. Which was quite a contrast to his ex-wife, who'd grabbed and snatched anything and everything she could, then expected more.

"Don't you think you're going a little overboard?" she asked after a long moment.

"Not really. When I think back through some of the secretaries I've endured in the past, hiring a nanny to keep a good one like you is nothing more than smart business sense."

Actually, there was nothing businesslike going through Conall's mind at the moment, yet he was playing it that way. Otherwise, he knew Vanessa would balk like a stubborn mule at his suggestion.

"Things have happened so quickly I've not yet had time to think of day care for the babies. There might be someone in Hondo to care for the twins while I'm at work," she said a bit tentatively. "Or Lincoln."

He smiled to himself. "Vanessa, we both know you'd be lucky to find a babysitter in either community. And making such a long drive every morning and evening with the babies wouldn't be practical."

She absently pushed at the egg on her plate. "Sometimes a person has to do things that are…well, not the most convenient."

"Why would you need to do that when I can hire someone to watch the babies right in your home? You wouldn't have to disturb them or drag them in and out in the weather. As far as I can see, it's the perfect solution."

She nodded briefly and he could see a range of emotions sweeping across her face. She clearly wanted to resist his help and Conall couldn't understand why. If he'd ever been harsh or cold with the woman, he didn't recall it. And though they'd never visited about things out of the office, he'd never treated her with indifference. He could understand, up to a point, her wanting to be independent. But now wasn't the time for her to worry about showing off her self-reliance. She had more than her own welfare to consider now. Maybe the only way she could think of him was as her boss, instead of a friend offering help. The idea bothered him greatly, although he couldn't figure why it should. He'd stopped caring what women thought of him a long time ago.

She let out a deep breath, then lifted her coffee cup from its saucer. "I'll be honest, Conall. I've been trying to budget in my head and the cost of child care is going to take a big hunk out of my salary. I'd be crazy to turn down your offer of a nanny. At least until the babies get older and I can get my feet planted more firmly."

Relief put a smile on his face. "Now you're making sense. I'll start making calls as soon as we finish breakfast."

"There is one condition, though, Conall."

He paused in the act of reaching for a second piece of toast. "Yes?"

Her brown eyes met his and for a split second his breath hung in his throat. He was slipping, damn it. None of this should feel so important to him. Yes, the babies were adorable and yes, Vanessa's kiss had been like sipping from a honeycomb. But Vanessa and the children weren't supposed to be his business or responsibility.

Her answer broke into his uneasy thoughts. "I also want to have a say in who you hire for the job."

In spite of his internal scolding, Conall began to breathe again. "I wouldn't have it any other way," he assured her.

By the time they finished the last bit of business at the lawyer's office, picked up the babies and boarded a plane back to Ruidoso, Vanessa felt as though she'd gone around the world and back again. The excitement of becoming an instant mother had finally caught up to her, along with the fact that she had no idea of how to deal with this new and different Conall.

The cool, aloof boss that she'd worked with for the past two months appeared to be completely gone. On the flight home, he'd been attentive, reassuring and helpful. When Rick had stirred and began to cry, he'd insisted on cradling the tiny boy in his arms and feeding him one of the bottles the nuns had prepared for their flight.

Seeing the big rancher handle the baby with such gentleness had overwhelmed her somewhat. He was such a man's man and she'd never seen him display much affection toward anyone or anything, except his grandmother Kate and the baby colts and fillies that were born every spring on the Diamond D.

She'd often wondered if his hard demeanor was the thing that had sent his ex-wife, Nancy, running to other pastures. But seeing him interact with her new son had given Vanessa a glimpse of a Conall that she'd never seen or knew existed. There was a soft side to him. So there must have been another, more complicated reason for his divorce.

For weeks now, Vanessa had told herself she didn't want to know what had happened to end her boss's marriage. After all, it wasn't her business and she'd had her own heartbreaking divorce to deal with. But now that Conall had kissed her, now that she'd seen for herself that he could be a hot-blooded man with all sorts of feelings, she'd grown even more curious about his marriage and divorce.

Trying to shove aside the personal thoughts about Conall, Vanessa glanced over her shoulder to see the twins sleeping soundly in the two car seats they'd purchased back in Las Vegas for the trip.

"I doubt the twins will feel any jet lag," Conall commented as he skillfully steered the truck over the mountainous highway toward Tinnie. "They've slept for nearly the entire trip."

She straightened in her seat and as she gazed out the window, she realized she was nearly home. So much had happened since they'd left for Vegas that she felt as though she'd been gone for weeks instead of two days. "That's what newborns mostly do, sleep. Unless they have colic and I'm praying that doesn't happen."

He glanced her way. "You know about babies and colic? I thought you were the youngest of the family."

"I am. But my mother used to reminisce to me about her babies. She said two of my brothers cried with the colic until they were six months old and she hardly got any sleep during that time."

"I don't suppose she had anyone to help, either. I mean, your dad worked hard and probably needed his rest at night. And she didn't have any older daughters to help out with a crying infant."

"No. My mother didn't have much help with anything. But she was a happy woman." Wistful now, she glanced at him. "I wish Mama could've seen the twins. She would have been so thrilled for me and so proud to have been their grandmother."

To her surprise he reached over and touched her hand with his. "I figure somewhere she does see, Vanessa."

Many of her friends and acquaintances had expressed their sorrow to Vanessa when her mother had died unexpectedly and she'd appreciated all of them. Yet, these simple words from Conall were the most comforting anyone had given her and she was so touched that she was unable to form a reply. The best she could do was cast him a grateful little smile.

He smiled back and she suddenly realized he didn't need or expect her to say anything. He understood how she felt. The notion not only surprised her, but it also stunned her with uneasy fear. She couldn't allow her feelings for this man to tumble out of control. She had to keep her head intact and her heart safely tucked away in the shadows.

Minutes later Conall parked the truck near the short board fence that cordoned off the small yard from the graveled driveway. After he cut the motor, he said, "Give me the keys and I'll open up before we carry the babies in."

Vanessa dug the house key from her purse and handed it to him. "I'll be unstrapping the twins," she told him.

When he returned, he gathered up Rose from her

car seat while Vanessa cradled Rick in the crook of her arm.

Nudging the truck door shut with his broad shoulder, he said, "I'll come back for your luggage and diaper bag later. Right now let's get the babies inside and settled."

Vanessa started to the house with Conall following her onto the tiny porch and past the open door leading into a small living room.

Pausing in the middle of the floor, she glanced around with faint confusion. "Someone has been inside and left the air conditioner on," she said. "I told Maura where the key was but when I last talked to her she didn't mention driving over here."

A sheepish expression stole over his lean face. "I confess. I sent Maura over here to…take care of a few things. I guess she had the forethought to turn on the air conditioner so it would be comfortable when you arrived." He inclined his head toward an arched doorway. "Are the bedrooms through there?"

Vanessa wanted to ask him what sort of things Maura would be doing here. She'd already arranged for a young neighbor boy to feed the goats and the chickens. But seeing he was already changing the subject, she let it pass. She'd be talking to Maura soon enough anyway, she thought.

Nodding in response to his question, she walked past him and he followed her through the doorway and into a tiny hall. As she made a left-hand turn that would lead them to the bedrooms, she said, "My bed is queen-sized so I guess for now, until I get a crib, I'll have to put the twins with me and surround them with pillows."

"Vanessa, why don't you put them in the spare bedroom?"

"Because there's only a narrow twin bed in there. And everything in there needs to be dusted badly."

"It couldn't be that dusty. And a small bed might work better. Let's look at it."

Vexed that he wanted to argue the matter, she paused to frown at him. "Conall, I told you—"

"Just humor me, Vanessa," he interrupted. "Let me see the room. That's all I'm asking."

How could she deny him such a simple request when he'd just interrupted the past two days of his life to help her? Not to mention absorbing the expense of the trip.

With an indulgent shake of her head, she muttered, "Oh, all right. But I'm beginning to think you'd have been better suited to raise mules than Thoroughbreds, Conall."

He chuckled. "I have a lot of Grandmother Kate in me."

The door to the spare bedroom was slightly ajar and she reached inside to flip on the light before pushing the door wide.

Glancing around at him, she pointed out, "Your grandmother Kate is wonderful. Not stubborn."

"That's what I mean."

The grin on his face made her heart flutter foolishly and she quickly turned her attention away from him to push the bedroom door wide.

"Oh!" The one word was quietly gasped as she stared in complete shock. The dusty drab room that she'd been planning to refurnish one day had been transformed into a fairy-tale nursery. Twisting her head around, she said with stunned accusation, "You knew about this!"

He motioned for her to step inside the room. "Perhaps you should take a look before you decide to chop off my head."

Dazed, she moved slowly into the room while her gaze tried to encompass everything at once. The walls had been painted a soft yellow and bordered with wallpaper of brightly colored stick horses. A classic crib made of dark cherrywood with carved spokes stood in one corner while on the opposite wall a matching chest and dresser framed a window draped with Priscilla curtains printed with the same theme as the wallpaper. Behind them, in another available corner, a full-sized rocking horse made of carved wood, complete with a saddle and a black rag-mop mane and tail waited for little hands and feet to climb on and put him in motion.

"This is…unbelievable," she said in a hushed voice. "It's lovely, Conall. Truly lovely."

"The crib is especially made to connect another one to it later on," he said. "Maura tells me most parents let their twins sleep together until they get a little older. So we thought the one would do for now."

Vanessa stepped over to the bed to see it was made up with smooth, expensive sheets and a yellow-and-white comforter. At the footboard, a mobile with birds and bees dangled temptingly out of reach.

"I think—" She paused as a lump of emotional tears clogged her throat and forced her to swallow. "It's all perfect, Conall."

She pulled back the comforter and placed Rick gently on the mattress. Conall bent forward and laid Rose next to him. Her throat thick, Vanessa watched as he smoothed a finger over the baby girl's red-gold hair, then repeated the same caress on the boy.

Once he straightened away from the babies, he rested

his hand against her back and murmured, "I'm glad you think it's perfect, Vanessa. I wanted this little homecoming to be that way for you."

She looked up at him as all sorts of thoughts and questions swirled in her head. "I don't know what to think…or say. The cost, all the work—"

"Don't fret about any of that, Vanessa," he said quickly, cutting her off. "The cost wasn't as much as you think. And the two stable hands that Maura borrowed from the ranch to help her were only too glad to get out of mucking stalls for a couple of days."

Even though Maura and others had worked to prepare the nursery, no one had to tell her that Conall had been the orchestrator of the whole thing and the fact left her totally bewildered. For a man who said he would never have children, Conall was behaving almost like a new father.

What did it mean? Was he doing all this for her? Or the babies? None of it made sense.

Yes, innately he was a good, decent man, she reasoned. And he could afford to be generous. Being his secretary, she personally dealt with the charities he supported, and the people he helped, some of whom he didn't even know. She could almost understand him paying for the trip, the nursery, the nanny. Almost. But the kiss, the touches, the smiles and easy words, those hadn't been acts of charity. Or had they?

"Vanessa? There's a tiny little frown on your forehead. Is something wrong?"

Hoping that was all he could read on her face, she said, "I'm just wondering."

"About what?"

She couldn't answer that, Vanessa decided. If he

knew her thoughts had been dwelling on his kiss he'd most likely be amused. And she couldn't stand that. Not from him.

"Nothing. Just forget it," she said dismissively.

He studied her face for a quiet moment, then bent his head and placed a soft kiss on her forehead. "I'm going to go get the rest of your things from the truck," he said gently.

As Vanessa watched him leave the nursery, she realized the twins had done more than made her an instant mother. For now, they'd turned her boss into a different man, one that was very dangerous to her vulnerable heart.

Chapter 5

A week and a half later, Conall stood inside the only barn on the Diamond D that was still the original structure their grandfather, Arthur Donovan, had erected back in the 1960s when the ranch was first established.

The walls of the structure consisted of rough, lapped boards while the wide span of roof was corrugated iron. Down through the years loving attention had allowed the old building to survive the elements and to this day the building was, in his opinion, the prettiest on the ranch.

Conall would be the first person to admit he'd always been attached to the old barn. It held some of his earliest and fondest childhood memories, many of which included his stern grandfather warning him not to climb to the top of the rafter-high hay bales.

"This old building is a tinderbox just waiting for

a match or cigarette to come along and ignite it," his brother Liam commented as the two men stood in the middle of the cavernous barn.

For the past few years Liam had been the sole horse trainer for the Diamond D and for the most part Conall allowed him to dictate how the working area of the ranch was laid out and what equipment was needed to keep the horses healthy, happy and in top-notch running and breeding condition. But the old barn was a different matter. It was full of history. It was a point of tradition and Conall was just stubborn enough and old-fashioned enough to insist it remain the same.

"Liam, I've heard this from you a hundred times. You ought to know by now that I have no intention of changing my mind on the subject."

Rolling his eyes with impatience, Liam answered, "Fine. If you don't want to tear the firetrap down, then at least you can renovate and replace the lumber with cinder block."

Conall groaned. "Sorry. I'm not doing that, either. I don't want our ranch to look like the grounds of a penitentiary."

Slapping a pair of leather work gloves against the palm of his hand, Liam muttered, "I don't have to tell you what a fire would do to this place."

The sun had disappeared behind the mountains at least forty-five minutes ago and for the first time in months Conall had left his office earlier than usual with plans to drive to Vanessa's. He didn't want to waste his time going over this worn-out argument with Liam.

"Liam, I might not have my hands on the horses every day like you do, but I do understand their needs and how to care for them. You damn well know that I'm aware of the devastation a fire causes to a horse barn or stables. But—" he used his arm to gesture to the interior of the building "—we're not housing horses in here now. Besides that, we have the most modern and up-to-date fire alarm system installed in every structure on the ranch. Not to mention the fact that we have security guards and stable grooms with the horses around the clock. The horses are safer than our own grandmother is when she's sitting in a rocker on the back porch. So don't give me the fire argument."

Liam let out a disgruntled grunt. "You've got to be the biggest old fogey I know, Conall. What about the argument of updating the barn to make it more usable and efficient? Right now all we have in here are hay and tractor tires!"

"This barn worked for Grandfather and it's still working for us. And right now, it's getting late. Let's get to the house," Conall told him.

With both men agreeing to let the matter drop for now, they stepped out into the rapidly fading light. As they walked to the main house, Liam kept his steps abreast of Conall's.

"I'm going over to the Bar M after dinner," he announced abruptly. "Want to come along?"

Mildly surprised, Conall glanced at him. "The Bar M? The Sanderses giving a party or something?" he asked, then shook his head. "That was a stupid question of me, wasn't it? You don't do parties."

Beneath his cowboy hat, Liam's lips pressed together in a grim line. "Why do you have to be a bastard at times, Conall?"

Conall bit back a sigh. It was true he'd purposely

asked the question to dig at his younger brother. But he'd not done it out of meanness as Liam seemed to think. He'd done it out of care and concern. But trying to explain that to his younger brother would be as easy as making it rain on a cloudless day, he thought dismally.

"I don't know—just goes with my job, I suppose," he quipped.

Liam grunted. "Compared to my job, yours is like a day off. You should be smiling and kicking your heels."

Even though Conall put in long, stressful hours, his job couldn't begin to be compared to Liam's. His younger brother was up at three in the morning in order to be at the stables at four and most nights he didn't fall into bed until long after the rest of the household was sound asleep. When Ruidoso's racing meet wasn't going on, he was shipping horses to tracks in the mid-south and on to the west coast. And their health and racing condition was only a part of his responsibility. He had to make sure each one was strategically entered in a race that would enhance his or her chances of winning.

"I know it," Conall admitted. "That's why you're going to have to give in and replace Clete. Or you're going to end up in the hospital with a heart attack."

Three years ago, Liam's longtime assistant, Cletis Robinson, had died after a lengthy illness. The death of the seventy-five-year-old man had shaken the whole ranch and especially the Donovan family, who'd valued Clete's friendship for more than thirty years. Liam grunted again. "According to Bridget I don't have a heart."

"She doesn't believe I have one, either," Conall half

joked. "I guess our little sister thinks we should be like those namby-pamby guys she went to med school with."

"Bridget is too soft for her own good," Liam muttered.

"So why are you going over to the Bar M this evening?" Conall asked as they approached a side entrance to the main ranch house.

"Chloe has a two-year-old gelding she's thinking about selling. I think he might be good enough to earn some money."

Pausing with surprise, Conall looked at him. "There has to be a catch. Chloe would never sell a good runner."

"Normally, no. But she was forced to geld this one. And Chloe doesn't like to invest time or money into a horse that can't reproduce."

Conall tried not to wince as he reached to open the door. "Yeah," he said, unable to keep the sarcasm from his voice. "Throwing offspring is the most important thing."

Close on his heels, Liam cursed. "Hell, Conall—"

"Forget I said that," Conall quickly interrupted. "You do what you think about the gelding. I have plans to see the twins tonight."

The two men entered the house and started down a long hallway that would take them to the central part of the house.

"The twins," Liam repeated blankly. "You mean Vanessa's new twins?"

"What other twins do we know?" Conall countered.

Liam stepped up so that the two of them were walking abreast of each other. "Well, there's the Gibson twins. You know, the ones we dated in high school."

Conall chuckled. "So you haven't forgotten them, either?"

Liam grunted with faint humor. "Forget two blonde tornadoes? They might have been short on intelligence but they were long on entertainment," he said, then glanced at Conall. "So what's the deal with Vanessa's twins? I thought after that trip to Las Vegas you had everything taken care of?"

Vanessa and the twins were settled now and from what she'd told him over the phone, everything was going fine. So why was he giving in to the urge to tear over to her house, Conall asked himself? Because ever since that evening they'd returned from Vegas he'd been dying to see the babies again. And more than that, he missed Vanessa, missed seeing her at her desk and talking with her, however briefly, throughout the busy day.

"They're fine. I have a gift for the babies that I want to deliver."

Liam studied him faint dismay. "Making a trip out to Vegas and bringing them home wasn't enough of a gift?"

Apparently Liam didn't know about the new nursery he'd funded for the twins or the fact that he was in the process of hunting for a full-time nanny. And Conall wasn't about to tell him. What went on between him and Vanessa was none of Liam's or anyone else's business, he decided.

"No. I wanted to give them something personal. After all, Vanessa is my secretary. And it's not like she had a baby shower." Seeing they'd reached the staircase that led up to the floor where his bedroom and several others were located, he broke away from his brother's side. As he started the climb, he threw a parting comment over his shoulder. "Good luck with Chloe. You're going to need it if you try to deal with her. She's tough."

"She might be tough, big brother, but she's not dangerous."

Conall glanced behind him to see Liam was still standing at the bottom of the stairs staring thoughtfully up at him.

"What does that mean?" Conall asked.

With a dismissive wave, Liam began to move on down the hallway. "You figure it out," he called back to Conall.

From the Diamond D to Vanessa's place, the highway meandered through pine-covered mountains then opened up to bald hills spotted with scrub pinion, twisted juniper and random tufts of grass, and this evening he took in the landscape with renewed appreciation. It wasn't often that Conall left the ranch for any reason. Unless there was an important conference or horse-racing event for him to attend, there wasn't a need for him to leave the isolated sanctuary of his home. Clients came to him, not the other way around.

Going to Vegas with Vanessa had definitely been out-of-character for him. And this trip tonight was even more so, he admitted to himself. Especially since he'd sworn off women and dating.

So what was happening to him? he wondered as he rounded a bend and the turnoff to Vanessa's house came into view. Had two little babies reminded him that his life wasn't over? Or was he simply waking up after a long dormant spell? Either way, it felt good to be getting out, good to think of seeing the babies, and even better to envision kissing Vanessa again.

* * *

Vanessa was at the back part of the house in a small alcove used for a laundry room when she heard a faint knock at the front door. Surprised by the unexpected sound, she used her hip to shove the dryer door closed and hurried through the house. In the past few days she'd had a few old friends and acquaintances stop by to see the babies, but it was getting far too late in the evening for such a neighborly visit.

Before opening the door, she peeked through the lacy curtain covering a window that overlooked the front porch. The moment she spotted Conall standing on the tiny piece of concrete, her heart momentarily stopped. He'd not been here since the evening they'd returned from Las Vegas and a few days had passed since she'd talked to him on the phone. It wasn't like her rigidly scheduled boss to show up unannounced on her doorstep. But then it wasn't like Conall to leave the Diamond D, much less leave it to come here.

Momentarily pressing a hand to her chest, she drew in a bracing breath, then pulled the door wide to greet him. This evening he was dressed in old jeans and a predominately white plaid shirt with pearl snaps. A black Stetson was pulled low over his forehead and she was struck by how much younger and relaxed he looked. This was Conall the horseman—not the businessman—and rough sexuality surrounded him like an invisible cloud.

She released the breath she'd been holding. "Hello, Conall."

A sheepish smile crossed his lean features. "Sorry I didn't call first, Vanessa, but I didn't want you thinking you needed to rush around and tidy things before I got here. Am I interrupting?"

Her insides were suddenly shaking, making her feel worse than foolish. For weeks she'd worked with this man every day. It wasn't like he was a stranger. But actually he was a stranger, she thought. This man on her porch wasn't the same as the tough-as-nails boss who ran a multimillion-dollar horse ranch; he was a man she was just beginning to know and like. Far too much.

"Not at all. Won't you come in?" she asked.

"Thanks," he murmured as he stepped through the door.

As he walked to the middle of the small living room, his male scent trailed after him and as her eyes traveled over his broad shoulders and long muscular legs, Vanessa felt her own knees grow ridiculously weak.

"Please have a seat," she offered, "or would you rather take a look at the babies first? They're in the kitchen. Asleep in their bassinet."

Two days after they'd returned from Las Vegas, a delivery truck had arrived at the door with a double bassinet fashioned just for twins. The card accompanying it had simply read, *I thought you might need this, too.*

She'd immediately called Conall and thanked him for the gift, but now that he was here in the flesh, now that his gaze was on her face, she felt extremely exposed and confused. Why was he really here? For her or the babies?

With a guilty little grin, he pulled off the black Stetson and placed it on a low coffee table in front of the couch. "If you don't mind I'd love to see the babies."

"Sure. I was just about to eat. Have you had dinner?" she asked as she motioned for him to follow her out of the room.

"I didn't take time to eat," he admitted. "Liam had me cornered and then it was too late to join the family at the dining table."

"I'm sure Kate wasn't too pleased about that."

He chuckled. "You've heard about Grandmother's strict rules of being on time for dinner?"

Vanessa smiled fondly. "Years ago, when I visited Maura at the ranch, Kate's rules were the first things I learned about the Donovan household. I remember being very scared to enter the dining room."

"Why? Grandmother always loves having young people around."

Shrugging, she entered the open doorway to the kitchen while Conall followed closely behind her. "I always thought I looked too raggedy to sit at her dining table or that I'd say something stupid or wrong."

He shook his head. "Grandmother has never been a snob. Strict, yes, but not a snob. And she made sure the rest of us weren't, either."

"I know. But I always felt a little out of place in your home, Conall." She laughed softly and gestured to the small room they were standing in. It was neat and clean, but the wooden cabinets were more than fifty years old and the porcelain sink chipped and stained. The ceiling was so low that Conall had to duck in order to keep from hitting his head on the light fixture and though the appliances were still chugging along, they'd seen better days. "This isn't quite the same as the kitchen in the Diamond D."

"No," he admitted. "But it's very homey and inviting. And it's yours. That should make you proud."

His comments made her feel warm and good. "It does," she agreed, then motioned to the bassinet sitting near a double window. "I know the babies can't see yet, but I put them by the window just in case they can pick up the movement of lights and shadows. But I think they notice music more than anything. Whenever I sing to them they usually fall right to sleep. To end the torture, I guess."

Chuckling, Conall crossed the small room and bent over the sleeping babies. "They've grown," he said just above a whisper. "And their skin doesn't look as ruddy."

"They're losing that just-born look," she told him.

He said, "Before you know it they'll be rolling, then crawling and walking. It seems incredible that they start out so tiny and grow into big people like us."

He gazed at them for several long moments before he finally straightened to his full height. When he turned away from the bassinet Vanessa caught sight of his profile and was immediately struck by the wistful expression on his face.

Were the twins softening him? she wondered. Perhaps changing his stance about not having children? She wanted to think so, although she didn't know why the issue was important to her. Whether Conall ever raised a family or not would depend on the next woman he married. Not her and the twins.

He walked over to where she stood by the cabinet counter. "I don't mean this in a bad way, Vanessa, but you look exhausted. I assume the babies are keeping you up at night?"

Unwittingly, she touched a hand to her bare cheek. Without makeup and her hair pulled into a messy knot at the back of her head, she no doubt looked terrible.

She hated having him see her like this, but it was too late to worry about her appearance now.

"Some nights are more broken than others," she admitted. "If the babies would both wake at the same time it would be a big help. But Rick always wakes far before his sister and then about the time I get him fed and asleep and I'm about to crawl back into bed, she starts fussing." She smiled at him. "But I'm not complaining. Having the babies...well, it's like a dream come true."

He reached out and rubbed a hand up and down her arm in what was meant to be a comforting gesture. But for Vanessa, it was like flint striking stone. The friction was igniting a trail of tiny flames along her skin, making it difficult for her to breathe.

"You need help, Vanessa. You can't continue to handle two infants alone. I'm sorry it's taken so long for me to find a nanny, but things have been hectic in the office since you've been away."

She sighed. "I'm sorry I've gotten everything out of whack. I did call Fiona and thank her for filling in for me at the office. I hope the job isn't wearing her out."

Conall chuckled. "Wearing Mom out? Not hardly. She thinks she's still in her twenties instead of entering her sixties."

"She had six children and I'm letting two wear me down," Vanessa said with a grimace. "That makes me feel like a wimp."

"She didn't have two at once. That would wear anyone out. But today I think I might have found a nanny and if things go as planned she'll be over tomorrow or the next day for your approval."

Her interest sparked, Vanessa asked, "Do I know this woman?"

"I doubt it. Her name is Hannah Manning and she's a retired nurse that Maura used to work with at Sierra General."

"Oh. Well, if she's a nurse, she ought to be qualified for the job. I'll look forward to meeting her."

His hand was still on her arm, sending sizzling little signals to her brain, and she could only hope he couldn't guess how much she wanted to touch him, kiss him again. In spite of her days and nights being consumed with caring for the twins, she'd not been able to quit thinking about the man.

"I've stewed a pot of *carne guisada* for dinner," she said, her gaze awkwardly avoiding his. "Would you like to join me?"

"I'd love to," he murmured, "but I'd like to do something else first."

She was wondering what *something else* could possibly be when his forefinger slid beneath her chin and lifted her face up to his. Their gazes clashed and Vanessa's heart began to thud so hard she could scarcely breathe.

"Conall, this…is…not good," she finally managed to whisper.

His mouth twisted to a sexy slant. "How do you know that? We haven't done it yet."

She groaned with misgivings but the sound didn't deter him. Instead, both his hands came up to frame the sides of her face. The tender intimacy shot her resistance to tiny pieces and as his head lowered toward hers, she closed her eyes and leaned into him.

This time the meeting of their mouths was not the fragile exploration they'd exchanged in Las Vegas. No, this time it was all-out hunger, and what little breath

Vanessa had beforehand was instantly swept away by the crush of his hard lips.

Instinctively her hands grabbed for support and landed smack in the middle of his chest. She gripped folds of his cotton shirt as the heat of his body infused hers with heady warmth and his hands began a lazy expedition against her shoulders.

Certain she was going to dissolve in a helpless puddle if the kiss went any further, Vanessa frantically tore herself away and turned her back to him.

She was fiercely trying to fill her lungs with oxygen, when his lips pressed against her ear and she closed her eyes as he began to whisper, "I'm not going to apologize for that, Vanessa. It felt too right."

She couldn't argue that point. Until now, until Conall's lips had touched hers, no man's kiss had ever spun her away to such a fairy-tale world. And that was the problem, she thought desperately. Conall was a prince and he wasn't looking to make her his princess.

She swallowed hard. "I don't expect you to apologize," she said in a faint voice. "I'm just—" Stiffening her resolve, she turned back to him. "I don't know what's going through your mind, Conall. But I think you should understand that I'm not a woman who plays around."

For a fraction of a second, he looked astounded and then a grimace tightened his features. "Do you think I'm a man who plays around?"

Her eyes searched his. "I've never thought so. But you're starting to make me wonder."

He let out a mocking snort. "I haven't touched another woman in a long, long time. Does that sound like a man that's on the prowl?"

It sounded like a man who was still in love with his ex-wife, or one that had been wounded so badly he'd turned away from love altogether. Either way, Vanessa thought, the notion was a bleak one.

Sighing heavily, she stepped around him and crossed over to a small gas range. Giving one of the knobs a savage twist, she ignited a flame beneath a blue granite pot.

After a moment, she answered his question. "No. It sounds to me like a man that's confused."

"Confused, hell," he muttered.

She glanced over her shoulder to see him striding toward her and before she could stop it, desire washed through her like a hot wave, knocking down her defenses before she could even get them erected.

"Well, if you're not mixed up, I am," she admitted.

He stopped within a few inches of her and though he didn't touch her, Vanessa could almost feel his hands, his gaze, roaming her face, her body.

"Explain that, would you?"

A war exploded inside her and she was trying to decide if she wanted to throw herself in his arms or scurry out of the room, when he shifted closer.

She tried to swallow but her throat was so dry she nearly choked in the process. Finally, she managed to say, "I don't understand any of this, Conall."

He was looking at her with that same stony expression she'd seen on him in the office when things weren't going his way.

"It would help if I knew what *this* was," he stated.

The fact that he was deliberately being ignorant made her clench her jaw tight and suddenly all the doubts and emotions that had been swirling around in her for the past two weeks boiled to the surface. "You know what I'm talking about, Conall!" she burst out. "I've worked for you every day for more than two months and you hardly took a moment to look at me, much less touch me. Now all of a sudden you behave as though I'm irresistible. It's—it's ridiculous! That's what it is."

Behind her the stewed beef began to boil rapidly and the sound matched the blood pounding in her ears. Twisting around to the stove, she automatically lowered the flame as she sucked in a deep breath and tried to calm herself. But the effort failed completely as soon as his hands settled upon her shoulders.

"Vanessa, I don't understand why you're so worked up over a kiss," he murmured. "I'm not asking you to jump into bed with me."

The mere idea of making intimate love to this man was enough to make her face flame and her body burn. And she suddenly felt terribly, terribly embarrassed. Maybe she was acting foolish and naive. Maybe she was making a mountain out of a molehill.

Forcing herself to turn and face him, she said, "I'm sorry, Conall, but this change in our relationship has caught me off guard. I wasn't expecting any of this and—"

"Do you think I was? Hell, Vanessa, like I said before I've not even looked in a woman's direction in years. And even after you came to work for me I wasn't thinking of you in this way, but…"

She waited for him to finish, but he appeared to be lost for words.

"But what, Conall? I receive word about the babies

and suddenly you're looking at me as though you've never seen me before."

"That's true," he admitted.

Incredulous, Vanessa stared at him. "It is?"

Clearly frustrated, he swiped a hand through his dark brown hair. "I can't give you a solid reason for my behavior, Vanessa, except that the day you fainted in the office I began to see you as a woman."

Grimacing, she peered around him to the opposite side of the room. Thankfully, the twins were still sleeping soundly in their bassinet.

"And what was I before?" she asked dryly, "A robot that answered the phone and dealt with your correspondence?"

He groaned. "I'm trying to explain."

"You're not doing a very good job of it," she pointed out.

His hands slipped from her shoulders and slid down her arms until they reached her hands. Then, like a pair of flesh-and-bone handcuffs, his fingers clamped around her wrists.

"You're not making the task any easier, either," he countered.

Nervously moistening her lips, she focused her gaze to the middle button on his shirt. "I suppose I'm not," she admitted. "But try to see things from my angle, Conall. Suddenly you're making the twins a nursery, buying them gifts and—and handling me as though… you want to! What am I suppose to think? Are you playing up to me just so you can be around the twins?"

"That's damned stupid!"

Surprised by sharpness in his voice, her gaze flew up to his face.

"I care about the twins," he went on. "But I'm pretty sure you'd let me visit them whether I kissed you or not."

Desperate for answers, she spluttered at him, "So why are you kissing me? Because your libido has woken up and I'm handy?"

His nostrils flared as his fingers tightened on her wrists. "Vanessa, none of this is hard to understand. I'm simply being a man. A man that has found himself attracted to a woman. A kiss is...well, I'm trying to tell you that I think we should get to know each other better. On a more personal level."

She groaned with disbelief. "That wasn't a get-to-know-you kiss, Conall. That was more like an I-missed-you-like-hell kiss."

To her amazement, a tempting little grin spread across his lips. "Finally, you're getting something right," he murmured, his eyes settling softly on her face. "I have missed you like hell."

His admission sent a foolish thrill rushing through her, spinning her heartbeat to a rapid thud.

"That's very hard to believe," she said, in a breathless whisper.

"Then maybe I'd better give you another demonstration. Just to prove my point."

Making his intentions clear, his head bent toward hers and though Vanessa told herself she'd be smart to make a quick escape, she couldn't make a move. Instead, she stood transfixed and waited for his lips to capture hers.

Chapter 6

Just a few more moments, Vanessa promised herself, and then she'd gather the strength to step away from the heated search of Conall's lips. She'd get her breath back, along with her senses, and then she'd remind herself why being in his arms was as dangerous as sidling up to a sizzling stick of dynamite.

But so far the minutes continued to tick away and she'd not taken that first move to end their kiss. Instead, she couldn't stop her lips from parting beneath his, her arms from sliding around his waist.

She was leaning into him, her whole body buzzing with the anticipation of getting even closer to his hard body, when she caught the sound of Rick's faint whimpers.

The pressure of Conall's lips eased just a fraction, telling her that he must have picked up on the baby's subtle call. Even so, he didn't bother to end the kiss until the tiny boy let loose with an all-out cry.

Lifting his head, he drew in a ragged breath and glanced over his shoulder toward the bassinet. "That child needs to learn better timing," he said with humor, then glancing back to Vanessa, he added, "Sounds like duty calls."

Struggling to regain her composure, she said in a husky voice, "It's Rick. I can tell by his cry. He's probably thinking it's time for his supper, too."

After switching off the fire beneath the *carne guisada*, she walked over to the bassinet. Conall followed close on her heels.

"Can I help?" he asked.

She lifted the fussing Rick from the bed. "It would be a big help if you could hold him while I heat a bottle."

Conall eagerly held out his arms. "I'd be glad to hold him, just don't expect me to make him stop crying," he warned. "I wouldn't know how."

She carefully placed the baby in the crook of Conall's strong arm. "Just rock him a little," she suggested. "And don't worry if he keeps on crying. He's not hurting, just exercising his opinion."

Chuckling, he looked down at the fussy baby. "Oh, well, we men have to do that from time to time."

Pausing for just a moment, Vanessa couldn't help but take in the sight of Conall with tiny Rick cradled against his broad chest. The man looked like a born father, she thought, certainly not a guy that had sworn off having children.

Shaking away that disturbing notion, Vanessa hurried to the refrigerator to fetch the bottle. She was about to place it in the microwave, when Rose decided to let loose with a wail.

"I think you'd better make it two bottles," Conall said, raising his voice above the crying.

"So I hear."

Vanessa collected another bottle from the refrigerator and quickly heated them to a wrist-warm temperature. By the time she handed Conall one of the bottles and went to gather Rose from the bassinet, the girl was howling at the top of her lungs.

"I think you'll find it easier to feed him if you're sitting down," Vanessa told Conall, then she picked up Rose and crooned soothingly to the baby while carrying her over to the dining table.

After taking a seat, Vanessa propped the baby in the crook of her arm and offered her the bottle. Rose latched on to the nipple and began to nurse hungrily.

On the opposite side of the table Conall was trying to emulate Vanessa's movements. "I've never fed a baby before," he admitted. "I'm not sure I'm doing any of this right."

From what Vanessa could see the Donovan family had been having babies left and right with Maura's two boys and Brady's little girl. She found it difficult to believe that Conall hadn't given at least one of them a bottle. Especially Brady's daughter, since the two brothers lived together in the main ranch house. Sure, he was a busy man, she reasoned, but not that busy. Perhaps the babies had all been breast-fed. That might account for his lack of experience, she thought.

"There's nothing to it," she assured him. "Just keep his head supported and the bottle tilted upward so he won't suck air. He'll do the rest."

He shifted Rick to a comfortable position and offered him the bottle. Once the baby was nursing quietly, Conall looked over at Vanessa and smiled. "Hey, that's quite a silencer. Does a bottle always do the trick?"

Vanessa chuckled. "Unfortunately, no. Sometimes they cry when they aren't hungry and I have to try to figure out what's wrong and what they're trying to tell me."

He nodded. "Like a horse. They can't talk with words, but they have other ways of communicating."

It wasn't a surprise to Vanessa to hear Conall use equine terminology. Even though he didn't spend his days down at the barns as Liam did, he was equally as knowledgeable about the animals. In fact, the first time she'd seen Conall up close was when she'd visited the Diamond D and she and Maura had walked down to the training area where Conall had been breezing a huge black Thoroughbred around an oval dirt track. At the time he'd been a lean teenager, not the muscular man he was now. Yet she'd remembered being impressed by his strength and the easy way he'd handled the spirited stallion.

Needless to say, from that moment on he'd been her dark, secret prince and she'd dreamed of how incredible it would be to be the object of his affection. But then he'd graduated from high school and left for college. Vanessa had put away her crush for the rich Donovan boy and focused on the reality of her future, one that included leaving Lincoln County, New Mexico, and her adolescent dreams behind.

"Vanessa, you've gone far way. What are you thinking?"

Unaware that she'd gotten so lost in her thoughts,

her face warmed with a blush as she glanced over at him. "Actually, I was thinking back to the first time I saw you," she admitted.

The lift of his dark brows said she'd surprised him.

"Really? You remember that?"

Clearly his memory bank didn't include the first time he'd seen her, but then she hardly expected him to recall such a thing. He'd been older and had moved in much higher social circles than she. He'd always been associated with the brightest and prettiest girls on the high school campus. He would have never bothered to give someone like her a second glance.

"I do. You were on the track, exercising one of your father's horses."

He chuckled with fond remembrance. "Hmm. That must have been when I was thirty pounds lighter."

"You were about seventeen."

With a shake of his head, he murmured, "So long ago."

"I had a huge crush on you."

The moment the words passed her lips, Vanessa expected amusement to appear on his face, or even a laugh to rumble out of him. Instead, he studied her thoughtfully for a long, long spell and Vanessa got the impression he was thinking back to those carefree days before either of them had met their respective spouses.

"I didn't know," he said finally.

She felt the blush on her face sting her cheeks even hotter. To escape his searching gaze, she bent her head over Rose's sweet little face.

"No," she murmured, as she absently adjusted the receiving blanket around the baby's shoulders. "I would have died with embarrassment if you'd found out. In fact, I never told anyone about my feelings for you. Not even my mother."

"And why was that?" he quietly asked.

That pulled her attention back to him and she smiled wanly. "Mama was a realist. She would have given me a long lecture about crying for the moon."

His brows formed a line of disapproval. "You make it sound like I was some sort of unattainable prize, Vanessa."

"To me you were."

His head swung back and forth. "I was just a young man, like millions of others in the world."

Not to her. Not then. Not now, Vanessa thought. With a shake of her head, she gave him a patient smile. "Conall, look around. You didn't pick your girlfriends from this sort of background. Nor would you now."

Rolling his eyes toward the ceiling, he mouthed a curse under his breath. "I don't have girlfriends now. I've already told you that." He lowered his gaze back to her face. "Unless I count you as one."

Her heart gave a jerk. "Is that what I am to you?"

A slow grin tilted the corners of his lips. "I think that's a subject we need to discuss, don't you?"

Was he serious? No. He couldn't be. But, oh, his kiss had felt very, very serious. And that scared her. She wasn't emotionally capable of dealing with a man like him. "No. That's out of the question."

"Why?"

She couldn't stop the tiny groan from sounding in her throat. "I could give you a whole list of reasons. The main one being we have to work with each other."

"So? I can't see that posing a problem. Neither of us are married or committed to someone else."

"It would make things awkward," she said flatly. "Impossible, in fact."

Seeing that Rose had quit nursing and fallen asleep, Vanessa placed the near empty bottle on the table. Rising to her feet, she carefully positioned the baby against her shoulder and gently patted her back. As soon as she heard a loud burp, she carried the sleeping girl back to the bassinet.

"I think he's finished eating, too," Conall told her. "But he's not asleep. His eyes are wide open."

"He probably won't cry now if you put him back by his sister," she suggested as she crossed the room to pull dishes from the cabinet. "But you need to burp him first."

"I might need a little help with that."

Leaving the task of the dishes behind, she walked back over to where he sat holding the baby. "Place him against your shoulder or across your lap," she instructed.

Slowly, he adjusted the boy so that he was reclined against his shoulder.

"Now what?"

"Pat him gently on the back."

He frowned at her. "I don't know what you consider gentle."

She rolled her eyes. "Well, I don't mean pat him like you would a horse's neck!" Deciding it would be easier to show him, she picked up Conall's hand and placed a few measured pats against Rick's back.

"Okay, I get—"

Before he could complete the rest of his sentence, Rick made a belching noise, which was immediately followed by Conall's yelp.

Vanessa didn't have to ask what had happened. She could see a thick stream of milk oozing from Rick's mouth and rolling down Conall's back.

"Uggh! Is that what I think it is?" he asked, twisting his head around in order to get a glimpse of his soggy shoulder.

"Sorry," she said, and before she could stop herself she began to laugh.

He flashed a droll look at her. "I didn't know being vomited on was so funny."

"It isn't. But—" She was laughing so hard she couldn't finish, but instead of him getting angry, he began to grin.

He said, "I didn't know you could laugh like that."

She calmed herself enough to say, "I didn't know you could look so...dumbfounded, either."

He thrust the baby at her. "Here, you'd better take the little volcano before he erupts again."

Still chuckling, Vanessa lifted Rick from his arms. While she cleaned the baby's face, Conall snatched up several paper towels and attempted to wipe the burp from the back of his shirt.

"I'll help you do that," Vanessa told him. "Just let me get Rick settled back in the bassinet."

Once she had both babies nestled together in their bed, she walked over to where Conall stood at the kitchen sink.

"You smell like formula," she said.

"No kidding."

She motioned for him to turn his back to her. When he did, she groaned with dismay.

"Oh, Conall, this is beyond wiping. You're going to have to take off your shirt and let me wash it for you."

"That's too much trouble. Surely the mess will dry."

"Eventually," she agreed. "But I don't think either of us will enjoy eating our supper with that smell at the dining table." She motioned with her hand for the shirt. "Give it to me. I have other things to wash anyway. And if you're worried about sitting around half-naked, I'll find you one of Dad's old shirts."

"All right, all right," he mumbled, then quickly began to strip out of the garment.

Vanessa tried not to stare as the fabric parted from his chest and slipped off his shoulders. Still, it was impossible to keep her gaze totally averted from his muscled chest, the dark patch of hair between his nipples and the hard abs disappearing into the waistband of his jeans.

"I'll put it right in the machine," she said in a rush, then hurried out of the room before she made a complete idiot out of herself.

A man's anatomy was nothing new to her, she reminded herself as she tossed Conall's shirt into the washing machine and followed it with a few more garments. She'd been married for five years and Jeff had been a physically attractive man. Yet looking at him without his shirt hadn't left her breathless or tongue-tied, the way looking at Conall had a moment ago.

Trying not to reason that one out, Vanessa went to a closet where she'd stored some of her father's clothing in hopes that one day he'd get well enough to come home and wear them again. Now she pulled out a dark blue plaid shirt and hurried back to the kitchen.

When she stepped through the doorway, she spotted Conall sitting at the table and she swallowed hard as she walked over and handed him the shirt. "Here's something to wear while you're waiting. It might be a little big," she warned. "Dad was pretty fleshy before he had the stroke."

"Thanks, I'm sure it'll be fine."

Rising to his feet, he plunged his arms into the sleeves of the cotton shirt. To her surprise the shirt wasn't all that big, proof that her eyes hadn't deceived her when they had taken in the sight of his broad shoulders and thick chest.

"So now that the babies are settled and you don't smell like a half-soured milk factory, are you ready to eat?" she asked.

"Sure. Can I help with anything?" he asked as he followed her over to the cabinets.

"Have you honestly ever done anything in the kitchen? Besides eat?"

"Well, I—" He thought for a moment, then gave her a sly grin. "I put the teakettle on to boil whenever I need steam to reshape my hat."

She let out a good-natured groan. "Oh. So you know how to boil water. That's something."

He chuckled. "Maybe you could teach me a few things. Just in case the Diamond D kitchen staff ever go on strike."

His comment reminded Vanessa of the privileged life he led, the fortune he'd been born into.

"I wouldn't worry about it," she replied. "You can always hire someone else to do the job for you."

As she began to pull down plates again, he came to stand close behind her.

"Do you resent that fact, Vanessa? That I…and my family have money? I never thought so. But—" One hand came to rest against the back of her shoulder. "We've never talked about personal things before."

She gripped the edges of the plates as unbidden desire rushed through her.

"We were always too busy to make personal chitchat." She glanced over her shoulder. "But as far as you being wealthy, I don't resent that. You work harder than anybody I know."

"Not Liam," he corrected.

With the plates pressed against her chest, she turned to face him. "No. Maybe not Liam," she agreed. "But you're just as dedicated."

He gently brushed the back of his knuckles against her cheek and Vanessa wanted to slip into his arms.

"I'm glad you think I earn what I have. And I'll tell you something else, Vanessa, I like spending it on you—and the babies. I like making things better for you. It makes all the work I do mean more to me."

Every cell inside her began to tremble. "That's not the way it should be, Conall. We're—the babies and I…well, you should be doing all of that for a family of your own. Not us."

Slowly, he eased the plates from her tight grip. "Yeah," he said, his quiet voice full of cynicism. "That might be good advice, Vanessa. But I don't happen to have a family of my own."

He carried the plates over to the table and all of a sudden she was struck by the fact that in spite of Conall's wealth, in spite of his long list of valuable assets, he didn't have what she had. He didn't have two tiny babies who needed and cried for his touch or quieted at the soothing sound of his voice. He didn't have anyone to call him Daddy. And from what he'd told Vanessa, he never would.

Hot moisture stung the back of her eyes and as she turned to fish silverware from a small drawer, she wondered whether the unexpected tears were for Conall or herself.

Chapter 7

Nearly two weeks later, Conall was sitting at his desk, watching dusk settle across the ranch yard when Fiona stepped into the room and announced she was quitting for the day.

"Your father and grandmother will be ready to eat in thirty minutes. Will you be there?" his mother asked.

"Uh...no." Struggling to focus his thoughts back to the moment, he glanced over to Fiona. The woman had been working nonstop all day at Vanessa's desk, yet she looked nearly as fresh as she had when she'd started at eight this morning. Her graceful femininity was a guise, he couldn't help thinking. She was actually a lioness, always fierce and never tiring. "I'm afraid not. I still have a few calls to make before I leave the office."

She grimaced. "Have you talked to Liam?"

"No. Why?"

"He wanted to speak with you about Blue Heaven—the two-year-old. Something about paying her futurity fees."

Leaning back in his chair, he looked at her with puzzlement. "Why would Liam want to talk to me about the filly? Liam is the trainer, he enters any horse he wants into whatever race he wants. He certainly doesn't ask my opinion on the matter."

Frowning with impatience, she stepped farther into the office until she was standing at the end of his desk. Conall felt as if time had traveled back to when he was ten years old and he'd slipped off to the horse barn instead of doing his homework.

"Does it ever cross your mind that your brother needs your support? That he might want your advice on these matters?"

His gaze dropping away from his mother, he picked up a pen and began to tap it absently against the ink blotter. He wasn't in the mood for one of Fiona's family lectures. He was missing Vanessa like hell and though a nanny for the twins had been hired more than a week ago, she'd not yet returned to work. And damn it, he wasn't going to push her, even though he wanted to. "Not really."

To his surprise Fiona muttered a curse under her breath. It was rare that he ever heard his mother utter a foul word and he couldn't imagine this trivial matter pulling one from her mouth.

"Not really," she mimicked with sarcasm. "I should have known that would be your answer. I doubt you actually think about your brother for more than five minutes out of the day!"

Startled by her unexpected outburst, he jerked his

head up to stare at her. "What in the world are you talking about, Mom? Is this 'feel sorry for Liam' day or something?"

"Don't get smart with me, Conall. This is as much about you as it is about Liam working himself to death."

Conall tossed down the pen. "Maybe you haven't noticed, but I'm not exactly taking a vacation here," he muttered, then immediately shook his head. "Sorry, Mom. I…shouldn't have said that."

"No. You shouldn't have."

Sighing with exasperation, he swiveled his chair so that he was facing her head-on. "Liam is working too hard. But what can I do about it? I've been after him to hire an assistant. But he doesn't think anyone could measure up to Clete. Until he decides that he's not going to find another Clete and hires someone to help him, there's not much I can do."

Fiona sighed. "That's true. But I wish…well, that you would take time for him and he would take time for you. You're both so damned obsessed with work that—" Pausing, she shook her head with regret. "Forget it, Conall. I can't change either of you and it's wrong of me to try. I just want you to be happy. But Liam goes around pretending everything is just dandy when it's anything but. And you—sometimes I think you've simply given up. A son of mine," she added with disgust, "I never thought I'd see it."

It wasn't like Fiona to be so critical. Even when she was angry with her children, she managed to display it in a loving way. But something seemed to have stirred her up. As for him giving up, it was no secret that his parents wanted him to get back into the dating scene and find himself a wife. To the Donovans, a person had nothing unless they had a family. And they both had the Pollyanna idea that if he found the right woman, she would understand and accept his sterile condition. Maybe there were a few out there, he thought dully. But would one of them be a woman he could love?

Hell. What kind of question is that, Conall? You don't believe in love anymore. Not after Nancy. Why can't you settle for someone to simply cozy up to and grow old with? Your heart doesn't have to be involved.

His jaw tight, he said firmly, "I'm sorry you've had to work so hard these last few weeks, Mom. I thought Vanessa would have been back by now. But—"

She looked at him sharply. "I can manage this office with one hand tied behind my back. That's not—" She waved a dismissive hand at him and started out the door. "I've got to get back to the house for dinner. And you won't be seeing me at Vanessa's desk in the morning. She called a few minutes ago to say she'd be returning tomorrow."

His boots hit the floor with a thump. "Vanessa called? Why didn't she speak to me?"

"You were on the phone with the fencing company. She didn't want to disturb you."

Or maybe she'd simply wanted to avoid talking to him, Conall thought as his mother slipped out the door. But that was a stupid notion. She was coming back to work tomorrow. She'd be spending her days with him. But it wasn't exactly the days that Conall had been thinking about before his mother had walked in and abruptly interrupted his musings.

With a heavy sigh, he rose from the deep leather chair and walked over to a large framed window overlooking part of the stables. Resting his shoulder against the window seal, he gazed out at the lengthening shadows. Ranch hands were busy with the evening chores and no doubt Liam was in one of the barns, making sure his latest runners were pampered and happy.

Liam goes around pretending everything is just dandy when it's anything but. And you—sometimes I think you've simply given up.

Fiona's words were still rattling around in his head and though Conall tried to tell himself they were simply a mother expressing dissatisfaction with her sons, he had to admit she was, at least, partially right. He couldn't speak for Liam, but as for himself, he supposed he had given up on some aspects of his life.

Didn't his mother realize it was easier for him to focus on his work instead of the mess he'd made of his personal life? The mess he would make if he tried to marry again?

You should be doing all of that for a family of your own. Not us.

Close on the heels of his mother's words, Vanessa traipsed through his mind, reminding him just how much she and the twins had changed his life, had reopened the old dreams and wishes that he'd started out with as a young man.

Although he'd talked with Vanessa on the phone about hiring the nanny, he'd not seen her since the night Rick had burped all over him. Every night since then, he'd wanted to go back to her house. He'd wanted to sit across from her at the little table, eat warm tortillas, talk about mundane things and simply watch her beautiful face. Over and over he'd thought about the way she'd felt in his arms when he'd kissed her and the way she'd looked afterward. For the first time in a long time he'd wanted to make love to a woman. And though he'd told himself he'd been too busy to make the trip over to Tinnie to see her, a part of him knew he'd been hiding these past few days, afraid to admit to himself or to her that she and the babies were the family he'd wanted for so long.

Three days later, Vanessa was relieved that Friday had finally arrived. If she didn't get out of the office and away from Conall soon, she was either going to break into pieces or throw herself into his arms and beg the man to make love to her. Neither option was suitable for a secretary who'd always considered herself a professional. And she was beginning to wonder if the job she'd once loved was now going to have to come to an end.

Drawing in a bracing breath, she rapped her knuckles on the door separating their offices. The moment she heard him calling for her to enter, she stepped into his domain and shut the door behind her.

"I have the contract for the trucking company ready for you to sign," she said as she approached his desk. "I've also alerted Red Bluff that a new trucking company will be in place at the mine by the middle of next month."

"Good. I'm glad to get that settled." He glanced up as she leaned forward to place the papers in front of him. "Did Red Bluff seem to have any problem with the idea of new haulers?"

It was after five in the evening and though he'd started out the day in a crisply starched shirt and matching tie, the tie was now loosened and the top two buttons of his shirt were undone while the sleeves were rolled back on his forearms. His nearly black hair was rumpled and she knew if she were to rub her cheek against his, she'd feel the faint rasp of his beard.

"Not at all," she said as she straightened to her full height and tried to bring her thoughts to the business at hand.

"Good. I only wish raising racehorses was as easy as digging gold from a mountainside." He picked up a pen and scratched his name on the appropriate lines. Once he was finished, he handed the document back to her and smiled. "But my grandfather used to say that nothing was worthwhile, unless it was earned. Gold mines eventually peter out. Horses will always be."

"Yes, well, I'll get this in the outgoing mail before I leave this evening," she told him, then quickly turned to start out of the room.

She'd taken two steps when his hand closed around her upper arm and with a mental groan, she turned to face him.

"Was there something else?" she asked.

Grimacing at her businesslike tone, he muttered, "Hell, yes, there's plenty more! I want to know why you've been acting as though I have a contagious disease. Ever since you've started back to work, you've been tiptoeing around me like I'm some sort of hulking monster."

Shaking her head, she looked away from him and swallowed hard. "I'm sorry if it appears that way, Conall. But I'm just trying to keep things in order."

"What does that mean?"

"It means—" Her gaze slipped to her arm, where his fingers were pressed like dark brown bands around her flesh. "I'm trying to keep our relationship professional here in the office."

He stepped closer and her heart began to knock against her ribs. "What if I don't want it to be professional?" he asked softly.

She cleared her throat, but it didn't clear away the huskiness in her voice when she spoke. "Like I told you before, Conall, we can't—"

Before she could get the rest of her words out, he jerked her forward and into his arms. The instant his lips covered hers, Vanessa understood why she'd been fighting so hard to keep this very thing from happening.

Tasting his kiss again, having his arms holding her close against his hard body, felt incredibly delicious and impossible to resist. She couldn't hide or ignore the desire rushing through her, urging her to open her mouth to his and slip her arms up and around his neck.

All at once the kiss heated, deepened and surrounded her senses in a hot fog. The room receded to a dim whirl around her head. She heard his groan and then his hands were sliding down her back, splaying against her buttocks and dragging her hips toward his.

Crushed in the intimate embrace, Vanessa forgot they were in his office and that anyone could walk in on them. She forgot, that is, until the phone in her office began to ring and stop, then ring again.

Summoning on all the strength she could find, she jerked her mouth from his. "Conall—the phone, I—"

"Forget the phone," he ordered huskily as his mouth descended toward hers for a second time. "The caller can leave a message."

Panicked by just how much she wanted to do his bidding, she burst out, "No!"

Twisting away from his embrace she started to hurry out of the room, but halfway to the door, she realized at some point during their kiss she'd dropped the contract.

Turning back, she groaned when she spotted it lying to one side of his boots. As she walked toward him to retrieve it, he said softly, "That was a quick change of mind."

"I haven't changed my mind." She bent down to retrieve the typed pages that were held together with a heavy paper clip. "I'm retrieving the contract. That's all."

Gripping the document with both hands, she straightened back to her full height and before she could step away his hand came out to catch her by one elbow.

"All right, Vanessa, you can pretend you're indifferent, but I won't believe it," he murmured.

She swallowed as her heartbeat reacted to his nearness. "Conall, I'm not going to deny that I like kissing you. But—"

"Good," he interrupted before she could go on. "Because I plan on us doing a lot more of it."

"No," she repeated. "It won't take us anywhere. Except to bed!"

A corner of his mouth curled upward. "For once we agree on something."

She stared at him as her mind spun with questions and images that left her face burning with red heat. "Well, you might as well go over to your desk and write this down on your calendar, Conall—it ain't gonna happen!"

He laughed in a totally confident way, but instead of

the sound irking her, it sent a scare all the way down to her feet. To make love to Conall would be the end of her. He'd have her eating out of his hand, waiting and begging for any crumbs of affection he might throw her way.

"You look very pretty when you use bad grammar. Did you know that?"

She muttered a helpless curse and then the phone began to ring again. "The one thing I do know is that I have to get back to work and—"

"No. You don't. It's quitting time," he said, his voice quickly slipping back to boss mode. "And right now I want to speak with you about tomorrow night."

She arched her brows at him. "Tomorrow night? Are you having a special meeting or something and I need to attend to take notes?"

He shook his head. "Not even close. Sunday is Grandmother Kate's birthday and the family is throwing her a party. Not anything as huge as we did for her eightieth. But since this is her eighty-fifth we thought she deserved more than just a cake and a few gifts from her family."

"What does this have to do with me? You'd like for me to pick up a gift or flowers for you to give to her?"

He frowned. "Not hardly. I know how to buy gifts for women. Even one as hard to please as Kate." His hand departed her elbow and began a hot glide up her bare arm and onto her shoulder. "I'd like for you to attend the party with me. Will Hannah be available to watch after the twins?"

He was inviting her to his family home? As his companion? She couldn't believe it. Sure, as a young teenager she'd been inside the small mansion many times.

But that had been totally different. She'd been there as Maura's friend, not as a so-called date for the eldest Donovan son.

"So far I can't get Hannah to take any time off, so she will be available. But I'm not keen on the idea of being away from the babies for that long. I know that probably sounds silly to you, but just being apart from them while I'm here at the office has been hard for me to deal with these past three days."

He smiled with understanding. "It's not silly. You're a new mother. But it's not a problem, either. You can bring the twins to the party with you."

Her jaw dropped. "To the party? Conall, they're only a few weeks old."

"I'm well aware of how old they are. Everyone will love seeing them. In fact, the whole family has been asking about them."

How could she turn down the invitation now, she wondered, without appearing to be indifferent to his family? She couldn't. "If you think no one will mind," she said hesitantly.

"Grandmother will love seeing the babies. Bring Hannah, the nanny, too," he added. "That way you won't be babysitting the whole time. And Hannah is acquainted with Maura and Bridget, so I'm sure she'll enjoy the outing, too."

Another reason why she couldn't refuse, Vanessa thought wryly. Hannah, the nanny that Conall had hired for the twins, was a lovely widow and worked tirelessly to keep the babies healthy and happy. So far she'd not taken a night off for any reason and Vanessa knew the woman needed a break of some sort.

"All right. We'll be there. But I don't understand any

of this, Conall. Why invite me? Now? Since I've come to work for you, your family has held several parties for one reason or another. You didn't ask me to attend any of those," she couldn't help pointing out.

"Look, Vanessa, whatever you might think or want, the two of us aren't going back to the impersonal relationship we had before the twins arrived. Things have changed with you and with me. Surely I don't have to spell that out to you."

Things have changed. That was certainly an understatement, she thought. If she wasn't with the man, she was thinking about him. And when she was with him all she could think about was being in his arms. She was in a predicament that was very unhealthy to her state of mind and try as she might, she couldn't seem to do a thing about it.

"I think—" She broke off abruptly as the phone began to ring again.

"You think what?" he prompted.

She shook her head. Now wasn't the time or place to say the things she needed to say to him. Tomorrow night would be soon enough to let him know he was sniffing around the wrong tree. "Nothing. I'll be at the party, Conall. With Rose and Rick. Right now I'm going to get this contract in the mail, then go home."

He looked like he wanted to say more, or maybe it was more kissing he had on his mind. Whatever it was she read on his face, she didn't hang around to let him put his wants into action. She hurried out of the room and purposely shut the door between them.

Apparently Mother Nature didn't want to disappoint the Donovans. With Kate's party being held in the backyard beneath the pines and the cottonwood trees, the early August weather couldn't have been more perfect. Even the mosquitoes seemed to forget to come out after night had fallen and the colorful party lanterns were glowing festively over the tables of food that had been served more than an hour ago.

Conall had told her the party was going to be small, but to Vanessa it was anything but. People, most of whom she didn't know, filled the yard and the back porch where Kate was presently ensconced in a rattan chair surrounded by family and friends. Music was playing and down by the pool the more active guests were laughing and splashing and swimming in the crystal blue water.

Tilting the long-stemmed glass to her lips, Vanessa drained the last of her punch while wondering how soon she could leave without appearing unsociable. She'd already spoken to Kate and expressed her well wishes. She'd chatted at length with Maura and exchanged a few words with the rest of the Donovans. Except for Conall. So far she'd seen him for all of two minutes and that had been when his grandmother had blown out the candles on her cake. After that, he'd disappeared into the house and left her wondering for the umpteenth time why he'd invited her in the first place.

Moving from her spot beneath a giant pine, she started walking toward the far end of the porch where the twins were sleeping in their double stroller. A few steps away, Hannah and Bridget were engaged in a lively conversation, but both women looked around as she approached.

"Vanessa, come have a seat with us," Bridget insisted. "Hannah was just telling me what it's like at the twins' bath time."

Vanessa laughed. "I can tell you in one word. Chaos. And in a few weeks I'm sure it's going to get a lot wilder and a whole lot wetter."

She started toward an empty chair to the left of the two women, but before she reached the seat, a hand came down on the back of her shoulder. At the same time Bridget said, "Conall, it's about time you showed your face around here. Where have you been anyway?"

"Business, as usual," he answered. "A phone call I couldn't ignore. But that's finished and now I'm more than ready for a piece of cake. What about you, Vanessa?"

Turning toward him, she tried not to notice how sexy he looked in close-fitting jeans and a black T-shirt that clung to his hard torso and exposed his muscled arms. "I've already had more than my share," she told him.

"Then you can come watch me have my share," he said with a grin for her, "but first I want a look at Rose and Rick. Are they enjoying the party?"

"At least they're not howling," Hannah answered with a laugh.

He moved over to the stroller and squatted on his heels in front of the twins. Rick was asleep, his head tilted toward his sister's. But Rose was awake, her blue eyes wide, her arms pumping through the air as though she could hear the music.

"Hey, little doll, your brother is missing the party. But you'd like to dance, wouldn't you," he said in a soft voice to the baby girl. Not bothering to ask permission, he eased Rose from her side of the stroller and cradled her in the crook of his arm. Then after letting her tiny fingers curl around his forefinger, he began to slowly two-step around the porch.

"Aww, look," Bridget gushed, her gaze resting fondly on her brother and the baby in his arms. "She loves that, Conall."

"So do I," he replied with a broad grin. "I've never had a better dance partner. She's not even complaining about me stepping on her toes."

"We need him around when Rose is crying at two o'clock in the morning," Hannah joked to Vanessa.

Her eyes taking in the precious sight of Conall dancing with her daughter, Vanessa felt her throat thicken with unexpected emotions. Years ago, she'd often dreamt of Conall waltzing her around a ballroom floor. Back then she could have never imagined him holding her baby, dancing her around as though she was a special princess.

"He wouldn't be any use to you then," Bridget observed. "My brother sleeps like a rock."

Dismissing his sister's remark with a chuckle, Conall carried Rose back to the stroller. After he'd placed her back beside his brother, he pressed a kiss on her chubby cheek. "Thank you for the dance, little Rose."

To Vanessa it seemed as though he remained bent over the babies for an exceptionally long time before he finally straightened and walked back over to her. After placing his hand around Vanessa's arm, he nodded to the other two women. "Excuse us, ladies."

He guided Vanessa off the porch and across the yard to where a table held a massive three-tiered cake and an assortment of beverages.

"Sorry I had to leave the party," he said as he gathered a plate and fork. "Have you been bored?"

"No. But I should be leaving soon. By the time Hannah and I get home with the babies, it will be getting late."

"You can't leave yet."

She watched him ladle a huge hunk of cake onto the plate. "Why? Is your family waiting to give your grandmother a surprise gift?"

"No. Kate doesn't want gifts. Says she has everything she wants. Personally, I think she needs a man in her life, but then she'd be hell to put up with, if you know what I mean."

Vanessa folded her arms against her breasts as he began to wolf down the cake. "No. I don't know what you mean. Kate might be strict and opinionated, but she wouldn't marry a man unless she loved him."

His brows lifted faintly as he looked at her. "You're probably right. She was crazy about Granddad, which always amazed me because he was a mean old cuss most of the time."

"I doubt he was mean to her. Kate is too strong of a woman to put up with that."

"Yes, but—"

"But what?"

His expression was nothing but cynical as he glanced at her. "Love makes people put up with behavior they wouldn't ordinarily tolerate."

Was he speaking from experience? Vanessa wasn't about to ask. Even though things had changed between them these past few weeks, he wasn't the type of man who poured out his personal life to anyone, including her.

Raking a hand through her hair, she looked away from him and over toward the twins. In spite of the night being pleasantly cool, she felt uncomfortably hot. "You haven't explained why I need to stay at the party a little longer," she reminded him.

He placed the now empty plate on the table and reached for her arm. "I'll explain as we walk. Let's go to Kate's rose garden. It'll be quieter there."

As the two of them disappeared into the shadows, Vanessa wondered if anyone had noticed their leaving. But why that should even matter, she didn't know. She was a grown woman and what went on between her and the manager of the Diamond D Ranch was no one's business but theirs. Yet at the same time, she had to concede that other people's opinion of her did matter. Maybe because as a poor girl growing up she'd heard the nasty whispers at school, she'd heard the gossip that Vanessa Valdez would turn out no better than her worthless brothers. And down through the years she'd worked hard to prove those people wrong, to make herself respectable and successful.

"If you needed to say something to me, you could have said it back there at the party," Vanessa told him as they trod along a graveled path that was lined with dim footlights and wound through head-high rose bushes.

"Not what I want to say."

The softness to his voice caught her attention and she paused to swing her gaze up to his shadowed face. Her heart jerked. He looked so serious, yet so sexy that her breath flew away and refused to come back.

"Conall—"

"Not here," he said. "Let's go sit in the gazebo."

Maura had told her that the gazebo had been built the same time as the huge ranch house. Now, after more than forty years, the board seats were worn smooth, along with the planked floor. A pair of aspen trees sheltered one side of the structure and as they sat down together on one of the secluded benches, the leaves rattled gently from the evening breeze.

Vanessa welcomed the cool air against her hot skin, yet it did little to chill her racing thoughts. Was he about to suggest that the two of them become lovers? That she become his mistress? She didn't know what to expect. Only one thing was clear to her—sitting in the dark with the heavenly scent of roses wrapping around them was going to be a heck of a test on her resistance.

"When my sisters were teenagers I used to tease them about sitting out here dreaming about marrying a prince or a frog. Whichever they could catch first," he said with amusement. "But after we all got older, I realized the place had a nice, calming effect. Now I think I visit the place more than they do."

"Is that why you brought me out here?" Vanessa asked wryly. "To calm me down?"

He chuckled as he reached for her hand. "That's one thing I like about you, Vanessa, you make me laugh. Something I'd almost forgotten how to do."

As his warm fingers tightened around hers, Vanessa wasn't about to let herself think she had that much of an effect on the man. To do so would simply be dreaming. And during her doomed marriage she'd learned that a person had to be responsible for their own happiness, instead of relying on someone else to provide it for them.

She sighed. "Sometimes that's easy for a person to do—forget how to laugh." She glanced over at him, but the shadows were too deep to pick up the expression on his face. "So why are we here instead of mingling with the party guests?"

"I wanted to talk to you about…several things."

The humor was gone from his voice now and her heartbeat slowed to a heavy dread of drumbeats. "Is this about my job?" she asked.

"Actually, it is."

He'd never been evasive or short on explanations before and she wondered yet again what had brought about this change in him. Before the twins he'd been cool, work-driven and predictable. Now she couldn't begin to anticipate what he might say or do next. It was more than unnerving.

Finally, he said, "I think I need to find a different secretary."

She sucked in a sharp breath and bit down on the urge to scream at him. "You invited me to a party to fire me? Why?" she demanded. "Because I refused to make love to you?"

His lazy chuckle infuriated her.

"No. Because I've come to realize that you were right. It's too damn hard to get any work done in the office when all I want to do is lock the door and make love to you all day."

Feeling the desperate need to escape, she tried to pull her hand from his, but he held her tight, making it clear that he had plenty more to say and expected her to hang around and listen.

"Conall—"

"Wait, Vanessa, before you get all huffy, this isn't… well, it's not just about the two of us making love. It's more than that."

Confused now, she squared her knees around so that she was facing him head-on. "What *is* this about?"

He looked away from her and if Vanessa hadn't known better she would have thought he was nervous. But that couldn't be so. Conall Donovan didn't allow anything to rattle him.

Eventually he began to speak and his husky voice slid over her skin like warm, summer rain and filled her with the urge to shiver, to lean in to him and invite his kiss. She clamped her hands together and tried to concentrate on his words.

"I've been thinking about us, Vanessa. A lot. And the more I think about it the more I realize there's a perfect solution to our problem."

She swallowed as all sorts of questions raced through her head. "Problem? You mean now that you want to fire me and get another secretary?"

He grimaced. "I don't want to fire you. I mean, I do, but only because I have something different in mind—for you…for us."

Bending her head, she sucked in several deep breaths and prayed the nausea in her stomach would disappear. "Look, Conall, I like my job. I like being here on the ranch and you Donovans are excellent people to work for. But I don't appreciate the fact that you're trying to…extort sex from me! I'm not that needy. Like I told you, I can easily get a job at the casino at Ruidoso Downs and—"

"Extort sex from you! What are you talking about?"

His interruption whipped her head up. "Why, yes, isn't that what this is all about? You want me to quit my job and be your mistress?"

With a groan of disbelief, he clasped his hands over

both her shoulders. "Oh, Vanessa, I'm sorry. I must be doing this all wrong. I don't want you to be my mistress. I want you to be my wife."

Chapter 8

If he'd not been holding on to her, Vanessa was sure she would have fallen straight backward and onto the floor of the gazebo.

"Your wife!" she said in a shocked whisper. "Are you…out of your mind?"

There was no smile on his face, no glimmer that he was anywhere near teasing.

"Not in the least. The twins need a father. And you and I…well, we obviously get on together. I think it's the perfect solution for all of us."

Stunned, she rose to her feet and walked to the other side of the gazebo. In her wildest imaginings, she'd not expected this from Conall. Twenty years ago, when she'd viewed him as a knight on horseback, she'd fantasized how it would be to receive a kiss from him, or even go on a date with him, but even her fantasies had known when and where to stop. Men like Conall didn't marry women like her.

She heard his footsteps approaching her from behind and then his hands came to rest upon her shoulders. As their warmth seeped into her skin, she closed her eyes and wondered why she suddenly wanted to weep.

"Vanessa, what are you thinking?"

Her throat was aching, making her voice low and strained. "I'm...very flattered, Conall. But marriage needs to be more than a solution."

His sigh rustled the top of her hair. "I'm trying to be practical, Vanessa. Marriage—making a family together—would be good for all four of us."

Maybe it would, she thought sadly, but what about love? He'd not mentioned the word, but then he hardly needed to explain his feelings. She already understood that he didn't love her.

Turning, she demanded, "How would it be good for you, Conall?"

His arms slipped around her waist and drew the front of her body up against his. "Just having you next to me would be good," he murmured.

She groaned as a war of wanting him and needing his love erupted inside of her. "I'm sorry, Conall, but it hasn't been that long since I got out of a horrible marriage. I don't want to jump into something that...well, I'm just not sure about."

He frowned. "Do you think I'm taking this whole thing lightly? That I proposed to you on impulse? Hell, Vanessa, my marriage turned out to be a nightmare. For a while after the divorce I tried to date again, to find a woman I could build a relationship with. But the past refused to let that happen so I finally gave up trying.

So if you think you're the only one who has a corner on being hurt by a spouse, then think again."

"That's exactly why this is all so crazy!" she exclaimed. "Why would you want to marry a divorced woman with two newborns when…"

"Finish what you were going to say, Vanessa. When…?"

Pressing her lips together, she looked away from him. Through the lattice covering the side of the gazebo, she could see the lights of the party twinkling through the pine boughs. Shrieks of laughter were coming from the pool and closer to the house she could hear several voices singing "Happy Birthday" to Kate. The fact that Conall had chosen this night to propose to her while his family was celebrating seemed surreal.

Biting back an impatient curse, she turned away from him. "Don't play dumb with me, Conall. It doesn't suit you at all. You know what I was about to say. You're a Donovan. You don't have to go around looking for a woman to marry. All you have to do is get the word out and they'll come running to you. You certainly don't have to settle for your secretary."

His face stony, he caught her by the shoulder and spun her back around. "Why are you doing your best to insult me and yourself? Me being a Donovan has nothing to do with us marrying!"

Amazed, her head swung back and forth. "Conall, that's a fact that can't be buried or swept under the rug!"

His nostrils flared. "Why do you think so little of yourself?"

Tears were suddenly burning her eyes. "Because… oh, you can't understand anything, can you? I've already had one husband who didn't love me! Do you honestly think I want another?"

Before he could answer, she twisted away from him and dashed out of the gazebo. As she hurried along the lighted footpaths, she did her best to stem the hot moisture threatening to spill onto her cheeks.

She'd made a fool of herself, she thought bitterly. Of course, Conall couldn't understand her reaction to his proposal. He couldn't know that she loved him and, perhaps, had always loved him. She was just now beginning to realize that herself.

At one time in his life, long before he'd learned of his sterility, Conall had been comfortable with women. As very young men, Liam had struggled to converse with the opposite sex, while Conall had instinctively known exactly what to say or do to make a woman adore him. Long before he'd met Nancy, he'd dated a lengthy list of beauties and he could safely say that each of the relationships had eventually ended on his terms, not his partner's. Whether his success with women had been partly due to his being a Donovan was a question he'd not considered that much. Until last night when Vanessa had flung the fact in his face.

Obviously he'd lost his touch. Or maybe the long marriage battle he'd endured with Nancy had taken away his innate ability to deal with a woman. Whatever the reason, he'd clearly done everything wrong when he'd proposed to Vanessa last night.

Glancing at his watch, he noted it was a quarter to eight. Normally Vanessa had arrived by now. Especially on a Monday. But he'd not heard any stirrings in the outer office and he was beginning to wonder if she'd decided to skip work altogether today. Or maybe she was going to quit and was planning to call and let the gavel drop on him.

Thrusting fingers through his dark hair, he pressed fingertips against his scalp. Tiny men were pounding sledgehammers just beneath his skull, a result of drinking too many beers last night after Vanessa had taken the babies and gone home, he thought grimly. He'd never been one to indulge in alcohol, but after the fiasco in the gazebo, he needed some sort of relief. Now he was paying for it with a doozy of a headache.

A hard knock on the doorjamb had him wincing and he glanced around to see Liam striding into his office.

"What's with all the roses in Vanessa's office? Did someone break into a florist shop this morning or something?" he asked.

With an awkward shrug, Conall admitted, "I broke into Grandma's rose garden. I knew it would be useless to drive to town and try to bribe a shop owner to open up and deliver this morning."

His brows arched with curiosity, Liam glanced over his shoulder toward the outer office. "I didn't realize your secretary was that important to you. What is today, secretary's day or something? If it is, Gloria is out of luck."

Conall grunted. "The only thing Gloria ever expects from you is win photos to put on the wall behind her desk."

"That's all?" he countered with sarcasm. "It would be a hell of a lot easier to raid Grandma's flower garden and blame it on the gardener."

Conall walked over to the coffeepot and refilled his mug. "Coffee?" he asked his brother.

"No. I'm in a hurry. I'm missed you at breakfast, so I wanted to let you know I was shipping Red Garland to Del Mar today, along with a few others."

He looked around at Liam. "To Del Mar? Now?"

Liam rolled his eyes with impatience. "Have you forgotten she's entered in the Debutante? That's only a month away and I want her to get accustomed to the Pacific climate and the Polytrack before race time."

Actually it had slipped Conall's mind that the filly would be traveling to the west coast to run in the prestigious race at one of the most famous tracks in California. "Sorry, brother, I guess the time has slipped up on me."

"Geez, Conall. What's going on with you? From the moment she was born Red Garland has always been your darling. And you've forgotten about her first stakes debut?"

Conall had been in the foaling barn, watching when Red Garland entered the world. Only hours later, the baby girl had left her mother's side to investigate Conall's outstretched hand and something about her trust had touched him, had gotten to him in a way no human ever had. Since then, she'd grown up to be an outstanding runner that had quickly stunned race fans with her ability to outdistance herself from the rest of the pack. Conall was extremely proud of her. He was also very attached to the filly. Something he normally didn't allow himself to be with the horses they raised and raced.

Conall glanced at his brother's incredulous expression. "Maybe you haven't noticed but I've had a lot going on here lately," he said, then shoved out a heavy breath. "Anyway, I'm glad you came by to say you were leaving. I…well, I'll be honest, I hate for her to be shipped all the way to California."

Liam frowned. "Why? We ship horses out there all the time."

Conall felt like a soppy idiot. "I know. It's just that… anything might happen. That Polytrack surface is unpredictable."

"So is the dirt."

"She might hurt herself. With an injury that could end her career or even kill her," Conall pointed out, even though both men were already well aware of that fact. "But you're the trainer. You know what she can handle best."

Liam shook his head. "Hell, Conall. You're my brother. I don't want to do anything against your wishes."

With a self-effacing grunt, Conall placed his coffee mug on the edge of the desk. "What's the matter with me, Liam? I've never gotten this soppy over any of our horses before. I've never let myself. Because…well, we both know anything can happen to lose them."

"Sometimes something or someone comes along to remind us we're not machines," Liam said thoughtfully, then added, "I'll scratch Red Garland from the Debutante and leave her here. We'll lose the entry fee, but what the hell. She's already won that much a thousand times over."

"No, she's going," Conall said with sudden firmness. "She deserves her chance to be great."

A wry smile touched Liam's lips. "Well, she stands a good chance to win a pile of money."

"Yeah. But money isn't everything," Conall replied.

Liam grunted in agreement. "Sometimes it doesn't mean anything at all."

Satisfied that things were settled with the situation, Liam turned to leave the room, but before he disappeared out the door, Conall called to him, "Thanks, again, Liam. For coming by and reminding me about Red Garland's race. Will you be following the horses out today or tomorrow?"

"Today and I'm taking three grooms with me."

Conall lifted his hand in farewell. "Travel safely and I'll see you when you get back."

"You want to drive to the airport and see Red Garland off this afternoon?" Liam asked in afterthought.

"No. I'd rather meet her there when she gets back."

With a nod of understanding, Liam left the office and Conall forced himself to sit down at his desk.

Five minutes later, he heard the outer door to the office open and close and then Vanessa's light footsteps cross the tile. Normally, she went straight to the closet they shared to store away her purse and whatever sort of wrap she was wearing but so far the closet hadn't opened.

He forced himself to wait another minute before he walked through the open door and into her section of the office. He found her standing in front of the desk, staring at the massive vase of pink roses he'd left for her.

Upon hearing his approach, she whirled around to face him. "What are these?"

Conall walked toward her. "Roses. To say I'm sorry if I hurt you last night. I didn't mean to. I didn't have any idea a marriage proposal would be so harrowing to you."

Bending her head, she closely examined the petals on the tea roses. "I'll be honest, Conall, I considered not coming to work this morning. But I didn't want Fiona to have to fill in for me. So I made myself drive over here." Turning slightly, she leveled her brown eyes on him. "I'm sorry, too, Conall. I overreacted about you— about everything. I was expecting too much from you. I realize that now."

Relieved that she no longer appeared angry, he walked over to her. "I'm glad you're here," he confessed. "And if you don't want to talk about things right now, we won't."

Her glaze flickered away from his face and back to the roses and Conall was struck by how very beautiful she looked this morning. Her hair was swept up and off her neck, while a heavy fringe fell in a smooth curtain over one eyebrow. Her dress was white, the neckline fashioned in a deep V. Faint freckles dotted her chest and lower down a hint of cleavage teased his senses. The pale pink color on her lips reminded him of a seashell and he realized he'd like nothing better than to kiss the shimmery color away, kiss her until her lips were ruby-red and swollen.

"There's nothing to talk about," she said wearily. "I can't marry you."

Desperate to touch her, he planted his hands on either side of her waist. "Listen, Vanessa, I have no idea what happened in your marriage or what kind of man your husband was, but please don't compare me to him."

To his surprise she laughed with disbelief. "Oh, Conall, you can't imagine how…well, how opposite you are from Jeff. He didn't have an ounce of ambition. He was perfectly content to let me support him."

Trying to understand, he shook his head. "I'm guessing you didn't know this about him before you married?"

Grimacing, she stepped away from him. "Of course I didn't! When I first met him he was doing contract electrical work for the casino where I was employed. At that time he owned a small building company and he and his men had more jobs than they could handle. He made very good money, plus he was from a nice respectable family that had resided in Bullhead City for many years. There was nothing about Jeff that warned he would turn out to be a deadhead."

She started into his office and Conall followed her to the coffee machine. As she poured herself a mug and stirred in a measure of half-and-half, he couldn't stop himself from asking, "When did you learn he was less than ambitious."

Cradling the mug with both hands, she turned to face him. "About six months after we were married. He began to find all sorts of reasons not to take jobs. Mainly he would use the excuse that he wanted to spend more time with me—because I was so irresistible he didn't want to leave me for a minute of the day," she added with sarcasm. "Dear God, was I ever stupid to believe his lines. But he…well, he had a charming, lovable way about him that was hard to resist and I—" Pausing, she shook her head with self-reproach. "I guess he'd come along in my life at a time when I was feeling very alone. My brothers were long gone and I was watching my parents grow old. I wanted a family of my own and Jeff kept promising we'd have one. I hung on hoping and praying he'd change. But in the end, I think all he ever wanted was to have fun and a woman to take care of him while he was having it. I should have seen that from the very beginning, but I didn't. And it's taken me a long time to convince myself that I'm not a fool. That I'm worthy of better than…him."

The faint quiver Conall heard in her voice touched a spot in him that he'd long thought dead and he was amazed at how much he wanted to take her into his arms, to whisper how beautiful and precious she was to him. Did that mean he loved her? No. It couldn't mean that. He'd forgotten how to love. But he'd not forgotten how to want and he wanted Vanessa in his life. He wanted to be a father to Rick and Rose.

I wanted a family of my own.

Her words had pierced him right in the heart and twisted home the reality of his condition, his failed marriage and the total emptiness he'd carried inside him for all these years. Maybe he should confess to her right now that he couldn't father a child. But she was already reluctant to trust him, to believe they could have a good marriage together. He didn't want to wham her with that kind of revelation. She would automatically think he was only interested in the twins. Later, he told himself. Later, after he'd convinced her to marry him, he would explain it all. He would make her understand just how perfect the four of them were for each other.

"Oh, Vanessa," he said lowly, "you are worthy of better. And I like to think I can give you better."

Her gaze dropped awkwardly to the brown liquid in her cup. "Yes, you could give me better in so many ways," she conceded. "Except you can't give me what I need the most."

She sounded so defeated, so sure, and that worried Conall more than any words she could have said to him.

"What is that?" he asked.

She looked up him and he spotted a mixture of defiance and resignation swimming in the depths of her brown eyes.

"Love."

The one word caused Conall to rear back and unwittingly drop his hands from her waist. "Love," he repeated, rolling the word around on his tongue as if he'd never spoken it before. "You mentioned that word last night, but you didn't give me a chance to have my say on the matter."

"All right," she said in a faintly challenging tone. "I'm giving you the chance right now."

Finding it difficult to face her head-on, Conall moved away from her and over to the huge plate glass window overlooking the stables. "And I'm telling you right now that love is a fairy-tale state of mind. That's all. It's just a euphoric condition that doesn't last. In fact, it only makes living with a person worse."

Her light footsteps sounded behind him and he turned to see she'd joined him at the window, but she wasn't looking out at the busy shed row, she was looking at him with so much disappointment that she might as well have struck him physically.

"No wonder your marriage crumbled."

Now, a voice inside his head shouted, *now is the time to explain everything, to defend yourself and your actions.* But he couldn't push the words off his tongue. She was already looking at him with disenchantment; he didn't want to add even more to it.

The tiny hammers pounding at his skull grew harder and he wiped a hand over his face in hopes of easing the pain. "I loved Nancy when we married," he said with gruff insistence. "And I loved her for a long time afterward. But love can't hold up to life's interventions. At least, it didn't for me."

She didn't reply and he used her silence as an opportunity to plead his case. Latching a hand over her shoulder, he pressed his fingers into her warm flesh. "Think about it, Vanessa. Love didn't give your marriage a happily-ever-after ending. Nor did it mine. But you and I have the chance to build a marriage on a solid foundation. Not something that crumbles at the slightest hint of trouble."

Her nostrils flared with disdain as she drew in a deep breath and let it out. "I've never heard of anything so…unfeeling," she muttered.

Before she could guess his intentions, he took the mug from her hands and placed it on the wide window ledge.

"There is nothing unfeeling about this, Vanessa. Maybe I ought to show you."

Pulling her into his arms, he fastened his lips roughly over hers. A moan sounded in her throat at the same time her mouth opened like flower petals seeking the hot sun. His tongue thrust past her teeth and began to explore the sweet, moist contours.

With his hands at her back, he pulled her closer, until her small breasts were flattened against his chest, until he felt the mound of her womanhood pressing into his thigh. Heat was rushing through him, gorging his loins with the unbearable need to get inside her. His sex was rock-hard and pushing against the fly of his jeans.

He couldn't remember the last time, if ever, he'd wanted a woman like this, and when her arms slid around his waist and her soft body arched into his, it was all he could do to hang on to his self-control, to lift his head and speak.

"Let me go lock the door," he said hoarsely.

His words must have hit her like a cold wall of water. Jerking away from him, she stumbled backward and pressed a hand against her throat. "No! You've made your point, Conall. You want me physically. And I admit I want you. But that's not enough. I'm not going to let it be enough. Not now. Not again."

She started toward the door and though Conall wanted to go after, he realized it wasn't the time or the place to press her. But, oh, God, he desperately wanted to.

"I'm going to work," she said over her shoulder. "If that isn't enough for you, then hire yourself another secretary!"

He stood where he was until the door between their offices shut firmly behind her. Once it was obvious she wasn't going to reappear or change her mind, Conall stalked over to his desk and sank into the lush leather chair.

Damn, damn, damn. What would it take to make her cozy up to the idea of marrying him? Or would she ever come around to his way of thinking? She wanted love, but how could he give her the one thing he didn't have?

With a frustrated oath, he picked up the phone and punched in Liam's cell number. His brother answered after the third ring.

"Yeah. What's up?

"I…just wanted to see what time the plane with the horses would be departing the airport."

"Probably around eleven this morning. Why?"

Pinching the bridge of his nose, Conall closed his

eyes. "I've changed my mind. I've decided I want to see Red Garland off."

Liam grunted. "What's brought this on?" he asked bluntly.

Conall grimaced. "Do I have to explain myself?" he countered gruffly. "Maybe I want to see her one last time. In case…she doesn't come home."

The line went silent for long moments, then Liam gently cursed, "Hell, Conall. I promise I'll bring the filly back."

"You can't make promises like that." He swallowed hard and glanced at the closed door between him and Vanessa. "Don't let the plane leave until I get there."

The next two days Vanessa was bombarded with an extra flurry of work while Conall was continually tied up with issues both in and out of the office. She'd done her best to deal with tractor dealers, feed suppliers and tack salesmen even as she plowed through mounds of paperwork.

Being busier than usual was a good thing, she supposed. That gave her less time to dwell on Conall. Since that fiery kiss they'd exchanged, they'd been polite and civil to each other, but the words and the touches they'd exchanged had hung in the air between them like a heavy humidity, leaving Vanessa uncomfortable and emotionally drained.

At the end of the second day, Vanessa was sitting at her desk, finishing a phone call and wrapping up her work for the evening, when Conall strolled through the door and eased a hip onto the edge of her desk. After two days of tiptoeing around each other, his casual nearness jolted her.

Looking up at him, she asked briskly, "Is there something you need?"

"I need a lot of things, but I won't have you make a list now." He gestured toward her work. "Are you nearly finished?"

"Yes. As soon as I make a few notes in my message book. Why?"

The faint grin on his face was the warmest thing she'd seen since the morning he'd wanted to lock the two of them in his office and his gray eyes had been hot with lust. She had to wonder about the abrupt change.

Folding his arms against his chest, his expression turned sheepish. "I wanted to see if you've forgiven me enough to have dinner with me this evening?"

Forgiven him? She'd not been expecting anything like this. Maybe a request for her to work later than usual, but not anything sociable, like having dinner together.

"You've been all business the past couple of days," she bluntly pointed out.

"So have you."

Her gaze dropped from his face to the vase of roses he'd given her a few days ago. She should have thrown them out or at least taken them home and given them to Hannah. But they were still as pretty as the morning she'd found them on her desk and she couldn't bring herself to get rid of them.

When she didn't reply, he said, "I thought we both needed some time to cool off."

That was an understatement, Vanessa thought wryly. Her gaze flickered back up to his face. "And you think we've *cooled off* enough to have dinner together? Alone?"

"We've eaten together alone before," he reminded, as if her memory needed refreshing. "At your house. And in Vegas."

She sighed. He'd been so sweet, so helpful during that trip to Las Vegas and for as long as she lived, she would never forget the look on his face when he'd held the twins for the first time. He'd looked at them with affection and tenderness and for those few moments she'd seen the part of him that she admired, wanted, loved.

"I remember," she told him.

"I'd like to do it again. Would you?"

She'd be lying if she told him no. These past couple of days as she'd kept her distance, she'd constantly argued with herself that it was better that way. The only thing she could ever expect to get from the man was sex. Yet even knowing that hadn't been enough to stop the hunger inside of her, the need to be near him in all the ways a woman could be near a man.

"Yes," she answered. "But—"

"What? Afraid you might find out that you like me after all?"

In spite of her torn emotions, she chuckled. "Oh, Conall, you know that I like you. Very much. That's the whole problem." She closed the small book where she scribbled down daily notes and stuffed it away in the top drawer of the desk. "We… Well, I'm not going to go into any of that tonight. Going out with you is out of the question. I've already promised my father I'd visit him after I got off work. And I'm not going to disappoint him for any reason."

"I wouldn't want you to disappoint him. We'll go by and visit him together," he said.

While she looked at him her thoughts swirled. "He's in the nursing home."

"I'm well aware of that, Vanessa."

Jeff would have never stepped foot in a nursing home, she thought. Not for anyone. In that way he'd been a thoughtless man. Unfortunately, she'd learned about Jeff's unpleasant traits after they'd been married, a fault she could only place squarely on herself. She'd been so eager to be loved, so anxious to be a wife and mother, that she'd been blinded by Jeff's charms and his quick press for them to marry.

With a mental sigh, she did her best to shove away the dark memories before she glanced down at the simple wrap dress she was wearing. The pale green geometric print still looked fresh enough, but it wasn't exactly what she would have picked to wear for a date with Conall. A date? If that's what this was supposed to be then he was going backward, she thought. Dates were supposed to come before marriage proposals, not after. But then she could hardly forget that Conall's proposal had not been the conventional sort, where a man promised his love for a lifetime.

"We can't go anywhere fancy," she finally said. "I'm not dressed for it."

He reached over and plucked one of the dark pink roses from the bouquet he'd given her. "You are now," he murmured as he tucked the flower behind her left ear. "A rose in your hair to match the roses on your cheeks."

Clearing her tight throat, she said, "I didn't know you could flirt."

He grinned. "I'll be happy to show you what else I can do."

Forbidden images raced through her mind. "I'll go get my handbag so we can be going."

Rising from the chair, she purposefully moved away from him and the desk before she lost all sense and reached for him, before she could tell him that the only place she wanted to go was straight into his arms.

Chapter 9

A few minutes later they were traveling toward Ruidoso in Conall's plush black truck. Only moments ago they'd watched the sun slip behind the mountains, and now in the western sky rich magenta threads laced together a cloak of purple clouds.

Being cooped up in the cozy cab with Conall was a temptation in itself and so far she'd been doing her best to concentrate on the scenery instead of his long, lean presence. But since they'd departed the ranch, he'd been in a surprisingly talkative mood and she'd found her gaze lingering on him far more than it should have.

"How long has Alonzo been in the nursing home?" he asked as he capably maneuvered the truck over the steeply winding highway.

Back at the office, he'd tugged a black cowboy hat low on his forehead and now as Vanessa glanced at his profile, she could only think that this man was living his days out not really in the way he wanted, but as he thought he was expected to. As a teenager she'd spent enough time on the ranch to see that Conall had been an outdoorsman, a horseman. She sensed that deep down, he would much rather be working hands-on with the horses than dealing with business issues. But apparently he considered managing the ranch his family duty and from what she could tell about the man, Conall would never shun his family responsibilities. In that aspect, he would be an excellent husband and father. But did duty mean more than love? Not to her.

"About six months," she answered. "After his stroke he was in the hospital for nearly a month before he was well enough to go to the nursing home. He's doing much better now, but he still has a way to go. I've hired a speech therapist to work with him and that's made a great difference. He's actually beginning to talk again with words that are understandable."

He nodded. "Do you think he'll ever get to come home?"

"If he continues to improve, his doctor says it's highly possible. But he'll not be able to live alone." She sighed. "I'm hoping when, or maybe I should say if, that happens, the twins won't be so demanding of me."

Chuckling lowly, he shook his head. "I'm sorry, Vanessa, but I don't think it's going to work that way. I have a feeling that the older the twins get, the more they're going to demand of their mother. Especially since—"

He broke off as though he had second thoughts about his next words. Vanessa didn't press him. She simply waited.

"Well," he finally said, "no matter about the twins.

I'm sure you'd love to have your father well again and back home. If it was my father, I certainly would."

She smiled wanly. "More than anything. He's all alone. And I have a feeling the twins would be good for him."

"The twins are very special," he said with undisguised warmth. "But you would be good for him, too. You have a way of making people around you feel better about themselves."

With a shake of her head, she said, "You don't have to overdo it, Conall."

He mouthed a curse under his breath. "I'm not overdoing anything, Vanessa. If you... Well, you've made me realize that divorcing Nancy didn't make me a criminal or a devil. Nor did it end my life."

Curiosity sparked in her and she couldn't stop herself from asking, "You were the one who wanted the divorce?"

He grimaced. "Yes," he answered bluntly.

"Why?"

Sighing, he said, "We had fundamental differences in what we thought was important to our lives and our marriage. But in the end she...betrayed me in a way that was unforgivable."

Had Nancy cheated on Conall with another man? She'd never met the woman who'd once been in the Donovan family, but she found it hard to imagine her committing adultery on a man that was breathtakingly sexy, unless the cheating had been more about her unhappiness. "You don't believe in forgiveness?" she asked.

A wry twist to his lips, he said, "I can forgive, Vanessa. But forgiving wouldn't have fixed the problem."

"Oh."

He looked at her. "Let's not waste this evening talking about such things. It's in the past and that's where it's going to stay. So tell me some of your favorite foods and we'll decide where to eat."

He obviously wanted to change the subject and Vanessa could understand why. She didn't particularly enjoy talking about Jeff and the mistakes she made with him. No doubt Conall felt the same.

"All right," she agreed, "I like anything I can eat with my hands. How about a hamburger?"

He flashed her a grin. "I knew we'd be perfect together. You just proved it."

Groaning inwardly, Vanessa could have told him there wasn't such a thing as being perfect together. Maybe for a few minutes at a time, but not for a lifetime. But she kept the cynical thought to herself. Now that she'd agreed to spend the evening with Conall, she didn't want to spoil their time together with more useless arguments.

Once they reached town, Vanessa started to give Conall directions to the nursing home, but he quickly interrupted.

"I know where it is, Vanessa. I've been there many times."

She looked at him with surprise. "I didn't realize any of your family had been incapacitated. From what Maura's told me, your grandfather's death was rather quick."

"I've not had a family member living in Gold Aspen Manor. But Liam's assistant stayed there until…his death."

By now they had reached the one-story, ranch-style building that sat in a carved out area of a wooded foothill. Slanted parking slots skirted a wide front lawn where sprinklers were going and a gardener was meticulously edging the sidewalk. It was a quiet and beautiful place, but Vanessa cringed each time she walked through the doors. She wanted her father to be whole and well again. She wanted him to be back on his little patch of land, scratching out a small garden and tending his goats.

"I didn't realize Liam ever had an assistant," she admitted. "I took it for granted that he'd always worked alone."

Conall cut the motor, but didn't make any hurried moves to depart the truck. "No. Before Liam was experienced enough to take on the task of being head trainer, Cletis—we called him Clete—was the man. He mentored Liam, then after handing the reins over to him, continued to work alongside my brother until about three years ago when his health began to fail. Liam's not been the same since the old man passed away."

"I can understand that. I've not been the same since my mother passed," Vanessa sadly admitted. "Everything that once was important to me now looks so different, almost trivial."

His expression suddenly sober, he let out a long breath. "Yeah. Well, Clete didn't have a family. He regarded Liam as a son. And Liam doesn't think anyone could ever fill Clete's boots. That's mainly why he continues to work himself to death instead of hiring a new assistant." With a wry expression, he reached over and touched her hand. "Come on, that's enough about that stuff. Let's go see your father."

To Vanessa's delight they found Alonzo outside, seated around a patio table with a group of men who were also patients at the Gold Aspen Manor. As soon as the older man spotted her approach, he rose from his chair and held out his arms to her.

Leaving Conall's side, she rushed to her father and hugged him tight. After he'd kissed both her cheeks, he put her away from him with a strength that surprised her.

"Wow, you're awfully spry this evening," she said with a happy laugh. "What have they been feeding you around here, spinach?"

Alonzo's dark wrinkled face split into a grin for his daughter. "Can't stand that stuff. Meat. Fresh meat. That's what's done it."

Pressing her cheek against his, she hugged him once again, before gesturing toward Conall, who was standing a few steps behind her. "I brought someone with me tonight, Dad. You remember Conall?"

The old man's brown eyes flickered with surprise, quickly followed by pleasure. "Sure, sure. Donovan. That right?"

Smiling, Conall stepped forward and reached to shake her father's hand. "That's exactly right, Mr. Valdez. It's good to see you again."

The other man nodded with approval. "Good to see you. Yes."

Looping her arm through his, Vanessa asked, "Do you think you can make it over to that empty table where we can sit down and talk?"

To her surprise, he pushed away her helping hand. "Show you. Watch," he said proudly.

Moving aside, she stood next to Conall and watched as Alonzo walked slowly but surely the twenty-foot distance to the empty table.

"Your father looks like he's doing great to me," Conall said under his breath.

She glanced up at him with pleased wonder. "I've never seen his back so straight and he's actually lifting his feet and putting them down instead of shuffling. He's improved so much from just a week ago."

Giving the side of her waist an encouraging squeeze, he inclined his head toward Alonzo. "Let's join him."

For the next forty minutes the three of them talked about the twins, then on to several local happenings, until finally the two men began to reminisce about the time Alonzo restored one of the Diamond D horse barns. Vanessa hadn't been aware that her father had ever contracted work for the Donovans or that he'd known the family so personally. But that didn't begin to describe the shock she felt when Conall suddenly scooted his chair close to Vanessa's and curled his arm around her shoulders in a completely possessive way.

"Alonzo, has your daughter told you that I've asked her to marry me?"

The old man appeared stunned and then he turned accusing eyes upon his daughter. "She did not tell me."

Conall shot her a devilish smile. "Why haven't you told your father about us?"

It was all Vanessa could do to stop herself from kicking his shins beneath the table. "Because it—" Jerking her eyes off Conall's expectant face, she looked over to her father. "Because I told him no!"

Alonzo studied her closely. "Why?"

"Yeah, why?" Conall echoed the older man's question.

She wanted to kill the man for putting her on the spot like this in front of her father. And yet, a part of her felt ridiculously warm and wanted and a bit like a princess to have Conall Donovan declaring to her father that he wanted to marry her.

"Because I—" She turned a challenging look on Conall. "I want a husband who will love me."

Alonzo's sharp gaze leveled on Conall and then after a moment he chuckled. The sound didn't just stun Vanessa, it also angered her.

"That'll come," Alonzo said with beaming confidence. "Later."

Jumping to her feet, she tugged on Conall's arm. "We've got to be going. Now!"

Conall didn't argue and after she gave her father a quick goodbye, the two of them hurried around to a side exit of the building and on to the parked truck.

As he helped her climb into the cab, she hissed under her breath, "What the hell were you doing back there?"

"Telling Alonzo my intentions toward his daughter," he answered easily. "As far as I'm concerned, that's the respectable thing for a man to do."

"But you did it on purpose!"

"Of course I did it on purpose." As she settled herself in the seat, he shut the door and rounded the truck. Once he was under the wheel and starting the engine, he said, "I don't say things just to be saying them, Vanessa."

Groaning helplessly, she swiped a hand across her forehead. "Now Dad is going to be wondering about us and expecting—"

"What?"

"Me to marry you. That's what. He likes and respects you and he's been telling me that I need a husband. It's all simple logic to him."

Conall smiled. "He did appear pleased about the whole thing. But I always did think your father was a wise man."

Latching on to his last words, she jerked her head around to stare at him in wonder. "You never cease to surprise me, Conall."

"Why?" he asked with a puzzled frown. "What have I done now?"

Suddenly her heart was melting like candy clutched in a warm palm. Maybe he didn't love her outright, but he was good in so many other ways that she was beginning to wonder if she was crazy for refusing to marry him. "Nothing. You complimented my father. Did you really mean that when you called him wise?"

He backed the truck onto the street and directed it down the steep street. "Like I said, I don't say things just to be saying them. Your dad has weathered plenty of storms and he's done it without bending or begging. He's worked hard all his life and managed to hold his land and his home together. That takes wisdom." He glanced at her. "Plus he knew how to keep your mother happy. I could see that each time I saw them together in church. They looked at each other the same way my parents look at each other."

She swallowed hard as emotions thickened her throat. "You mean...with love?"

His features tightened ever so slightly. "I'd rather call it respect."

Vanessa couldn't argue that respect was a key ingredient in a marriage. But it wasn't enough to keep her heart warm and full. It didn't thrill her or fill her with hunger or need or joy.

"By all means call it that if it makes you feel safer,"

Vanessa told him as she unconsciously reached up and touched the rose he'd placed above her ear. "I prefer to call it what it is."

They ate at a tiny café on the northwest side of town called the Sugar Shack, in tribute to the decadent home-made desserts that were served there. Over the casual dinner, all mention of love and marriage, or anything close to it, was avoided by both of them and eventually Vanessa was able to relax and enjoy the good food.

Once the meal was over and they exited the building, she pressed a hand to her stomach and groaned. "I've not eaten that much in ages. I'll probably have nightmares tonight after stuffing myself."

"I have a perfect place for you to walk some of that meal off," he suggested slyly.

Spend more time with this man? Alone? The sane, sensible and smart thing for her to do would be go straight home. He made her crazy and on edge, yet at the same time he made her undeniably happy. She was at a loss as to how to deal with the contradictory feelings, especially when a part of her was screaming to simply give up and give in to her desires.

"I really should get back home and give Hannah some relief."

He moved his arm around the back of her waist and guided her toward the truck. "I promise you, Hannah and the twins can make it without you for a little while longer. And if you don't feel like doing any walking, we can always do a little stargazing."

Her mouth opened to utter another protest, but that was as far as her resistance would take her. "All right," she conceded. "It would be nice to stay out a little longer."

"That's exactly what I was thinking."

Once they were back in the truck, he drove northwest until most of the town was behind them. After turning onto a narrow dirt road, they wound upward through a tall stand of pines and spruce trees until they were near the crest of the mountain. Just when she'd decided he was probably taking her to a state campground, the road ended and the forest opened up. Beyond the beam of headlights she could see some sort of house constructed of cedar wood and native rock.

"Is this your place?" she asked as he parked the truck near a big blue spruce.

"It belongs to the Diamond D," he answered. "We have guests, horse buyers, or out-of-town friends fly in to attend the races and this place is a lot closer to the track than the ranch. Our city friends especially enjoy the privacy." He reached to release his seat belt. "Let's get out and I'll show you around."

Once he helped Vanessa down from the truck, he took a firm hold on her hand. "Be careful and watch your step," he warned as they started toward the house. "Dad doesn't want to install a yard light up here. Says it would ruin the effect. So at night it's dark as hell."

"The moon is rising," she remarked as she cast an observing glance at the eastern sky. "That gives us walking light."

The back part of the structure sat on the edge of the mountainside, while the front was supported with huge wooden pillars. She figured the Donovans considered this a mere mountain cabin, but to regular folks like her it was more like an opulent getaway.

The two of them climbed long steps up to a wide planked deck that also served as a porch. Conall led her over to the far end and they leaned against a waist-high wooden railing to gaze beyond the surrounding forest to a majestic view of the valley below.

"It's beautiful up here!" she said with quiet wonder.

He said, "Well, you can't exactly get the full effect of the view in the moonlight, but we'll come back again when the sun is out and the weather is nice. You'll really appreciate it then."

His suggestion implied that he planned to spend more personal time with her. The idea thrilled her, yet troubled her. No doubt the more time she spent with him, the more she would fall in love with him. And where would that eventually leave her? Loving a man who was unable to love her in return?

No. She didn't want to think about that right now. Since her divorce more than a year ago, she'd kept a high fence around herself. Before she'd taken even the tiniest of steps, she'd stopped and looked in all four directions to make sure she wasn't about to be waylaid by something or someone. Careful, cautious and controlled, that was how she'd lived her life since her marriage had ended. Now she was struck with the reckless urge to break free of those cold boundaries, to let herself live and feel again. No matter the painful consequences.

Sighing, she turned toward him. "I'm glad you asked me out tonight," she admitted.

His smile was full of doubt. "That's hard to believe. I haven't exactly been one of your favorite people since… well, since that morning at the office when I wanted to make love to you."

The memory of that incident still had the power to heat her cheeks and she was grateful the darkness masked the telltale color on her cheeks. "Make love to me? Don't you mean you wanted to have sex with me?"

In the silver moonlight she could see a grimace cross his face. "I was trying to be tactful. Making love sounds better."

"I'd prefer honesty over sounding nice." She directed her gaze away from his face to a dark corner of the deck. "Actually, I should tell you that I was angrier at myself that day than I was with you."

His hand released hers only to wrap around her upper arm. Since her dress was sleeveless, the feel of his fingers against her bare skin was like throwing drops of water into a hot skillet. The sizzle vibrated all the way down to her toes.

He said, "I don't understand."

She dared to look up at his shadowed face. "You should understand, Conall. It's not smart of me to want you. But I do," she added in a whisper.

Suddenly the hand that had been burning a ring around her arm slid upward until his long fingers were curved against her throat. No doubt he could feel the hammering of her pulse and knew exactly what his touch was doing to her. But then, he'd probably always known how weak and utterly helpless he made her.

"You shouldn't have been angry with either one of us," he murmured. "And if it's honesty you want, I can truthfully say I want you, Vanessa. More than I've ever wanted any woman."

From any other man, a trite line like that would have garnered a groan of disgust from Vanessa, but coming from Conall she wanted to believe it was uttered with sincerity. Oh, yes, to think he desired her over any other woman was more than a heady thought. But thinking, wondering, deciding what was right or wrong was quickly taking a backseat. Instead of her brain, her heart had taken control and it was urging her body to press against his, begging her arms to wrap around his waist.

"Don't say any more, Conall. Just show me."

She heard him suck in a sharp breath and then his lips were suddenly hovering over hers.

"Vanna. Vanna."

The repeated whisper of her nickname was like a warm, sweet caress and she sighed ever so slightly before his lips latched on to hers, his hands slid to the small of her back and pressed her body into his.

She'd expected his kiss to be a lazy, searching seduction, but it was anything but. His lips were rampaging over hers, taking her breath and searing her senses with the depth of his desire. She tried to match his movements, tried to give back to him, but he'd taken total control and all she could do was surrender to the ravaging passion.

By the time he lifted his head, her legs were trembling and she was clutching the front of his shirt just to keep herself upright.

He whispered, "I think we should go inside, don't you?"

Her lips felt swollen, prompting her to run the tip of her tongue over them at the same time she sucked in deep, ragged breaths. And though she should have taken the time to regain her senses and consider his loaded question, she didn't wait. She was tired of waiting.

"Yes," she murmured. "We should."

She followed him over to the door, which he quickly unlocked with a spare key hidden beneath a pot of cacti. Once they were inside, he switched on the nearest table lamp and beneath the dim glow Vanessa caught a brief glance of expensive, rustic-style furniture, a polished pine floor scattered with braided rugs and a wall of glass overlooking the deck. Beyond that, she saw nothing but Conall's dark face as he pulled her into his arms and began to kiss her all over again.

For long, long moments, they stood just inside the door, their bodies locked together, their lips clinging, tasting and searching for a closeness they couldn't quite attain. Unlike his ravaging kiss on the deck, this time his lips were slow and hot, luring her to a place where there was nothing but mindless pleasure.

The concept of time faded, along with their surroundings. When he finally ended the embrace and took her by the hand to lead her out of the room, she followed blindly and willingly down a narrow hallway with doors leading off both sides.

At the far end, they entered a bedroom with a wall of glass similar to the one they'd just left. Beyond it, the moon was a bright orb in the sky and its silver light illuminated the layout of the room, the king-sized bed and matching cedar armoire, a pair of stuffed armchairs by the window and a nightstand that could also be used as a desk.

Leading her toward the bed, Conall said, "This is the room I stay in whenever I'm up here. But that's not often."

"Why is that?" she asked huskily.

Their legs bumped into the side of the mattress and

he quickly spun her into his arms. "Because you're not here," he said with a hungry growl.

She groaned with disbelief. "Oh, Conall."

He pulled her down onto the mattress and with the two of them lying face-to-face, he cupped a hand against her cheek. "It's true, Vanessa. Until you came to work for me, I think I'd forgotten about living. And I'd sure as hell forgotten about this."

With his arm around her waist, he urged her forward until the front of her body was pressed tightly to his. Vanessa's heart was pounding like a drumbeat deep in a hot jungle as his lips settled against her cheek, then slid open and wet to the side of her neck.

Desire bubbled within her before spreading like fingers of hot lava to every part of her body. Certain she was paralyzed by the incredible heat, she moaned and waited for a sense of normalcy to return to her limbs. It didn't. And in the back of her mind, she suddenly realized that everything about this and about Conall was different and new.

"I think…I might have forgotten, too," she whispered as his lips continued their heated foray against her throat. "Or maybe I never knew that it could feel like this."

Lifting his head, he gazed wondrously at her. "Vanna. Oh, baby."

It was all he said before his lips moved over hers and then his kiss was telling her how much he needed and wanted her. And for the moment that was enough for Vanessa. Words could come later.

Like a man wandering through a parched desert, Conall craved to drink from her lips, to bury himself in the moist folds of her body and restore the dry emptiness inside him. And though he was trying his best to control himself, to give her time to get used to being in his arms and to accept the idea of making love to him, the weeks, days, hours of wanting her had left him simmering far too long.

Before he could stop himself, he was tugging at her clothes, tossing them every which way until his hands and mouth had nothing but smooth skin beneath them. She felt like the petal of a flower and tasted even sweeter. Without even knowing it, a groan rumbled deep in his throat as he explored her tight nipples, then on to the hollow of her belly, the bank of her hipbone and the tender slope of her inner thigh.

Above his head, he could hear her soft whimpers of need and the sound fueled him, thrilled him, empowered him in a way he'd never felt before. And when her fingers delved into his hair, her hips arched toward his searching mouth, he realized that without even trying she was giving him everything his body, his soul, had been craving for so long.

Desperate to have her, yet please her, he slipped his hand between her thighs, then his fingers into the very warm center of her. Her reaction was to suck in a harsh breath and then she released a guttural groan as his slow, tempting strokes caused her to writhe and beg for relief.

"Conall...please...I can't...wait!"

Her choked plea prompted him to pull his fingers away and quickly replace them with his tongue. As he lathed the moist folds, she began to pulsate and he supped at her pleasure, inhaled the unique scent of her until the ache in his loins threatened to overtake him.

While her body was still riding on a crested wave,

he moved up and over her, then sealing his lips over hers, he thrust deep inside her.

The intimate connection was so overwhelming it took his breath, and not until her legs wrapped around his waist and her hips arched toward him did he realize his body had gone stock-still. He used the moment to lift his head and gaze down at her face and for one split second he wished he'd looked elsewhere, anywhere but at the tenderness, the raw emotion radiating from her eyes. What he saw in the deep brown depths looked so much like love that he wanted to embrace it and run from it all at the same time.

Cupping a hand against her cheek, he tried to speak, to tell her with words exactly how much this moment meant to him. But nothing would form on his tongue except her name and it came out on a hoarse whisper.

"Vanna. My beautiful sweetheart."

Reaching up, she curled a hand around the back of his neck and pulled his face down to hers. "Make love to me, Conall."

Love. She wasn't labeling it as sex anymore. She was calling it love. And Conall couldn't argue the point. In spite of his effort to put a brake on his free-falling emotions, everything inside his heart was shouting that he loved this woman. And he could no more put a halt to his feelings than he could stop his body from moving against hers, from seeking the pleasure that only she could give him.

Chapter 10

With her cheek resting against his damp chest, the sound of his rapid heartbeat merged with the blood rushing through her ears. Her hair was a damp tangle around her face while the rest of her body was covered with a fine sheen of sweat. Beyond Conall's shoulder she could see the glass wall, which was partially covered with dark drapes.

Sometime after they'd entered the bedroom, clouds had covered the moon and now bolts of lightning were streaking across the peaks of the distant mountains. The ominous threat of rain matched the turmoil going on inside of her and though she tried to push the dark feelings away, tried to focus on the sheer wonder of being in Conall's arms, she couldn't prevent a wall of tears from stinging her eyes and thickening her throat.

When his hand rested on her head and his fingers

began to push through her hair, she did her best to speak. Talking would break the spell, she told herself. Talking would make her realize that what just happened between them was normal and nothing out of the ordinary. The earth hadn't shattered nor had her heart. It was still beating in her chest and the world was still turning on its axis. So why did she feel as though everything had suddenly changed?

"It's going to rain," she said.

He murmured, "Not in here. We're dry and cozy."

His hand left her hair to settle on her shoulder and Vanessa's eyelids drifted closed as his fingers made lazy circles across her skin. She wanted to stay in his arms forever. She wanted to pretend that he loved her, that each time he'd touched her, his heart had been guiding him. But that would be fooling herself. And she wasn't going to be a fool a second time around. No matter how good he made her feel.

"It's getting late," she reminded him. "I have to be going home soon."

His sigh ruffled the top of her hair. "It's already late. Being a little later isn't going to make much difference."

Tilting her head back, she looked at him. "Explaining this to Hannah is not going to be easy."

One side of his lips twisted upward. "Hannah isn't your mother. And why don't you simply tell her the truth? That you were out with me?"

She bit down on her bottom lip. "I don't know."

"Why? Are you ashamed of being here with me?"

"Not exactly."

His jaw thrust forward. "What is that supposed to mean?"

She swallowed as the raw thickness returned to her

throat. "I guess what I'm trying to say is…that I'm feeling more sad than anything."

A puzzled frown puckered his forehead and then his expression quickly turned to one of concern. "Sad? Why, did I hurt you? Did I do something wrong and you're too embarrassed to tell me about it?"

A rush of pure love for him overcame her and she scooted her body upward until she could press her lips against his cheek. "Oh, Conall, you did everything right. Perfect. I could make love to you over and over if…well, I suppose I'm just feeling sad because I know this is the end."

Next to hers, she could feel his body tense.

"End?" he asked inanely. "I thought it was just the beginning."

Easing out of his arms, she sat up on the side of the bed. Except for the intermittent flashes of lightning, the interior of the bedroom was completely black. She was glad the darkness was there to hide her tears.

"I can't keep being your secretary now, Conall. Not after this. It would never work."

The sheets rustled as he shifted toward her and then his hand was pushing the hair away from the back of her neck. As he pressed a kiss against her nape, he murmured, "I'm glad you said that, Vanessa. Like I said before, I don't want you to be my secretary. I want you to be my wife."

Groaning, she bent her head and squeezed her eyes against the burning tears. "Oh, Conall, please don't do this to me," she pleaded in a whisper. "Not tonight."

With his hands on her bare shoulders, he twisted her upper body toward him. "What am I doing to you that's so wrong, Vanna? I'm asking you to be my wife, to be at my side for the rest of our lives. A few minutes ago you said you could make love to me over and over. Did you mean that?"

"Yes. But marrying you—I can't. I can't live in a loveless marriage." She gestured toward the center of the bed. "Yes, the sex between us would be good—for a while. But after the initial luster wore off everything would feel empty…be empty. I want more than that."

His hand smoothed the hair back from her forehead and as her gaze flickered over his shadowed features, she suddenly felt as though she was looking at a different man. The soft and gentle expression in his eyes was something she'd never seen before and she didn't know what to think or expect.

"I want more than that, too, Vanna."

Wide-eyed, with her lips parted, she stared at him. "What are you saying?"

One corner of his mouth lifted. "You don't want to make any of this easy for me, do you?"

"Easy? Nothing about this is easy for me," she said flatly. "I've made too many mistakes, Conall. I don't want to keep making more."

A heavy breath slipped past his lips. "Neither do I," he admitted. "That's why…you have to know…that I love you."

Stunned, she shifted her body so that she was facing him directly. "Love? Who are you trying to kid? Me or yourself?" Angry and confused, she slipped off the bed and reached for her dress. "Either way, Conall, I'm not sure I can forgive you for this!"

Leaping off the bed, he snatched the dress from her hands before she could step into the garment. "What the hell are you talking about?" he demanded. "I'm trying to tell you how I feel about you—about us!"

"Sure. Sure you are." Since he'd confiscated her dress, she glanced around for something to cover her nakedness. Luckily his shirt was at her feet and she quickly jammed her arms into the sleeves and buttoned the front between her breasts. "What do you think I am? An idiot? A fool?"

Tossing her dress aside, he reached for her and though she wanted to resist, she couldn't. As soon as his hands wrapped around her shoulders, as soon as the front of his hard, warm body was pressed against hers, she was lost to him.

"Vanna," he began gently, "maybe I did pick the wrong time to confess my feelings. Maybe it does look all contrived to you. But I can't help that. I'm a rancher not some sort of Romeo or playboy that knows exactly what to say or how to say it."

She wanted to believe him. Every beat of her heart was longing for his words to be true. But the scarred, wary side of her held back, refused to believe that this man could have changed. Especially for her.

"Maybe you're forgetting, Conall. You told me that you didn't believe in love. That it was a fairy-tale existence. Not a firm foundation for a marriage."

A mixture of regret and frustration twisted his features. "That was the bitterness in me doing the talking, Vanna. For a long time now I'd quit looking for a woman to love. I'd decided it wasn't worth the pain. But then you walked into my life and…oh, Vanna, believe me, I've tried not to love you. I've tried telling myself that you're just another woman, you're nothing special and I could do without you. But none of that has worked. I want you by my side. I need you in my bed, my life, in every way a man can need a woman. I love you. Pure and simple."

Even though she felt the safety barriers inside her begin to crumble, she tried her best to withstand his gentle persuasion. "And us just having sex had nothing to do with this sudden realization of yours," she said with skepticism.

His hands left her shoulders and began to roam against her back and farther down to the curve of her bottom. The familiar touch of his hands, even through the fabric of his shirt, was heating her flesh, reminding her body of the delicious pleasures he could give her.

"Would you call what just happened between us sex?" he countered. "You don't believe that. And neither do I. And as for realizing that I loved you—" dipping his head, he nuzzled his cheek against hers "—I think that happened a long time ago, Vanna. Even before that day you fainted in my arms. That's why I did my best to keep everything between us business. I didn't want to give myself the chance to let my feelings for you grow."

In spite of all the misgivings traipsing through her thoughts, Vanessa's heart began to beat with hope. Tilting her head back she gazed at him through shimmery eyes. "I didn't want to love you, either," she whispered, "but I do."

With a groan of relief, he captured her lips with his and with their mouths still locked, he lowered them both back onto the bed.

As he shoved his shirt off her shoulders and began to nibble eagerly at one breast, she groaned in defeat. "Conall, the babies—"

"Are going to have me for a daddy," he murmured, his words muffled by her heated skin.

"But tonight—"

"You'll be getting home late. Very late."

More than a week later, Conall was standing beneath the shady overhang of a long shed row talking with Walt. In his early seventies with a face as wrinkled as a raisin, he was rawhide-tough and as dependable as the rise and fall of the sun. For longer than Conall had been alive, he'd been the man who made sure the barns, the stalls, the gallopers, the hot walkers, the grooms and everyone in between had what they needed to make their jobs easier and keep the horses in top-notch condition.

A stickler for making lists, Walt's hand-scribbled notes normally went to Liam's office first and then on to Conall's. But with Liam still out in California at the Del Mar track, he was making sure Conall was personally handed the written requests.

"Not asking for much this time, Mr. Conall," he said as Conall scanned the short piece of paper. "Mainly shavings and clippers. Had two pair of them burn up this week. They just ain't made to last like they used to be."

Even though it had been more than forty years since Walt had migrated over to New Mexico from South Texas, he still insisted on the mannerly form of putting the *Mr.* in front of Conall's name.

"Shavings, huh?" Conall mused out loud. "I just had a thousand yards of those delivered to the ranch last week. We already need more?"

"Yes, sir. That brother of yours has stalled nearly

every two-year-old on this place and I think half of 'em needs to be turned to pasture. Save plenty of shavings like that. But you know Mr. Liam, he thinks they're all runners."

Conall grunted with amusement. "He's supposed to think like that, Walt. Otherwise, he might accidently turn a champion out to pasture."

The older man's grin was sly. "Well, we couldn't have that, could we?"

Giving Walt a companionable swat on the shoulder, Conall said, "It's time I got back to the office. Why don't you take the rest of the day off, Walt," he suggested. "You work too hard."

A scowl wrinkled Walt's features even more. "Look who's talkin'. Besides, I gotta help Travis repair the water trough in the yearling pen. Anything mechanical boggles that boy's mind. This younger generation is helpless. Slap-dab helpless."

Still muttering about Travis's incompetence, Walt turned and walked away. Conall headed in the opposite direction and was nearly at the end of the shed row when he spotted Brady, his younger brother, striding toward him.

Being a deputy for the Lincoln County sheriff's department kept Brady working random shifts, which didn't give Conall much opportunity to spend time with him. This evening Brady was still dressed in his uniform and Conall didn't have to ask if his day had been long. The man put in an extraordinary amount of hours on the job, yet even now there was a grin on his face, albeit a weary one.

If Conall was being totally honest with himself, he'd often been envious of his youngest brother. Brady had grown up to be the strong-minded, independent one of the Donovan boys. He'd chosen to go outside the family tradition of horse racing and take on a job that he quite obviously loved. Moreover, Brady had never experienced a moment's guilt over the decision. Whereas Conall had often felt bound, even restricted, by the duty of being the eldest son; the one that was meant to hold the Diamond D together for future generations.

"Hey, Conall," he greeted. "Are you heading toward the house or the office?"

As Brady took off the felt hat he was wearing and slapped it against his thigh to remove the dust, Conall gestured toward the part of the ranch yard where the office buildings were located.

"The office. And I'm glad you interrupted. I get damned tired of being cooped up."

Brady chuckled slyly. "With Vanessa? That's hard to believe."

Conall frowned. "Vanessa took the day off to go shopping with Maura. Mom's been sitting in for her, but she's already left me, too. One of these days I've got to take the time to hire an assistant to take over whenever Vanessa or Mom can't be around."

Clearly amused, Brady walked over to the nearest stall where a chestnut horse was poking his nose eagerly over the wooden gate that had him safely fastened inside the small square space. As he stroked Hot Charlie's nose, he said, "Mom probably hightailed it to the house 'cause you were too cranky to put up with."

Smiling, Conall walked over to join his brother. "What are you talking about? I'm always Mr. Nice Guy."

"Well, maybe now that Vanessa has tamed you," he conceded. "You two set a wedding date yet?"

"Not yet. But we will soon."

"That's good." Brady glanced at him. "I haven't had a chance to tell you how glad I am that you're getting married again. I've been hoping for a long time that you'd find somebody special—like I found Lass."

Conall smiled ruefully. When Brady had first fallen in love with Lass, Conall had been worried sick about his younger brother and the whole situation he'd gotten himself into. At the time, Lass had been suffering from amnesia and hadn't known who she was or even if she had a home somewhere. Conall had been certain she was going to take Brady for a disastrous ride. He and Brady had even had cross words over the woman. But Conall would be the first to admit he'd been dead wrong about Lass. She'd made Brady a loving and devoted wife.

"Well, I didn't find her on the side of the road like you found Lass," Conall joked, "but she's definitely the right one for me."

Turning away from the horse, Brady gave him a weary smile. "That's all that matters. When's Liam coming home?"

"I don't know. Probably not until Del Mar closes on Labor Day. So let's hope he's taking a liking to all that sun and surf."

Brady laughed out loud. "Liam in the surf? That'd be the day. He's spending every waking moment on the backside of the track. That's what he's doing." He slapped a hand over Conall's shoulder. "I've got to get going. Dallas is staying at Angel Wings an hour later tonight to accommodate a little girl who's just gotten over a long illness, so Lass is expecting me to drive over and fetch her before dinnertime. And since my wife and I haven't had dinner together in the past two weeks, she'll kill me if I'm late."

"I doubt it. Other than Vanna, I don't know of any woman who's more understanding than Lass."

Brady started to stride away, then at the last minute turned back toward Conall. "Oh. By the way, I came down here to tell you that we found out who crashed their vehicle through the fence—a teenage boy from over around Alto. The father found the damage to the truck and pressed his son for answers. The man is offering to pay for the fence repairs. I told him I'd discuss it with you and let him know."

Conall shook his head. "Money isn't the issue. I'd rather the boy do the labor to repair the fence. Teach him a hell of a lot better lesson than his dad bailing him out with money."

"That's exactly what I was thinking. I'll have a talk with the father and see what we can work out," Brady said, then grinned. "By the way, I hope Vanessa knows what a hell of a daddy those twins are getting."

Brady lifted his hand in farewell, then turned to hurry on to his waiting truck. Conall remained beside Hot Charlie's stall as all sorts of emotions swirled inside of him.

These past few days, he'd been torn between complete euphoria and stark terror. When Vanessa had made love to him and agreed to marry him, the joy he'd felt had put him on a cloud. She was everything he'd ever wanted in a woman and wife. Being with her, loving her, made his life complete. Yet in his quieter moments, nagging fear tried to intrude on his happiness.

There was going to be trouble—big trouble—if he didn't take Vanessa aside and talk to her about his condition. But since their night at the mountain cabin, when she'd agreed to marry him, things had quickly begun to barrel out of control. Not that he could use a hectic routine as an excuse. If he'd been any sort of man at all, he would have told her that night. But at the time, he'd not had the courage or the confidence to risk smashing the progress he'd made with her. He'd felt… no, he'd *known* that Vanessa needed more convincing of his love and he needed more time to do that convincing.

But that had been more than a week ago and now his mother and grandmother were already planning an engagement party for the two of them. In a matter of days, the ranch house would be full of friends, family and acquaintances. Everyone would be expecting them to announce their wedding date. But would there even be a wedding, he wondered, once Vanessa discovered he was sterile?

Once he returned to the office there was a stack of business calls he still needed to make. But business would have to wait, he decided, as he reached for the cell phone in his shirt pocket. Talking to Vanessa couldn't. If she was the wonderful, understanding woman that he believed her to be, then she would accept and empathize with the circumstance that had never been his fault.

Buoyed by the thought, Conall punched in Vanessa's cell number. After the fourth ring he was expecting her voice mail to end the call when she suddenly answered.

"Hello, Conall," she said. "This is a surprise. I expected you to still be working."

"I am. Sort of. I've been down at the shed rows talking with Walt. But I'm on my way back to the office to make a few calls before I quit for the evening."

"Oh, do you need information? Maura and I are at the Blue Mesa having coffee. I can probably talk you through it."

He smiled to himself. No matter what the situation, Vanessa was always the consummate secretary. "Everything is okay here. I'm calling to see about us getting together tonight. I thought I'd drive over to your place. That way I could see the twins. And we could...talk."

Her low chuckle was sexy enough to curl his toes. "Talk? You really think that would happen?"

He closed his eyes as the images of her naked and writhing beneath him rolled into his mind. Talking to Vanessa tonight was going to be difficult. In more ways than one. "Well, we do have things to discuss. Important things. Like making a date for our wedding. And... other things," he added. He drew in a deep breath and blew it out. "Will you be in town for much longer?"

"Not much, I don't think. Let me check with Maura," she told him. She went off the line, but in the background he could hear the faint sounds of music and the casual chatter of voices, intermingled with street traffic. When she finally returned, she said, "We'll be leaving here soon, Conall. So I'll be home by the time you get there."

"Great. I'll see you then, darlin'."

Vanessa closed her cell phone and reached for her cooling coffee. Across the outdoor table, Maura smiled shrewdly.

"So what's my brother doing? Already giving you orders before you even get married?"

Chuckling, Vanessa said, "He's my boss. He's supposed to give me orders."

With a good-natured groan, Maura shook her head. "It's clear that he has you right where he wants you."

After a long sip of coffee, Vanessa looked over the rim of her cup at her longtime friend. "I can truthfully say I'm right where I want to be."

Smiling with approval, Conall's eldest sister sliced her fork into a piece of blueberry pie. "Hmm. Well, I can honestly say that Conall appears to be right where he wants to be, too." She chewed, swallowed, then released a sigh of contentment. "This is so nice, Vanessa, the two of us getting out like this together. Since you've returned to Lincoln County we've hardly had any time to spend together. I hope that changes and we can have more days like this. You've not even been out to see the Golden Spur yet."

"I will soon," Vanessa promised. "After we're married Conall wants to find someone to help me in the office. He thinks I need to be home with the twins for at least half of every workday and I agree with that. I want the twins to bond with me and know me as their mother, not just a woman they see in the mornings and at night. Still, I don't want to give up working completely. Does that sound selfish?"

"Not to me," Maura said between bites of the rich dessert. "After Riley was born I cut my weekly work hours down to half. And since Clancy arrived back in April I've cut them even more. But I've not quit nursing entirely. I believe some women need outside interest, too. Like me. Otherwise we'd become as dull as dishwater. And no man wants a dull wife."

Vanessa took a long sip of coffee before she replied,

"Well, working a half day will be plenty for me until the twins get older."

Maura smiled suggestively. "And who knows, by then you and Conall might want more children."

Vanessa felt a blush creep across her cheeks. If she'd not had the forethought to stay on the oral birth control she'd used during her marriage, she would probably be pregnant with Conall's child at this moment. That night they'd first made love, she'd been so besotted and lost in the man she'd forgotten to mention she was protected and apparently he'd forgotten to ask. Later, when she tried to assure him that there was nothing to worry about, that she was on oral contraceptives, he'd quickly dismissed the whole thing. As though getting her pregnant would be a welcome idea with him.

She'd not yet talked with him about having any future children. But she had no doubts that he would want them. As crazy as he was about the twins, she couldn't imagine him wanting to stop with just the two.

"Maybe," Vanessa said, then before she could stop it, a happy laugh slipped past her lips. "Oh, Maura, it's still hard for me to take everything in. First the twins and now becoming Conall's wife. In my wildest imaginings I couldn't have pictured this happening to me. I look back now and wonder why I was fighting Conall so hard and refusing to accept his proposal."

Her pie gone, Maura pushed the plate aside and reached for her coffee. "I remember the feeling well. I fought Quint for a long time before I ever agreed to marry him. But a woman wants to know she's loved for herself, not because of a baby. And Gilbert had done such a job of deceiving me that I…was scared to trust any man. Thank God Quint was persistent."

"I'm very happy that Conall didn't give up on me, either."

Vanessa placed her empty cup back on its saucer and reached for her handbag. "If you're ready we should probably be going. I need to tidy up the house—and myself—before Conall gets there."

Reaching across the table, Maura placed her hand over Vanessa's. "Before we go, I just wanted to say how glad I am that you're going to be my sister-in-law. I couldn't have picked any better woman for my brother. He's been so…well, dark and lost after the mess he went through with Nancy. I was afraid he'd never let himself love again. But you've made him so happy and I know you always will. You'd never try to hurt or manipulate him like she did. And you'd certainly never stop loving him just because of his condition."

Vanessa suddenly froze. "Condition?" she repeated blankly.

Maura's auburn brows pulled together. "Why, yes. You know—*his condition*."

Thrown for a loop, Vanessa's mind began to race down a tangle of dark roads. If there was something personal about Conall that she wasn't aware of, something he should have told her already, the last thing she wanted was for Maura to explain. That could only cause trouble between brother and sister. And whatever it was, she wanted to hear it directly from the man she planned to marry.

"Oh, yes," she said with feigned dawning. "That… None of that matters to me."

Maura's smile was full of approval and relief. "That's one of the reasons I've always loved you, Vanessa. You don't expect a person to be perfect."

Her mouth suddenly felt like she'd walked through Death Valley in mid-July. She reached for her water glass and after a long drink, tried to speak casually. "I'm hardly perfect myself, Maura. I can't expect others to be."

Just as Maura started to reply, her cell phone went off and the other woman quickly began to fish the device from her handbag. Vanessa was grateful for the diversion. She couldn't continue to fake this train of conversation.

"Excuse me, Vanessa, it's Quint. I'd better see what he needs."

While Maura exchanged a few short words with her husband, Vanessa's mind tumbled end over end. What could be wrong with Conall? A recurring health problem? That was hard to believe. During the time she'd worked for him, she'd never seen him sick or even close to it. He appeared as healthy as the horses he bred and raised.

The snapping sound of Maura's phone being shut jerked Vanessa out of her whirling thoughts and she looked across the table at her friend's apologetic face.

"I hate to end the day so abruptly, Vanna, but Quint's grandfather is feeling a bit puny and he wants me to drive out to Apache Wells and check on him before I go home. It's forty minutes from here, so I need to hit the road."

As she stood up, she tossed several bills onto the table. "That ought to take care of everything here."

Rising to her feet also, Vanessa quickly grabbed up the money and thrust it back at the other woman. "Here. I'll take care of things."

"No arguments. It's my treat today, sweetie." She

pressed a quick kiss on Vanessa's cheek. "See you soon. And I promise you that Conall's eyes are going to pop out of his head when he sees you in the dress we found today."

Smiling as brightly as she could, Vanessa waved her friend off, then went to pay the check. A few minutes later, she was on the highway, driving home to Tinnie as fast as the speed limit would allow.

Conall had never been known for being a nervous person. In fact, his brothers had often accused him of having ice water in his veins and his mother had regularly referred to him as a piece of unmoving granite. But if they could see his insides now as he drove to Vanessa's place, they would all believe they were looking at some other man, not him. His stomach was clenched into a tight, burning knot and his heart was hammering at such a rate, the blood was pounding like a jackhammer against his temples.

He'd never agonized over discussing anything with anyone. Especially when he knew he'd be talking to a level-headed, sensible person. And Vanessa was definitely both of those things. Plus, she was understanding. So he had nothing to worry about, he told himself as he pulled his truck to a stop in front of the small Valdez house. Except his whole future.

Chapter 11

Vanessa answered the door after his first knock and before he stepped over the threshold, he pulled her into his arms and placed a long, reckless kiss on her lips. "Mmm," she exclaimed with a little laugh. "Gauging by that greeting I'd say you've missed me a little today. Maybe it's a good thing I told Hannah she could have the evening off."

His arms tightened briefly around her waist and as the sweet scent of her rose to his nostrils, he desperately wished the only thing he needed to say to her were words of love and longing.

He peered over her shoulder. "She's not here?"

Vanessa stepped back and allowed him to enter the house. As she shut the door behind him, she said, "No. She left a half hour ago. I've been feeding the twins and now they're both down for the count."

"Oh. I was hoping they'd still be awake," he said as they gravitated away from the door, to the middle of the small living room. "It seems like ages since I've had a chance to hold them."

"It seems like ages since you've held me," she replied.

With an eager groan he pulled her into his arms and kissed her again, but this time he sensed she wasn't fully focused on him and when he lifted his head, he could see there was a tiny frown creasing her smooth forehead.

"What's wrong?"

"Nothing. I hope." Turning away from him, she gestured toward the kitchen. "Would you like something to eat?"

"No. Maybe later."

She clasped her hands in front of her. "All right. You said you wanted to talk. Let's talk."

For some reason he couldn't figure, she was on edge, even a tad cool, and he realized her unusual mood was only going to make his task harder.

"I'm trying to decide if we should discuss anything right now." Rather than make his way toward the couch, he continued to search her face. The closer inspection revealed a paleness he'd not noticed when she'd first answered the door. "You're not yourself tonight."

Her shoulders suddenly sagged and she let out a long breath. "Okay, I confess. I'm not myself. I'm actually worried sick about you."

Conall frowned with amused confusion. "Me? I'm great. Everything about me is great. And it'll be even better after we set our wedding date."

With a look of enormous relief, she sagged limply

toward him and rested her cheek against the middle of his chest. "Oh, thank God. I thought...well, I've been imagining all sorts of horrible things."

Totally confused, Conall wrapped his arms tightly around her. "Why would you be doing that, honey? Surely you can see that everything is fine with me."

"I know," she said with a tiny sniff. "But I was afraid that...well, after what Maura said, that you might have a recurring disease or something. Since she's a nurse and—"

For once Conall felt as though there was actually ice water in his veins and it was freezing him with dread. "What exactly did Maura say?" he asked stiffly.

Leaning back, she looked up at him. "Nothing particular. Just something offhand about your condition. I didn't press her to explain. Whatever it is, I wanted to hear it from you."

With a sinking feeling in the pit of his stomach, he took her by the arm and led her over to the couch. "I think we'd both better sit," he said.

By the time they were settled and facing each other on the cushions, her brown eyes were dark with concern. Conall reached for one of her hands and clasped it tightly between the two of his.

"What is it, Conall? The way you're looking at me— it frightens me."

"I'm sorry. I didn't mean to." He shook his head, then lifted his face toward the ceiling and closed his eyes. "I'm not doing this right. But then, I don't guess there is a right way," he murmured. "I should have told you about this days ago. Weeks ago, even. But I couldn't bring myself to."

"Why?"

Struggling to keep the bitterness from his voice, he said, "Because the information has always produced a negative reaction. Especially with women."

Her brows arched with surprise. "Women? I don't understand. You're certainly not frigid or impotent."

If he hadn't felt so sick inside he could have laughed. "No. I'm glad you figured that out."

Her free hand moved over his and squeezed tightly. "I don't know what this is about. But there's nothing you could tell me that would make me stop loving you, Conall."

"I hope to God that's true, Vanessa. I hope a few days from now we'll remember this moment and smile."

Her lips gently curved at the corners. "Being with you anytime makes me smile," she said, then laughed softly. "I sound like a hopeless cornball, don't I?"

Leaning forward, he pressed a kiss against her forehead. "And I've never seen a more lovely cornball."

She sighed. "Oh, Conall, even if you are ill I can deal with it. We'll deal with it together."

Easing his hand from beneath hers, he touched the side of her face. "I'm not ill, Vanessa, I promise. But I was once. When I was a very young child just learning to walk I had a viral infection that caused me to have a very high fever. I ended up having convulsions and my parents feared for my life. But eventually my body fought off the infection and I got well without any lasting effects, it seemed."

Her head swung back and forth. "Why are you telling me this now, Conall? I don't understand."

His eyes caught hers as he forced the words off his tongue. "Because you need to know why—why I can't have children."

She stared and he could see from the confusion crossing her face that she was having difficulty absorbing what he'd just said.

"Do you mean…you—"

"I'm sterile, Vanessa. The fever affected my reproductive system. It doesn't occur often, but it does happen from time to time. And I didn't even know that anything was wrong until Nancy and I tried to get pregnant."

"Oh. Oh, Conall…this is—" Her whole body sagged as though the air had literally been knocked from her. "I wasn't expecting anything like this."

Slowly, she pulled her hand from his and rose to her feet. Conall stayed on the couch and watched as she began to absently move about the small room. Eventually she stopped at a small end table and picked up a framed photo of her parents. There was raw pain on her face as she studied the image and in that moment Conall hated himself. If he'd not fallen in love with her, if he'd not pushed her to marry him, she would have eventually found someone else, someone who could give her everything. Now, God only knew what all this was doing to her.

"I'm sorry, Vanessa," he said hoarsely.

She didn't respond and after a moment he rose to his feet and walked across the room. As he came to stand beside her, she placed the photograph back on the table, then turned to face him.

"I'm sorry, too, Conall, that such a terrible thing ever happened to you. But mostly I'm sorry that you felt you couldn't tell me—long before—before I fell in love with you!"

Tears began to stream down her face and he realized there was an ache in the middle of his chest that made it almost impossible to breathe. If he was having a heart attack he probably deserved it, he thought. But he wasn't ready to die. No, there was so much that he wanted for the two of them and the twins.

"You're right. I should have. But...you weren't exactly warming up to the idea of having any sort of relationship with me. If I'd suddenly blurted out the fact that I was sterile, you would have turned your back on me and not given us any chance for a future together."

Her mouth fell open. "How do you know that I would have reacted that way? You didn't try!"

He curled his hands over the top of her shoulders. "Would you have given us a chance, Vanessa? Answer me truthfully."

Her tear-filled eyes were full of agony as she searched his face. "I don't know. I've always wanted children. Jeff wouldn't give me any and—"

"You have two children now," he pointed out. "Two beautiful, wonderful children. I want to be a father. Just like you want to be a mother."

A perceptive light suddenly flickered in her eyes. "Ahh. I wasn't thinking. But I am now," she said stiffly. "You want to be a father and I have two babies." She rapped her fist against side of the head. "What a fool I've been! That's what this has been about all along. Everything you've done and said was all for the babies! I was just a...side dish for you!"

His face felt like a stiff clay mask as he spoke in a low, purposeful tone, "I thought...I hoped and prayed that you would be different from the others. That's one of the reasons why I fell in love with you. Because deep down I believed you would accept me for the man that I am instead of persecuting me for what I can't be. I can see now that I was wrong. Again," he added bitterly.

Her expression incredulous, she shook her head. "Don't try to make me the culprit, Conall! You asked me to marry you because of the twins!"

In spite of the pain ripping through him, the corners of Conall's mouth tilted into a wan smile. "You finally got something right about this whole situation, Vanessa. The twins were the very reason I proposed to you. I like to think they need me just as much as I need them. But mainly I figured you having the twins would make my sterility easier for you to accept. You already had two children and I was hoping they and me would be enough for you. I can clearly see we're not."

Not bothering to wait for any sort of reply she might give him, he snatched up his hat, levered it onto his head and quietly let himself out of the house.

The next morning, after a night that had passed like a wide-awake nightmare for Vanessa, she dragged herself out of bed before daylight, and chugged down a cup of coffee before she finally found the courage to reach for the phone.

As she'd hoped, Conall wasn't yet in the office and she felt a measure of guilt when the voice mail answered. But she was in such a raw, emotional state she knew the mere sound of his voice would break her into sobs. Talking directly to him would only make matters worse.

Her throat aching, she swallowed and forced herself to speak. "This is Vanessa. I'm calling to let you know I won't be in to work today. If you…feel you need to replace me permanently I'll understand. Goodbye."

As soon as she snapped the phone shut she began to weep and when Hannah walked into the kitchen, tears were still seeping from Vanessa's eyes.

On the way to the coffeepot, the woman yawned and swiped a tangle of dark hair from her face. "My, you're up early," she exclaimed. "Do you have to go into work earlier than usual this morning?"

Vanessa hurriedly made an effort to wipe her eyes. "No, I'm not going in today. I—I'm not sure I'll be working for…the Diamond D anymore."

Pausing as she reached for a mug, Hannah glanced over her shoulder and suddenly noticed Vanessa's tearstained face. "What in the world is going on?"

Swallowing hard, Vanessa answered in a hoarse voice, "I don't know where to begin, Hannah. Everything is…over."

Forgetting the coffee, the woman hurried over to where Vanessa sat at the small dining table and curled an arm around her shoulders. "Are you ill? I'll get the babies ready and drive you in to town to see a doctor."

Since Hannah had become the twins' nanny, the two women had grown to be fast friends and Vanessa was beginning to think of her more as a sister than anything. At this very moment she felt like falling into Hannah's arms and sobbing her eyes out.

"No. I—I'm not ill." She looked away from the other woman and struggled to gather her composure. "Something happened last night—between me and Conall. I— We're not going to be getting married…like we'd planned."

Stepping back, Hannah looked at her. "Oh, no! I'm not going to believe this, honey. You two—why, you're perfect for each other."

Closing her eyes, Vanessa pressed fingertips against her burning eyelids. Last night when Conall had walked out the door, she'd felt her heart rip right down the middle and for a few moments, she'd almost run after him. She'd wanted him to understand just how wrong he was about her. It wasn't his sterility that was a problem with her. It was the fact that being a father to the twins appeared to be far more important to him than being a husband to her.

But she'd not run after him. Pride, confusion and anger had all stopped her. Now, as the morning sun was beginning to creep across the kitchen floor, she wondered if she'd saved herself from another loveless marriage, or ruined the best thing that could have ever happened to her.

Sighing, she said, "Nothing is perfect in this world, Hannah."

"It's clear you're not thinking straight this morning, Vanessa. And I'm not going to pry into what happened. I'm just going to tell you to give yourself time. Whatever happened between the two of you will work itself out. I just know it."

Vanessa wished she had the other woman's optimism, but at the moment all she could see was a long bleak road ahead of her. Even if she'd misjudged Conall's motives for marrying her, she'd hurt him deeply with all her accusations. She seriously doubted he would ever want anything else to do with her.

"I seriously doubt it, Hannah. And I…well, I hate to bring it up, but if Conall fires me then I won't be able to keep you on as the twins' nanny." The idea of losing both Conall and Hannah brought a fresh spurt of tears to her eyes. "I'm so sorry."

Squeezing Vanessa's shoulder, she said, "Look, honey, quit borrowing trouble. Conall is the one who hired me for this job and he's the one who signs my checks. Until he tells me otherwise, I'll be here. Now put your chin up and help me fix us a bit of breakfast before the twins start yelling for theirs."

Almost two weeks later, Vanessa was surprised by a call from Gold Aspen Manor. The doctor had pronounced Alonzo fit enough to leave the nursing home for a few hours and she'd wasted no time in fetching him away from the facility and bringing him to the only home he'd known for the past sixty years.

Playing with the twins had left a sparkle in his eyes and now that they'd fallen asleep, her father was exploring the backyard, the patch where he'd grown vegetables and the acre-sized pen that held his beloved goats. At the moment, one of the nannies had trotted up to him and Vanessa's eyes misted over as she watched him stroke the goat's head.

Having her father home again, even for a few short hours, was the only bright thing that had happened since her break with Conall.

Break. Was that the right word for it? she wondered bleakly. It felt more like a dead-end crash to her.

With a heavy sigh, she turned her gaze to the pot of white daisies sitting in the middle of the patio table. *He loves me. He loves me not.* Plucking the petals couldn't tell her, Vanessa thought sadly. And as for Conall, he'd not even bothered to try.

Since the morning she'd called and left a message, she'd only talked to him once and that was when he'd called her later that same day. He'd been cool and brusque as he'd informed her that he'd gotten her message and that she needn't worry about coming in to work today or any day—he could handle things without her. She'd tried to get in a reply, to explain that she needed time to think things through, but he'd not given her a chance to say anything. Instead, he'd quickly ended the call with a cool goodbye and she'd not seen or heard from him since.

Had she really expected to hear from him? she miserably asked herself. Perhaps. Deep down she'd hoped and prayed that she'd been wrong about him, about his motives, about all the harsh things she'd accused him of. But he'd not made any effort to prove her wrong. And she couldn't humble herself to ask him to.

I believed you would accept me for the man that I am instead of persecuting me for what I can't be.

For the past couple of weeks Conall's low voice had sounded over and over in her head. His words continued to haunt and confuse her. Was she blaming him, punishing him for simply being unable to have children? No. She wasn't that sort of woman. She was using common sense. She was simply refusing to jump into another loveless marriage.

The feel of her father's warm hand on her shoulder had her looking up and she did her best to smile at him. "The goats are happy to see you," she said.

"They're fat. You've been feeding them good." He eased onto the chair opposite his daughter while glancing over to a shaded part of the patio where the twins were sleeping in a portable playpen. "The babies are growing fast. They'll soon walk."

Vanessa's gaze followed her father's and as she watched the sleeping babies, her heart swelled with a mixture of emotions. Even if she'd given birth to the twins herself, she couldn't love them any more. They were her children to raise and nourish, to teach and guide, to love and cherish. No matter how a child came in to a person's life, it was a precious gift and she'd been given not one, but two gifts.

Now, each time she looked at Rose and Rick, she thought of Conall. Unless he married a woman who already had children, or adopted some of his own, he would never know the joys of being a father. It wasn't right or fair and her heart ached for his loss. But the ache didn't stop there. Missing him, wanting and needing him, filled her with such pain she doubted she would ever recover.

Pulling her thoughts back to her father's remark, she said, "Yes, in a few months they'll be walking and I'll be chasing after them."

Even though Conall hadn't formally fired her, when he'd told her goodbye over the phone there'd been finality in his voice. He'd obviously decided she couldn't bring herself to work for him. And he clearly wasn't going to ask her to return to her job. As for Hannah, the woman had stuck to her guns. Unless Conall terminated her position, she insisted on staying with Vanessa and the babies. And so far, he'd not told Hannah that her job as the twins' nanny was finished.

Vanessa didn't know what to think about the situation. Did he love the twins that much?

"What are you going to do about a job?"

Caught off guard by Alonzo's remark, she looked across the table to see he was studying her closely. It was almost like her father had been reading her thoughts. But then, she'd never been able to keep anything from either of her parents. She was as transparent as a piece of cellophane tape, until it came to Conall. He'd been unable to see how much she loved him, how much she wanted his love in return.

"What do you mean?"

He grimaced. "I know about your job at the Diamond D, my daughter. And your fight with Conall."

Vanessa drew in a sharp breath. Since she'd picked up her father earlier in the day, he'd not mentioned anything about Conall or even asked why she wasn't working today. Vanessa had been putting off telling her father that she'd quit her job and her relationship with Conall. She'd known it would upset him and she'd been trying to think of some way to approach the subject without making it sound like her life was in a mess.

But it was in a mess. And avoiding the issue wasn't going to make her or her father feel any better about it, she decided.

"Who told you?"

"Conall. He came last week to see me. And explain." Alonzo shook his grizzled head. "I'm not happy, Vanessa. You're wrong. Wrong."

Sighing heavily, Vanessa looked away from her father's penetrating gaze. "I'm sorry I've disappointed you, Dad. But things…just didn't work out for us. That's all. I'm moving on. He's moving on. I'll get another job soon. In fact, Eric has already offered me a job at the Billy the Kid and I'll probably take it. So everything will be okay."

"Will it?"

Her lips pressed together, she rose from the chair and walked over to the playpen. Rick was beginning to stir, so she reached down and picked up her son. The warm weight of the baby cradled against her breasts was momentarily reassuring.

"Why not?" Vanessa countered his question with one of her own. "I've been supporting myself for years now. Jeff rarely lifted a hand to help me make ends meet. I'm not worried."

Alonzo spit out several curse words, further proof that his speech and his health was rapidly returning.

"What is this? You talk about money? Money is nothing. Nothing."

With Rick snuggled in her arms, she walked back over to her father. "It's something when you don't have it." She cast him a censuring glance. "Isn't that why you wanted me to marry Conall? So that I'd be financially secure?"

More curse words slipped past his lips and Vanessa shook her head. "It's a good thing the twins aren't old enough to hear you, otherwise I'd have to cover their ears."

"Hearing me cuss—you think that's bad?" He snorted. "Not near as bad as you explaining to them why Conall won't be their daddy."

Vanessa sat back down and positioned her son against her shoulder. As she patted Rick's back, she asked, "Just why do you think I'm not...marrying Conall?"

"Because he can't give you any more babies. The twins aren't enough for you, I guess."

Vanessa had thought she couldn't hurt any more than she had these past two weeks, but she was wrong. Her father's impression of her had always been important to her. Ever since she was a tiny girl, she'd wanted him to admire her, be proud of her. When she disappointed him it cut something deep inside her.

Trying to swallow away the tears burning her throat, she said, "You have this all wrong, Dad. I'm not marrying Conall because he's sterile! Even if I didn't have the twins, that wouldn't matter to me. It's because he doesn't love me—he was using me to become a father. That's all!"

Alonzo sadly shook his head at her. "I hope to God your mama is not hearing you. Tears would be in her eyes."

"I guess as a daughter I've been a disappointment to you both," Vanessa said flatly. "But can't you see, Dad? I made a bad mistake with Jeff. I don't want to repeat it with Conall. I—" Her eyes pleaded with him to understand. "I just can't go through that sort of pain again."

"You think Conall only wanted the twins? I thought you were smarter than that, my daughter. Conall isn't ugly or stupid or poor. There're plenty of single women around that need a daddy for their children. You aren't the only one. Wonder why he isn't proposing marriage to them?"

"Probably because he hasn't gotten off the ranch to meet any of them yet," Vanessa retorted.

Alonzo snorted. "And what about all those orphanages with babies that need a home? If all he wanted was to be a daddy, he could do that without you. He asked you to marry him because he loves you. But you can't see that. All you can see is Jeff. You're still hung up on that sorry excuse for a man."

Outraged, Vanessa shot straight to her feet. "That is not true! I love Conall! You know that!"

Nodding, Alonzo said, "I know it. But does Conall? Maybe you should be telling him instead of me."

Vanessa sank weakly back into the chair. Her father was making sense, a lot more sense than she'd made this past couple of weeks. Which made her feel even more like a fool. But what could she do about it now? Conall appeared to have already washed his hands of her. "I'm not sure he'd want to hear it," she mumbled uncertainly.

For the first time since he'd sat down at the table, Alonzo smiled. "It'd be worth a try."

Easing Rick from her shoulder, she cradled the baby against her breasts and as she gazed down at her son's tiny face, she knew she had to see Conall, she had to convince him that she loved him for the man he was and nothing else mattered.

Chapter 12

The next morning, shortly after daylight, Conall broke from the normal routine of reading his messages and walked the quarter-mile distance to the training track. Now, as he stood next to his father at the pipe railing, he tried to focus his attention on one of the ranch's most promising runners.

Like a gull skimming the ocean, the dark brown filly was moving smoothly over the track, floating as though she had wings on her hooves. Her neck was level and outstretched, her ears perked with reserve energy. On the last turn, she lay close to the rail and then sprinted down the homestretch.

"Look at that!" Doyle practically shouted. "Juan didn't even have to ask her to change leads!" His father punched the button on the stopwatch before turning to look at Conall. "Kate's Kitten is going to be a queen, boy! She's not only fast, she's smart. When was the last time we got a combination like that?"

"When Red Garland was born," Conall was quick to answer.

Doyle stared at him with surprise and then he chuckled. "You got me there. But Kate's Kitten is right behind her. We're going to have two queens on our hands."

A wan smile touched Conall's lips. Even though the sight of the galloping filly had been beautiful, he couldn't work up near the enthusiasm that his father was displaying. But then, there wasn't much of anything that could lift his spirits these days. Not since he'd walked out of Vanessa's house. He'd not looked back that day. But he'd not needed to look back to see that he'd left his heart in her hands.

Everything you've done and said was all for the babies! I was just a...side dish for you!

Even now, after nearly two weeks had passed, the accusation that Vanessa had flung at him still had the power to hurt. Unlike an aching tooth that could be pulled out and thrown away, the words continued to claw at him and he didn't know what to do to dull the pain, much less make it go away.

"Liam will be thrilled to hear you say that about Kate's Kitten," Conall remarked. "And Grandmother will be happy to hear that her namesake has yet to disappoint."

Doyle frowned at his eldest son. "Hell, Conall, *you're* supposed to be thrilled, too. Instead you look like you did when you were a kid and I just ordered you to your bedroom to study for exams."

Conall held back a weary groan. With Vanessa no

longer sitting at her desk, nothing seemed the same, felt the same. He'd walked down here to the track this morning in hopes of giving his mind a short reprieve of her image, of the tortured thoughts he couldn't cast away. But so far he'd not felt one moment of relief.

"Sorry, Dad. I am excited about Kate's Kitten. It's just that…I've had a lot of things on my mind here lately."

Doyle stuffed the stopwatch in his shirt pocket as Conall absently watched the jockey jump to the ground and hand the filly's reins to the waiting hot walker.

"Guess it doesn't have anything to do with that little secretary of yours."

Conall grimaced. "She was more than my secretary, Dad. She was the woman I was planning to marry. Now she…well, she's not even my secretary anymore."

The tall dark-haired man's expression turned to one of concern as he eyed his son. "Hell, Conall, we all knew you were planning to marry Vanessa and we all know those plans went awry. But no one has mentioned anything to me about Vanessa quitting her job."

Conall's gaze dropped to the toes of his boots. "I haven't exactly told anyone that Vanessa has quit. Since Mom is filling in at the office, I just explained to her that Vanessa was taking some time off, that's all."

"Instead, Vanessa quit. Is that it? Because you two can't see eye-to-eye on your romance." Squinting at a far off group of horse barns, he said in a gentler voice, "Well, that's not surprising. When a woman gets angry she doesn't want a man getting too close. If he does get near, she'll raise her hackles and hiss. I can see where she wouldn't want to be cooped up in an office with you."

Conall wiped a hand over his face. He couldn't remember the last time he'd slept the night through and his lack of rest was only compounding the mental agony he was going through. "She accused me of wanting to marry her just for the twins."

Doyle sighed. "In case you didn't know, your sister Maura is heartsick. She thinks she's the cause of all of this."

Shaking his head, Conall turned his gaze back on the exercise track. At the moment a chestnut colt was being trotted around the mile oval, but Conall wasn't really seeing the beautiful Thoroughbred, he was seeing Vanessa's face, the way she'd looked when he'd told her that he couldn't have children. It was like he'd punched her in the stomach.

A grimace tightened his weary features. "Maura isn't to blame for anything. I wasn't planning to marry Vanessa without telling her about my condition. Maybe I should have done it sooner, but I kept thinking our relationship needed to be more solid before I sprung something like that on her. Apparently there wasn't anything solid about it," he added bitterly.

Stepping closer, Doyle rested a comforting hand on Conall's shoulder. "You think she turned her back on you because you can't give her children, don't you?"

Filled with agony, he looked at his father. "Oh, God, Dad, what hurts the most is that I really thought she was different. That she would accept me just the way I am. I don't want to believe that she's like Nancy or the others that backed away from me like I was a ruined man."

"Conall, just because I'm your father doesn't make me an expert on women. God knows I've only loved one all of my life and she's more than enough to keep me confused. But from the little time I've been around her, Vanessa seems like a very sensible woman."

Conall grunted. "What does that make me, an idiot?"

"Sort of."

"Thanks, Dad," Conall said with sarcasm. "That really makes me feel better."

"Hell, son, I'm not trying to make you feel better. I'm trying to help you fix things. Forget about Nancy and what came about with her. Forget about the other women that turned tail and ran. Nothing is going to be fixed with you and Vanessa until you first start accepting yourself. You need to realize that siring a child doesn't necessarily make a man a man or a father a father. You're much a man in my eyes, son. And I think you are in Vanessa's, too. Don't give up on her."

Doyle gave him one final pat on the back, then strode off in the direction of Kate's Kitten and the hot walker. Watching him go, Conall continued to lean against the white railing as his father's words reverberated in his head.

Had he been too hard on himself all these years? God knows, he'd tried hard to live up to the role of being the eldest Donovan son. He'd tried his best to always be the strong one, the one who rarely, if ever, failed, the one who would leave an admirable pattern for his younger brothers to follow.

When he'd learned of his inability to have children, he'd felt like a total failure, like he'd let his family down in the worst kind of way. But in the tradition of his role, he'd glued on his iron-man image and pretended to his family and acquaintances that he was tough enough to swallow anything life handed him.

Scrubbing his face with one hand, he turned away from the track and lifted his gaze toward the far mountain range where Vanessa's little house sat near a shrubby arroyo. It was no wonder, he thought, that Vanessa had struggled to believe that he truly loved her. For most of his adult life he'd been pretending, making an art out of hiding his feelings.

If he ever hoped to have another chance with her, he was going to have to go to her, open himself wide and hope that she could see what was truly inside of him.

His strides long and purposeful, he hurried back toward the office. If his mother had arrived to fill in at Vanessa's desk, he would send her home and reroute all his calls to the ranch's general office, he decided. If he hurried, he could drive over to Vanessa's house in twenty minutes.

His thoughts were so caught up in his plans that when he arrived back at the block of offices, he didn't notice the car parked next to his Ford truck at the side of the building. When he stepped inside, he glanced over, expecting to see his mother. Instead, Vanessa was sitting at the desk, sifting through a stack of correspondence as though she'd never been gone.

"Vanna!"

He didn't know whether he'd shouted her name or whispered it. All he knew was that she looked like a beautiful dream come true and his boots couldn't carry him across the room fast enough.

She looked up as he approached her desk and as their gazes met, her lips parted and he could see the movement of her throat as she swallowed.

"Hello, Conall."

"Where is Mom?"

She tried to smile and he was amazed to see that she was pale and nervous. Didn't she realize that she was holding all the cards, his very heart in her hands?

"When Fiona found me here, she went back home." She placed the papers she'd been holding back on the desktop and then with her eyes still on his face, folded her hands together in a tight steeple. "Since you never formally fired me I was hoping you needed your secretary back."

Amazed and shocked, he stared at her while his heart began to bump and thump with hope. "Did you honestly think I wouldn't want you here?"

Her head jerked back and forth. "I...didn't know. You walked out and—"

"That was a stupid stunt on my part."

Her eyes wide and hopeful, she rose to her feet. "You were hurt," she said in a raw whisper. "And I should have never said those awful things to you."

Fast as lightning, he streaked around the desk and tugged her into his arms. "Vanna! Oh, God, I'm so sorry. I've done everything wrong and—"

She placed a shushing finger against his lips. "So have I. Maybe we both have. But that doesn't matter now. Does it?"

For an answer, his lips swooped down on hers. The sweet, familiar taste of her kiss was a soothing balm to his battered heart and it was a long, long time before he ever lifted his head.

"My darling, I...when I stepped through the door a few moments ago I was about to tell Mom to forget about working today. I'd already planned to drive over to see you—to see if you'd be willing to listen to me."

"Listen? You don't need to explain anything, Conall. I—"

Before she could finish, he grabbed her by the hand and led her into his office. After shutting the door behind them, he urged her over to the couch. After they were sitting, their knees together, hands clasped tightly, he said, "I need to explain a lot of things, Vanessa. I need to say them as much as you need to hear them."

Nodding, she said, "All right. But first, I just want to say...I love you. That I never stopped loving you."

His heart was so full he thought it would burst; he lifted a hand and reverently touched her cheek. "Vanessa, I was wrong in not telling you about my condition long before anything started to develop between us. But I guess it was something—well, I was trying to convince myself that with you it wouldn't matter."

Through a mist of watery tears, she smiled at him. "It doesn't matter if we can't have more children the conventional way," she assured him. "I don't care about that. I didn't care the day you told me about it. I wanted to be the reason you wanted to marry me. Not the twins. That's all. And I was quick to jump to the wrong conclusion. Because I guess I never believed I was good enough to deserve your love. I never could totally believe that you wanted me, needed me in that way."

Amazed by her confession, he shook his head. "Oh, Vanna, that's awful. How could you think such a thing? You're the most precious woman I've ever known."

Bending her head, she murmured, "Jeff squashed my ego, Conall. He never saw me as a wife that he loved and cherished. He saw me as a workhorse, a provider for him. And I could only think that you saw me as a way to have children—not as a wife."

Sighing, he pushed his fingers gently into the rich brown hair at her temple. "And I thought you couldn't love me because I was sterile." His mouth twisting to a wry slant, he went on. "You see, when Nancy and I married, I had no idea that I was unable to father children. When we started trying to get pregnant and nothing happened, we both went through a battery of health tests. The minute the doctor gave us the news, something twisted inside of her, warped her into someone that I hardly recognized."

Lifting her head, Vanessa searched his face. "Didn't she stop to think that the two of you could adopt?"

Conall snorted. "She wouldn't even consider the option. She wanted a baby of her own and she was determined to get one no matter what she had to do."

Vanessa's brows peaked with questions. "So what options did that leave?"

Fixing his gaze to a spot on the floor, he said, "She wanted to go to a fertility clinic and get impregnated by a donor."

"Oh."

"Yeah. I understand that's a suitable solution for some childless couples. But at the time, the whole idea revolted me. I was young and full of masculine pride. I didn't want to see my wife pregnant with another man's child, much less have her giving birth to one. I tried to explain that it would leave me feeling as though I was on the outside of things. I argued that adoption would be a better option for the two of us. An adopted child wouldn't be more hers than mine—it would be ours."

"She couldn't understand your feelings? Or she didn't want to try?"

Dropping his hand from her hair, he released a long, heavy breath. "Nancy was a headstrong woman determined to have her way. She accused me of being selfish and robbing her of the right to be a mother. A 'real' mother in her terms."

Sickened by what she was hearing, Vanessa laid her hand on Conall's forearm. "So she didn't believe an adopted child would be a 'real' child," Vanessa mused out loud. "Well, I could tell her, or anyone, that the twins are just as much my children as if I'd given birth to them."

As he turned his gaze back on her, a wan smile tilted his lips. "Yes. But you're not Nancy. It took me a few horrendous days without you to figure that out." He turned his gaze to the picture window framing the wall in front of his desk and this time when he spoke his voice was reflective and full of doubts. "I suppose I was equally responsible for the breakdown of our marriage. Perhaps I was selfish for not letting her have her way. Anyway, I've stopped trying to figure it out. We wanted different things and nothing could change the way each of us felt."

Her fingers slid back and forth over the warm skin of his forearm as she searched for the right thing to say. "You both had different values and ideas about things. That never works—unless one of you sacrifices everything. And that wouldn't have made you happy, would it?"

"No." His expression pained, he said, "You know, I believed I'd married a woman that loved me, but after a while I realized I didn't really know her at all. And that made me the biggest fool who ever walked down the aisle."

A self-deprecating frown turned down the corners of Vanessa's lips. "Forget it, Conall, I hold that honor," she told him, then asked, "What finally happened? You two could never come to terms about having children, so you agreed to divorce?"

"I wish it had simply ended that way."

"What do you mean?"

"Like I mentioned before, something twisted in Nancy—I don't know what. I'm not even sure a psychiatrist could tell you. But she became an obsessed woman. She wanted to become pregnant. Anyhow, anyway that she could. She kept hounding me about going to a clinic and selecting a donor. I kept refusing and she continued to hound."

"I'm surprised she didn't ask for a divorce," Vanessa mused. "But love binds and I'm sure she didn't want to lose you."

His grunt was a cynical sound. "Nancy probably did love me in the beginning. At least, I want to think so. But after she learned I was sterile, I think all that died. She hung around because she liked being in the Donovan family. She liked the luxuries and privileges, the social standing that went along with the name."

"I see," Vanessa murmured thoughtfully, "Was she originally from a poor family?"

Conall shook his head. "No. Her family wasn't rich by any means, but they were financially comfortable. Nancy was the youngest of three children and I think after the other two grew up and left the nest, her parents doted on her. I'm guessing she learned at an early age that she could bat her eyelashes and quiver her lips and get most anything she wanted. After a while I grew weary of her demands, but I didn't ask her for a divorce. I wanted our marriage to make it and I suggested that we needed counseling to help us work out our problems."

"So did she agree? Did you two go for counseling?"

Rising to his feet, he crossed the room and rested his shoulder against the window frame. As he stared out at the busy ranch yard, he spoke in a flat voice. "She laughed and said that all we needed was a baby to make us happy again. At that time I didn't know what was going on in that head of hers. And I would have never known if Liam hadn't come to me and told me."

Frowning, Vanessa asked, "Liam? What did he have to do with any of this?"

Turning his head, he looked straight at Vanessa. "Nancy went to him and begged him to get her pregnant. In her twisted mind, she was sure that I would accept the baby. After all, it would be a true Donovan, she reasoned."

Vanessa gasped. "That's—insane! And how did she plan to explain her pregnancy?"

His lips took on a wry slant. "Divine intervention. She believed she could convince me that the medical tests were wrong and by some miracle I had gotten her with child. And if she couldn't convince me, then she was gambling that I could never turn away from my own brother's baby."

"How terribly sad," Vanessa said pensively. After a moment, she went to him and rested her palms against his chest. "Oh, God, Conall, I didn't know that any of this had ever happened to you. Maura or anyone in your family never spoke to me about your marriage or why it ended. And I've not asked. You must have been so crushed when Liam revealed what Nancy had done. And I can't imagine what it must have done to him to have to tell you that your wife…well, that she was disturbed."

He cupped her face with his hands and she was relieved when the dullness in his eyes flickered to a bright and shining light of love.

"Actually, in some strange way the whole incident brought him and me closer. But that was the only good thing to come out of the mess. After the divorce, everything else about me was pretty much numb and I guess I stayed that way until I met you." He lowered his head until their foreheads met and his lips were hovering close to hers. "For years, I got damn good at hiding my feelings. I didn't want anyone guessing that I might be vulnerable or hurting. I didn't want anyone thinking I was anything less than a man. I guess I must have perfected my acting ability. Otherwise, you would have seen how much I love you."

"Oh, Conall, yesterday evening I got to bring Dad home for a visit and while he was there we had a long talk about you and me. He made me see how stubborn I was being and how much the twins and I were going to lose if I didn't get you back in our lives."

Smiling now, Conall rubbed his nose against hers. "Thank God for fathers. Not more than an hour ago, mine pretty much said the same thing to me."

Rising on her toes, she brought her lips up to his. "And thank God you're going to be the twins' daddy. And if they're not enough to turn your hair gray we can always adopt a whole house full of babies to go with them."

Wrapping his arms around the back of her waist, he clamped her tightly against him. "Hmm. You'd do that for me?"

"Only if you think you can handle the double duty."

He chuckled as he pressed his cheek against hers. "Double duty? I think you'd better explain, my darling."

She sighed as the warmth of his body and the goodness of his love filled her with pure, sweet contentment.

"That you'll always love me just as much as you love our children."

His lips moved to the side of her neck where he began to mark a trail of kisses. "You're going to quickly learn, my lovely, that I always honor my family duties."

A month later, early autumn had moved in to predict the winter to come. The night air was sharp and clear and sometime before dawn frost would lace the fading roses in Kate's garden. But inside the Donovan ranch house no one cared about the chilly weather. The lights were blazing, music filled the great room and there was no end to the dancing and plates of good food. Family and friends had gathered to celebrate the marriage of the eldest heir of a horse-racing empire and no expense had been spared for the party.

Two weeks ago, Conall and Vanessa had decided they couldn't wait for a big, traditional wedding to be planned. Instead they'd flown to Las Vegas and married in a little wedding chapel not far from the spot where they had first kissed. Afterward, Vanessa had insisted they spend their week's worth of honeymoon, not in Jamaica, where Conall had initially planned to take his new wife, but at Del Mar, where they'd played in the sand and surf and watched Red Garland race to victory in the Debutante.

The fact that Vanessa had remembered how Red Garland held a soft spot in Conall's heart, much less that she'd be willing to accommodate their honeymoon to catch the filly's race, had amazed him. And he knew those special days they'd spent loving each other on the California coast would be relived in his mind on each and every wedding anniversary.

Now, as Conall moved Vanessa around the dance floor to a romantic waltz, she gazed up at him, her face glowing. "When your mother said she was planning a little get-together for us, I was expecting a gathering of twenty to thirty people. This reception is incredible. I never expected to see so many people. So much food. So much…everything!"

Happy that she was so pleased, Conall squeezed her hand. There was never a time that Vanessa didn't look beautiful to him, even in the mornings when her face was puffy from sleep and her skin bare of makeup. But tonight, dressed in an ice-blue concoction that provocatively draped her curves, she looked especially lovely. And as they danced, he kept asking himself why he'd been so blessed, while at the same time thanking God that he had been.

"And I never expected to be enjoying it all so much," he confessed. "Normally when my parents throw parties, I'd always find an excuse to make a quick exit. But not tonight. We're going to dance until dawn."

The sparkling light in her brown eyes warmed him with loving promises. "Just dance?" she teased.

Grinning, he whirled her out of another couple's

path. "Ask me that question later—when we're climbing the stairs to our bedroom."

Since their marriage, he and Vanessa and the babies had taken up residence in an upstairs suite of rooms that were connected to his original bedroom. As for the little Valdez house where Vanessa had been living, Alonzo had been able to move back home, thanks to live-in assistance that Conall was only too happy to provide. His father-in-law's health was continuing to steadily improve and tonight the older man was clearly enjoying being here at the party, chatting with friends and acquaintances and watching his daughter dance with her new husband.

As the music finally paused, she said, "I'm having a lovely time, Conall, but would you mind if we took a few minutes to slip upstairs and check on the twins? A couple of hours have passed since Hannah had them down to meet the guests."

"You've been reading my mind," he agreed. "Let's go give Hannah a little break, so that she can come and enjoy the festivities."

With his hand still wrapped around hers, he led her out of the crowded great room and down a long hallway until they reached a polished staircase. Side by side, they climbed the steps until they reached the second floor. At the end of the landing, Conall tapped lightly on a carved door. When they entered the room, Hannah was sitting at the end of a long couch. The dim glow of a table lamp illuminated the book in her hands.

She looked up in surprise. "Don't tell me the party is already over."

"It's just now getting fired up," he assured the devoted nanny. "We thought we'd better come see how you and twins have been getting along."

"In other words, you wanted to come up and play with your son and daughter," Hannah teased.

Vanessa laughed. "How did you ever guess?"

Laying her book aside, Hannah gestured toward a nearby door that led into a room that had been transformed into a beautiful nursery. "The last time I peeked in they were both asleep."

His hand still latched around his wife's, Conall began to urge her toward the nursery. "Get out of here, Hannah. Go on down and enjoy the party. We'll take care of things up here for a while."

The woman glanced down at her jeans and fitted sweater. "I'm not dressed for a party. But I will go down to the kitchen and test the food," she told him. "Whenever you need for me to come back up just let me know."

As Hannah slipped out the door, they both thanked her before making their way into the quiet nursery.

Near the head of the crib, an angel-shaped nightlight illuminated the slumbering babies and Conall's throat tightened with emotions as he leaned over the rail and touched a finger to each sweet face.

"I never dreamed I would have one child," he said murmured. "Now I have two."

Vanessa's arm slipped around his back and as always, whenever she touched him, he felt strong and sure of himself. But most of all he felt loved. Utterly loved.

"Whenever we first went to the orphanage to see the babies, you told me then that you were certain you'd never have children. I thought it was because you didn't want any," she admitted. "And I couldn't fit that notion with the Conall I knew and loved."

Rick's tiny fist was lying outside the blanket. Conall picked it up between his thumb and forefinger while imagining how his son's hand would look in a few years after he'd grown to be a man. Other than being a husband to Vanessa, being a father was the richest gift he'd ever been given and he was cherishing every moment with his new family. "I'd already decided that I would never find a woman I could love again, much less one with children. I'm so happy you proved me wrong, my darling."

After placing a kiss on each baby's cheek, he pulled Vanessa over to a wide window that faced the southwest part of the ranch. Through the boughs of the pine trees, a ridge of mountains could be seen reaching up to the star filled sky.

Vanessa sighed with pleasure as he pulled her into his arms and kissed the crown of her head. "See that break in the mountain? Way over to the west?" he asked.

Vanessa's gaze followed his instructions. "Yes, I see it."

"I want to drive you over there tomorrow," he said, "I want you to take a look at the view and see if you like the spot enough to build our new home there."

Leaning her head back, she stared wondrously up at him. "New home? You don't like living with your family here in the big house?"

"I love living with my family. It's the only home I've ever known. But the Donovan family is changing and growing. Brady and Lass already have a daughter and I suspect they're already planning for another baby. And who knows, Liam might shock us all and marry again. Plus, there's Bridget and Dallas. This old house can't hold us all. Besides," he added, as his hands moved to the small of her back to gather her closer, "our children deserve a home of their own, one that they can pass on to their children."

"Mmm. Family tradition. I wouldn't expect anything else from you, my dear husband." She slipped her arms around his waist. "I only ask that our new home be simple and homey. And that you make a big fenced yard for our children to play in."

Smiling, he brought his lips down to hers. "You're such a demanding woman."

She kissed him softly, then easing slightly back, whispered, "How long do you think it will be before our guests realize we're missing?"

With a wicked chuckle, his arms tightened around her. "Long enough."

At the same time, down in the kitchen, Brady was doing his best to persuade Hannah to join the rest of the merrymakers while Bridget was at the far end of the cabinet, holding one hand over her ear while straining to hear the voice on the other end of the telephone.

With her hand over the receiver she scolded, "Brady! Shhh! I can't hear a thing." Turning her attention back to the caller, she finally managed to pick up the sound of a male voice and as she did her face grew pale, and her heart kicked to a rapid thump. "On the res, you said?…Oh.…Yes.…Yes, I remember.…I'll be there as soon as I can make the drive."

When she hung up the telephone, she started toward a door that exited to the outside of the house. Thankfully, she'd left her coat and medical bag in her car and wouldn't have to waste time fetching it or dealing with prolonged goodbyes.

"Sis! Are you leaving?" Brady called after her.

Her hand on the doorknob, she paused to glance over her shoulder. "Yes. An emergency has come up."

Leaving Hannah, he trotted over to his sister. "Is it that important? This is your brother's wedding reception," he pointed out, as though she needed reminding.

Tossing him an impatient look, she said, "You know as well as I do that emergencies don't pick and choose their times to happen. Explain to the family why I had to go and give my love to Conall and Vanessa."

"Sure." He gave her quick kiss on the cheek. "Are you headed to the hospital?"

Shaking her head, she stepped through the door and out into the cold night. "No. But I might end up there," she called back to him.

Before he could ask more, Bridget hurried away from the house. She didn't want her brother to know that it had been his old friend Johnny Chino that she'd been speaking with on the phone. And she especially didn't want Brady to know that she was driving straight to the Mescalero Apache Reservation. He wouldn't understand why Johnny had summoned *her*. And frankly, Bridget didn't, either.

* * * * *

Tina Leonard is a *New York Times* bestselling and award-winning author of more than fifty projects, including several popular miniseries for Harlequin. Known for bad-boy heroes and smart, adventurous heroines, her books have made the *USA TODAY*, Waldenbooks, Ingram and Nielsen BookScan bestseller lists. Born on a military base, Tina lived in many states before eventually marrying the boy who did her crayon printing for her in the first grade. You can visit her at tinaleonard.com, and follow her on Facebook and Twitter.

Books by Tina Leonard

Harlequin Western Romance

Bridesmaids Creek

The Rebel Cowboy's Quadruplets
The SEAL's Holiday Babies
The Twins' Rodeo Rider

Callahan Cowboys

A Callahan Wedding
The Renegade Cowboy Returns
The Cowboy Soldier's Sons
Christmas in Texas
A Callahan Outlaw's Twins
His Callahan Bride's Baby
Branded by a Callahan
Callahan Cowboy Triplets

Visit the Author Profile page at Harlequin.com for more titles.

The Rebel Cowboy's Quadruplets

TINA LEONARD

Much love and gratitude to the generous
and supportive readers who have embraced my
families and communities so enthusiastically—
I have the best readers in the world.

Chapter 1

Justin Morant recognized trouble when his buddy Ty Spurlock texted him a link to a dating website. This was what happened when you had to leave the rodeo circuit thanks to a career-ending injury: your friends decided you needed a woman with whom to share your retirement, and maybe a spread to call your own because you were going to need something to do with your new spare time. The woman would run your life and the spread would rule your life, and maybe it was one and the same. You'd work hard, be tied to the land and the woman, never have two nickels to call your own. You'd have children and, suddenly, you were up to your neck in obligations and debt.

He'd seen it happen too many times. At twenty-seven, Justin was in no hurry to be fobbed off on a woman who was so desperate for a man that she'd use an online service.

He packed up his duffel, tossed it in his seen-better-days white truck and headed away from Montana, destination unknown, knee killing him this fine summer day.

His phone rang and Justin pulled over. This was a conversation that was going to follow him every step of his self-imposed sabbatical if he didn't stamp it out now.

"I'm not going to answer the ad, Ty," he said, skipping the greetings.

"Hear me out, big guy. I'm *from* Bridesmaids Creek. I know where the Hawthorne spread is. It's the Hanging H ranch, or, as we locals fondly call it, the Haunted H. Go check out the place. You've got nothing better to do, my friend."

"What kind of a name is Haunted H?"

"The Hawthornes used to run a yearly haunted house for kiddies there, and folks remember that. It was bad to the bone, and rug rats to small-fry attended like bees at a hive. Mackenzie's folks did everything they could to turn a dime with it. Her family raked in dough nine months a year with puppet shows, petting zoos, pony rides and lots of good treats."

"Nine months a year?"

"Well, three months a year it was turned into Winter Wonderland at the Haunted H, to go with the town's annual Christmastown on the square," Ty said, as if Justin didn't understand the importance of holidays. "You have to appreciate that a haunted house wouldn't be as much of a draw as Santa Claus for the youngsters."

"So what happened to the place?"

"Hard times hit us all, buddy," Ty said, a little mysteriously for Justin's radar. "Give Mackenzie a call. You're burning daylight on this deal. Someone's going to answer that ad, which will come as a shock to her because she doesn't know what's been done on her behalf." Ty laughed. "The only thing I haven't been able to figure out is why someone in Bridesmaids Creek hasn't already gotten her to the altar. I'm not suggesting you try to do that, of course. Small towns usually keep their own pretty well matched up, and judging by her profile on the dating site, that should happen soon enough. Good luck, my friend."

Ty hung up. Justin tossed his Stetson onto the seat with some righteous disgust and pulled back on the road.

He wasn't going to Texas. Not to Bridesmaids Creek to a woman whose family had operated a haunted house.

Just because a man could no longer ride didn't mean he had to make a laughingstock of himself.

Mackenzie Hawthorne smiled, looking at the four tiny babies finally sleeping in their white bassinets. "Whew," she said to Jade Harper. "Thanks for the help."

"That's what best friends are for." She arranged soft white blankets over each baby, protecting them from the cool drafts blowing from the air conditioner, which seemed to run almost constantly this baking-hot July. "Who would have ever thought Tommy possessed the swimmers to make four beautiful little girls?"

Mackenzie smiled at her adorable daughters, all scrunchy-faced in their tiny pink onesies. "Don't talk to me about my ex. Every time I think about him dating that twenty-year-old, I want to eat chocolate. I'm trying very hard not to do that. Your mother keeps me busy enough with desserts I can't resist."

Jade laughed. "Tommy Fields was never right for you. What you need is a real man." She hugged Mackenzie. "You rest while these little angels are asleep. Mom will be over this afternoon with dinner and to help out. I've got to get down to the peach stand and help make ice cream. 'Bye, darling."

"Thanks for everything."

Jade flopped a hand at her. Mackenzie was grateful for all the friends she had in Bridesmaids Creek. Everyone had been pitching in almost nonstop, bringing food, baby clothes, and giving their time so she could shower and even nap sometimes. She hated to be a burden, but when she mentioned that to anyone, she was reminded that she gave generously of her time to the community, as had her parents.

Mackenzie walked through the huge, heavily gingerbreaded old Victorian mansion, wondering how she was going to fix the fences that were rotting and sagging, not to mention the gutters on the house. Never mind run the horse operation. With four-month-old babies, she was constantly running, taking care of them.

But she wouldn't trade her babies for anything. Tommy might have turned out to be a zero as a husband, but Jade was right: he'd left her with four incredible gifts.

And a lot of bills.

But her parents had been entrepreneurs, smart with money. She had a small cushion, if she was very careful with those funds. She wasn't destitute, thank God. Raising four children was going to take everything she had and then some.

She needed a miracle to keep herself from going into debt, and with no income coming in and no way for her to work until the babies were older, things could get tight fast.

Justin was nobody's idea of a miracle, certainly not from his point of view. If the little lady was looking for one, she was doomed to disappointment. Yet here he stood on the porch of the strangest-looking house he'd ever seen two weeks after Ty had tweaked him about it, wondering what in the hell he was thinking by letting his curiosity get the best of him.

The house hovered tall and white on the green hilly land several miles outside Austin. Four tall turrets stretched to the sky, and mullioned windows sparkled on the upper floor. A wide wraparound porch painted sky-blue had a white wicker sofa with blue cushions on it, and a collection of wrought-iron roosters in a clutch near a bristly doormat with a big burgundy *H* on it.

Quaint. The place was homey in a well-worn sort of shabby way, and he'd be sure to tell Ty that he didn't appreciate him sending him out here to see a doll's house in the middle of nowhere. Miles and miles of green pastureland badly in need of mowing surrounded the house, wrapped by white-painted pipe fence so it wasn't totally hopeless, but still. No man would live here willingly.

The door opened, and a petite brunette stared out at him. She didn't come up to his chest, not totally. Brown eyes questioned why he was taking up space on her porch, and he asked himself the same. She was cute as a bunny with sweet features and a curvy body. The matchmaking ad had probably gotten hundreds of interested hits. Not to mention the nice breasts—and as she turned to answer someone who'd asked her some-thing, he noted a seriously lush fanny—yeah, her ad would get hits. He wondered if she knew what Ty had done on her behalf with the dating ad and pulled off his hat, telling himself he'd just introduce himself and go.

This was no place for him.

"Can I help you?"

"I'm looking for Mackenzie Hawthorne. My name's Justin Morant. Ty Spurlock sent me by."

"I'm Mackenzie."

Her voice was as pretty as she was. Justin swallowed. "Ty said you might need some help around here."

Pink lips smiled at him; brown eyes sparkled. He drew back a little, astonished by how darling she was smiling at him like that. Like he was some kind of hero who'd just rolled up on his white steed.

And, damn, he was driving a white truck.

Which was kind of funny if you appreciated irony, and, right now, he felt like he was living it.

Sudden baby wails caught his attention, and hers, too.

"Come on in," she said. "You'll have to excuse me for just a moment. But make yourself at home in the kitchen. There's tea on the counter, and Mrs. Harper's put together a lovely chicken salad. After I feed the ba-bies, we can talk about what kind of work you're looking for. Mrs. Harper will love to pull your life story from you while you eat."

She made fast introductions and then the tiny bru-nette disappeared, allowing him a better look at that full seat. Blue jeans accentuated the curves, and he figured she was so nicely full-figured because she'd just had a baby.

Damn Ty for pulling this prank on him. His buddy was probably laughing his fool ass off right about now, knowing how Justin felt about settling down and family ties in general. Justin was a loner, at least in spirit. He had lots of friends on the circuit, and he was from a huge family. He had three brothers, all as independent as he was, except for J.T., who liked to stay close to the family and the neighborhood he'd grown up in.

Justin was going to continue to ride alone.

Mrs. Harper smiled at him as he took a barstool at the wide kitchen island. "Welcome, Justin."

"Thank you," he replied, not about to let himself feel welcome. He needed to get out of there as fast as possible. The place was a honey trap of food and good intentions. Another baby wail joined the first, and Justin's ears perked up. Two? Maybe she was babysitting. He looked at Mrs. Harper, worried.

Mrs. Harper laughed. "Yes, she probably does need a hand," she said, misunderstanding the question on his face. "Run on in there and help her out for a second, and I'll serve up a lunch for you that'll take the edge off any hunger pangs you've got." She pulled a fragrant pie from the oven—an apple pie, he guessed—and his stomach rumbled.

Okay, he could go check on the little mother for the price of lunch. But then he was heading out, with a "Sorry—this job doesn't fit the description of my talents," or something equally polite.

He was going to kick Ty's butt hard, over the phone, which wouldn't be nearly as satisfying as doing it in person. He'd driven a day out of his way to apply for what he'd thought might be bona fide employment.

He walked into the den, guided by the baby cries.

Mackenzie glanced at him from the sofa. "Don't be scared—they'll calm down in a moment," she said, but he was anyway, unable to stop staring at the four white bassinets, three babies tucked into them like pink-wrapped sausages working free of their casings. Mackenzie held a fourth writhing baby close to her chest, and Justin realized she was nursing.

Holy crap. She had four babies. He backed up a step, belatedly removed his hat. "I'm not scared. I'm something else, but I'm not sure I can identify the emotion." He looked at the three squalling babies, clearly deciding they all wanted their mother's attention at once. "What can I do?"

He hoped she'd say nothing, but instead she pointed him to a bottle. "If you're sincerely asking, Holly's next in line."

Holly? He glanced back at the baskets. Tiny nameplates adorned the bassinets, which for some reason reminded him of the carved beds of the seven dwarves. Only Mackenzie was no Snow White under an evil spell, and he was certainly no handsome prince.

But the lady did need help; that much was clear. She was in over her head by any reasonable metric, whether it was the ranch (which she probably would lose, if he were a betting man) or these tiny babies (which would require an army of assistants that he figured she couldn't afford—again, no hard bet for a man who liked betting on sure things). This would only take an hour, he figured, and an hour he certainly did have, damn his torn PCL.

Justin studied the nameplates to make certain he picked up the right baby. Holly, Hope, Haven and Heather. All chosen, no doubt, to go with the Hanging

H of the ranch, which was sort of a hopeless exercise because they'd all get married one day and their last names would change. To Thomas or Smith or whatever. Then he remembered that Mackenzie's last name was Hawthorne, and she must not have ever changed her name when she got married.

If she'd been married.

Gingerly he picked up Holly, who had a pretty annoyed wail going, grabbed one of the bottles off a wooden tray and slipped it into her mouth. Oh, yeah, that was exactly what she wanted—food—and what he wanted—golden silence.

"Thank you," Mackenzie said. "They all decide they want to eat at once, every time."

He sank onto a sofa, carefully holding the baby. "My brothers and I were the same. It lasted through our teens and drove our parents nuts." He glanced at the other two babies, who were now occupying themselves with listening to the adult voices in the room. "I guess these are all yours."

She smiled, and he noticed she had very shapely lips. He avoided staring at the blanket at her breast, not wanting to catch an accidental glimpse of something he shouldn't see. He was a gentleman, even if he found himself at the moment feeling like a fish out of water.

"They're all mine." She smiled proudly at her children. "We're still working out some things, but the girls are coming along nicely now. They have a little better routine, and the health issues are more manageable."

He turned his gaze back to Holly so the doubt wouldn't show on his face. The overgrown paddocks, the sagging gutters and the chipping paint stayed on his mind. These four children—was the father totally useless? Did he not care about the state of his property? Or these four sweet-faced babies? Not to mention the sexy mother of his children.

"Their father is in Alaska," she said, somehow reading his thoughts. "Working on an oil rig. And when he's not working, he's otherwise engaged. We don't hear from him," she said. "Not before the divorce or after. I'd been on a drug to help me get pregnant, and he was unpleasantly surprised by the results." She put a now-content baby into the empty basket marked "Heather," diapered her, kissed her and picked up Hope. "This one was born with lung issues, but we're slowly getting past that. And Holly has struggled with being underweight, but time has been the healer for that, too." She smiled at Justin, and he saw how beautiful she was, especially when her face lit up as she talked about her children. "So tell me what kind of work you do, and we'll see if our needs match."

He held in a sigh, wondering how to extricate himself from this dilemma. He could help this woman and her brood, but he didn't want to. Justin glanced at the four babies. They had calmed some as they were getting either bottles or a breast—there was a thought he had to stay away from.

Mrs. Harper bustled in with a tray of food for him and took the baby he was holding. "I heard you say that you need to talk business. I'll feed this one, and you eat. Your plates say you're from Montana, so you've come a long way to talk about work. I know you're starved."

No, no, no. He needed a job, but not this job. And the last thing he wanted to do was work for a woman with soft doe eyes and a place that was teetering on becoming unmanageable. From the little he'd seen, there was a lot to do. He had a bum knee and a bad feeling about this. And no desire to be around children.

On the other hand, it couldn't hurt to help out for a week, maybe two, tops. Could it?

He ate a bite of Mrs. Harper's chicken salad, startled by how good it was. Maybe it had been too long since he'd had home cooking. He smelled the wonderful cinnamon aroma of apple pie, and his stomach jumped.

Mackenzie bent over to put the fed, diapered and happy baby she was holding back into the bassinet. He watched her move, looked at her smile, admired her full fanny and breasts—stopped himself cold.

He had no business looking at a new mother. He really had been on the road too long. Glancing around him, Justin took in the soft white-and-blue curtains, the tan sofas, the chairs in a gentle blue-and-white pattern that complemented the drapes. A tan wool rug lay under a blocky coffee table, the edges rounded and perfect for children who would be learning to pull themselves up in a few months.

Taking another bite of Mrs. Harper's delicious meal, he focused on the food and not the homey atmosphere. That's what was wrong: this felt like home. It could draw in a man who wasn't careful, who wasn't aware of the pitfalls.

Maybe Ty hadn't sent him here because of Mackenzie's ad. Maybe she simply needed a grievous amount of help, and Ty had known he needed employment.

He could do this job—or at least he was comfortable with the work he could see that needed to be done.

But he needed to know.

"So about your ad," he said, and Mackenzie and Mrs.

Harper looked at him curiously. "On the dating website."

She shook her head. "What dating website? I didn't advertise on a website. I talked to some friends about the position for ranch foreman." She straightened. "Are you saying you came all the way here from Montana because you think I'm looking for a man?"

Chapter 2

Mackenzie planned to give Ty a piece of her mind at the first opportunity. A phone call to express her dismay at his ham-handed matchmaking was tops on her list.

The cowboy who'd clearly been sent on a mercy mission seemed supremely uncomfortable at the outraged question.

"I thought you were looking for help around here," Justin said. "So, yes, I was under the impression you were looking for a man. Though not in the manner in which you may have mistaken."

"Ty put me in a dating website, and you show up here. How would you feel if you were me?"

Mrs. Harper drifted from the room with a baby in her arms. Mackenzie was too upset to cool her temper.

"Probably grateful that one of my friends cared enough to reach out to try to get me some help. Incidentally, I haven't seen the ad. Didn't look." He shrugged, dismissing it.

That was a man for you. It was all about the practicalities, when the mousetrap was perfectly clear to her. You didn't live in Bridesmaids Creek and not know that people plotted to get you married. Always done lovingly in your best interests, of course.

Which was how she'd ended up married the first time—not that Tommy hadn't been a sinfully gorgeous, totally lazy man more interested in pleasure than anything resembling work.

There was a lot of work to be done around the Hanging H, so named when one of the Hawthorne *H*'s had partially fallen off the sign. The name had stuck—though she knew very well that Daisy Donovan—one of the town's most notorious bad girls—liked to say the ranch was called the Hanging H because the Hawthornes were barely hanging on. Mackenzie did need help, which would have been quite obvious to the handsome cowboy meeting her gaze without hesitation. Tommy might have been handsome in a hedonistic sort of way, but this cowboy had him beat for raw sex appeal.

"You're right. If you're here just for work, and not because of a matchmaking website, I'd like to talk to you more about the position." She decided to give him the benefit of the doubt. Hazel eyes stared at her, unblinking. Justin didn't look like he had romance on the mind. Broad shoulders complemented a trim waist, the sinewy body of a man who spent his time actively. He had a square jaw that hadn't been shaved today—or maybe even yesterday—and shaggy dark hair that hadn't seen a barber in many months.

All in all, the kind of man who would turn women's heads.

"I'd be interested in hearing more about the kind of help you're looking for," he said.

She looked at her babies, tried to turn off the zip of sex appeal that was overruling her ability to think clearly. "Why would you want to work here? There must be a lot of ranches hiring."

He nodded. "I'm sure I can find a job if this doesn't work out. But Ty seemed to think you could use a foreman."

"A foreman position would be a long-term proposition." She looked at him, curious. "Somehow you don't strike me as a long-term kind of man."

"Things change."

Okay. She'd noticed he had a bit of a limp, and there was probably a story to that. In fact, there was no doubt a story to Justin in general, but she wasn't looking for a colorful background. She needed help here, and the fact was Ty's reference counted for a lot. There was no doubting that Justin didn't want to answer a lot of questions about himself, which was fine because she could ask Ty whatever she wanted to know. She could simply negotiate an open-ended employment offer with Justin.

"Yes, things do change. Thanks for helping out with the babies. If you give me ten minutes to get them settled and grab the books, I'll go over the job requirements with you."

He nodded. "Thanks."

She gazed into his hazel eyes, seeing nothing there but appreciation for a chance of employment. No attraction, no flirtation; just level honesty.

Whatever it was she'd felt from the moment he'd

walked into the room, he didn't seem to be affected by it.

Which was fine.

She went to find Mrs. Harper to watch the babies while she talked to Justin. If she hired him, she was going to call Ty.

Whether Mackenzie thanked him or yelled at him about the cowboy in the other room remained to be seen.

Two weeks had gone by, and Mackenzie hadn't seen much of Justin since he'd moved into the foreman's house. But evidence of his presence was obvious: the gutters no longer hung sad and neglected, the paint on the house gleamed, the paddocks were mown and hay was bundled into round bales that studded the landscape outside her window.

It was beginning to look like the Hanging H of old, which brought back a lot of happy memories.

Jade came into the kitchen, peering over her shoulder at the paddocks. "Looks like a postcard, doesn't it?"

Mackenzie nodded. "Maybe I should have thanked Ty for sending Justin my way."

Jade laughed. "You didn't thank him?"

"I was too annoyed when I found out he'd put my name in a dating registry."

"To be fair, that was a tiny fib on his part. He didn't really do that. It was just a little intrigue he threw in for Justin's sake."

Mackenzie shook her head and returned to the babies, who sat in carriers, all four of them, on top of the wide kitchen island. They gazed at different things around the room or their toes, content for the moment. "Ty can get a little crazy at times. But, yes, I should thank him now. The ranch looks like it's in recovery mode."

"And then there's other kinds of recovery," Jade said, still staring out the window. "Is this your daily view?"

Mackenzie turned to see what Jade was goggling at.

Justin. Hot, dark skin gleaming with sweat, bare to his blue-jeaned waist. Muscles for miles. Mackenzie stared at the man wearing a straw Resistol, amazed to feel her heart beating like mad. "Actually, no. That's never been the view."

"Too bad." Jade laughed. "If it was, I'd be eating lunch over here every day with you."

"You do eat lunch with me almost every day. You make the lunch." Mackenzie tore her gaze away from Justin and sat at the island. "I've been meaning to tell you that I feel like things are much more under control. You and your mom don't have to come over here every day anymore to help me out. I'm going to be okay." She smiled at Jade. "You've been amazing friends. You and everybody who's sent food over."

"Pooh," Jade said. "Don't think you're going to run me off now that you've got a bona fide beefcake on the ranch. I'm single, you know."

Mackenzie held Heather's tiny foot in her hand. "By all means, come by if you want to. I just hate to keep taking up your life."

"Believe me—this is a joy and pleasure. And it would kill Mom if you cut off her visiting privileges." Jade stood beside her. "She dotes on these babies. Says they may be the only grandchildren she has because I'm so slow about finding a husband."

"You could try Ty's matchmaking registry."

Jade laughed. "I'll meet my handsome prince when

it's meant to be." She went back to staring out the window. "Did you notice his limp?"

Mackenzie sighed. "Yes. It's more pronounced when he doesn't know I'm watching him, which tells me he doesn't want to talk about it. So I don't ask." She tucked the blankets around the babies and smiled. "He does his job. I don't see him. He came into the kitchen last Friday, and I handed him an envelope with his pay in it. Your mother gave him a lunchbox, so I think she's feeding him. That's the relationship we have, and now you know everything I know."

Maybe that would settle Jade's curiosity.

"You have to wonder about that matchmaking story, though. Something brought that handsome stud here. He could have gotten a job where he came from, right?" Jade asked, curiosity clearly not abated.

"Don't ask me. I took Ty's word as a reference and didn't ask too many questions. As you may have noticed, I needed help around here, and if he was looking for a job, I was happy to give him a try." It had nothing to do with the fact that he was, as Jade mentioned, quite handsome. Sexy. Breathtaking, if a woman was looking for a man.

But she wasn't.

"I had a husband," Mackenzie said, looking at her babies with adoring eyes. "And while I wouldn't say I wish I'd never met Tommy—I have him to thank for my sweet children—I can't say a husband is something I'm looking to put on my shopping list. But speaking of shopping, I'm taking you up on your offer to babysit while I go into town to grab some things."

Jade gave up watching Justin and picked up a baby. "I was hoping you were still going to let me babysit. An afternoon out will do you good. And my first-timer's nerves will be calmed."

"You'll do fine! You've helped me almost every day with the babies." Mackenzie hugged her friend.

"My nerves are due to my suspicion that you might not be able to leave your babies for the first time," Jade said, laughing. "Mom's coming by for backup. We have everything under control. Go."

A knock sounded on the kitchen door, and Jade pulled it open. "We don't knock on the back door—just come on in," Jade said, and Justin entered. Even a little sweaty and a bit dirty, he was a sexy, handsome man—just as Jade had noted.

"Ladies," he said, removing his hat.

"Hi," Jade said. She poured him a glass of tea from the pitcher on the counter. "I'm going to put these babies down for their nap."

She left the room carrying Hope. Mackenzie smiled at Justin as he put the empty glass back on the counter. "Would you like some more?"

"No, thank you."

He had the most amazing eyes, the nicest hands—

Mackenzie pulled her gaze back where it belonged. "The house looks great. And it's nice to see the lawn mowed. Thank you."

He nodded. "I was going to head into town. I figure there's a hardware place and maybe a tractor supply in town so I can get some parts." He glanced at the remaining two babies on the kitchen island after Jade came in and removed Heather. "I thought I'd see if there was anything you need."

Him, maybe? "Thank you. Actually I'm being sent into town myself."

"That's right," Jade said, sailing into the kitchen to pick up Haven, cuddling the baby to her. "It's high time my friend got out. She's a wonderful mother, but everybody needs a break. Although I'll believe that she leaves these babies behind when I see it. Try to help ease her out the door, will you?" She grinned and left.

Justin shrugged. "I can drop you off in town."

Mackenzie hesitated. "That's all right. I can drive."

"I could use a tour."

She looked into his eyes, surprised. "Haven't you been into Bridesmaids Creek?"

"Just ran in to grab some feed for the horses."

There was a lot of lore in Bridesmaids Creek. She was half tempted to go with him so she could tell him all the wonderful stories.

On the other hand, she was tempted to go with him simply because he was the hottest man she'd ever laid eyes on.

Which wasn't the best reason, but it was a reason. She could feel herself melting under his gaze. He seemed so solid, so strong...so unlike Tommy.

"I really—"

"Go," Jade said, coming back into the kitchen to collect the final baby. She cradled Holly as Mrs. Harper came in the back door bearing a pie.

"Hello, everyone," Mrs. Harper said. "I brought something for Justin because I know how much he likes apple pie."

"Yes, ma'am," Justin said. "I can find room for that."

Jade handed Holly to her mother after she put the pie on the counter. "Justin and Mackenzie are just leaving."

"Oh, good," Mrs. Harper said. "That will give me

time to make up some fried chicken to go with it for later."

"I think we're not getting any of that pie until we get our chores done," Justin said, his gaze turning to Mackenzie again.

"I think you're right." She also sensed a heavy helping of matchmaking, too, but forewarned was forearmed. She gave Jade a wry look, who returned that with an innocent look. When Justin opened the kitchen door, Mackenzie went out, telling herself that all the matchmaking in the world wasn't going to make her fall in love again.

"After hearing Ty sell Bridesmaids Creek," Justin told Mackenzie as he drove into town, "I'm anxious to get the tour. Ty brags about the Bridesmaids Creek swim, he talks about the Best Man's Fork, and a few other bits of lore, but I was never sure if he was just pulling my leg or not. Ty likes to hear himself talk, and talk big."

"There's a lot of history in BC," Mackenzie said. "Some good, some bad. Just like any place, I guess."

He nodded, pulling his truck into a parking spot in the wide-set, clean town square. Families with kids milled in front of the shops, but not as many as one might expect to see if one were in a city.

Still, it felt like a comfortable town where everyone knew each other, celebrated each other's hopes and joys. "The Wedding Diner?" Justin peered at the white restaurant with its pink-and-white-striped awning, big windows and flashing pink Open sign.

"Home cooking, and, if you're interested, Mrs. Chatham will tell your fortune for you."

Justin grunted. "I don't believe in fortune-telling."

"Oh, she doesn't do read-your-palm kind of stuff. Mrs. Chatham has a completely different method." She got out of the truck and he followed suit, meeting her on the pavement.

"So, shall we meet back here at four?" Mackenzie asked. "I know you said you wanted to go to the feed store. By the way, Ralph Chatham, Jane Chatham's husband, runs that."

"Does he tell fortunes, too?" Justin asked, telling himself to relax and enjoy the small-town ambience.

"Not exactly. But he does do a Magic 8 Ball kind of thing where you pay a small fee, his steer drops a cowpat on a square for you and you win a prize. Or you can trade the prize for one of Mrs. Chatham's sessions."

Justin laughed. "Cow-pie-drop contests are done in lots of places."

"You laugh," Mackenzie said, "but Mr. Chatham's steer is well loved in this town. The steer's name is Target thanks to his aim and the fact that he's made some folks a good bundle of money. Target always hits a mark. See you at four." She smiled and walked away, stunning him when she walked into a shop with a bouquet-shaped shingle that read "Monsieur Unmatchmaker. Premier Unmatchmaking Service."

Was the whole town backward? Off its collective rocker?

It was none of his business why Mackenzie would need an unmatchmaking service. *Ugh.*

The unforgiving rodeo circuit had been more sane than this town.

Still, he'd been serious about getting a grand tour from Mackenzie, though she obviously hadn't thought he'd meant it. How better to learn about Bridesmaids Creek than from one of the town's favorite daughters?

He glanced toward the unmatchmaking service, seeing that next door to Monsieur Unmatchmaker's dove-gray-painted shop was a pink store with a cheery window and painted scrolling letters that read, "Madame Matchmaker. Premier Matchmaking Service. Where love comes true."

He laughed out loud, startling some passersby. Suddenly he understood why Ty had worked so hard to sell him on this town: the whole place was set up on gigs. Sleights of hand. Fairy tales. From the rumored special steer with excellent aim to The Wedding Diner with the fortune-teller owner to the matchmaking–unmatchmaking rivals—everybody had a gig.

So did Mackenzie, now that he thought about it. Her parents had run a successful haunted house for years, and, according to the talkative fellow at the feed store, parents from miles around had brought their very young kiddies to enjoy the place. No real spooky stuff was allowed. Just down-home bobbing-for-apples fun. Puppet shows, piñatas, a parade with characters.

Until a local murder near Mackenzie's place had spooked folks. That year, attendance had gone way down. So far down they'd had to close the haunted house. They'd been virtually bankrupted, or so the story went.

"You still here?" Mackenzie asked, shaking him out of his reverie.

He snapped his gaze to hers. "Yeah. Your errand was fast."

Mackenzie nodded. "I just wanted to check in on

Monsieur Lafleur. He had gall bladder surgery recently."

"Rough."

"It was rough." She started walking and he followed, more out of a desire to be with her than to hear about Mr. Lafleur's funky gall bladder. "It was gangrenous and they couldn't get to it laparoscopically, so they had to do it the old-fashioned way. Not much fun."

He felt a little sympathy for Mr. Lafleur after all.

"But his wife is wonderful and she took good care of him. They bicker like crazy, but they've been married for fifty years and love blooms in spite of the bickering." She looked up at him, and Justin felt something hit him somewhere near his gall bladder—not his heart—that felt suspiciously like something bordering on attraction.

All this talk of wonky gall bladders was stirring up his desire to eat. That was all it was. He glanced toward The Wedding Diner, wondering if it was safe to go inside and eat without prognostications of marital bliss being preached at him.

"Madame Lafleur runs the matchmaking service," Mackenzie said, snapping his attention back to her and away from the people filing inside the diner.

"The Lafleurs run rival businesses?"

"Complementary businesses. Some people want love, and some people want relationships ended. Monsieur Lafleur doesn't get as many clients as his wife, of course, so he teaches French at the high school and tutors privately in his shop."

"If the divorce rate is around fifty percent, how is it that Monsieur Lafleur has to supplement with teaching and tutoring and his wife doesn't?"

"Because this is Bridesmaids Creek. When matchmaking occurs here—and it occurs often—the relationships tend to stick. Madame Lafleur takes great pride in her ability to bring people together who are perfect soul mates."

He idly wondered if Mackenzie had utilized the services of Madame Lafleur. If so, she didn't seem bothered by the irony of her marriage not lasting. He looked away for a moment, trying to shake off the charm of the town. His rational side said it was just all so ludicrous, and the first chance he got he was going to tell Ty that he'd sent him to a place where people were clearly just one car short of a crazy train.

"Can I buy you a snack? Seems a shame not to take my boss to get a soda and a slice of pie, or whatever is served in The Wedding Diner."

"Sure." She looked at him curiously. "You realize you'll be setting yourself up for the gossip mill."

"Putting myself right in the line of fire." He opened the door for her. "After you."

Chapter 3

Mackenzie and Justin were greeted warmly by the proprietress of The Wedding Diner, an amply shaped woman with a big smile.

"Jane Chatham," Mackenzie said, "I'd like to introduce you to Justin Morant. He's been helping out at my place."

Jane's smile widened as she swept them over to a bright white booth inside the diner. "Welcome, Justin. Those four darlings running you off your boots over there?"

He removed his hat and took the seat she indicated. "It's a nice place."

"Sure it is." Jane laughed. She looked at Mackenzie with a fond smile. "I'm sure you're happy for the help."

"You have no idea."

Justin felt a slow warmth steal up the back of his

neck. It was just a job like any job. He rubbed his knee surreptitiously under the table, glad it wasn't aching much today. It wouldn't matter if Mackenzie had twelve kids—he was glad for the work.

And the chance to work for himself. Under a blue sky with no one talking to him.

"Still thinking about selling the place?" Jane asked Mackenzie, and Justin listened hard in spite of himself.

"We'll see what happens," Mackenzie murmured. "In the meantime, can we talk you out of some of that delicious pie I smell?" She looked at Justin, and he felt a tiny zap hit him around his chest cavity again. Really weird, because he'd never been much of a heartburn sufferer.

He told himself he'd grab some antacids later.

"You order what you like," Mackenzie told him, "but I'm not about to pass up that blackberry pie."

"I'll have a slice."

"Two, please," Mackenzie said, and Jane ambled off with a pleased nod.

"You didn't mention you were selling your ranch," Justin said, so startled by the news he forgot he'd intended to mind his own business.

She nodded. "It would probably be best. It's hard for me to keep up with on my own, to be honest, and since I'm not working, I need to keep my savings for my daughters." She smiled. "Selling the Hanging H would mean college educations and a few other things comfortably. I'd like to not stay awake at night worrying about money."

He cleared his throat. "Your ex doesn't pay any child support?"

She shook her head. "Hard to squeeze blood out of

a turnip, especially a turnip that stays on the move to avoid child support."

Ouch. Justin sipped the coffee Jane brought over, glad for the dark steaming brew. He then busied himself with the flaky, rich blackberry pie, delicious enough to draw a sigh of pleasure from him if he weren't so caught by Mackenzie's story.

Her plans made total sense. A woman with four brand-new babies, who'd been born with some challenges, was going to need cash. A lot of cash. She was being wise, had clearly given her situation a lot of thought. It was what he'd do were he in her boots.

Seemed a shame to sell a family home, though. He thought about his childhood home, and how much it had hurt when it was gone. He and his rowdy brothers had grown up there, enjoyed the benefits of living and working on a family ranch. When his father had taken up with another woman, scandalizing the town, his mother had booted him out of the house and sold the family ranch—her right as it was the home she'd grown up in. Though his father had tried to make amends, Dana Morant was made of sterner stuff. She'd taken her boys to Montana to be near her sister, and life had changed forever. Mainly for the better but always with the lingering shadows of what might have been. Jensen Morant now lived on a thousand acres of rich Montana ranchland. Justin didn't go near the place.

He looked at Mackenzie's soft hair and gentle smile.

"You were way far away," she said.

He took another bite of pie, sipped his coffee. "Let me know what I can do to help."

"You have already. I can put the ranch on the market now, thanks to the wonderful shape you're getting it in. I really appreciate it."

A sudden pound on his back had him looking over his shoulder. "Ty!"

"Me in the flesh." Ty slapped him on the back again and nodded at Mackenzie. "Jade told me I'd find this devil here."

"I have things to discuss with you, Ty," Mackenzie said, and he grinned.

"You can thank me later for sending you this guy," Ty said.

"That's just it," Mackenzie said. "You really shouldn't have."

"Getting attached to him?" Ty teased, and Justin decided the conversation had gone far enough.

"Join us," Justin said.

"No. No time." Ty looked at him. "I'm in town for one thing and one thing only. And that's to help you back to the rodeo circuit."

Justin frowned. "How am I going to do that? I'm a bit physically challenged at the moment."

"In a different capacity than riding," Ty said. "You and I are going to travel the country recruiting talent."

"Talent for what?" Justin didn't like the idea of that at all. Correction: once upon a time he might have jumped on it enthusiastically. Traveling the country with one of his best buddies, seeing his friends on the rodeo circuit, giving back to the sport he loved so much—dream-come-true stuff.

His gaze slid to Mackenzie, who watched him with gently smiling eyes as she listened to Ty go on and on with his plans. Justin couldn't work up the same excitement.

He felt like he had plenty to do here in Bridesmaids Creek that was important. Mackenzie smiled at him, a slow, sweet smile. Her big eyes were looking at him, so trusting, and that heartburn he'd been experiencing felt more like his heart was melting into a big soupy puddle. *Dang.* This was new. Different.

Maybe hitting the road with Ty was the right idea.

He looked at his friend. "Why don't you stop by the house later and tell me about this harebrained plan of yours?"

Ty looked at Mackenzie. "Would you mind? I know you've got a lot going on over there."

"You're welcome anytime." Mackenzie got up. "Just know that if you take my cowboy, who has become indispensable to me, I'm going to offer you up as a candidate for the Best Man's Fork run. All in the name of charity, of course." She winked at Justin. "I'm going to talk to Jane for a moment."

She headed toward Jane at the cash register. Ty studied his friend.

"You've got the strangest look on your face," Ty said as Justin returned his gaze to Mackenzie. He just couldn't seem to get enough of looking at her. "I'd say you have indigestion, except you're smiling."

Justin relaxed his mouth so the smile would disappear. He *had* been smiling, because his muscles ached a bit. Like he'd been smiling a long time—watching Mackenzie walk and chatter with some friends who came over to talk to her.

"I'm not smiling, but I may have indigestion."

Ty snorted. "I see what's going on here."

"Do you." He made the comment as flat as possible. His buddy's opinion didn't really matter. Ty had no idea what was going on, because Justin had no idea.

"You're tired," Ty said. "Being around those babies and that falling-down farm has worn you out. You better hit the road with me. You'll be back to your old self in no time."

"What was my old self?"

Ty put his hat on, prepared to leave, which was fine with Justin. Then he could go back to surreptitiously staring at Mackenzie. "Grumpy, cranky, annoying."

Justin grunted. "Thought that was you."

"Not me." He peered at Justin. "I really hope this wasn't too much for you, old buddy. I didn't mean to bring you down. Figured some time in a small town with a real job would do you good."

Justin put his hat on, too, because if he didn't get out of there, people were going to notice that he couldn't stop staring at his beautiful boss. "That's what you get for thinking. See you at the house. Don't get there too soon. I'm taking the boss lady shopping."

Ty stared at him, stunned. "What's happened to you?" he whispered. "You're a shadow of your former self!"

Well, that was a question he didn't care to ponder too much. Mackenzie came to stand beside him, smiling up into his face, and his poor stupid heart felt like it took the final dive into his stomach.

What had happened to him, indeed.

Mackenzie and four babies were happening to him, and they were going to require a great deal of consideration. This was a bad idea, this tiny woman with the big eyes and her sweet family. A very bad idea, because he wasn't a family man; he wasn't a staying man.

"You ready?" he asked Mackenzie, and she nodded.

"If you're not going to chicken out," she teased.

Oh, he might. He was thinking about it. Thinking about it hard.

But something told him he probably wouldn't.

Four hours later, when Ty stopped by the house, Mackenzie wondered what her old friend was really up to. Ty had sent Justin to her, now he wanted him to hit the road?

It all seemed very convenient. As if Justin might have conned his buddy into helping him escape the Hanging H with a good reason.

"Anyway," Ty said as the three of them sat at the wide wooden kitchen table, "the reason I stopped by is to get a game plan going with Mackenzie."

"Game plan?" Mackenzie glanced at Justin. If Justin had been part of Ty's game plan, she wasn't sure she wanted to know what the next play was.

"I wouldn't leave you here without backup," Ty said. "I know that in spite of his knee—"

"My knee's fine," Justin said, clearly annoyed.

Mackenzie glanced at him. Occasionally she saw Justin favor his knee, but it did seem as if he'd been limping less since he'd arrived at the Hanging H. The doctor in town had given him a soft knee brace, which he wore without hesitation. Now there were days when Justin walked like he wasn't in any discomfort at all.

"I know your knee's getting better," Ty said. "I'm just saying that in spite of your knee, you've been a big help here. I can see a lot of improvement." Ty shook his head. "Still, I wouldn't leave Mackenzie in the lurch, so I was wondering if you mind, Mackenzie, if I swap cowboys on you."

Mackenzie hesitated. "Swap cowboys?"

"Replace Justin, in a manner of speaking," Ty said. His words ceased entirely when the kitchen door opened and Jade walked in.

"Howdy," Ty said. He stood up to greet the tall, sexy redhead, removing his hat for a moment. "Jade Harper, long time, no see…and clearly I've been missing out."

Jade laughed. "No sweet talk from you, Ty." She gave him a hug and he might have tried to pinch her bottom, but Jade was too fast for him. "Hi, Justin. Mackenzie, who are the three hunky guys who just pulled up in the black truck outside?"

Mackenzie got up to look out the window.

"*That's* the game plan," Ty said with a glance at Justin. "I don't want you to miss my buddy Justin when I take him with me, so I thought I'd trade you, three for one."

"Wow," Jade said. "Grab this deal, is my advice, Mackenzie." She laughed at Justin's smirk.

"Ty, I don't know if I need three—" Mackenzie began.

"You need help out here," Ty said.

Justin didn't say anything, and a bit of unease began to hit Mackenzie. Did he want to leave? Maybe he'd told Ty that he wanted to. She looked at his face, hazel eyes giving away nothing, his dark hair awry as he ran a hand through it. He looked distinctly uncomfortable.

As Ty had noted, Justin's knee was better—not well enough to ride or run a fast race, maybe, but better—

and the last place he wanted to be was stuck here with her and four little baby girls.

"I'll get that," Mackenzie said when knocking erupted on the front door. "Might as well give the candidates a grand tour, let them know what they're getting themselves into."

Justin glanced at her, his eyes widening like he was surprised by her comment. She went through the den, checking the babies quickly—still sound asleep, as was Mrs. Harper in the corner chair—and opened the front door.

Whoa. So much testosterone, so many muscles. "Hi," Mackenzie said, a little startled by all the masculinity crowded on the front porch.

They took off their hats.

"Ty sent us," the tallest one said with a rascally grin. "He said the Haunted H was looking for help to get ready for the county's biggest haunted house and pumpkin patch for miles around."

Mackenzie blinked. What had Ty meant by that? She was selling the place, not going back into business.

"Hello, fellows," Justin said from behind her. "If you're looking for Ty, you'll find him in the side paddock."

"Thanks."

They tipped their hats to Mackenzie and left the porch. Mackenzie turned to look at Justin.

"I don't want to get in the middle of things," Justin said, "but if you want me to leave, just say the word."

"I don't want you to leave." That was the last thing she wanted. "Do you want to go?"

"No. Not if you don't want me to." He shrugged as if he could go either way, whatever she decided. Still, she had the feeling her answers mattered. "I'm not going to say that I know everything about your town or your ranch. But so far things have been working pretty smooth. Or at least I thought they were."

"Ty seems to think he needs you with him." Mackenzie stepped off the porch.

"I'll make that decision." Justin followed her. "Or you will."

Something about this whole thing felt like a setup. Ty's story to the three hunks who'd come riding into town in their big black pickup, that she needed to restart the old family business, felt fishy. Never had she mentioned breathing life back into the haunted house to anyone. It was a dream she'd kept buried, knowing it wasn't practical. She couldn't run that kind of people-intensive business herself, and especially not with four newborns. The small remaining funds she had needed to go into their care—not the vague hope of bringing back the Haunted H.

And yet she had to admit restoring all her family traditions would be a wonderful way to raise her girls. She had had a storied childhood, full of wonder and magic and fairy tales.

But for a fairy tale, one needed a prince.

She looked at the five men leaning against the corral, studying her, waiting for something, some signal. Big, strong, handsome men. They all had rugged appeal, Justin most of all, in her opinion.

A prince had no reason to stay in Bridesmaids Creek—not unless there was a quest, something to make him stay and fight.

"So, Ty," Mackenzie said slowly as Jade came to put

her arm through hers for support, "maybe you'd like to explain why you're offering me three cowboys for the price of the one I've already got?"

Chapter 4

"These fellows here," Ty said, grandly waving his arm to indicate his friends, "go by the names of Sam Barr, Squint Mathison and Frog Grant."

"I'm sorry." Mackenzie stared at the last big man who'd been introduced. He was a broad-shouldered man with bright blue eyes and a shock of saddle-brown hair that wouldn't lay flat even if he used molasses on it. "Frog?"

The men laughed. "Gets 'em every time," he said, not minding the attention. "That's not my real name."

"We call him Frog because he looks like he's hopping around like a frog on the back of a bronc." Ty slapped the man on the back. "Anyway, he kind of looks like an amphibian, so it fits."

"I don't see any frog about him," Jade said, and silently Mackenzie agreed.

"These gentlemen have come to apply for the position of hanny," Ty said, delighted to have a stage to sell his snake oil from.

"Hanny?" Mackenzie tried not to laugh. "Is that what you call a working hand now?"

"It means, Miss Mackenzie," Squint said, his brown eyes earnest, "that Ty tells us you need hands to work this place and sometimes some occasional babysitting."

"Oh, a *manny*," Jade said.

"No." Ty shook his head. "A manny is a male nanny. These men are hands. They're also willing to help out with Mackenzie's munchkins."

"That wouldn't be necessary—" Mackenzie began, but Ty shook his head.

"These men haven't seen the inside of a home in so long that a little babysitting would make them happy as clams." He looked at his friends. "And they don't have any problems cleaning up stuff."

"Stuff?" Mackenzie echoed.

"Oh," Jade said. "You promised you wouldn't mention what I told you on the phone, Ty."

Mackenzie glanced at Justin, who shrugged, his whole demeanor screaming, *I had nothing to do with this.*

"Baby spit," Ty said helpfully.

"Upchuck," Squint elaborated.

"Hurl," Sam said.

"Giveback," Frog said, and Mackenzie held up a hand.

"Thank you, but I have it under control," she said with a glance at Jade.

Jade looked guilty. "She handles poo just fine. It's the other that gives her a little trouble."

Embarrassment swept Mackenzie. She couldn't meet Justin's gaze, though she could feel him looking at her. "It was tough in the beginning, but I'm fine now. Anyway, I don't need help with my children."

"And I'm not going anywhere," Justin said.

Mackenzie glanced at him. "You don't have to stay if you need to go with Ty. I'll totally understand. But I haven't got a need for three hands, fellows. Sorry."

"Darn," Jade said. "I wish I'd known that all I had to do to get three handsome hunks to show up in their black truck was have babies. I'd have given that a shot."

The three newcomers seemed to appreciate Jade's comment. Some of the bravado had gone out of them at Mackenzie's refusal of their services, but at Jade's words their air of jauntiness returned.

"You could always give us a free trial," Frog said.

Mackenzie shook her head. "I don't need any help. But come into the kitchen. Let me at least feed you lunch before you go."

"That's an offer I won't refuse," Sam said.

All three gentlemen grouped close around her as she turned to walk to the house.

She looked at them. "I'm okay, guys, really I am."

"You should be resting," Squint said.

"We'll take care of you," Frog told her.

"Guess you're stuck with me, beautiful," Ty told Jade. He put his hand around Jade's arm as they walked.

"I've got some work to do," Justin said, and Mackenzie turned.

"Lunch first. Then you can work all you like." She didn't want him leaving her with Ty. His buddy was working on a plan—maybe big plans—and anyone from

Bridesmaids Creek knew that when plans were afoot, you'd better have backup around.

Justin was really handsome backup.

"Sure. I'll come along."

She flashed him a grateful smile. The group went inside, crowding the kitchen, and Mrs. Harper smiled at them.

"Are these the hands Ty was telling me about?" she asked. "I'm Jade's mother, Betty Harper. It'll be nice having more help around here. Now sit down and eat before Mackenzie puts you to work."

Mackenzie started to say that she wasn't hiring anyone, but Jade gave her arm a light pinch.

"What?" Mackenzie said.

"Don't send them away yet," Jade whispered.

"It's not fair to keep them here when I don't have work for them!"

"You have work for them. You could hire a dozen of them and it wouldn't be enough."

Mackenzie looked at the five strong, large men sucking down huge quantities of food. "If I hire these hannies—really harebrained idea of Ty's, by the way—I'd have to pay them. And that's not in my budget."

"We'll figure something out. An idea will come to you," Jade said, comforting her.

"No, it won't." She went into the den to check on her babies, who were all asleep except Hope, who was gazing at the mobile over her playpen. Mackenzie picked her up. "If I had spare money, I'd be putting it away for college educations. Besides, I'm selling the Hanging H."

"Don't be so hasty." Jade took Hope from her. "Give Justin and Ty a chance to help you."

Mackenzie watched as Mrs. Harper fed the big men

seated on the wooden barstools around the island. Her gaze wandered to Justin. "If I thought there was a way, I might give it a shot."

"You don't want to get rid of the family home, do you? Wouldn't you like the girls to grow up here?"

"It's just me and four babies," Mackenzie said. "I have to be practical. My folks were a team, and they only had me for many years before my sister was born. My focus needs to be on my children, not running a business and a ranch." She knew from experience that good times could be few and far between when it came to running what amounted to an amusement park.

"You're overlooking one small detail," Jade said. "According to Ty—"

"And that reminds me, you seem to be getting chatty with Ty."

"Not chatty. We talked once. I let slip about the baby spit-up bothering you. Sorry about that."

"I'm past that now," Mackenzie said. "I don't get queasy anymore. I think it just scared me because Hope did it so often."

"The thing you might not be aware of is that these men are looking for a place to stay," Jade said, glancing at the muscled hunks at the kitchen island. "Ty told them they had to pay rent. You'd essentially be a landlord. In other words, money coming in right away. They'd throw in some ranch work, some babysitting, for their meals."

Mackenzie looked at her. "Why is Ty so involved in my business?"

"He says you need help. He needs help. *They* need help." Jade went to the counter, then returned with two pieces of pumpkin spice cake in one hand and a baby in the other arm. She handed a plate to Mackenzie. "Ty says that if you sell, some developer is going to grab this place and cut it up into tiny lots for houses. I'm pretty sure he's right. You're sitting on five hundred acres, Mackenzie. If each house is put even on a large one-acre lot, that's five hundred homes. A thousand homes if they built smaller."

"Is that a bad thing? More housing for Bridesmaids Creek?" She got the image Jade was trying to draw.

"Not necessarily. You think about whether that's what you think should happen in our small, friendly community."

"We don't know that would happen." Mackenzie took a bite of the cake. As always, Mrs. Harper's cake was scrumptious. "The land might go to a hospital, or we could use a new elementary school. Something more beneficial than the Retirement Home for Beat-Up Riders Ty seems to have in mind." She studied the cowboys. Fit, handsome, hunky. But definitely not young enough to keep up on the circuit. And that's what this was really all about. "Justin says he's not going anywhere. So this is all really moot. I don't need help with the babies, and I don't need any more help than Justin." If he was planning on staying.

"Are you counting on him too much?" Jade asked.

Her gaze slid to Justin. She was startled to find his eyes on her. "I don't know," she murmured. "Maybe."

Jade had a good point. It was a mistake to count too much on another person. Witness her ex. She couldn't allow herself to get overly comfortable again.

She heard a motorcycle roar outside, glanced at Ty. Was he having yet another buddy come by? She looked at the cowboys having a great time eating Mrs. Harper's food and regaling her with rodeo stories. Maybe one couldn't have too much of a good thing.

A knock on the paned window of the back door sounded above the laughter. Jade opened the door and Daisy Donovan sashayed in, long brown hair spilling from her helmet, short black leather skirt swinging, black cowboy boots showing off shapely legs even Mackenzie had to admire.

Daisy Donovan had always had radar for hot guys.

"Hello, fellows," Daisy practically cooed. She basked in the sudden stares from the hunks. Ty's buddies had ceased eating, ceased talking and maybe ceased breathing, stunned by the wild-child vision that was Daisy Donovan.

"I brought you a baby gift, Mackenzie," she said, handing her a pink-and-silver wrapped box she pulled from the band of her skirt. The men's gazes never left her. "Hello, Mrs. Harper. Jade."

The guys jumped off their stools to allow Daisy to sit. She smiled and went to stand beside Justin. "I'd love a piece of your delicious cake, Mrs. Harper," Daisy said, her eyes on Justin. She then made certain every man in the room got the full benefit of her smile. Mackenzie was astonished that they all didn't faint from the feminine firepower launched at them.

"Thank you for the gift, Daisy," Mackenzie said. She unwrapped it to find four engraved silver teething rings. A very nice gift, indeed—for a woman who had never really been her friend. Daisy was a natural-born competitor for the male eye, and guys adored her.

"It's just a little something for those sweet babies of yours," Daisy said, smiling at the men. She took a bite of her cake, Marilyn Monroe–sexy, and Mackenzie imagined she heard hearts popping in the kitchen.

"Wonder what the Diva of Destruction wants?" Jade muttered under her breath.

The answer to that was obvious. Daisy was man-hunting. And by the looks of how she was staking her claim, she appeared to be hunting Justin.

Mackenzie told herself it didn't matter if Daisy was hunting Justin or not.

She didn't quite convince herself.

"What are you up to, buddy?" Justin had managed to catch Ty in an unguarded moment in the barn, where he was showing the three new guys the layout of the Hanging H. "It's time you share the plans that are buzzing around in that brain of yours."

"The plans are for you and me to hit the road," Ty said, giving him a genial thump on the back. "I told you—we're going to hunt up recruits."

"Yeah, but you didn't say what we're going to be recruiting talent for." Justin glanced toward Sam, Squint and Frog. "Did those guys make your recruitment list?"

Ty laughed. "Them? No way. They're just replacing you, which I think is fair, considering I brought you here. I couldn't leave Mackenzie without help."

Justin leaned against a post, crossed his arms. "Why are you so interested in Mackenzie's welfare?"

"It's not just her. It's you, too. And Bridesmaids Creek, if you really want to know."

"You're trying to bring men into Bridesmaids Creek." Justin shook his head. "They have a match-maker here, you know. Aren't you kind of bumping the competition?"

"Just giving the matchmaker some material to work with."

"Why?" Justin's curiosity was getting the best of him.

"You'd had to have grown up here to understand." Ty shrugged. "The Haunted H was a great draw. Lots of jobs were lost when the Hawthornes had to close it down."

"That's what this is all about? Bringing jobs back to your hometown?"

"Not exactly." Ty wouldn't meet his gaze.

"Oh, I get it." Justin thought he suddenly saw into the cracks of his buddy's mercurial brain. "You're trying to find a man for *Mackenzie.*"

Ty shrugged. "It's complicated."

"Not that complicated." Justin snorted. "When did you decide to play guardian angel to Mackenzie?"

"Since I was the guy with the not-too-swift idea of setting her up with her ex. My onetime good buddy, who turned out to be a weasel of epic proportions."

Justin stared at his friend. "Have you ever considered that maybe Mackenzie doesn't want another husband?"

Ty snorted. "Don't be silly. She's a woman. A woman needs a husband to feel complete."

"I'm not sure I ever saw this chauvinistic side of you before."

"Yes, you did. You just didn't recognize it, because you and I were thinking alike." Ty laughed. "Don't worry, good buddy. I'm not including you in my plan. Just the opposite. I'm clearing you out to make room for some cowboys who don't wear the rebel badge as enthusiastically as you do."

If being a hard-baked bachelor earned him that

honor, he supposed he'd go with the rebel badge. "And that's why I'm being dragged on a recruiting tour? You want me out of the way so your matchmaking has a better chance of succeeding?"

"Look. The idea came to me after I'd sent you here." Ty looked at him patiently. "I realized that Mackenzie didn't just need help bringing back the old place—she needs a husband and a father to those children. I'm the man who fixed her up with the loser, so I'm going to put it right."

"Why don't you just put your own neck into the marriage noose and save everybody some agony if you feel so guilt-ridden?"

Ty put up his hands as if to ward off the very idea. "My conscience is guilty but not stupid."

Justin stared at his friend. It was true. Ty wasn't husband material.

Neither was he.

Justin sighed heavily. "I think you're nuts. But whatever. It's not my town. Nor are these my friends."

Ty brightened. "So you'll do it? The lead stallion agrees to head off and leave the pen to the lesser junior stallions?"

"You make it sound like Mackenzie's ever looked my way twice in a romantic way, which I can assure you she hasn't. We haven't spoken that much since I've been here."

"Call it a hunch. Clearing out the pen, as they say. The ladies always want the one they can't have. Mysterious types seem romantic. Like Zorro."

Justin shrugged. "I think you took one too many falls off the mechanical bull, Ty, but whatever. I'll go with you," he said, "but you better hope Mackenzie never finds out what you're up to. I have the feeling that little lady doesn't think she needs any man to rescue her."

"Mechanical bull! I was no dime-store cowboy," Ty said, following Justin as he headed back to work. Justin couldn't stand around examining the holes in his friend's head any longer. Mackenzie hadn't given one signal that she might be interested in him in more than a foreman–boss lady relationship.

Still, he had a slightly uneasy feeling about leaving her to the romancing of the Three Dating Daddies—a thought that totally brought him up short.

That's what one of those men might become: a dad to Mackenzie's four little girls.

Maybe the most troubling thought of all.

Chapter 5

"You're going to have to keep an eye on Daisy," Jade told her as Mackenzie settled her daughters down for an afternoon nap. Late-day sun filtered through the windows of the family room, twilight just arriving at nearly seven o'clock. Mackenzie loved summer days when there was so much cheery sunshine.

She couldn't be bothered to think about Daisy Donovan.

"I'm not going to keep an eye on Daisy. I don't care what she does."

"You do care. All of Bridesmaids Creek cares. Her and her band of rowdies are bent on making certain this town drops off the map for families. That way Daisy's father can keep buying up the land around here in his quest for mineral rights and selling huge land parcels to the government. Or worse." Jade flopped down onto a flowered sofa, fanning herself. "As our town bad girl, Daisy lives for herself. My guess is she didn't come here today to bring you a gift, but to check out the new foreman. Everyone is town has been chattering about the hot guy you've got working the place."

"It doesn't matter. I'm not even going to think about Daisy's shenanigans. Even if Justin decided to hop on the back of her motorcycle and roar off into the sunset, I wouldn't think about Daisy."

Jade laughed. "Methinks you protest a bit too much. So what did you think about the three new guys?"

"That Ty and I are going to have to talk. The men are welcome to stay here and bunk in the bunkhouse, but I don't know if I have enough work here for three more men."

"Not unless you reopen the haunted house."

"Which I'm not going to do."

"It's August. We have plenty of time until October," Jade said.

"I know. But my only priority right now is my babies. We'll do fine living in a small cottage in town."

"There might be a miracle. You never know." Jade got up to stare out the window. "She bugs me—I swear she does. Why are men always so blinded by Daisy?"

"Because she's beautiful and has a wild streak. There's nothing blinding about it. It's human nature." Mackenzie smiled at her babies. "You girls, however, must promise your mother to grow up to be teachers, nurses and librarians. No motorcycles for you!"

"My goddaughters won't be Daisies," Jade said, laughing. "However, I think Daisy may be about to kiss a frog."

"Not Frog?" Mackenzie hurried to the window. "Poor

Frog! Of all of the new cowboys, I'm pretty sure he's the least suited to Daisy's charms."

"Hate to watch a good man fall." Jade walked away from the window. "In fact, I can't look."

"Can't look at what?" Justin asked, entering the room.

Mackenzie glanced over her shoulder, struck again by how handsome Justin was. She'd gotten a little used to him at the Hanging H, even if she wouldn't share that with a soul. Still, if he wanted to move on with Ty, she'd understand. She'd be sorry—but she'd understand. "We're spying."

"I can see that." He joined her at the window, and Mackenzie was shaken by the sudden warmth of proximity. Almost intimate, their arms nearly touching. She smelled spicy cologne and strong male, felt body heat and strange sensations sweep over her.

She was awfully glad it wasn't Justin out there getting far too close to Daisy Donovan's heart-shaped lips.

"I'll take the night shift," Justin told Mackenzie as she finished bathing the girls. She put them into soft nighties and touched a towel gently to the light fuzz atop their heads. A little baby oil for the dry spots, and they were like angels ready to be tucked in for the night.

"You don't have to," Mackenzie said. "But thank you, Justin. Babysitting isn't part of your job description."

"I've been thinking about my job description." He carried Hope and Holly down the hall, so Mackenzie picked up Heather and Haven and followed. She watched the big man settle her daughters ever so gently into their white-ruffled cribs. "This business of Ty bringing on hannies for you, for example."

"Ty is nuts, and there'll be no hannies around here, nor mannies. Silliest thing I've ever heard." Mackenzie covered her daughters with light pink blankets and kissed each of them. "Ty doesn't want to bring those cowboys here to help me as much as he's looking for a place for some of his buddies to work. I'll ask around town, see if anybody needs a couple of hands."

"You know I'm leaving with Ty. Probably day after tomorrow."

She felt a slight prick at that news. "Then I'll only need one of the men. Maybe Frog. He seems pretty harmless." She sighed to herself. And maybe if he were here he'd be less likely to fall into Daisy's clutches.

"Frog, is it?"

"I can't get used to a grown man being called Frog."

"Hiring him on here isn't going to save him from Daisy."

She looked at Justin. "Who says I want to?"

"I know something about the female mind. And I heard you and Jade talking about saving him."

"Jade was talking about it. I personally think Frog can probably take care of himself just fine." She didn't look at Justin directly. Just too much sex appeal, too much closeness.

It was the babies. She loved the way he took care of her daughters, handling them like they were delicate treasures.

He moved a strand of hair away from her face, and she tucked it up into her ponytail. "I should catch a shower while they're down. We've hit the four-hour mark at night now, and I take full advantage of those four hours."

Justin moved away, sat in the rocker. "Go. Get some rest. I'll keep an eye on them."

"There's no need," she said quickly. "The monitor is on, and I'll hear them—"

He waved a hand at her to leave. "You need four hours to yourself. I'll wake you when they start looking for dinner." A smile tugged at his lips. "Better take me up on my offer. Ty's taking me out of here tomorrow or the next day."

"Oh. Okay. Thank you." She backed up slowly, then turned to hurry down the hall. He was actually leaving. She'd always known he would, and yet she'd hoped— Well, it didn't matter what she'd hoped.

The fact was, she'd gotten used to Justin being around. But it was more than that, and she knew it. Something about the big man made her feel safe and protected and happy. They weren't a family, but they'd gotten into a groove that worked, and she'd come to rely on that comfort. Rely on *him*.

Maybe Jade's right with that protesting too much stuff. I've got a major thing going for this cowboy. I was just trying to ignore it because I knew he'd leave one day.

And now it seemed that day had come.

Justin slept off and on, dozing in the room with the babies. It was weird how much he found himself enjoying taking care of them. As a man who'd never been interested in having children—not one bit—he was surprised by how Mackenzie's four little daughters tugged on his heartstrings.

He hated the idea of leaving them—all of them. And, somehow, he even hated the idea of Frog staying behind to take his place. Or any of the three men Ty was bringing on to replace him, for that matter.

The only reason he was leaving with Ty was because Ty had brought him here in the first place. He owed it to him out of a sense of brotherhood. Ty wouldn't ask him if he didn't need him. Mackenzie didn't really need him—not like Ty did.

He needed to talk to Ty a bit more, dig into the mission to settle the questions in his mind. But the thing that unsettled his mind the most was how much he hated the idea of three men he didn't know all that well roaming around the Hanging H and falling for Mackenzie and the girls.

Just as he was beginning to fall for them.

Whether he liked it or not, that was the truth. Justin closed his eyes as he rocked in the chair. The tiny night-light sent a soft glow over the room. An occasional baby snuffle or sigh reached him, the sound somehow comforting and not intimidating at all, not the way he'd thought it would be. During his wilder, crazier rodeo days, the idea of a family had been distinctly unappealing.

Mackenzie was recently divorced. No doubt the last thing she wanted was another man in her life. He couldn't blame her if that was the way she felt.

At dawn, when Betty Harper appeared in the nursery, Justin felt strangely rested. He smiled at Jade's mother. "Good morning."

"Go get some rest. I'll take over from here. Mackenzie said the babies didn't even move last night."

He felt like he hadn't, either. In fact, he couldn't remember the last time he'd felt so relaxed. "I thought I was awake all night. I didn't even realize Mackenzie came in the nursery."

Betty smiled. "I checked on you at five. Everybody was sound asleep, which is a first for the girls. They probably feel comforted with a man's presence around. Babies do that sometimes. You have a nice deep voice with is probably soothing to them."

She disappeared from the room. Justin rose and stretched. Haven peered up at him from her blanket, and he had the uncanny notion that she was watching him. Did babies see anything at this tender age?

"Hello, little one," he said, approaching her crib. Gently he picked her up, held her close. "Good morning to you, too."

He kissed the top of her head, breathed in the sweet baby freshness of her skin, the scent of baby powder.

"Hi," Mackenzie said, her voice soft.

He turned and saw she was wide-awake and looking refreshed. "You're up bright and early."

"I got a lot more sleep than I have since before I became pregnant." She came to take Haven from him, and he smelled an entirely different smell: strawberry shampoo, delicate floral soap, sexy woman.

His heart did one of those funny flip-flops he'd gotten used to feeling around her.

"Thanks for watching them last night." She gazed up at him. "I think I slept so well because I knew you were standing guard."

Oh, boy. There went the heart. "It was no problem. Part of the job."

"Not part of the job I hired you to do." She looked at him funny.

He backed up a step when he realized he was staring at her pink, glossy lips. "It's the job Frog and Fellows are applying for."

"That's Ty's bright idea. And by now, you know Ty can be a bit of a squirrel." She smiled. "Babysitting isn't part of your job description. But thank you."

Warmth expanded in his chest at her smile. He wondered if he'd ever met a woman he was so blindingly attracted to—and decided in a hurry that was a terrible thought to have about his boss. Definitely a dead end. There was no way on this planet he had any business being attracted to her.

"I'm going to get some coffee. You want a cup?"

"No, thank you. You go on."

He nodded and turned to leave.

Turned back around, met her gaze. Started to say that sitting up with her daughters hadn't been work; he hadn't done it because of Frog and Friends. He'd done it because he'd wanted to. Wanted to make her happy, help her out.

But it was a bad idea to make such a confession. No purpose to it at all, and he didn't do anything unless he knew the purpose.

Shutting his stupid yap tight before it could say weird, mushy things, he left.

Chapter 6

"Hello, handsome," Justin heard as he got out of his truck, which he'd parked right in front of Madame Matchmaker's small shop.

He turned, found Daisy Donovan just about too close for comfort, chest-high, tiny and dangerous. The brunette was dressed in a short denim skirt, brown cowboy boots and a white halter top. She smiled at him mischievously. All the sex appeal being aimed at him had warning bells ringing like mad inside his head.

"Hi, Daisy."

She wound an arm through his. "Where're you heading to?"

He wasn't about to tell her he'd been planning a visit to Madame Matchmaker. The kind of answers he was looking for required discretion. Daisy didn't look like she did discretion very well. "I was planning to grab lunch."

"Mind if I join you? I had some things I wanted to talk to you about."

He did mind—very much. Ty was hitting the road tomorrow and Justin was going with him, so he had a lot to get done. Lunch with Daisy wasn't on the to-do list.

"I'm leaving town tomorrow, so I'm grabbing takeout. Why don't you call the Hanging H and let Mackenzie know what you need, and maybe one of the new guys she's hired can help you out."

Daisy looked up at him, her dark eyes focused. "We need you here in Bridesmaids Creek."

He shook his head. If there was any reason he'd stay, it would be for Mackenzie. The reason he was leaving was Mackenzie—or, more to the point, the feelings he knew he was developing for his boss.

He extracted himself from Daisy's arm. "Bridesmaids Creek survived without me for many years."

He tipped his hat and pushed open the door of The Wedding Diner. It seemed as if every customer turned to stare at him. Conversation halted.

No, he wasn't imagining the stares. He nodded to the room at large and headed to the pink stand where Jane stared at him, too, her bright blue gaze curious.

Justin removed his hat. "If you have a booth open, ma'am, I'd appreciate it."

She nodded and took him to a white booth. He sat, noticing that everyone followed his progress. No one bothered to hide their curiosity. He hoped she'd bring him a cup of hot coffee sooner rather than later. His stomach rumbled. He could have eaten at the ranch—certainly he'd miss the good cooking there.

But today he really felt a need to put some space between him and the babies. And Mackenzie, most of all.

Jane gazed at him intently. "You're not a settling down kind of man."

"No, ma'am."

"But you're happy at the Hanging H."

The way she made statements instead of asking questions—like she already knew everything but was only giving him a chance to confirm her thoughts—forced his thoughts off the coffee he'd been hunting. "I've enjoyed my time out there."

"But you're not a family man."

He looked at her. "I wonder if I can get a cup of coffee, Jane."

She smiled. "You think I'm digging in your business."

"Yes, ma'am."

"That's what we do here. You'll get used to it. We're really pretty harmless here in Bridesmaids Creek." She cocked her head. "You don't need to worry about us matchmaking."

His brows rose. "I don't?"

"No. We're looking for family men in Bridesmaids Creek."

She strode off to get his coffee. Justin ran a finger around his collar.

A woman with pinkish hair piled high on her head slid into his booth. "Jane tell your fortune?"

He shook his head. "I don't think so."

"She just gave you the third degree." She nodded. "She'll tell your fortune to us later." She stuck a hand across the table for him to shake, which he did, slightly out of his element. "I'm Cosette Lafleur."

"Ah. Would you be Madame Matchmaker?" The

French name and the pink-frosted hair seemed like a giveaway.

She looked at him closely. "*Absolument.* And you should have come to see me."

"But I'm not looking for a match."

"That's what we hear." She indicated the diner, whose patrons weren't even bothering to disguise their interest in Cosette's interview of him. "So you're leaving."

"Yes. Tomorrow." He looked at the grilled cheese sandwich and tomato soup a young, bouncy waitress with a nose stud put in front of him. "I didn't order this."

"It's what you get. Miss Jane says you're looking peaky and some protein and calcium will set you right." Cosette shrugged. "Nobody really orders. We all get what Jane thinks we need. It works for us. Most of us never get even a cold!"

Great. He had to pick the one place to get away from Mackenzie where he couldn't get away from talking about her and couldn't even order a nice, greasy burger.

"Go ahead. Take a bite. That cheese is County Line cheese, made off a local farm. You'll never taste better."

A grilled cheese sandwich was just bread and cheese. Nothing fancy. He took a bite, not expecting much. "That's good stuff," he said, surprised.

Cosette looked pleased. "So, back to you leaving. It's too bad you have to go, but Ty said he misjudged you."

"Misjudged me?"

"Ty thought you were probably a man looking for a change in your life. A family man in disguise."

That would be odd. He and Ty had never discussed it. "I'm pretty certain I've never misled anyone about the fact that I like life on the road."

"That's the problem, then, isn't it? Expectations?"

She beamed. "Ty shouldn't have tried to put you in a position you wouldn't be comfortable with."

"Are you saying that Ty had me hired on at the Hanging H so I'd fall in love with Mackenzie?"

"Or at least the babies. It's very hard not to fall for those little angels." Cosette glanced up, her smile widening. "Hello, Mackenzie."

He started a little, surprised when Mackenzie slid in next to Cosette and hugged her.

"How are you feeling?" Mackenzie asked. "Your stomach virus has gone?"

"All gone. That soup you sent over for me did the trick. Thank you, dear friend."

Justin ate his sandwich, needing strength after everything he'd heard. Ty wouldn't have brought him to Bridesmaids Creek on a matchmaking mission. His buddy wouldn't have hung him out to dry like that.

But there was no denying that the "bait"—if Mackenzie had been Ty's bait—was worthy of any hook. If he were wired a little differently, if he could consider staying in one place with one woman, Mackenzie would be the one.

Whoa. That was a very strange thought.

She looked at him, her smile innocent and carefree, and he wondered why he hadn't seen it before. Apparently all of Bridesmaids Creek had seen it.

His buddy, best friend, old pal Ty had set him up.

It was a blind date without the date. Nothing more than the same service Madame Matchmaker might provide. And now Ty was pulling the plug, because Justin wasn't a settle-down kind of man, and Ty had found three better victims: Sam, Squint and Fish. No—Frog.

A jealous streak ran up his back.

Which was exactly why he had to leave tomorrow.

"It's such a shame Justin has to go," Cosette told Mackenzie. "He was just telling me how much he was going to miss your little girls."

He hadn't said any such thing. Justin's mouth opened to deny the woman's claim; then he realized what a schmuck he'd sound like if he did. So he nodded and spooned his soup a little faster. Maybe if he kept his mouth busy, he'd keep his foot out of it.

Mackenzie looked at him, her expression polite. "Justin has been a big help at the ranch. And with the girls."

Justin swallowed uncomfortably. Why did he feel so guilty? Did Mackenzie know that her friend Ty had tried to set her up? There were few secrets in Bridesmaids Creek. She had to suspect.

Then again, she'd never given him half a signal that she was interested in him. Hadn't put up much of a fuss when Ty had mentioned they were leaving town, had seemed okay with the new hands.

Maybe he should probe that little situation a bit.

"The new guy should work out well at the Hanging H," Justin said a bit gruffly, not completely able to work out the jealous kink he got about Toad. Or whatever the man's name was.

"You mean *guys*," Mackenzie said. "Ty talked me into taking all three of the new hands on."

Good ol' Ty. If one bachelor didn't pan out, Ty had planned for backup. His friend was almost diabolical with his matchmaking.

"I hear through the BC grapevine," Cosette said, "that your sister is coming home tomorrow, Mackenzie."

Sister? He looked at Mackenzie, noticing instantly that she didn't smile, only nodded gravely.

"Yes. Suz will be home."

Good. Then Mackenzie would have more help, and he'd feel less like a heel for running out on her. Wasn't that what he was doing?

"What are you going to do?" Cosette asked in her sweet, lilting, French-accented voice.

Mackenzie shrugged. "It's her home, too. She can always come home to the Hanging H."

"You don't need a fifth child," Cosette said, and Mackenzie stirred the tea she'd poured a half a packet of sugar into and shrugged.

"Maybe she's changed," Mackenzie said.

"How old is your sister?" Justin asked, curious. The ladies' chatting had turned a bit ominous.

"Suz is twenty-three," Mackenzie said.

And Mackenzie was thirty. Not an uncommon age gap between siblings, but it didn't sound like they were entirely close.

Still, Mackenzie's family problems were none of his concern, and as Cosette had pointed out—much to his chagrin—he had no need to worry. He was being dragged off by Ty because he wasn't looking for a family. And family skeletons were one thing he made every effort to avoid.

Justin kept himself from helping put the babies to bed that night, though it was a ritual he enjoyed. He liked the smell of lavender-scented soap and the sweet sounds they made when Mackenzie slipped them into their cribs. They always looked so darling in their little nighties. Strangely enough, although most people wouldn't find four babies peaceful, that was exactly how he felt at night in the nursery.

Peaceful.

He loved watching Mackenzie do her mom thing, too. It was such a soothing sight as she lovingly slipped her daughters off to dreamland.

He was going to miss it. He'd been lucky that she'd allowed him to become part of the nightly ritual. Part of him wished he could stay at the Hanging H, because he sure did like it here.

On the other hand, now that he knew the price of staying, there was no reason to do so.

They left the nursery, the night-lights glowing softly in the wall sockets, the girls conked out from their busy day and all the good loving from their mother.

So he didn't say he would miss the girls—and Mackenzie—though he knew he would.

Mackenzie went into the kitchen, and he followed. Here was where he usually said good-night every night, another ritual, this one more professional. They put the babies to bed, they walked into the kitchen and he said *sayonara*.

"Thank you for everything," Mackenzie said. "You've been a big help. I'll admit that when Ty sent you here, I had my doubts." She pulled a cake dish toward her. "Betty left the coffee on and a pound cake she baked. You don't want to leave without tasting Betty's pound cake."

He found himself nodding before he even sat down, glad of the excuse to stay. "I'll take you up on that offer. Thanks."

She poured him a steaming mug of coffee he suddenly realized he didn't want. She cut him a fragrant slice of cake he suddenly didn't want, either.

And when Mackenzie passed him to rinse off the knife, he reached out and caught her hand. "I'm going to miss this."

Her face held surprise—then she smiled. "Thank you."

He noticed she didn't take her hand from his, so he did the only thing he could. He set her cake knife on the counter and pulled Mackenzie to him. She stared up at him with those beautiful brown eyes, and he kissed her lips, ever so lightly, just in case she didn't want to be kissed. There was still time to stop before it was a full-blown kiss. He'd know in a second if he'd gone someplace she didn't want him to go.

Mackenzie didn't move—she stayed still as the night, waiting—and Justin was never so glad of anything in his life. He pressed his lips against hers, letting himself sink into the sweetness. He heard rain begin spattering against the windows, but that was the outside world. In this warm, cake-scented kitchen, he held the softest woman in the country in his arms, and she was responding to him.

The back door blew open. Mackenzie and Justin jumped apart. He stared at the woman in the doorway. She was dripping from her head to her toes, her boots muddy, her jeans ragged and pocked with deliberate tears. She dropped a dirty duffel bag onto the floor. But it was her short pixie hair, blond with blue streaks, that stopped him, not to mention the cheek stud and the dark glaring eyes.

"Suz!" Mackenzie flew to hug her sister, enveloping her.

Suz stared at him over Mackenzie's shoulder. "Who's he?"

"This is Justin Morant." Mackenzie sounded uncomfortable. "He's the foreman. Until tomorrow, that is."

Suz didn't move to shake his hand. Didn't leave her sister's arms.

"What's he doing in the kitchen at this hour?" Suz demanded.

Damn good question. He grabbed his hat, went to the door. "I'll say goodbye tomorrow before I go, Mackenzie."

Suz glared, willing him gone. Mackenzie nodded. "Thank you."

Ouch. He nodded and headed out into the rain, leaving the cake and the coffee behind.

The kiss stayed with him.

Chapter 7

Justin came upon Frog, Squint and Sam spying on the house from the bunkhouse. "What the hell, fellows?" he demanded.

"Didn't you see her?" Frog asked. "That little bit of darling that roared up on the motorcycle?"

He hadn't seen a motorcycle, hadn't heard one, wouldn't have noticed one if it had run over his foot. All he'd been focused on was Mackenzie in his arms. He didn't think he'd ever forget that.

She was all woman, gentle and sweet-smelling. Curves. Heaven.

No wonder her sister was so protective of her. He would be, too.

"That *darling* is too much for any of you to handle." He hung his hat on the hook and went into the kitchen for a much-needed beer, eschewing the temptation to spy on the kitchen, which faced the bunkhouse.

"Who was she?" Frog asked.

"Little sister. Nothing for you to worry about." Justin flung himself onto the leather sofa.

"I'm not worried about her," Squint said. "If I can't have Mackenzie, I'll be happy to—"

"Whoa, whoa, whoa." Justin scowled at the three stooges he was stuck with for the moment. "No one said you were getting Mackenzie or Suz."

"Suz," Sam said dreamily. "I could have guessed she had a pretty name."

Justin mentally rolled his eyes. "Again, who said those women were available? You work for them. You can't hit on them."

They looked at him, grinning.

"If you had understood your assignment," Frog said, "you would have known that romancing is what we're all here for. We're all bachelors looking for a good wife and a home."

Justin blinked. "What assignment?"

"Didn't Ty tell you? In this town, the ladies are looking for a husband any way they can find one," Squint said. "And we are all preapproved to join the race to the altar."

"Where did you get a name like Squint?" Ty asked.

"Name's John Squint Mathison," the tall man said. Justin supposed he was a decent-looking fellow, the kind a lady might call a hunk. "I got *Squint* in the military."

"I don't like it," Justin said. "It sounds a bit shady."

"Au contraire," Sam said with a flourish. "If you'd been in the mountains of Afghanistan with us, you'd

have wanted this one and his peashooter at your back. We called him Squint-Eye, Squint for short, for certain reasons best not discussed. But you can trust it was a badge of honor."

"Yeah, well." He looked at the gentle giant next to him. "I guess I don't want to know what Frog is derived from," he said, feeling a little sour that these gentlemen would be staying and he'd be going. Gentlemen, indeed. More like woman-hunting, non-commitment-phobic, nice guys.

They shook their heads solemnly, and he sighed.

"What makes Ty so sure that Bridesmaids Creek is so ripe for marriage-hunting males?"

"Did you get a load of that beauty that pulled up on the motorcycle yesterday?" Sam's eyes went round.

"Daisy Donovan? Yes, I did." Justin shrugged.

"She's *fine*. And she invited us all to a special gathering." Frog looked pleased. "I'd marry her in a heartbeat."

From what he'd heard about Daisy, Justin didn't think that was necessarily a good idea. He sipped his beer, studied the eager bachelors in whose capable hands he was leaving Mackenzie.

"Don't worry," Squint said, as if reading his mind. "We'll take care of everything. We've figured out your routine."

They knew what he did outside the house. Inside the house with Mackenzie and the babies, they had no idea.

He'd like to keep it that way.

"I'm so glad you're home, Suz," Mackenzie told her sister when she wandered back into the kitchen, freshly showered and wearing comfortable pajamas. Mackenzie passed her sister the slice of pound cake she'd cut for Justin and made her a hot cup of tea. "How was Africa?"

Suz sat on a barstool and glared at her sister. "Africa was beautiful. I think we did a lot of good with the limited resources we had. We can talk about that later, after I've seen my nieces again. And after we talk about that cowboy you were in here sucking face with."

"I was not," Mackenzie said, placing the teacup in front of her sister and pushing the sugar bowl close, "sucking face with the cowboy."

Suz shook her head. "I do believe if I hadn't walked in, this kitchen would have seen some action."

Mackenzie looked at her little sister with a noncommittal shrug. "I doubt that."

"Do not fall into another man's arms just because what's-his-face went off with what's-her-face."

That familiar sting lodged deep inside her, yet stinging less than it once had. "I am not falling."

Pants on fire. It had been wonderful for the few seconds Justin had held her in his arms. The feeling had shocked her when he'd pulled her close against his broad chest, right up to his hard body. She'd watched him many a time from this kitchen window, admiring the muscles and the quiet, steady, strong way he went about his work. Being held by Justin had sent her heart rushing out of control.

"Oh, no," Suz said, staring at her sister. "I've seen that look on your face before."

"What look?"

"That about-to-fall look."

"I am not about to fall. In fact, Justin's leaving tomorrow. So falling is out of the question."

Suz shook her head, started in on the pound cake. "It's rebound. Surely you know that."

"So what?"

"I mean," Suz said, her mouth full, "if you were the type of woman who would just kiss and quit, that would be one thing. But you kiss and marry. And that's a problem."

Mackenzie laughed. "If you knew Justin, you wouldn't worry. He is so not the marrying kind. Everybody knows that."

"Everybody can't know that, because he was only here a short time." Suz was being practical. "You don't know for sure."

"Regardless, he's leaving tomorrow." She wasn't entirely happy about that, but Ty could be inscrutable about anything and everything. Certainly Justin hadn't argued about leaving.

So it was for the best.

"Anyway," Suz said, sipping her tea, "how are my angel cakes? I peeked in on them, and they were sleeping hard. Haven sucks her thumb, you know. It's cute."

"She doesn't do that when she's awake." Mackenzie smiled. "They're amazing. There's not a day I don't thank Heaven that I have them."

"Yeah, well," Suz said gruffly. "It was the least Knucklehead could do for you." She sniffed. "You look good."

Mackenzie smiled. "Do I?"

"Yeah. You gained a little weight. You look rested." Suz sniffed again. "In fact, you look beautiful."

Mackenzie stared at her normally unsentimental sister. "Why are you buttering me up?"

Suz laughed. "I'm not. I'm being my typical honest

self. Some days it's brutal, and some days it's all good news. You really do look great. I'm sure I'm not the only one who's told you that recently."

"Believe it or not, the cowboy, as you call Justin, and I don't have some hot love affair going. Before today, we hadn't spoken more than twenty minutes at one time."

"I don't think talking's what's on his mind."

"He's been nothing but a gentleman. If you're done with your snack, I'm going to tuck you onto the sofa and turn on the TV. I may look great, but you look like the flight was long."

Her sister followed her from the kitchen. "It was long and hellish. I always say I'm quitting the Peace Corps. But then I don't. I can't. It's in my blood."

Mackenzie settled her sister in her old room, spreading a soft blue-and-white afghan over her that Betty had knitted. Suz had the reputation for being a wild child—she was tough and a little wild. But she had such a good heart. And she'd go places no one else would go, in the quest to do what few others wanted to do. Or could do. She gazed at her sister tenderly. "How long are you here?"

"Not long." Suz's eyes started to close. "Just until I determine that you're not suffering too much without me. And until I make sure you don't do something dumb, like fall for a cowboy with a restless leg."

Mackenzie brushed Suz's blue-streaked hair away from her forehead. "Restless side, darling. Restless leg is something entirely different."

"No, I'm pretty sure I'm worried about his restless leg." Suz's eyes drifted shut. "It's always so good to be home. This will always be our home, won't it?"

Mackenzie felt a pang of guilt. This was a discussion for another day. She patted Suz's hand, noted the cracked nails, the dry skin, the calluses. Suz was a warrior of a different kind, a misunderstood warrior, and Mackenzie would do anything to protect her.

But keeping the family home probably wasn't in the cards. "Rest now."

"I try," Suz said. "I try to rest, Mackenzie. But I always see them."

Mackenzie drew back a little. "Don't think about it. It's all over."

Suz nodded, and Mackenzie tucked the blanket close around her sister, cocooning her like she would one of her babies. Then she went into the kitchen and looked out toward the bunkhouse, staring into the darkness.

Suz was right about one thing—Justin had made it clear he was a footloose, rebellious kind of guy. There was no reason to fall for him. Suz walking in had probably stopped something that should never have been started.

But she was amazed by the feelings his kiss had awakened inside her, feelings she'd never had before. Suz was right. The kitchen table probably would have been used for something other than its intended purpose, because the last thing Mackenzie had wanted was for Justin to let her go.

And that's why it hurt so much that he was leaving.

Justin was awakened by the feel of something warm and curvy sliding into bed, curling right up against him. He blinked, realizing he wasn't dreaming.

But something was wrong. For one heavenly second he thought Mackenzie might have crawled into his bed. The perfume wasn't right. The hands were too greedy. He caught the hands and sat up, switching on the lamp.

"Daisy! What the hell?"

She blinked and hopped out of his bed naked as the day she'd been born. He averted his gaze from the flash of skin as she scooped up her clothes and began dressing. "I thought—"

"You thought what?" He got up, pulled on his jeans, annoyed. There were three other occupants of the bunkhouse. Any one of them would probably have been happy to find Daisy in his bed.

He was not.

"Never mind." Daisy had pulled on some of her clothes but definitely couldn't be called "dressed."

Which of course was when the three stooges entered the room. Their eyes bugged from their sockets.

"This isn't what it looks like," Justin said, zipping his jeans. "She's lost."

The stooges looked concerned.

"Not that lost," Frog said.

"Damn, son," Squint said. "You're exactly what we heard about you."

"Which is what?" Justin demanded.

"Emotionally unavailable," Daisy said, slowly pulling the straps up on her dress. "A real renegade."

Justin hesitated, realizing Daisy was putting on something of an award-worthy act. "What the hell is going on here?"

"Nothing," Sam said, "except that you were in bed with Daisy."

"I was not in bed with Daisy!"

"Someone was in bed with Daisy, and it wasn't us,"

Frog said. "One of us, I should say," he said; then he was suddenly shoved aside.

Mackenzie stared at him. "What are you doing here, Daisy?"

"Nothing," Daisy said, her voice too sweet. Too silky, a bit catty.

Justin sighed. "Everybody out of my room. Now."

Mackenzie turned to leave, too. "Not you," he said, grabbing her hand and pulling her back into the room. He closed the door, took the lunch sack from her hand and set it on his dresser. "Were you bringing me a snack bag for the road?"

She glared at him. "Yes."

"Bet you'd like to take it back."

"Yes, I would!"

"Well, you can't." He pulled her into his arms, taking her lips with his, kissing her the way he'd wanted to kiss her earlier.

She put her hands on his chest, pushed him slightly away—though not too far. "Why would I want to kiss you after Daisy Donovan's been in your room?"

"Because you're in my room now."

"Which begs the question what was she doing in here?"

He smiled. "I think she'd lost her way."

"I very much doubt it."

"I'm pretty certain I wasn't the intended target. And you sound like you may have a jealous streak, boss lady."

"I'm not jealous in the least. I'm *concerned*."

Now she did try to tug away from him, though he didn't allow that. She didn't try hard enough for it to count—and he was pretty intrigued by this *concerned* side of her. "*I'm* concerned that you don't leave without what you came for," he said, slanting his lips over hers, drawing her in for a deep kiss. He loved holding her, that was for certain; she was soft and, at this moment, a trifle annoyed, which he was going to enjoy kissing right out of her.

Her lips were sweeter than he'd ever imagined. Every kiss, every stroke, was more amazing than before. Mackenzie let out what sounded like a tiny whimper, and he wasn't about to stop now. No longer stiff in his arms, she was pliable and leaning into him, her hands reaching up behind his neck, pulling him closer.

God, he didn't think he could leave this.

The thought brought him right down to earth. He really had no right to be doing this. Not to Mackenzie. If Daisy played fast and loose, Mackenzie was the kind of woman a man didn't play with at all. "Hey," he said, pulling back. He moved away, jerked his head toward the lunch sack. "Thanks for bringing my lunch. I really appreciate it."

She put her hands on her hips. "Chicken much?"

He was—he was a chicken with all the trimmings. "Maybe."

"At least you admit it."

"What else can I do?"

"Whatever you want to."

What he wanted to do was drag her into bed. Make love to her all night long. But what would that solve besides momentarily easing the overwhelming attraction he felt for her? It wasn't fair—he couldn't make love to Mackenzie and then hit the road. Not with those four little babies at the big house who needed a father, not a man who made love to their mother and then disappeared.

"You make things hard, Mackenzie."

She raised a brow. "If anyone's making anything hard for you, it's just you. I only brought you a lunch."

She had him there. He was all kinds of torn up, and he couldn't blame it on her. "I hate the thought of leaving you with the three amigos."

"Why? Ty trusts them."

Justin wasn't certain how much he trusted Ty. Heck, he didn't trust him at all. Ty was running a matchmaking game to get Mackenzie to the altar.

"Maybe I'll stay," he said, the words popping out of his mouth before he'd measured them.

She looked at him a long time. "Whether you stay or go is your decision," she said, disappearing from his room. He heard the front door close and took a deep breath.

I screwed that up every which way from Sunday. Holy cow.

Daisy climbing into his bed had started off a chain reaction. Mackenzie didn't trust him now; he could feel that. Already burned by one man, she had her guard up. It had taken him weeks to get past those shields, and now they were going to be stronger than ever.

He went to find his bunkhouse mates. Daisy was long gone, and Frog, Sam and Squint loafed on the leather sectional.

"Boss lady just blew out of here like a whirlwind," Squint observed. "Guess she didn't like what you were selling."

Ah. Ribbing from the dating-challenged. "If you have a point, make it, fellows."

"No point," Frog said quickly. "Except it seems to us your chips are down."

"And you see an opening?" He leaned against the wall, staring down at them. "Maybe. Maybe not."

Sam grinned at him. "The only maybe is maybe you shouldn't be leaving. Field's going to be wide-open."

"Thanks for the advice." Justin grabbed his lunch, headed to his truck.

The three boneheads followed him out.

"The only reason we're trying to help you is that Daisy says without you, this dump's going down," Squint said. "Kinda hate to see that happen to the little lady. She's got those four tiny whinies, you know."

Justin glanced toward the house. "Are you going to follow me out of town?"

Sam shoved his hands in his pockets. "No. We're going into town to meet Daisy. She wants to show us her place."

Justin turned. "So which one of you was Daisy coming to see this morning when she accidentally got in my bed?"

Frog shook his head. "That was no accident. She was trying to get you in trouble with Mackenzie."

"How do you know that?" It was a very strange thought.

"She left without getting into any of our beds, didn't she?" Squint asked. "Though believe me, we wouldn't have thrown her out of bed for eating crackers."

"I didn't throw her out of bed," Justin said. "I didn't *want* her in my bed." He frowned. "She wouldn't have had any idea that Mackenzie was coming to the bunkhouse to say goodbye. So how do you know it was a setup?"

"It's the way ladies work," Frog said. "At your age, you should know this."

"Daisy sure did disappear once she stirred up trouble," Squint said. "So if Trouble won't come to us, we're going to Trouble."

"But why?" Justin was confused. "Why would you want to bother with a wild woman like Daisy?"

"For many reasons." Sam thumped him jovially on the back. "We shouldn't have to draw you a picture, but one of those reasons involve the benefits you were going to receive this morning."

"Sex?" Justin frowned. "That seems cold-blooded, doesn't it?"

"The world runs on sex," Frog said expansively. "Do you know we get hit with like a bajillion sexual messages a day?"

"It's sort of like subliminal phone calls," Sam said. "Only you don't seem inclined to pick up the phone. So one of us will."

Justin shook his head. "I don't care." He got into his truck.

"Anyway," Squint said, "the real reason we're going to see Daisy is that we consider ourselves something like spies. Spies with muscles and highly desirable—"

"Brains," Frog interrupted. "This is brain warfare. We're not going to let Mackenzie and those little girls down."

Justin's gaze narrowed. "You just said your interest in Daisy is sex."

"All good spies do what they have to do," Squint said. "But the mission is to keep Daisy from sinking Mackenzie. But go on—run off if that's what you were born to do. Born to run and all that. We get it."

"Back up a second," Justin said. "You're going to try to seduce Daisy so she'll tell you what she and her father are up to in their plan to get Mackenzie to sell out? Because apparently this isn't the first rodeo with the Donovan crowd."

"Not seduce, exactly. More like romance," Sam said. "Sweet talk."

"There's just one problem with your plan. Daisy got into my bed. Not one of yours. What if she's not interested in the bait you're dangling?"

"Well, we figure absence makes the heart go wander. The three of us can convince her you were never here," Frog said.

"Sounds like a plan," Justin said, not wanting to hurt their feelings. "You do know that Mackenzie is planning to sell the Hanging H, don't you?"

"Yes, but Ty says she can't. He says we have to help her. Because Daisy's family will buy it and carve it up into tiny land parcels. And the Hanging H means jobs and commerce when Mackenzie starts the haunted house back up."

"But she doesn't want to," Justin said. "Mackenzie has four babies she's juggling. This plan of yours has so many holes in it that it could be your heads."

"Ty says Mackenzie just needs time. That she's all emotional right now, hormonal and stuff. Worried about the future. But he says that what's good for Bridesmaids Creek is Mackenzie, and what's good for Mackenzie is Bridesmaids Creek. So we're men on a mission, brother."

Justin considered their words, caught by their earnest worry about Mackenzie and her daughters.

"Gives you pause, doesn't it?" Squint asked.

Justin grunted.

"Don't bother him. He's beginning to see the light," Frog whispered. "It's like watching a fire slowly coming to life."

Justin ignored the ribbing. He had to admit the points were salient—*if* he trusted Ty's machinations, *if* he wanted to fall in with men with names like Squint, Frog and Toad—er, Sam. *If* he wanted to spend more time in a place with a crazy, totally female name like Bridesmaids Creek. That would be the address his mail was sent to from now on. Justin Morant, Bridesmaids Creek, Texas. Mr. Badass Bull Rider from Bridesmaids Creek.

"Shall we help you unpack that duffel from your truck for you?" Sam asked.

Justin thought about Mackenzie's sweet lips against his, responding ever so cautiously—and then more warmly as she opened up to him. It had been a helluva rush.

Ty wanted to drag him away from Mackenzie, open the playing field up to more serious contenders. But the little lady had an awful lot of serious warfare being waged against her.

He looked at his three new friends earnestly awaiting his answer.

"Do the right thing," Frog said softly.

What the hell. He got most of his correspondence by email or text anyway. Justin got out of the truck.

He realized Mackenzie and Suz were standing in the driveway not forty yards away. Suz's arms were crossed, her posture belligerent. He had some smoothing over to do with little sister.

But it was Mackenzie he was staying for—and that was something the man he'd been even a week ago wouldn't have ever considered.

Chapter 8

"I don't need four ranch hands," Mackenzie told Suz as she watched the men return to the bunkhouse. "Frankly, I'm not even sure I want one."

"Looks like you've got them. Maybe it's time to tell Ty his plan's not going to work." Suz sat down on a stool at the kitchen island and pondered a tat on her inner arm Mackenzie hadn't known she'd added to her collection, a tiny heart with the initials *HH* scrolled inside.

Hanging H.

"Would you please quit getting tattoos?" Mackenzie said. "When you get to be a hundred, you're going to be a wrinkled mass of ink."

Suz laughed. "Live for today, sister."

She didn't have that luxury. "Don't you ever want to settle down? Find the right guy?"

"Didn't work for you." Suz brightened. "Although

I can tell my nieces are going to be amazing women, with love and direction from their Aunt Suz."

Mackenzie sat across from her sister and reached out to take her hand. "When's your next assignment?"

"I've decided there isn't going to be one. Africa was my last stop." Suz sighed. "Even a rolling stone with a mission has to grow moss sometime."

Mackenzie looked at her sister, worried. "This isn't like you. You never wanted to settle down."

"Dearest sister. I didn't want to settle down before I did something with my life. Now I've done a little." She shrugged, and they both glanced up as the kitchen door opened a crack.

"Can I come in?" Justin asked.

Mackenzie's heart did a funny little skip. "Sure. Have a seat."

"I saw the kitchen light was still on. Figured that meant the coffeepot might still have a few grounds left in it."

"Not really," Suz said.

"Suz!" Mackenzie said.

"Oh, all right." She got up ungraciously to get Justin a mug. "It's not coffee. It's tea at this hour. Can you deal with that?"

Justin smiled. "Sure."

"You want the milk and the sugar and the full deal, or—"

"Just hot. Thanks." Justin sat across from Mackenzie. "I don't think you need four hands."

"I just said that to Suz."

Justin nodded. "The three eligible bachelors have appointed themselves your guardians, courtesy of Ty."

"Told you you're going to have to talk to him," Suz

said, setting the mug in front of Justin. "I'm going to bed, kids. Don't do anything I wouldn't do."

"Night, Suz." Mackenzie shook her head. "Wait—come back here!"

Suz turned in the doorway. "Yes, sister dear?"

"Finish the story about your life now that you're done with the Peace Corps."

"Oh. That's easy." Suz grinned. "I'm going to finish college. I only have two years left. Then I'm applying to medical school." She drifted out of the room, humming.

College. Medical school. Mackenzie ran through the amount of money she had left from their parents' estate.

"Problems?" Justin asked.

"No." She got up to cut them both a piece of pound cake and set one in front of him. "Why did you decide to stay? You didn't have to."

"Yeah, I kind of did. Those gentlemen Ty sent out here are bent on rescuing you."

Mackenzie was annoyed. "From what?"

"Life." He shrugged. "Yourself? Daisy? I don't know."

"You mean because I'm a single mother."

"Sure. Apparently Ty believes—"

"Ty needs to get bent." Mackenzie forked her cake. "I don't even know what that means, exactly, but I heard someone say it one day and it totally describes what Ty can do to himself."

He laughed. "Good cake."

She watched him happily munching away, not caring at all that his decision to stay had completely upended her world. He had no idea how crazy she was about him—or she'd bet he'd run like the wind. She glared at him. "So you're going to rescue me from the three stooges?"

"No." Justin shook his head. "My role is the innocent bystander."

"So what was Daisy doing in your bed?" She hated to ask but had to know.

"Probably what any red-blooded female would want to do."

She sniffed. "Not any red-blooded female."

"You win. I think she may have had the wrong room."

Mackenzie gave him a cool look. "Daisy never, ever gets the wrong room."

"Really?" He perked up. "Thanks for the ego boost."

Her cool expression went straight to hard stink-eye. "None intended. Just fact."

"Truthfully, it wasn't the most pleasant experience."

"I don't think I believe you," Mackenzie said sweetly.

He put a hand over hers, startling her. "Enough teasing. You know very well I have as much interest in Daisy as I do in wearing wet socks."

His hand was so warm over hers, so strong. She nodded. "I know. I'm sorry. I have no business saying anything—"

"Stop." He squeezed her fingers lightly. "This is your ranch."

"Still, your personal life is your business. If you're really staying, we should establish that up front. You don't worry about my three new hands, and I won't poke my nose into your business."

"Maybe I like your nose—" he lifted her hand to his mouth ever so slowly, kissed it "—in my business."

Her breath caught. His gaze held hers, mesmerizing yet somehow gentle.

She pulled her hand away. "Listen, Justin. You're going—now you're staying. I don't know what to think."

"I understand." He got up and put his dishes in the dishwasher after rinsing them.

Drat. He would be a dish rinser. She silently approved.

"I'm going to hit the hay. By now maybe the fellows are asleep."

She raised a brow. "I can't tell if you like them, or if you view them as carbuncles you have to deal with."

"You don't have the corner on a little healthy jealousy," he said, winking at her before closing the door behind him.

Stunned, she sat glued to her stool for a second, then shot to the window. Justin walked across to the bunkhouse, his big shoulders visible in the darkness.

Unless she was mistaken, that big man had come on to her in a big way. Almost like he'd decided to stay because of her. A feeling of warmth spread over her.

"You like him, don't you?"

Mackenzie squealed and whirled around. "You scared me!"

Suz got back on her stool, her spiky hair awry. "I couldn't sleep. Decided to come get another piece of this cake. Carbs will do something for me, if not make me sleep, then wake me up enough to start filling out some college apps. By the way, I checked on the munchkins. Sleeping like lambs." She cut the cake, glancing up at Mackenzie. "I don't even have to ask if you like Justin. I can tell you do."

Mackenzie returned to her stool. "He's a nice man.

Can we talk about college? Where are you planning
on applying?"

"Everywhere and anywhere. I'll have to take the
MCAT first, the medical school examination." Suz
sighed as she ate her cake. "This, I missed."

"I have some money saved—"

"So do I. Thank you, sister dear. But you don't have
to take care of me anymore. I'm a big girl, you know."
She smiled at her sister. "I love you for it, though. You
just don't always have to be mother hen."

"Mom and Dad left us money. They wanted you to
have an education," Mackenzie said softly. "You've
never touched your part."

"I don't need my part. I don't need much to live on."
Suz looked around the kitchen. "If I never spent any of
what you call my part, would we have enough to hang
on to this place?"

"Suz—"

"Would we?"

Mackenzie looked at her sister. "I know what you're
trying to do."

"You *think* you know what I'm trying to do."

"You're trying to figure out how the girls can grow
up here and have the same wonderful childhoods we
did." Mackenzie looked at her little sister. "We had
good childhoods because Mom and Dad worked hard.
It wasn't about the ranch so much as it was about our
parents. They loved us. They took good care of us."

"It was partially the ranch," Suz said stubbornly.
"And you're not respecting the Hanging H when you
talk that way. Mom and Dad built this up from nothing.
It's the heart and soul of who we are."

Suz gazed at her, unblinking. She never wore

makeup. There were tats and piercings and hair dye but never makeup. And somehow her eyes were still so very expressive.

"I know you're right," Mackenzie said, "and I love that you're trying to honor our parents' memory. But I think they'd want you to have your money for a rainy day. So you don't have to take loans for college or medical school. For whatever you may need. Remember how hard Mom and Dad worked to build the Hanging H? They wouldn't want you to struggle as hard as they did."

"Do I get any say in this? A vote?"

"Of course you do."

"Good. Because it didn't feel like it there for a minute." Suz ate some cake, waved her fork. "I've lived in Africa for a year. I just don't have needs like other people do. It's hard to think about material things when I understand what people live without. And what I developed a great appreciation for was home."

Mackenzie sighed. "I haven't even had a chance to see your Africa photos yet. Let's leave this for another day."

"It's not a decision that's going to wait long. You've got four hands signed on. And Jade told me that you were planning on selling out by Christmas."

"I was going to tell you—"

"I know. You were going to tell me when you quit mooning after the cowboy."

"I really was going to discuss it with you. I wouldn't make the decision without you. But I didn't know if you planned on coming home, Suz. Truthfully, I had no way of knowing if you would stay with the Peace Corps. Your letters sounded like you were so happy."

Suz waved a hand again. "This is why Daisy's buzzing around here, trying to steal your man. She knows you're weakening."

"I am not weakening!"

"It's clear I came home in the nick of time." Suz carried her plate to the dishwasher, then, without rinsing, just placed it inside. She turned to grin at Mackenzie. "I know. Your pet peeve." She pulled the plate back out and gave it a swift rinse before replacing it. "I don't want to sell the family home or the ranch. None of it. I'd rather see you married to one of the three new guys than—"

"Married!" Mackenzie shook her head. "You can forget that nonsense right now. I'm never going through that again."

"Speak in haste—"

"It's not haste. Marriage isn't for me." Not even to the hunky man who'd just kissed her hand. Luckily he was a rebel who had no interest in settling down.

"One of us is going to have to run Daisy off for good," Suz said darkly. "Remember when our folks passed, she was like a vampire, hanging around looking to suck the dollar bills out of this place."

"There are no dollar bills to suck. If we keep the ranch, we're going to have to think of a way to make it profitable. It's big enough that we could take in boarders," she said, looking around the kitchen.

"No!"

Mackenzie blinked. "All right. No boarders."

"It wouldn't be right. We have the babies to think of. I don't want anybody around them that we don't know."

"All right. Any other ideas?"

"I'll work for a couple of years, then apply to medical school."

"No!" Mackenzie said, protesting as forcefully as her sister had about boarders. "*That* is not an option."

"We'll think of something." Suz drummed her fingers. "I can be very creative."

"That worries me." Mackenzie could hear the wheels turning in her sister's head.

"Whatever we do, it has to be something that keeps Daisy from catwalking around here all the time, annoying the crap out of me."

"She really bugs you, doesn't she?"

"Yes." Suz got up to look out the kitchen window. "She's after Justin."

Mackenzie shook her head. "It's doesn't matter."

"It does. I can't bear to let her win." Suz giggled. "At anything. In fact, I like to see her lose."

"Suz!"

"She deserves it." Her sister laughed again. "You're too tenderhearted. Be tenderhearted about our home, okay?" She kissed Mackenzie on the cheek and opened the kitchen door.

"Where are you going?"

"To see the three musketeers. They might be up playing cards or something. They look like the types that would have something going on in the wee hours. 'Night, sis."

Suz drifted out the door. Mackenzie watched her from the kitchen window. Sure enough, the bunkhouse door opened and shut with alacrity, and more lights went on inside.

The new guys had no idea what they were in for.

Mackenzie turned out the kitchen lights and went to check on her babies. Like Suz had said, they were sleeping like lambs. She loved her daughters so much.

It felt as if her heart was tied to them in some way she couldn't have explained to anyone.

Maybe Suz was right. The Hanging H would be a wonderful place for the girls to grow up. Deep in her heart, she'd like them to have what she and her sister had as kids. Yet it cost money—a lot of money—to pay the bills at a ranch that wasn't bringing in income. She'd been dipping into her own inheritance to cover expenses.

The nursery smelled like baby powder and freshly laundered linen. She sat down in a rocker for a moment, enjoying the gentleness and peace in the room. In the soft glow from the night-light, Mackenzie thought life could probably never get better than this.

She thought about Justin kissing her and about Daisy leaving his bedroom. He just didn't strike her as a dishonest man. And Daisy could be such a finagler. Suz was right: Daisy had long had her eyes on the Hanging H acreage. Set on prime real estate, near to usable roads but back far enough from town to feel private, the ranch had intrinsic value for those who might dream of large homes designed in the new architecture. Not like their traditional home now, with its quaint rooms and hidden staircase and wide window views.

This was home, full of happy memories and the misty patina of childhood dreams. The four men she'd hired would help her get the place back in shape to put on the market—there was no other way she could see to secure the future for her daughters, for Suz and even for Bridesmaids Creek. Maybe someone with money would buy the place, bring it back to its former glory, where it could once again give back to the community she loved so much.

As for Justin, she was just too close to the past to count on a man Ty had brought here for the specific purpose of rescuing her. Ty thought she needed that, but she'd do just fine on her own.

"It's not going to work, fellows." Suz stared at the four men lounging around the room, settled in leather recliners and on the huge circular sectional that, despite its age, still looked in good condition. Someone had been smoking a cigar, but Suz supposed it was likely that worse had been smoked under this roof.

With the three new guys, anything could happen. They had a bit of a wild look to them, not too long out of the heat of a war zone. Justin was his cool-cucumber self. Suz eyed him, and he eyed her in return. She didn't know the man well enough to say, but she had the feeling that cowboy wasn't a smoker. "I get the plan. I even appreciate that you've taken the time to dream something up to try to help my sister."

This she directed at Squint, Frog and Sam, as she was pretty certain Justin hadn't had any part in the idea they'd sprung on her. "My sister isn't going to get married to one of you in order to have a father for her children. She has one of those, and he's a louse, and I can tell you that even though you're offering to sign away any financial or gainful rights to the ranch, Mackenzie will never stand at an altar again. At least not in the near future, and I believe she's putting the ranch on the market as soon as you get the place fixed up. She mentioned something about wanting to be out of here by Christmas."

Sam glanced at Justin. "Do you have anything to say, or are you just going to sit there like a bump on a log?"

Justin looked at his newfound companions but didn't say a word. Suz supposed the question didn't merit an answer, and, anyway, Justin wasn't the type of man who would be pushed into any harebrained schemes.

Marrying her sister off was certainly the most foolish scheme that had been floated. "Got any more practical ideas under those Stetsons?"

Justin laughed, which she thought might be rude. Was he even trying to help her sister? At least the new guys were focused on the problem, which was dire.

"Dig out your folks' business model and records from the days of the haunted house," Justin said, stunning her.

"Well, Mr. Helpful, that's not going to work, either. My sister thinks we're moving. Not opening a business."

"Tell her it's just for this last season. Sort of a goodbye to Bridesmaids Creek." Justin's gaze gleamed, his eyes intent, and she realized he'd been working on the problem all along, just waiting for the right time to spring it.

She frowned. "With you four as ringleaders?"

"Well, we all need jobs," Frog pointed out. "And we'd like to stay here."

"I don't get what's in it for you," Suz said.

"Money," Squint said. "And this place is nice. It's kind of storybook."

"And you have your eyes on Daisy Donovan." Suz noticed none of the three new guys seemed bothered by that pronouncement, but then Frog spoke up.

"Not me. Not my type," he said, his tone certain. "I go for the real wild girls."

Wilder than Daisy? Suz wrinkled her nose, suddenly

aware that Frog was looking at *her.* Intently. Like he had something on his mind.

He wasn't suggesting that she was wild? What would make him think that? "Er—"

"Look, Daisy's a nice woman, I'm sure," Justin said, "but you fellows best cast your nets elsewhere."

"Why?" Frog demanded, his face a bit crestfallen. "We're not horning in on you. You've got a thing for the boss lady, anyone with one eye can see that—"

Frog fell silent, dead silent, at Justin's raised brow. Suz stared at the big man, ready to hear the truth. "Well, Cowboy? Do you have a thing for my sister?"

Chapter 9

Justin found himself in the hot seat unexpectedly, and he knew it was best to get off in a hurry. "Don't listen to our friends. I've learned they talk a lot but say little of importance."

"Maybe we talk a lot but say a lot of importance that you don't want to admit," Frog said.

Suz was staring at him. "You're not denying it, Justin."

"I don't have to." He met the eyes of each of his new friends, daring them to say another thing. They all looked away from him after a moment—except Suz.

"O-*kay*," Suz said. "Anyway, what we need to do is figure out how to get my sister out of her pickle. Get *us* out of our pickle," she amended. "Any and all good ideas will be considered. For the sake of my nieces."

A sideways sensation hit Justin at the mention of

those four tiny dolls. They deserved more than they were going to get out of life. He didn't need little sister to spell it out for him. Deadbeat Dad was long gone, and Mackenzie and her babies would be living off their wits. Suz was a different animal altogether, obviously a tough survivor. So was Mackenzie, but she had a soft edge to her. Soft, sexy, rounded edges.

"Aw, he's not going to step up to the plate," Frog said, staring at Justin derisively. "So here's my good idea. Marry me, Suz."

Suz blinked. Justin stayed out of this new twist. If Frog wanted to get tossed back into the pond on his head by Suz, that was no concern of his.

"Marry you?" Suz scoffed. "I said come up with a *good* idea."

Justin laughed. "She has you there."

Suz got up. "Marriage isn't the answer for anyone."

Justin crossed his legs. "You're too young to be so cynical."

"Not cynical. Practical," Suz replied.

He thought she was adorable in a little sister sort of way. "I agree marriage is a bad idea."

"Yeah," she said, looking at Frog. "Any woman who would marry a man named Frog needs to have her head examined."

Justin took pity on his new buddy. "Take it easy on the man. He's just trying to help."

"Yeah," Sam said. "Does anybody think that little Jade mama might be open to a date?"

Justin shook his head. "You have to ask to find out."

"Anyway," Squint said, "you're all too chicken. Let's head into town. Hunt up some trouble."

"We're trying to solve the Hanging H problem," Justin reminded the room at large.

"Yeah, but I want to find that ornery little brunette with the loud bike," Squint said. "I like my ladies loud and wild."

"If you go for Crazy Daisy," Suz said, "you deserve everything you get."

"Looking forward to that." Squint winked at them and went out the door. Sam looked disgusted, Frog surprised. Justin shook his head. "Let's table this meeting. We'll meet again when somebody has a real idea."

"I really think," Frog said, staring at Suz like he wanted to melt into her arms, "that you should let me take you into town for an ice-cream cone, Miss Suz."

"I've got ice cream in the freezer. Sorry, Frog." She drifted out the door, and Justin looked at his buddy with pity.

"Don't be discouraged. She's got a lot on her mind," Justin said.

"Pretty sure she shot me down," Frog said, his shoulders drooping.

"It'll work out, maybe," Justin said. "Good night, gentlemen." He headed off to his room, needing to disconnect from all the angst being shared. How to save the Hanging H—if Mackenzie even wanted it saved. He thought again about the murder near the Hanging H that had ruined the haunted house, wondered if that was the reason Mackenzie didn't want to open it again.

Maybe worrying about Mackenzie was a waste of time. Could be she didn't want him thinking about her situation. Maybe she'd shoot him down as hard as Suz had shot down Frog. Those Hawthorne girls seemed pretty independent. Wild child Suz with a guy named Frog? Not a chance.

For starters, Frog had to reveal his real name if he was going to get the girl. But Justin figured advice to the lovelorn should stay in Madame Matchmaker's capable hands, because he had no desire to get involved in small-town love affairs and soap operas.

Me? I'm going to have to get the girl the old-fashioned way.

I'm going to win her.

Mackenzie wasn't looking for another man, as Suz had pointed out. In fact, it might be easier to be Frog with his insane crush on Suz.

He'd never let long odds stop him before.

"You've got the whole thing wrong," Mackenzie told Ty a week later when she ran into him at The Wedding Diner. "You sent four bachelors to my place on purpose."

Ty looked amused. "Would you rather I sent four happily married men?"

Mackenzie glanced around the diner, remembering her father bringing her there to have lunch and a piece of cake. They'd had those father–daughter luncheons many times over the years, as he'd also done with Suz, calling them his special times with his children. Maybe he'd done it to give her mother a break from the kids, she thought fondly. She would have understood that—right now Betty and Jade were watching the quadruplets. As much as she loved her children, a mini-break was nice, too. "You won't believe this, but the last thing I want in my life is a man. I just don't have room for one."

He winked. "There is always room for the right man."

"But I didn't elect you my matchmaker," Mackenzie protested, knowing by the gleam in his eye that her friend wasn't listening to her with any remorse. "When I want a matchmaker, I'll go to Madame Matchmaker."

"I'm not stealing any business from her." Ty grinned. "As far as I'm concerned, I owe you one from the first time."

"No one could have foretold how Tommy would feel about becoming a father to four children."

Ty's expression turned dark. "Look, Mackenzie, not to rub salt in the wound, but Tommy Fields never deserved you. He'd always considered himself a hot item with the ladies. I just believed him when he said he'd changed."

She shrugged. "I don't care anymore."

"I guess you do a little," he said softly, "or you wouldn't be so annoyed about the perfectly macho specimens I put out at your ranch."

She made a face. "So you admit you were being a Nosy Ned when you put that package together and sent it my way."

"They needed a job. You deserve better choices for a father for your daughters. How am I a bad guy?" He winked at her. "Look, you're young, Mackenzie."

"Thirty."

"Young. You're beautiful, smart and talented. You deserve a great guy."

She sniffed. "Why not you?" she demanded, just to wind him up. Ty would never settle down, never.

He looked aggrieved and reached to hold her hand in his. "Your hand is warm from your coffee cup."

She raised a brow.

"Friends don't let friends marry inappropriately. And I'm so inappropriate."

She laughed. "Yes, you are."

"I would marry you, you know, if I hadn't sent you better options," he said, his tone convincing and yet the expression on his face somehow not.

"You're such a fibber. You'll never get married."

"Nope," he said happily, releasing her hand. "But I'd call it a day and go home happy if you'd get married again."

"You realize one of those men has a thing for Daisy—"

"That's a misfire," he said, frowning. "Squint needs to have his head examined. Think he left a critical part of his brain back in Afghanistan."

"And one might be developing a thing for Suz."

He pondered that news. "Not exactly a misfire, but not exactly encouraging, either."

"That's my sister," Mackenzie said. "Speak with respect."

"I'm just saying she's young—she's not pliable."

Mackenzie laughed. "You mean she wouldn't allow you to manipulate her. I'm completely on to you."

Justin walked into the diner. Everybody turned to look at him, and Mackenzie could easily see why he'd draw attention. He was so big and tall and he carried himself well, his aura strong and commanding. Her heart jumped a little.

If she was going to think about dating again, Justin would definitely be high on her list.

He'd be the only man she'd want on her list.

"Hi," Justin said, sliding into the booth next to her. "Who are we gossiping about today?"

He was muscular and warm beside her. Mackenzie told herself to ignore the sudden hormone surge. "I believe Ty was talking about you."

Justin eyed Ty. "Matchmaking again?"

Ty laughed. "You know me too well."

"Does Madame Matchmaker know you're horning in on her area of expertise?"

"She gave me her blessings." Ty winked at Mackenzie. "I have to go. Tell your sister no go on the new guys. Those are all for you."

Ty sauntered off, paid his tab and kissed Jane Chatham goodbye. Mackenzie wrinkled her nose. "He thinks so much of himself." She noticed Justin wasn't in a big hurry to shift to the other side of the booth.

After a moment he seemed to remember where he was and moved to the other side. She kind of wished he hadn't.

"Let me ask you something," Justin said. "Is there any circumstance under which you'd rethink bringing back your family's business?"

His question stunned her. "I haven't thought about it. All my time and energy is devoted to my daughters. In fact, I need to be getting back. It's about time for their lunch."

He caught her hand. "Give me five minutes. Then I'll head back and give you a hand."

"I didn't hire you to be a—"

"Hanny."

She sighed, put her shoulder bag back down in the seat. "That's such a stupid expression. Only Ty could have thought of it."

"I like the little ladies." He looked at her. "I have the strangest sensation you don't really want to move."

"Nobody ever wants to move. Sometimes you suck it up and know that life will be good anyway."

"Yeah." He rubbed her fingers, and tiny sparks tingled inside her. She realized the diner had gone totally silent, everyone focused on them.

Oh, boy. She discreetly pulled her fingers away, then hid them in her lap.

"Sorry," he said, glancing around. "I forgot we're in BC."

For a moment, she had, too. It had felt like they were in their own world.

Which was probably not a good thing.

The people in the diner—folks she'd known all her life—slowly turned back to their meals, but the buzz around them was low and excited. Definitely the gossip bandwagon was rolling merrily along now. "To answer your question honestly and fairly, I wish I could keep the ranch for the girls. But it's precisely because of the girls that I won't."

"I get it. I really do. I grew up in Whitefish, Montana. I'll never live there." He shrugged. "Life moves on."

"It's not just that," Mackenzie began, and the diner door opened again and Daisy walked in with Frog on her arm looking like the cat that ate the canary.

"That's not right," Mackenzie said, and Justin turned to see what was going on.

"No, it's not," he said.

Daisy and Frog slid into the booth.

"Hello, boss lady," Frog said. "Justin, thanks for the afternoon off. I'm putting it to good advantage." He beamed at Daisy, who gave him such a sexy look that Mackenzie thought the napkins at the table might combust.

But then Daisy's gaze slid to Justin, and Mackenzie knew it was all a show.

Jane Chatham came over. "What can I get everyone?"

"Spice cake and an iced tea for me," Daisy said. "I want a piece with as much frosting as you can manage, Jane."

Frog looked besotted. "I'll have the same. Not so much frosting, though."

"I'll just stick with iced tea," Mackenzie said, wishing she could take off. She would go, except that Justin was looking at her with such an intense stare that her heart pounded. She wasn't about to leave him to Daisy's wiles.

That was a terrible thought she shouldn't even be thinking.

Didn't matter. "And a piece of spice cake," she added. *Might as well go the whole mile.*

"I figured you'd be watching your weight, Micki," Daisy said, bringing up an old nickname Mackenzie had always despised.

"I'll have some pecan pie," Justin said, cutting through the sudden tension at the table. "Hot coffee with that, if you don't mind, Jane."

"You should let me tell your fortune, Justin," Jane said, and Mackenzie looked at Justin to gauge his reaction.

Which was slightly amused.

"If it comes with the pie, I might take you up on it," Justin said, his tone easy.

It hit Mackenzie that Justin was trying to fit into the ways of BC, which probably weren't like any other town he'd lived in. Mackenzie hid a smile.

"Do let her, Justin," Daisy said. "You'll be surprised what Jane can tell you."

"I don't really believe in fortune-telling and horoscopes and hocus-pocus. No offense, Jane," Justin said.

Jane smiled. "None taken. How's the family in Whitefish?"

He blinked. "They're fine, thank you."

"Knee hasn't been bothering you as much, has it?"

"No, ma'am, it hasn't."

Daisy giggled. Frog looked at her as if a goddess had landed in his sphere and he couldn't quite figure out how it had happened.

"Four drinks and desserts coming right up." Jane went off, her stride all-business, as it always was. Mackenzie looked at Justin.

"She doesn't really tell fortunes as much as she reads people," Mackenzie told him.

"She listens to gossip very well," Justin said. "But what the heck. I'll play."

"Gossip?" Daisy looked adorably confused; clearly she'd decided adorable was the key to Justin's heart. "What does gossip have to do with anything?"

"I told her husband down at the feed store today that my father was having a bit of trouble on the ranch in Whitefish," Justin said. His gaze hooked on Mackenzie's. "I also mentioned that my knee was doing a lot better."

Mackenzie shook her head. "When is Ty leaving, anyway?"

"You're not going with him, are you?" Daisy asked,

her tone sweetly horrified. Designed to suck up to Justin's ego.

"Staying right here." He leaned back in the booth, winking at Mackenzie. "Not going any place anytime soon."

Warmth ran all over Mackenzie. She didn't look away from Justin's gaze, even though it was hot, hot, hot. No, she didn't look away, even though Daisy and Frog were kind of gawking at the two of them. Jane dropped off their desserts and drinks, just as they'd ordered, which seemed to surprise everyone at the table.

Then Justin shocked the entire diner by reaching over and placing his cowboy hat on top of Mackenzie's head.

"Little mama," he said, "you're the sexiest thing I've ever laid eyes on, and that's a fact."

And that was the moment Mackenzie felt herself falling.

It felt unexpectedly wonderful.

"No, Frog," Daisy said, glaring past him. He'd tried to plant a kiss on her and she was having none of that, as Justin could have foretold. In the shadows cast by the declining sun just dissipating around the barn, Justin shook his head. In a minute, he'd save Frog from himself—but not quite yet. It wouldn't hurt him to figure out that he wasn't quite the gift Daisy had led him to think he was. Oh, there'd be a little bit of ego bruising, but it wouldn't last long. Frog would snap back.

Frog tried again, a bit oblivious to the fact that he was out of Daisy's league. He'd really bought into Daisy's flirtation, which was dumb. Daisy flirted with every man.

Justin walked from the barn to the house on his way

inside to find Mackenzie and the babies. "Frog, I need you to change out every single lightbulb in the spotlights and the lanterns on the corrals."

His demand seemed to jerk Frog out of his Daisy spell. "All right. Night, Daisy."

"Good night," Daisy said absently.

Frog ambled off, his shoulders slumping a bit. Mackenzie came outside, looking from Justin to Daisy. "What are you doing here, Daisy?"

"I heard a piece of gossip in town that you might be reopening the Haunted H, Mackenzie," Daisy said. "I was a little surprised when Jane Chatham told me, because I know how devastated you were when that man died out here. They never figured out what happened to him, did they?"

Mackenzie's face turned pale as the moon. Daisy looked pleased with herself.

"That was ten years ago, Daisy." She turned to Justin. "I got your text. You're welcome to dinner if you'd like." She closed the door, leaving Justin with Daisy outside.

"What was that all about?" Justin asked Daisy, knowing full well she had something up her tight sleeve.

"Well, if Mackenzie hadn't slammed the door in my face, I was going to tell her I'd be happy to help with the Haunted H. I'm good with kids," Daisy said, turning on the cute as hard as she could.

Daisy help Mackenzie? He doubted that. "I'm sure she got the message. Good night."

He went inside. Mackenzie sat at the kitchen table with the four babies in their carriers, gently wiping their faces. She didn't look at him.

"So," he said, going to pick up Haven—she'd already

been given the cleaning treatment, so she smelled like sweet lavender. "You going to tell me what happened out here? Or are you going to let Daisy keep digging at you?"

Chapter 10

Mackenzie didn't say anything, and Justin thought he heard a sniffle, like maybe she was trying to hold back tears. He didn't know her well enough to say definitely, but Mackenzie didn't strike him as much of a crier.

Suz wandered into the room. "Here, give me Thing One," she said, trying to take Haven from him.

"Get your own Thing," he said, holding the baby against his chest so Suz couldn't get her.

Shrugging, Suz took Thing Number Two—Holly—out of her basket, kissed her and then caught a glimpse of Mackenzie's face. "Hey! Is he making you cry?" She glared at Justin. "You put Thing One back in her carrier and get out!"

"No!" Mackenzie shook her head. "I'm not crying, and nobody's putting any Things back!" She laughed, wiping her nose on a baby washcloth. "I wish you hadn't started calling the girls Things. It makes conversation really interesting."

"Yeah, well. I've been reading Dr. Seuss to the girls as part of their early reading program." She glared again at Justin. "You'd best watch yourself, Cowboy."

"Suz." Mackenzie took Heather out of her carrier and sat down to feed her. Justin couldn't bear it because that meant Hope was left with nobody to hold her, so he picked her up in his other arm. "Justin didn't do anything. I just let stupid old Daisy drag up ancient history. I shouldn't, but it happened."

"Is she still here? Because if she is, I'm going to kick her ass." Suz went to the window, but Justin had heard Daisy's motorcycle roar off a few minutes ago, saving her from the ass-kicking he had no doubt Suz could dish out. "Anyway, what's she hanging around here for?"

"She had a little outing with Frog." Mackenzie's gaze met Justin's. He got that jolt he always felt around Mackenzie and wished she'd let down her guard just an inch. An inch was all he'd need to get inside her heart.

"Daisy and Frog?" Suz came back to join them. Justin thought it was interesting that Suz looked surprised, and maybe not pleasantly. "Why would he want to take out the wicked witch of Bridesmaids Creek? Quite stupid, if you ask me. But that's a man for you." She drifted out of the room with Holly, cooing softly to her.

Mackenzie kissed the top of Heather's head. "Why was Frog hanging around with Daisy?"

"Because your sister turned him down flat as a very old pancake." Justin sighed, but the feeling of the two babies in his arms was at least comforting. "He had a momentary brain fart is the best way I can explain it."

"Frog seems to suffer from that."

"Yes, but don't tell Suz. Injured pride has been known to send a man into other arms."

Mackenzie didn't look convinced. "Weak argument."

"I'm just saying I think Daisy has strong allure. Frog's pride was dented. He folded when Daisy asked him to go running around today. But I suspect he'd rather Suz look on him with some fondness."

Mackenzie didn't say anything to that. She carried Heather from the room, and he followed. Together they placed the babies on a soft pallet in front of the fireplace, joining their sister Holly.

"You ever going to tell me about this information Daisy threw out that upset you so much?"

He sat on the sofa; she sat on the floor with her babies. He wished he dared pull out his phone and snap a photo of her. There was just nothing more beautiful than Mackenzie and those babies, a perfect four of a kind. A man could get real used to being around this little family.

"I don't like to talk about it. Suffice it to say someone died here. It made everything ugly. Before that happened, everyone looked at our children's haunted house as a wonderful, safe event. When the murderer was never found, it really hurt business. Mom and Dad held off as long as they could, and the town tried really hard to help. But the next year, attendance really dropped." She took a deep breath. "It's hard to erase such a stain, and my parents' health went down fast after that. First Dad went, and then Mom about five months later." She looked at Justin. "So, no, I'll never, ever reopen the haunted house."

"I don't blame you." He could make a little more sense of Ty's eagerness to help Mackenzie—although he was just as certain that Ty's idea of finding her a husband wasn't as brilliant as Ty thought it was. What he wanted to do more than anything was hold her in his arms, protect her from the sad memories he knew she could never forget. "How can I help you?"

"You can't." She looked at him. "But it means a lot that you want to, and I thank you for that."

He wanted to help her. Justin had never felt helpless before, but the fact was, he had nothing to offer Mackenzie. He could work at the ranch as long as she needed him, but so could the new guys. They were good men, hard workers. Eventually Mackenzie would sell the place—she'd said by Christmas.

There wasn't anything he could do for her.

She shocked him when she got up off the floor and sat next to him on the sofa, gazing into his eyes. "You don't have to rescue me. You don't have to take care of me. I know Ty sent you here on a mercy mission and I appreciate everything you've done. But I promise you, we'll be fine."

We'll be fine. Her and Suz and the angels. He glanced at the four babies on the floor, secure in their soft blankets, in the process of either practicing opening their eyelids or dozing off.

"I know you will." It was true. He wanted to kiss her in the worst way, feel her lips underneath his. Wanted to hold her in his arms. Didn't dare. Making more moves on the boss lady was no way to make her feel good about him staying around. And there was no way he wanted to leave. Mackenzie and her small, seemingly defenseless family had thoroughly stolen his heart.

A tap on the back door caught their attention, and Mackenzie went into the kitchen. Justin stared at the babies, thinking that whatever the ex hadn't seen in being a father to four daughters was completely obvious to him.

Frog, Sam and Squint walked in, following Mackenzie like puppies. "What's going on, fellows?" Justin asked.

"I—we have an idea," Sam said, and Justin thought, *Oh, no.*

"What's going on?" Suz asked, wandering in. "Sounds like Grand Central Station in here. I just started watching *Pride and Prejudice*, the 1940 version, and I can hear you over the Bennet sisters. Which is no easy feat."

She sat down cross-legged next to the blanket and picked up Holly, shooting an annoyed look Frog's way. Justin wondered if she even knew she'd done it.

"Sam has an idea," Justin said, his tone ironic. He arched a brow at Sam. "Go ahead. Share."

Mackenzie waved the men to some flowery chairs near the sofa, and they gawked at the babies.

"Four," Frog said. "I would never have believed all those babies could come out of such a little lady."

"Nice," Squint said. "Graceful even, Frog."

"Sorry." He honestly looked like he might be blushing. "I'm not always gifted with speech."

"No fooling." Suz looked pleased to get a dig in. Justin wondered if she felt more for Frog than she was letting on.

"What's your real name?" Justin demanded. "I can't go on calling you Frog. It's just all wrong," he said to the dark-haired big man.

Frog looked uncomfortable now that all the attention was squarely on him. "Francisco Rodriguez Olivier Grant. Mom was French, Dad was Spanish. They had some debate about how many relations in the family needed to be honored when I was born. Therefore, Frog. Deal with it."

Justin stared at him. "You're definitely not a Francisco."

His buddies laughed. "He's an F-R-O-G," Squint said.

"I think it's lovely," Mackenzie said quickly, and Justin gave her an appreciative look. He found himself feeling a little sorry for the big man.

"It's just a name," Suz said, and Frog perked up a bit. "They're all good names, too."

"My high school and college friends called me Rodriguez," Frog said. "It wasn't until the military that I became Frog."

Suz smiled at him. Practically batted her eyes.

"Now that we have that solved," Mackenzie said with a glance at Justin, "what idea do you want to share, Sam?"

He took a deep breath. "A cattle base, for one thing. You have enough land here to run about two dozen head. Could do milk goats, too. The whole organic thing has really taken off, and you have a great place here for opening your own organic kitchen and label."

Justin was stunned. "I didn't know you had it in you, Sam. I've misjudged you."

"Easy to do because I'm so quiet," he said, and they all hooted at him.

"Part two of the plan," Squint said, "is to consider storytelling tours. Like survival tours. People are interested in learning how to make their own cheese and raise their own organic food."

"And we'll all dress in costumes," Suz said. "I see where you're going with this."

They all looked at Mackenzie for her reaction. "I don't know what to say," she said, and Justin could tell she was truly caught off guard. "It's actually a brilliant idea."

"It's in the early phase," Frog said. "We've been brainstorming. Once we develop a business plan, we'll bring it to you."

Suz went into the kitchen, then brought back a tray of cookies and a pitcher of milk. "All that brainstorming probably has you hungry," she said, setting the tray down on the coffee table.

Justin noticed she handed Frog a napkin, then flounced over to pick up Heather, who was starting to stir, as if she hadn't treated Frog just a little bit differently than the other men.

"I don't know what to think." Mackenzie went into the kitchen to get a bottle, brought it back and handed it to Suz. "Someone's tummy tanked out a little sooner than her sisters'."

"I know how she feels," Frog said earnestly. "I'm always hungry."

Justin looked at Mackenzie. "Any chance you could hang on to this place if a workable business model was drawn up? You're busy with the babies, but these three seem pretty eager to keep their bunks here."

"Yes, we are," Squint said. "I never imagined I'd like living in a small town, but I have to say after Afghanistan I have a whole new perspective on small-town friendly."

Justin leaned back in his chair, pondering Squint's words. He had to give the three amigos points for coming up with an idea—and maybe not even a half-bad idea—for trying to help Mackenzie and Suz out. He studied the sisters—polar opposites—and wondered how Mackenzie would feel if she knew he felt the same as the three amigos.

As if this had become sort of a home—and she was the person he wanted to come home to every night, forever.

Not long after the guys had shared their business idea, they left, and to Mackenzie's surprise her sister went with them. "You don't mind?" Suz had asked Mackenzie, and Justin said he'd stay and help put the babies to bed, so Suz had bolted out the door.

They were going into town to "hunt up trouble," as Sam said, and Suz had said trouble sounded good to her. Mackenzie wondered if Justin would have liked to go hunting trouble, too.

"You could have gone with them." Mackenzie closed the nursery door after making sure the baby monitor was on and the babies were totally settled.

Justin gave her a long look she couldn't quite read. "I could have. Didn't want to get in the way of Frog trying to figure out Suz."

She smiled as they walked back into the family room. "You really think she'll look at him twice after he was seen out with Daisy?"

"That did seem to tweak your sister a bit." He sat on the sofa, lounging, long and lean and sexy. "In fact, I'd bet that's why she so eagerly went with them tonight."

Mackenzie looked at the tray of cookies that had been polished off pretty well. "I'm going to get a cup of hot tea. Can I get you one?"

He followed her into the kitchen. "I'll take a glass of iced tea." He then proceeded to get it himself. Justin put the teakettle on to heat while she got down a tea-cup and saucer.

It struck her that she liked this, the sort of family feeling of togetherness that she felt with Justin.

"So what did you really think about the boys' idea?" he asked.

She put some loose-leaf tea into a tea ball and set it into her cup. "I'm going to think it over."

He turned her toward him. "I know you'd like to stay here, Mackenzie. When I look at this house, I think of you. It's like you're a part of it."

"Thank you." His hand lingered at her elbow for just a moment, a moment too short.

"Don't let Daisy drive you away," he said.

She hesitated. "Daisy has nothing to do with it."

"Felt like she struck a nerve today with that speech about the dead guy."

A chill ran over Mackenzie. "I don't like it, but it doesn't define whether I sell or not. It's just about finances."

"And leaving memories behind."

She studied him as he leaned against the counter, his boots crossed, his gaze on her. "Maybe. Sometimes."

He nodded. "I understand wanting a fresh start."

The kettle whistled and he reached behind her to turn it off, brushing her arm ever so slightly. He looked down at her and then lowered his mouth to hers.

Thankfully. Mackenzie didn't think she could have waited any longer to kiss Justin. He kissed her so sweetly, then turned more demanding as she melted into him. She heard a little moan, realized it was coming from her. Ran her hands around his back to hold him close—sank into his body as he devoured her mouth.

She'd never been kissed like this. *Don't stop—this time, don't stop.* She felt as though she was going to jump out of her skin if she didn't get closer to him.

Bed, she wanted to say, but her mouth wouldn't say the word. "Make love to me," she whispered, her mouth desperately getting out what she felt, and he scooped her into his arms to carry her down the hall.

He glanced at the old-fashioned four-poster bed dressed in sky blue and white. "Feminine. Just like you."

He placed her on the bed, making short work of her clothes. She just as quickly got rid of his, dying to get her hands on the muscles and tanned skin she'd watched working many times. His hands were work-rough but gentle on her, and she moaned again, pulling him into the bed with her. He stroked a strand of her hair from her face.

"You're beautiful," he told her, then kissed her, taking his time. Mackenzie closed her eyes, letting his lips work magic on her.

More magic as he held her in his arms and made long, gentle love to her. Mackenzie felt herself waking, coming to life, amazed by how much wonder a man could make her feel. Like a princess, kissed awake by a prince, Mackenzie wanted the magic to last forever.

Justin jerked awake at the sound of motorcycles roaring up the drive. Sudden baby tears and snuffles jerked him out of bed. He glanced at his watch—two o'clock in the morning. There shouldn't be motorcycles gunning outside at this hour.

"What's going on?" Mackenzie asked, sitting up, switching on a bedside lamp. "Oh, the babies are awake. They don't usually get up this soon. All that noise must have woken them." She jumped out of bed and pulled on a robe, giving Justin a brief glimpse of bare skin he wished he could drag back to bed to kiss for a few more hours.

"I'll check out what's going on," he said. "You get the girls calmed down and I'll come help you."

"Thank you."

She dashed from the room. He'd sensed her hesitation, like she didn't want to accept that she needed his help.

He went to the kitchen door and hauled it open, prepared to give someone heck for being rodeo-loud when there were babies asleep—everyone in BC would know that it needed to be walking-on-eggshells quiet around here at this hour.

About six motorcycles wheeled around at the top of the drive—damn it, six—then drove past him, heading down the road, gunning like mad. One did a wheelie as it went by, and he recognized Daisy's long bronze hair and tight black gear.

He waited, but they didn't return. Damn them, they'd done a drive-by on purpose, either to wake the babies or to haze Mackenzie.

He went back inside, locking the door behind him. He headed straight to the nursery. Mackenzie had four unhappy little girls on her hands, and he couldn't blame them.

"Come here," he told Hope, picking her up. "Bottles or breast at this hour?"

"Bottles, I think. They're too upset from the noise." She rocked Haven, feeding her. "What was that?"

He turned on some soothing music on his phone, Brahms's lullaby, as he popped a bottle into Hope's mouth, soothing the two remaining girls so they could relax long enough to wait their turns. "About six motorcycles."

"Daisy's gang."

"Gang?" He glanced at her. "A real gang?"

Mackenzie shrugged. "They've always hung out together. I don't know what they do exactly, but everyone calls them a gang."

Justin took that in. "She ever done a drive-by before?"

"Not like that."

He rocked Hope, who had begun to turn into a sleepy, content baby again. Mackenzie changed Haven, slipped her into bed and picked up Holly. One more to soothe. "I'll ask her not to do it again."

"I will. Thanks."

She met his gaze, her eyes determined. "You know, it's okay to accept help," Justin said.

"I appreciate your offer. But I know what Daisy wants, and I need to tell her she's not going to get it."

He could respect that. Still he wanted to protect Mackenzie and her babies all the more. "If you sell, won't she get this place eventually?"

"It's her father's conglomerate." Mackenzie stood, rubbing Heather's back with a hand to calm her. "Mr. Donovan is well-known to play dirty to get what he wants. He and his partners have made so much money chewing off the best parts of BC that they think they're invincible. I won't sell to them."

"Won't he just send in a dummy buyer?"

Mackenzie looked at him. "I'll figure it out."

He nodded. She would; she'd think of something.

"Then again," Mackenzie said, "I've been giving serious consideration to the suggestions you and the other guys have come up with."

"Yeah?"

She came to him, and, still holding the baby, leaned down and kissed him a sweet, hot one on the mouth. "Yeah. What do you think about that?"

He swallowed hard. Told himself it was time to face his future. Bad knee and all, he could handle this family. This amazing woman was basically saying she saw them as something of a partnership.

"I like it," he said, pulling her and the baby into his lap next to Hope. "I like it a lot."

Chapter 11

"This was just delivered to us by courier," Suz said the next morning, waving a large brown envelope at Mackenzie. "Or should I say served?"

A little ice slid down Mackenzie's back at the word *served*. "Who is it from?"

"A Dallas law office." Suz tore it open. "What do you know? It's a love letter from the Donovan Corporation, and your dear ex, Tommy. They have formed a dubious partnership to take over the ranch."

"How can they?" Mackenzie went to stare over her sister's shoulder.

"Because you were married to Tommy," Suz said, studying the papers. "Apparently, he feels entitled to half the ranch, which he wants to sell to the Donovan Corporation, Daisy's father, in essence."

"He never owned half the ranch," Mackenzie said.

"It wasn't in his name. And nothing came up about it in the divorce proceedings."

"Therein lies the rub." They sat down on the sofa together. Suz and Mackenzie glanced up when Justin walked in. "You're just in time," Suz said. "You might as well enjoy the next phase of the thrilling saga, Hanging H Tough, since this concerns your employment."

"It's nothing," Mackenzie said quickly.

"It's something," Suz shot back. "We're being sued by your pinheaded ex and Daisy's greedy father."

Justin sat down across from them. "Can I help in any way?"

"Well, I guess you could marry my sister," Suz said, still staring at the papers.

"Suz!" Mackenzie shook her head. "I don't think that will help. Please excuse my sister, Justin. Sometimes she has a mouth problem."

He grinned. "I'm okay with little sister."

"It says here," Suz said, "that we're behind on taxes. Is that true?"

Mackenzie's mind raced. "I don't think so, but I was in the last stages of my pregnancy at tax time, so there's a chance it slipped my mind." Horrified, she pulled out her laptop to check her records. "I guess I didn't pay them. But we're still in the grace window. I just have to pay interest on what I owed, which is a bummer but not the end of the world."

Suz looked up. "Which means Daddy Donovan has someone working in the records office if he knows we're behind by a couple of months. Dirtbag."

Mackenzie took the paperwork from her sister. "So I'll go down and pay them right now."

Suz hopped to her feet. "I'll go with you. In case there's any trouble."

"No. You stay here with the babies, if you don't mind." The last thing she needed was Suz raising hell in the tax office.

Justin stood. "I'll drive you."

She met his eyes, grateful for his calm, nonjudgmental strength. "Thank you."

"Please pop someone for me, Justin," Suz said, "if they give my sister any trouble. She's far too nice for her own good."

He laughed. "No popping will be necessary. Just a check will probably solve the whole matter."

"And then Daddy Donovan can shove this silly suit right up his—"

"Suz." Mackenzie grabbed her purse, making sure her checkbook was inside. "The babies will be up any second, but Jade and Betty are on the way. I'll be back in an hour."

"Take your time," Suz said cheerfully. "The girls and I will hold down the fort. When they wake up, we'll have a long chat about how they're not to ever fall for Daisy's—or anyone's—baloney. They have to be Hawthorne tough."

Justin walked Mackenzie to his truck and opened her door for her. "Your sister doesn't pull her punches."

"She never has. She's serious when she says she'd pop Robert Donovan a good one. And nothing good can come of spitting in your enemy's eye." She wasn't being entirely honest—she was so steamed with Tommy right now that were she to run across him, she certainly would pop him a good one. The man had no scruples.

The fact that he planned to rob his own daughters' of their birthright inflamed her.

"You're quiet. You sure you're all right?"

She tried to gather her temper into a neat, tidy ball. "I'm furious, to be honest."

"You're quiet about it. Suz is loud." He reached for her fingers, held them in his warm, comforting hand. "Maybe her idea is worth considering, Mackenzie."

"What id— Oh, no, Justin. Suz was teasing about us getting married. Actually, she was being annoying." Could this get any more embarrassing? She didn't think so. He clearly felt her circumstances were so dire that he had to sacrifice himself, which was noble, but he didn't know that she could survive the Donovans. "You working at the ranch is enough. Everything else you're doing is beyond the call of duty. Please don't let all the Bridesmaids Creek fun and games get to you."

He released her fingers after a moment. Didn't say anything. Mackenzie looked out the window, her hands tight on her purse, furious with Daisy and Tommy more than Mr. Donovan. Daisy and her gang riding through the ranch last night, deliberately trying to create a ruckus and wake the babies, had been the last straw.

She wasn't going to put up with being harassed out of the home that was her daughters' birthright—if they wanted it.

Of course they would—they'd love growing up at the Hanging H just as she and Suz had.

"The Donovans and Tommy Fields aren't getting my house," she said, and Justin laughed.

"That's my girl."

Mackenzie blinked. His girl? How did that work?

Wasn't he Mr. Never-Settle-Down? "I hope you know what you're letting yourself in for."

He wore a confident, amused smile just shaded by his cowboy hat, and Mackenzie slid her fingers back into his, just to let him know he'd best beat a hasty retreat now while he had a chance.

His fingers tightened on hers.

Suz saw Frog and Co. across the way, and since Jade and Betty were already in the house cooing at the babies, she struck out to chat up Frog. That man had the wrong idea if he thought he was going to bark up Daisy's tree. The long, tall, sturdy cowboy appealed to her, and, one day, she planned to steal a kiss from Rodriguez Grant. "Hi!" she yelled, waving at the men so they'd stop. They turned, and Frog headed her way—just as Daisy's motorcycle ripped up the drive. She pulled between them, parked her bike, got off and removed her helmet.

She was grinning at Frog with a sassy smile. "Hello, Francisco Rodriguez Olivier Grant," she said, and something inside Suz hit the boiling point. She leaped onto Daisy, pushing her down, and the two of them rolled over and over in the dirt.

"Chick fight!" Squint hollered.

"It's not a chick fight until they start pulling hair," Sam said, but Suz was too busy trying to grind Daisy and her dumb lawsuit into the ground to care. Suz was small, but she was tough—the Peace Corps had focused her—and there was no way Daisy was getting up until her hair was full of twigs and dust and her chamois skirt with the fringe was a darker shade.

She felt Frog pulling her off Daisy and she fought wildly to shake him off. "What are you doing?"

"Keeping you from going to jail, tiger." He set her on her feet behind him and let Squint help Daisy up, which Squint was only too glad to do by the mesmerized expression on his face.

"Ladies, ladies," Frog said.

"Oh, shut up!" Daisy said, abandoning all pretense of being a delicate flower. She glared at Suz. "What the hell was that for?"

Suz grinned at the mess she'd made of Daisy. "For waking the babies last night when you rode through here with your band of rowdies. Next time you pull that stunt, I'll pick you off with a well-placed BB—"

"Now, now," Frog said, covering her mouth with his hand and pulling her toward the house. "You have a nice day, Miss Daisy. Suz can't play anymore."

Suz ripped his hand off her mouth. "Have you lost your mind? That bimbo's suing my sister and me! The least I can do is make her think twice about what she's doing!"

Frog gazed at her admiringly as he dragged her into the house and into the kitchen. He retrieved a wet paper towel and proceeded to wash her face. She snatched the towel away from him. "Stop babying me."

He smiled. "I haven't babied you yet. You'll know when I do—and you'll like it."

She sighed. "You're so full of horse pucky. You had no right to stop me from doling out some just deserts on Daisy."

"I can't have you going to jail, cupcake. And that

little lady is the type to press charges. You know what would happen if you went to jail?"

"I'd go to jail," Suz said, annoyed.

"And it would break my heart," Frog said.

She blinked. "Full of crap, Rodriguez."

He laughed. "You'll never know, love, unless you find out."

She had no intention of falling for his cowboy blather. "You can show yourself out."

"Yes, ma'am."

He did so, and Suz crept to the kitchen window to watch him walk away. The fellows were still standing around talking to Daisy, who was no doubt whining about the ever-so-tiny can of whup-ass Suz had uncorked on her.

Baby.

She was relieved to see Rodriguez walk a wide circle around Daisy and go into the bunkhouse.

"Smart man." *And a smart man is right up my alley.*

Justin was afraid Mackenzie was in over her head with the Donovan/ex-husband problem. Nothing good could come of the deck being stacked against her to that extent, and from the sound of things, there couldn't be a much worse posse to be after the Hanging H.

He waited while Mackenzie paid the tax bill, noting her relieved expression when she came out of the courthouse. "It's paid."

"Sorry you had to go through that." He helped her into the truck.

"It was embarrassing but nothing more." Mackenzie smiled at him. "Thanks for driving me."

He didn't say he wanted to be around in case there was a problem. His suspicion was that merely paying the tax bill wasn't going to be enough to stop Donovan and Tommy from teaming up to get Mackenzie and Suz's ranch. Back taxes had been the first look into how vulnerable the Hawthornes were. They'd find another crack to try to wedge open.

Very bad to have greedy takers in cahoots against you.

"You're going to need to consider legal counsel of your own," he said quietly, steering the truck toward the ranch.

"You think this won't be the end of the lawsuit?"

"I think that you're in a vulnerable spot and they're going to try to exploit that."

"Excuse me, but I don't feel particularly vulnerable."

He smiled. "That's good."

She sighed. "Oh, who am I kidding? You're right. The Donovans are known to be ruthless, and God knows Tommy is dumb enough to go along with anything if there's a buck involved."

He shook his head. "Wrapping up the estate for you and Suz would be a good idea. Do you have a will?"

"I'll call a lawyer. Get everything done." He felt her perk up beside him. "Monsieur Unmatchmaker will know who would be good in this situation."

He wished he felt comfortable about her asking legal advice from someone who billed himself as an unmatchmaker, but that was hardly his business. Mackenzie was vulnerable right now—any new mom would be, never mind a mom of quadruplets holding down a ranch basically on her own—but she also had a strong sense of independence. He was pretty certain she wouldn't appreciate him putting too much of his nose into her business until—if and when—she asked. She'd been recently burned by her divorce, and he didn't figure Mackenzie was all that interested in being overly advised by a man.

"Hey, what's Daisy doing here?" He pulled up the drive, surprised to see Daisy with Squint and Sam.

"Being her typical man-magnet self." Mackenzie hopped out of the truck. "Daisy, hit the road. Get off my property before I file a restraining order against you."

Justin switched off his truck right in the drive and strode after Mackenzie, whom he sensed was in no mood to be baited by Daisy. Mackenzie waved the brown envelope containing the lawsuit at Daisy.

"This isn't going to work," Mackenzie told Daisy. "I paid my tax bill. You're not going to get my ranch."

"You paid it?" Daisy looked at Justin. "Did he loan you money?"

Justin saw Mackenzie take a deep breath to contain her temper.

"Why would my employee need to loan me money, Daisy?" Mackenzie demanded.

"Everyone knows you're dead broke. Anyone would struggle with four kids. So it stands to reason—"

"Daisy, go away. Right now. I very seriously will file a complaint against you—what happened to your face?"

Justin had wondered the same thing.

"Your crazy sister happened to my face." Daisy looked to Squint and Sam for confirmation, and both men nodded.

"Suz?" Mackenzie headed toward the house.

"You put a muzzle on Suz, and I won't file charges

for physical violence, whatever it's called," Daisy called after her. "I've got three witnesses."

Mackenzie turned around, marching right back to the group. Justin steeled himself in case he was needed to protect Daisy.

"If you file anything against my sister," Mackenzie said, "you will wish you hadn't, Daisy."

"Why?" Daisy asked. "You have nothing. My father can buy and sell you all day long."

"And you think life is all about money?" Mackenzie asked.

Silently, Justin applauded this. "You'd best go, Daisy. The Hanging H is closed. You're trespassing."

Daisy glared at Justin. "I'll go, but this isn't the end of anything. Not by a long shot, Mackenzie."

Justin winced. Bad combination: Daddy's money and a spoiled brunette.

Daisy glared at all of them before she hopped on her motorcycle. "See you later, Squint, Sam."

He hauled ass after Mackenzie, who was long gone. Justin found her in the nursery, her hands on Suz's face, staring at the scratches on her sister's cheeks and arms.

"I just saw Daisy," Mackenzie said. "It looked like you won."

Suz looked pleased. "Never doubt it."

"Here's the thing," Justin said as Mackenzie hugged her sister. "I'll do the fighting from now on."

"You're a mom," Suz told Mackenzie before turning to Justin. "And you're not family. I'll do the fighting for the Hanging H."

"The next fight is going to be in a court of law." Mackenzie forced Suz to sit in a rocker. Smiling at her babies, she lifted Holly out of her crib when she started to stir. "Justin says we need to get some legal counsel, make certain everything is tied up tight."

"All of my portion can go to the girls," Suz said.

Mackenzie gasped. "Absolutely not!"

"It's not like I'm ever going to have kids." Suz glanced at Justin. "While the stork may not be finished visiting you."

Mackenzie blushed, which Justin thought was cute. She didn't look his way.

"Give me Holly," he said, reaching for the baby. "You girls have a lot to talk about. Holly and I will take a walk."

"There's no need." Mackenzie looked at him. "We're not talking anymore today. Suz needs to call up some friends and get out of the house for a change. Be a young person."

"I'll take care of your sister," Justin told Suz. "I agree with Mackenzie, though. I wouldn't make Daisy's life too miserable. We don't want her figuring out a way to have you arrested."

"The sheriff is a family friend," Suz said. "That's why the Donovans went straight to a lawsuit. They knew the sheriff's office would never bring any nonserious complaints to us. The town has been evenly split for a long time, with most folks siding with us instead of the Donovans. It chaps Daddy Donovan's big-bucks ass."

He looked at Mackenzie. She studied him for a minute, reached out to take Holly back. "You go, too."

Justin wasn't going anywhere. "I'd rather stay, if you don't mind."

Suz slipped out of the room. "I'm going into town," she called back down the hall.

"Suz is right," Mackenzie said. "You shouldn't try to fight our battles."

Justin shrugged. "I'm not fighting anything. But I'm here should you need anything."

"You've done enough." She kissed the top of Holly's head, and Justin felt something tug at his heart. "We weren't looking for a knight in shining armor."

"Well, I'm no knight, and I wouldn't be caught dead in medieval armor." He glanced around the room at the babies suddenly stirring. Heather tried to roll over without much success—she was too young for that but she gave it her best shot, craning her neck around—Haven blew a bubble, then spit up, which Mackenzie was quick to wipe away, and Hope looked like she was about to let rip an ear-stunner. "You're sure you want me to go?"

"Yes." Mackenzie nodded, juggling burp cloths and babies. "We'll manage."

He had no doubt of that. Still, he cruised down the hall into the kitchen to give her privacy but to remain within earshot in case baby pandemonium hit a freakish level. But all sounded calm down the hall: infant wails were addressed, and he could hear Mackenzie singing and cooing to her babies.

Maybe she didn't need him. Actually, he knew she didn't, but he was hoping he fit somewhere in her life.

Mackenzie had a lot on her plate. Perhaps the best thing to do would be to give her some space. He understood needing space—if he didn't, he'd be in Whitefish right now, on his father's ranch, taking over the family business. There was no reason to do that, not with three other able-bodied brothers who were more interested in it than he was, even if the old man said Justin was his top choice to take over.

Sometimes space was necessary.

He left the house, closing the door quietly behind him.

Mackenzie was startled when the front doorbell rang, since everyone always used the back door and most people walked right in, anyway. So it couldn't be Jade or Betty, or even Daisy, who used the back door as if she were one of the close-knit circle that visited the Hanging H. Casting a quick eye over the babies to make certain they were all secure for the two minutes she'd need to be gone, Mackenzie picked up Hope and took her to the door with her.

"Who is it?"

"Robert Donovan."

"Lovely," she said to Hope. "Gird yourself for the first true annoyance in your young life." She pulled the door open. "I thought you do all your talking through a lawyer."

Robert Donovan cast a tall shadow, and he wasn't a particularly friendly-looking character, either. He had buzzed short hair—too impatient to be bothered with combing it, she supposed—and a self-righteous smirk.

"I should have called on you sooner," Robert said. "Instead of sending my request through my lawyer, for which I apologize and hope to make amends. May I come in?"

"Absolutely not."

"It's difficult to discuss what I have to say standing on the—"

"Mr. Donovan, I have four babies. I don't have time for this. Say what you came to say."

His smirk widened. Mackenzie stared at him, wondering if the man might be an idiot. She was two seconds from slamming the door when he sighed.

"I'm an old man, Mackenzie."

"That sounds like a personal problem to me."

He laughed. "Indeed. But old men like to build kingdoms."

"All well and good, but not my problem." She glanced over her shoulder, wondering if she'd heard something. One ear stayed cocked to listen for the babies. In her arms, Hope stayed very still, gazing out into the sunlight, which tall Mr. Donovan mostly obscured. "Can you get to your point?"

"I'll send all four of your daughters to private colleges or university, and pay twice the offer I made you on your property, if you agree to sell it to me by September."

"This September," Mackenzie said flatly. "Less than thirty days."

He nodded. "I'll buy all your equipment, horses and so on. And I'll buy whatever house in town you would like, in your name, if you're out before the end of September."

She'd been wanting to sell, hadn't she? Said she would? It was a generous offer, more generous than any she'd ever get for the Hanging H most likely. "What makes you think the Hanging H is for sale?"

"I heard in town you're not interested in reopening your family's business and that you've got your hands too full to run the place. Noticed you've hired on new hands." Robert shrugged. "Wanted to see if I could help you out. As you may know, I'm a generous man where Bridesmaids Creek is concerned. I try to be very civic-minded."

"If you're so generous, why didn't you make me this offer instead of roping my ex into a deal with you?"

Robert smiled. "Actually, Mr. Fields contacted me on the matter."

Mackenzie's body tightened to perfect stillness. Hope bobbed a little in her arm. "It was Tommy's idea to file the lawsuit?"

The big man shrugged. "I generally prefer to work things out in person. Mr. Fields seemed to believe that as you'd parted on poor terms, as I believe he put it, the professionalism of legal papers would be a better instrument to conduct business."

That rat bastard. No scruples at all at trying to take his own daughters' inheritance.

"Mr. Donovan, the Hanging H isn't for sale. I'm not overwhelmed, contrary to what you might have heard." Mackenzie took a deep breath. "You're not the only one who likes to help out Bridesmaids Creek. My family spent many years building up this town, as you know, even though you only came here when Daisy was what? Two, three years old?"

Robert Donovan hated to be reminded that he wasn't born and bred BC, despised knowing that the town still considered him an outsider in spite of his money and the weight he liked to throw around.

"Daisy and Suz were in class together," Mackenzie said. "I remember it well when she came to the haunted house that year. She was afraid of the puppets, and one of the chickens pecked her finger and made her cry. City girls don't see that many chickens, of course, and she didn't know not to pull its feathers. But she's grown up a lot since then." Mackenzie kissed the top of Hope's head. "I do appreciate you stopping by and discussing your offer in person." She shook her head. "But if I were you, Mr. Donovan, I'd avoid doing business with Tommy Fields. No matter what he tells you, I'm difficult to deal with on any terms, whether legal instruments or face-to-face."

He looked frozen, not certain how to proceed.

She took another deep breath. "And the Haunted H will be open for business by October, so you're welcome to spread that news all over Bridesmaids Creek."

Mackenzie closed the door and walked into the kitchen, where she knew Justin would be sitting.

"I knew it was you I heard," she said. "Eavesdrop much?"

"I eavesdrop a lot, particularly when black Bentleys pull into your drive." Justin grinned. "Opening the Haunted H, huh?" He reached out to take Hope from her, snuggled her in his arms. "Your childhood just changed, sugar. You're going to grow up with a mother who runs a haunted house. How cool is that?"

Mackenzie shook her head and went to check on the other babies.

Cool? He had no idea.

Chapter 12

"I don't know what got into me, but I know it's the right thing to do, if all of you believe it's a good idea to bring the Haunted H back," Mackenzie told the people gathered in her kitchen. "I realized that this ranch isn't just mine—it's Bridesmaids Creek's, too. A lot of people have happy memories of this place, and I want my daughters to share those, as well as your children and grandchildren."

She pushed away the only bad memory she had of the Hanging H and looked at Frog, Sam, Squint, Suz, Jade, Betty and plenty of other townspeople who had showed up for the meeting.

"We'll all help," Jane Chatham said. "Let's open on a Sunday night, when our shops and diners are closed in town, so we can all be here. I, for one, look forward to celebrating the grand opening!"

"Good idea," Madame Matchmaker said. "Let's start small, get our feet wet. Not overpromise at first. It took your parents years to get the Haunted H built up to being the best children's harvest fun around."

"Agreed. Good idea." Mackenzie nodded. Suz grinned, delighted by Mackenzie's change of heart, and waved Haven's fist at her mother. Justin held Hope, Monsieur Matchmaker had Heather tucked into his arms and, for some reason Frog had ended up with Holly. Since Frog was wedged in as tight to Suz as he could get, maybe it wasn't all that surprising he'd ended up with a baby.

"What about the dead man?" Daisy's voice called from the back. "No report was ever filed on how he died. How do we know that doesn't happen again? It was a real black eye on Bridesmaids Creek, and we don't want another, bigger, black eye."

The room went deathly silent. A dark cloud seemed to rush past Mackenzie's eyes. "Why would anyone else die here?"

"We never knew what killed him. Could have been food poisoning. Could have been murder," Robert Donovan said.

Since she'd opened the meeting to anyone in BC who might be interested in learning more about the Haunted H reopening, Mackenzie wasn't all that shocked that the Donovans had showed up. Justin winked at her, fortifying her resolve.

"Food inspections are done routinely. It wasn't food poisoning."

"I'll say it wasn't!" Jane Chatham hopped to her feet. "Since my restaurant provides fifty percent of the food that comes to the haunted house, I sure hope you're not accusing me, Daisy Donovan!"

"Nor my cooking," Betty Harper said. "If Jane does half, I'm sure I contributed around twenty percent. Most of my ingredients are organic or grown by me and prepared by me." She stared around the room. "There's not a person in this room who has ever complained of food problems from my cooking!"

"Someone killed him," Robert said, throwing his weight around as usual. "And it didn't take too much digging to find out that the cause of death was undetermined on the death certificate."

"How would you know?" Sheriff Dennis McAdams said. "Death certificates can only be ordered by the family. Cause of death is private."

Robert sniffed. "Reporters dug that information up, Sheriff. Be fair. You've been covering for the Hawthornes long enough."

Mackenzie frowned. "Excuse me, no one covers for the Hawthornes. We pull our own around here."

"You're just mad," Suz piped up, "because we won't sell to you. Isn't that harassment or something, Sheriff?"

"There's probably a good case for it." Sheriff McAdams looked unimpressed by the Donovans' claim. "That man who died here was an out-of-towner, an unfortunate soul with no kin to claim him. The autopsy revealed nothing. Not sure what you're working at, Robert."

"Just saying that there was a stain on this place ever since that day, and everybody here knows it." Robert sat down, pleased with the trouble he'd caused.

"Anyway," Mackenzie said, refusing to let him get to her. "I want to open this to a vote. No one has to like the idea or participate. I'm doing this for my daughters, but if our town doesn't like the idea, if it no longer fits the needs of Bridesmaids Creek, I'm just as happy to be simply a mother and not the owner of an amusement park."

"All in?" Sheriff McAdams asked, and all hands went up but the Donovans' and their cronies'.

"Fine, fine. We're back in business, friends," Sheriff Dennis exclaimed.

Mackenzie met Justin's gaze, startled to see him smiling at her as he'd abstained from the vote. She'd expected that—he wasn't from here, and no matter what he said, he might not stay—but she felt his support, and it warmed her.

After the guests left, Justin waved and headed out the back door, as well. She hated to see him leave as she peeked out the window at him. Watched Daisy accost him, doing her best to crack his armor. Justin shook his head at her before he headed into the bunkhouse.

Daisy turned around, catching Mackenzie spying on her. Daisy glared and Mackenzie waved cheerfully, then went to check on her babies, still smiling.

Justin walked into the bunkhouse, his mind completely on the meeting that had just been conducted and the warmth he'd realized the town felt for Mackenzie and Suz. Favored daughters, for sure.

He'd never been a favored son, so seeing it in real life made him a little wistful for the family situation he didn't feel that he'd ever had—except for rodeo. Rodeo had been a different kind of family, but it had been all he'd had. It had sufficed.

Ty walked into the bunkhouse, slapped him on the back. "Mooning?"

"Have you ever known me to moon?" Justin demanded, returning the greeting. "Why are you here again?"

"BC is my home. You know that. I came to check on the boys." He glanced around. "Where is everyone?"

"Off working or finding trouble." Justin didn't really care. Sam, Squint and Frog had proved themselves able and hard workers. He didn't keep too close an eye on them.

"So you're happy with them."

He shrugged. "Sure. I don't think Mackenzie would have reopened the Haunted H without them being here."

Ty nodded. Grabbed himself a beer out of the fridge. "I've got a message to pass along from your family."

"Why?" Justin barely glanced his way. "Can't they call my cell?"

"It was just an offhand thing. I was out there doing some horse trading—"

"Stirring up trouble."

Ty shrugged. "I did need a new horse. And your father and brothers have the best around."

"I don't know anything about that."

"Yeah, you do. You can't go on being the rebel forever."

"Sure I can, if being a rebel means staying away from a place where you're not really wanted."

"Yeah, about that." Ty took a long drink of his beer. "Your dad's not doing too good. He didn't say it, but I think he wishes your mother would at least take a phone call from him."

"Can't help you much, old buddy."

"Justin, it's your dad. If you went home, you could set a lot right."

Justin fell into the nicely worn leather sofa, eyeing his friend. "Look, you brought me here. This was all your idea."

"Yeah, because Mackenzie needed help, and you needed a job. You were never going to rodeo again."

That stung more than it should have. "I'm twenty-seven. You don't know what might happen." He knew exactly what was going to happen. His knee injury was severe enough that surgery might fix it, but there'd be no guarantees of how stable it would be. He'd never rodeo again.

"But getting you on here wasn't a way to keep you away from your family. Now that you're not rodeoing anymore, they'd like to see you."

"You mean now that they've forgiven me for not staying to work the family business?" Justin shook his head. "I'm fine here." He wasn't about to leave Mackenzie and the babies just because his father had decided he finally wanted to acknowledge the prodigal son.

"You might think about it. No one is getting any younger, and you're not exactly barking up Mackenzie's tree. Believe me—I had high hopes on that," Ty said with a sigh. "But things would have happened between you by now if it was meant to be."

"Wait a minute." Justin glared at him. "You don't know that nothing's happened."

"Suz says it hasn't."

Great. Chatty little sis. "Let me worry about my personal life, okay? One thing has nothing to do with the other."

"Okay." Ty gave a melodramatic sigh. "Are you sure you're not bothered by the age thing?"

Justin blinked. "What age thing?"

"You know." Ty waved a hand in grandiose fashion. "You're twenty-seven. Mackenzie's thirty. She's already got four kids and you might want one yourself and she may have had enough of pregnancy."

"You're riding down a ridiculous road right now, bud."

"It all weighs on a man, I'm sure."

"I'm fine," Justin growled. "The reason nothing's happened is because the woman has plenty on her plate. Why do you think she's looking for a husband? To be honest, that seems like the last thing she wants."

"You have to change her mind."

"No, I don't," Justin said. "And you seriously need to butt out."

"All right," Ty said. "Don't say I never tried to help."

"There's help and then there's being freaking annoying."

Ty laughed. "So, Daisy and Frog, huh?"

"I doubt it very seriously. The lady in question is hot to trot for any man who may look her way. And if I didn't know better, I'd think Frog has eyes for Suz. But what do I know? I'm a cowboy, not Madame Matchmaker." He perked up. "I still think she'd be unhappy if she knew you were operating solo on this gig."

Ty laughed. "I have my marching orders from Madame Matchmaker—believe me."

Justin studied his friend. "Are you saying the two of you are working together?"

"You haven't been in BC long enough to know how things work, but this town is a team, old buddy. And once you're in the team's crosshairs, you're probably going down. Loner, rebel, family issues, financially independent, moody," Ty ticked off. "Then there's hardworking, determined, stubborn, good friend, loyal, daredevil. Catnip around here."

"BC's matchmaking is nothing more than coincidental. No more real than Jane Chatham's fortune-telling." Justin laughed. "Or that business about ladies swimming in Bridesmaids Creek and finding their soul mate."

"Okay, that one's a stretch. It's really just a charity function. But we like to see the gals in their bathing suits. And the week before it happens, we get everybody together to clean up the creek and we test the water. It serves many purposes, so don't critique our ways."

"I'm not." Justin held up a hand. "Just trying to figure out why BC runs so much on lucky charms and rabbits' feet."

"Don't knock it until you try it." Ty went to the door. "Be sure to call your father and brothers at some point. They're ready to hear from you."

He wasn't ready to hear from them.

"Do you know Suz is out there sucking face with Frog?" Ty suddenly whispered.

"I don't care."

He slapped Ty on the back, a brotherly pat, hardly anything at all. Ty coughed and said something about friends shouldn't damage other friend's lungs. Shaking his head, Justin went outside, where he saw Mackenzie loading the van with her babies.

He strode to help her, lifting the carriers into the van, securing seat belts, tucking in blankets. Holly and Haven writhed around, not happy to be stuffed in a car seat and placed backward; Heather looked around at whatever she could focus on. Hope fell right asleep, unconcerned.

"An outing for the girls?" Justin asked.

"Yes. I've taken the idea under advisement that I need to secure my paperwork for my daughters' future." She looked at him. "Now that we've definitely decided to stay."

"I was glad to hear you say it in the meeting." Relieved had been more like it. He couldn't bear the thought of this little family heading off without him, because it was for sure that wherever they went, they wouldn't need a foreman.

Which meant he had some thinking to do. Justin looked at Mackenzie. Her eyes were on him, and all he could think of was how badly he wanted to kiss her.

So he did.

Gently, softly, he kissed Mackenzie's lips, kissing her again and again when he felt her lips moving against his, seeking the same response he was looking for.

Then, to his disappointment, Mackenzie turned away. "I have to go, Justin."

After getting in the car, she switched it on, looked at him one last time and drove away.

She was fighting it hard. That was clear.

But why?

Chapter 13

"We hear that handsome cowboy is living with you," Jane Chatham said after helping her settle the babies in The Wedding Diner. They sat in a quadruple row of darling, and Mackenzie couldn't believe they had a father who wanted to take everything away from them. "Of course, I told everyone that wasn't true," Jane continued.

Mackenzie stared at Jane, stunned. "Why would people think that?"

"Probably because he's a hunk with your name written all over him. Maybe they're hoping for a wedding in this town." Jane smiled. "Most likely, folks want you to be happy. Everyone knows Tommy's been giving you a rough road."

"How is my name written on Justin?"

"I think it's the way he watched your every move in

that meeting. He's the real reason you're reopening the place, isn't he?"

Mackenzie shook her head. "My decision is about my daughters. And Suz. I know Suz can take care of herself, but the Hanging H is still her home and she wanted to remain there. Just about the easiest way I know to do that is to do what I know best, running a circus."

Jane smiled. "We'll all help you."

"Thank you."

"But you have powerful enemies in this town," Jane said, her voice suddenly changing. Mackenzie had heard that tone before. An icy premonition tickled at her.

"Enemies who would rather see the Hanging H burn than come back to life," Jane said softly. Mackenzie gasped and grabbed Jane's wrist. Jane jumped, her eyes settling on Mackenzie.

"Gracious! I've left you sitting with no tea and no cake, Mackenzie." Jane hopped up from the booth. "I got so excited to see the babies I forgot about serving you. Please excuse me!"

She hurried off, not taking Mackenzie's order, because she wouldn't have, anyway. But she also didn't remember a word of her warning, because that was how Jane's visions worked. She literally didn't remember having visions sometimes.

But Mackenzie would never forget it. Jane's words slid through her memory like an icy wind. Her premonition was too terrible to contemplate. Surely Daisy and her gang of rowdies wouldn't burn down the Hanging H just to make sure it never came back to its former glory.

But even she knew anything was possible.

Jane set a piece of frosted strawberry cake and a glass of iced tea in front of her. Mackenzie knew she couldn't eat a bite. She sipped at the tea, trying to clear the fear from herself. The babies lay still for the moment in their carriers, and Jane bent down to coo over them.

"You young ladies have no idea how much fun you're going to have as you grow up. It's not many kids who get to grow up in a true haunted house!"

Jane must be wrong. The Donovans didn't want the Hanging H enough to get it by foul means.

She remembered Robert Donovan with his astounding offer to take care of the girls' education, to buy her a home, and she swallowed hard. Jane knew everything. She'd been born here, as her mother and her grandmother had. The names of the first settlers who established and named Bridesmaids Creek were on a stone in the courthouse, and one of those names was Eliza Chatham, Jane's great-great-great-grandmother. "Why do you think Robert Donovan wants the Hanging H so badly?"

"It's very valuable real estate due to its location," Jane said without hesitating. "He's planning big things for Bridesmaids Creek."

Mackenzie sat very still. "Some of which we've managed to thwart."

"Yes, but he's still bought up a lot of Bridesmaids Creek establishments and land just the same." Jane smiled when Holly grabbed on to her finger. "Your ranch just happens to be the crown jewel."

She blinked. "How?"

"Mineral rights, I'd say. You've heard about all the new shale drilling going on." Jane got up. "There's some theory that your land might hold some undiscovered secrets. You should consider making certain the mineral rights to your land are held by you and nothing that Tommy can lay claim to."

"Tommy!" Mackenzie shook her head. "We weren't married long enough for him to have a claim. The divorce is final. He can't sue me for anything." Her mind whirled. "What else should I know?"

"That your cowboy has dubbed himself something of your protector, and that's nothing to sneeze at," Jane said and went off to serve some customers.

Mackenzie looked at the strawberry cake. Beautiful and no doubt tasty as always, but Mackenzie couldn't eat it.

Justin considered himself her protector? She didn't need a protector.

Who was she kidding? She needed all the friends she could get. And a man who really seemed to want to help take care of her ranch—wasn't that almost a fairy tale come true?

Daisy was waiting for her on her porch when she got home. Mackenzie lifted the carriers from her van and set them on the ground, trying hard not to wish that Daisy would simply turn into a toad and hop away.

She came over to help her carry the babies inside instead.

"It wasn't my idea to go after your land when you fell behind on your taxes," Daisy said as she carted Haven inside.

Mackenzie wished she had four arms so she could carry all her babies at once. She really didn't want Daisy near them, though she supposed she was being terribly ungrateful. But Daisy never gave without taking, and what she took usually left you with a painful hole somewhere. "You don't have to help. Thanks."

"I want to. I wish I had a baby." Daisy went back for Heather and set her inside the den beside Haven as Mackenzie toted Hope and Holly. The babies set up a huge wail, Hope spit up and Mackenzie had a strong urge to create a little mayhem herself.

"Look." Mackenzie sighed and tended to Hope's dirty dress. "It doesn't matter about the lawsuit. I'm just back from my lawyer's office, and the ranch and all its holdings are airtight and in no danger, from your father or Tommy or you. So, if you don't mind, please go away. I have a million things to do, and sparring with you isn't going to be part of the game plan."

Daisy looked at her as she went to the front door. "You know, when we were growing up, I always wished I was you and Suz. You had everything. You still do."

Mackenzie frowned. "What are you talking about?"

"You had two parents who loved you. A haunted house that was all anybody in Bridesmaids Creek ever talked about." Daisy shook her head. "You and Suz were like princesses."

Mackenzie had certainly never felt like a princess, and she knew Suz would laugh out loud at such a notion. "Your father wouldn't try to buy this ranch just because you want it, would he?"

"Of course not." Daisy shrugged. "Dad doesn't discuss his business deals with me. But I think he'd heard through the grapevine that you wanted to sell. He was trying to help you out, like he would a charity or a struggling business."

Mackenzie's eyes went wide. Suz came speeding into

the den, Justin not far behind. He came to stand beside Mackenzie, his warmth comforting.

"It's true," Daisy said. "You Hawthorne girls always had everything."

She left with a lingering, almost inviting, glance at Justin. He looked down at Mackenzie, searching her eyes, gauging her mood.

"Okay, Miss Fussbucket," Suz said, bending down to pick up Holly and comfort her. "Gracious, ladies, the wicked witch is gone. You can all relax and stop crying. Uncle Justin can't stand to see a woman cry."

"That's right," he said softly. "You're not going to, are you?" he asked Mackenzie.

"Of course not." She went to wash Hope up, trying to settle her nerves. Darn Daisy, anyway—always looking for a way to get under someone's skin.

And yet something about her story had rung so true, so honest.

"So what was Daisy doing here?" Suz demanded when she returned with a fresh dress on Hope. "Doing what Daisy does best, showing that the apple really doesn't fall far from the old tree?"

"You need a Daisy alarm," Justin said, bringing baby bottles from the kitchen. "She sat on the porch for an hour waiting on you. I couldn't convince her that you'd gone to visit family in another state."

"Because we don't have family in another state," Suz said. "Nice try. Unlike Daisy, we've been in BC since we first saw daylight."

Mackenzie sat on the sofa and picked up a bottle to start feeding Hope. "I think that's part of Daisy's problem. She claims she was always jealous of us."

"The girl who has it all? I doubt it." Suz plunked

down with Heather and grabbed a bottle from Justin. "Don't let her work on you. You know that's what Daisy does best, gnaw away at something until it finally cracks."

Mackenzie smiled at Justin as he carried Holly to the window to check the front of the house. "We could turn the tables on her. Include her."

Suz's jaw dropped. "Include her in what?"

"The planning and setup for the haunted house. Put her in charge of a committee." Mackenzie caught Justin's expression and had a sudden flash memory of his kiss that morning. Jane's words about the handsome cowboy living with her made her look away.

What a silly rumor.

"Jane had a vision while I was at The Wedding Diner today," Mackenzie said, and Justin made what sounded like a scoffing noise.

"Oh?" Suz perked up. "I hope it was a juicy one!"

"You don't really believe in that nonsense," Justin said. "Isn't that just another way to sell Bridesmaids Creek's many tales of make-believe? Kind of like the small towns who rely on their ghost stories and sightings for tourist trade?"

Suz gasped. "Justin! Those are practically fighting words in BC! Our livelihood depends on our small-town charms!"

He looked at Mackenzie, who shrugged. "It was a real vision." There was no mistaking it when Jane went into a trance.

"So? So?" Suz prompted.

"She said the Hanging H is going to burn to the ground," Mackenzie said.

The babies all set up a tremendous wail, despite their bottles, almost like a sudden attack of four-way colic.

"Gosh!" Suz scrambled to grab Haven, who'd been so patient about waiting her turn. "You'd think they knew what we were talking about!"

Justin's mouth was set in a firm line the next time Mackenzie looked up. It had taken a full five minutes to calm the babies, but what Jane had seen still hung in the air, a specter that probably wasn't going to go away anytime soon.

"Look," Justin said slowly, "I'm no expert on BC. But I don't believe in spells or magic or visions. A bull rider might be superstitious, sure, but most of the time he's thinking about winning, not getting crushed under a bull. He can't afford to think about negative karma. I think it's best if you don't let word become deed, in Jane Chatham's case." He shrugged. "Not that my opinion counts for anything."

Suz's eyes were wide. "It is a terrible thought, Mackenzie."

She felt horrible that she'd brought it up. She'd just wanted so badly to get it off her mind, out of her head and into the daylight where it could be laughed away.

It just wasn't a laughing matter.

"It's okay," she said quickly, wanting to soothe the horrified look from Suz's eyes. "I shouldn't have told you."

"Of course you should have," Justin said, crossing back to the window. "Because you can't handle everything yourself. That's what friends are for, to share the load."

"That's right," Suz said. "We can't let Daisy and Jane and other people deter us from our goal, which is to bring the Hanging H back to all its wonderful splendor. I think Mom and Dad would be proud of us, don't you?"

Mackenzie looked at her little sister. In spite of her worldliness, Suz would always be her best friend and her connection to the family they'd once been. Suz was tough, but she could also be that child who tagged along after her big sister looking for reassurance. She remembered the scare when Suz had fallen from a tree, breaking her arm, and the late-night run to the emergency room in Austin when Suz had come down with meningitis. It had been so scary, such a frightening time. Mackenzie had been terrified she might lose her only sibling—the tiny baby her parents had brought home one day and allowed her to name. Betty Harper had come to babysit Mackenzie while her parents had taken Suz to the hospital, and Jade had comforted her, telling her she'd always be her friend.

Mackenzie caught Justin's gaze on her, and she needed desperately to change the subject. "Jane isn't all about visions. She also mentioned some folks in town seem to think you're living with me."

"Oh?" He raised a brow, seemed amused.

"I just mention it in case you're worried about your reputation."

He laughed. "A lot of BC gossip tends to be about this place, doesn't it?"

"It's not surprising when it's a onetime haunted house and one of the owners has four children all at once. Tends to make folks talk," Suz said practically.

He shook his head and turned away. Mackenzie caught him smiling, though. The only reason she'd brought the rumor up was to get his reaction and test that rebel reputation he held so dear.

"Guess I'd have to be pretty thin-skinned to worry about a rumor," Justin said.

"One never knows how a man feels about being the subject of such a rumor," Mackenzie said, knowing she sounded prim.

Suz laughed. "Men love it when ladies talk about them. Justin has all kinds of a reputation in town for being a major ladies' man."

Mackenzie stared at her sister. "How do you know that?"

"Because people don't just gossip about the Hanging H," Suz said. "They also gossip about newcomers. And the newcomers du jour are Justin and the three hunks we've hired on. Justin's right about this place being a gossip factory." Suz kissed the baby she held as she looked at Justin. "I've heard everything from you're married, to you didn't really leave the circuit because of your knee but because your heart was broken by a cheating fiancée, to—"

Suz's teasing words came to a stop. Justin's expression had turned grim. He put his baby gently onto the pallet, astonishing all of them, and walked out of the room. They heard the kitchen door close.

"Gosh! Was it something I said?" Suz asked.

Apparently so. But clearly Justin wasn't about to deny any of the rumors.

Chapter 14

Ty strolled into the kitchen the next day, pretty much grinning from ear to ear.

"Why are you so disgustingly happy?" Suz demanded.

"Life is good. Why shouldn't I smile?" Ty glanced at the four babies Suz and Mackenzie had put in the kitchen in a playpen while they did some baking. It was never too early to begin baking and freezing the treats the Haunted H was known for. "Anyway, I heard the big meeting is being held here today to discuss opening this joint back up."

"You missed it by a day," Mackenzie said, slightly miffed with Ty. The way Justin had lit out last night made it obvious that he wasn't the no-strings-attached bachelor Ty had portrayed him as—which was worrying, since Mackenzie recognized she'd begun falling for her foreman. "How does it feel to know that your usually sterling gossip line has failed you?"

Confusion crossed Ty's face. "The meeting was yesterday?"

"Yes, it was. And we are open for business," Suz said. "Do you want an assignment? We could put you in charge of the petting zoo. Maybe the carriage rides or the toss-the-water-balloon-at-the-clown game. That would be my choice for you."

Ty sank onto a barstool. "You can't reopen."

Mackenzie looked up from diapering Hope. "Why not? Everyone who was here for the meeting voted the idea in unanimously. They're looking forward to bringing tourists back here. Except for the Donovans, obviously. They were 'no' votes, but they don't count."

"I get it," Ty said. "But Justin's leaving."

"We don't need Justin," Suz said. "We can stand on our own two feet."

"What do you mean, Justin's leaving?" Mackenzie demanded, her heart skipping a beat.

"He called last night. Said he was ready to take me up on my offer. I'm here to pick him up. Didn't you know?" Ty asked, looking at her closely.

"Like any employee, Justin's free to give notice whenever it suits him," Mackenzie said, fibbing through her teeth so Ty wouldn't know how stunned she was. She felt Suz's stare on her.

Ty shifted uncomfortably. "He didn't sound too good when he called. He sounded like he had a lot on his mind, needed to unwind."

"Justin's personal affairs are his own business," Mackenzie said, dying a little inside.

"You're not as smooth as I thought you were," Suz told Ty, who looked a little disturbed by this news.

"If you'll both excuse me, and keep an eye on the babies," Mackenzie said, "I'm going to go hunt up my foreman. I'll let him know you're here."

She went out the door, heading across to the barns, anger carrying her boots across the dirt-and-stone path quickly. Justin was in the paddock behind the barn, working with a large chestnut. Mackenzie went up to him slowly so she wouldn't startle the horse.

"Ty's here."

"Great. Thanks." He patted the horse on the neck, praising it for its good work. "Listen, about yesterday, I want you to know that none of that gossip Suz was teasing me about is true."

He walked the horse to the barn, and Mackenzie followed. "Is that why you're leaving? Because of the gossip?"

Justin shook his head. "I'm not going anywhere."

Mackenzie stopped, eyeing him as he hosed the horse down. "Ty says you called him to say you're ready to hit the road again."

Justin nodded. "I'm ready to help him out. But I have no intention of leaving anytime soon." He glanced at her. "Did you think I was leaving? Is that why you came out here with a full head of steam? I could tell by the starch in your march that you were pissed about something. Had no idea it was me." He grinned. "On the other hand, I kind of like the idea that it would matter to you if I left."

"Of course it would matter. You're the foreman."

He nodded. "Okay."

She put her hands on her hips. "Were you testing me? My feelings?"

"No. I think I know what your feelings for me are."

He couldn't possibly know. She didn't even know herself, not anything she could admit out loud, to him or anyone else. "What do you think my feelings are?"

Justin shrugged. "You don't trust a relationship enough to allow yourself to fall into one right now. So just about anything I do, anything you feel for me, won't be enough to change your mind."

Mackenzie caught her breath. She'd expected anything but his stark assessment—which hit so close to the truth she didn't know what to say. She watched as he put the chestnut in its stall. "So you're leaving because of me?"

He came out, peering back in at the horse, who was now munching hay, then turned to face Mackenzie. "Not today, not for a while. But it's for the best."

She stared up at him. "I don't know what to say."

He touched her face, gently stroking a finger down her cheek. "There's nothing to say."

That was also uncomfortably true. Mackenzie nodded. She wished it were different, but he was right. She wasn't in a place right now to fall headlong in love. She couldn't allow herself to do it. There were the babies to consider—if she was going to get involved in a relationship, it would be with a man who would be a good father to her daughters—and there was the ranch to think about.

"It's all right," Justin said. "I understand more than you think I do. And if you want me to leave sooner, I can. No questions asked."

She shook her head. "Of course not. You're an important part of the ranch."

"I'm training my backup as fast as I can," he said, his tone a little teasing, but Mackenzie didn't smile.

"Frog, Sam and Squint are nice and they're hard workers." She looked into his eyes. "I'd like to keep you on as long as you're comfortable staying."

"I'll help out until October. That's when Ty's planning to hit the road looking for recruits."

Ty had done this—he'd brought a man here he knew she might find irresistible. When she didn't fall fast enough, he'd sent three more to sweeten the pot, which had only made Justin seem even more appealing by comparison.

She'd fallen for Justin, whether she wanted to admit it or not.

"Can I ask you a question?" Justin said.

"Sure." She gazed up at him, wondering if it would be any easier to say goodbye to him in a few weeks than it would be today.

It wouldn't.

"Did you believe any of that silly gossip Suz brought home? That bit about me being married or having a broken heart or something?"

She couldn't look away from the intensity in his eyes. "I didn't know."

"You don't trust me." He touched her cheek again. "I'm sorry that you don't."

It was true—she'd been upset because she'd been afraid something in the rumors meant that he wasn't the man he appeared to be. They'd never discussed personal issues—for all she knew, he'd had a love life he didn't want to discuss. The fear had worried her, slicing into her feelings for him.

She couldn't deny the gossip had hit her hard. Justin was right: she hadn't trusted him, hadn't trusted the lovemaking they'd shared.

After a long look into her eyes, Justin nodded, turned and walked out of the barn.

Mackenzie went back to the house, the babies and the baking, her heart splintered and ragged.

Squint, Frog and Sam were gathered around the babies on the floor, playing with them and gazing up at Suz, who was too busy rolling out dough to pay attention to their adoring looks.

Suz was totally oblivious to the heartsick look on Frog's—Suz called him Rodriguez only—face. She would never believe he cared about her after she'd seen him out with Daisy. Mackenzie grabbed the basket of cookie cutters and began pressing them into the dough.

"You're stabbing it," Suz complained, removing the heart-shaped cookie cutter from her sister's hand. "It requires a delicate touch, and that's something you don't have today. You can press cookies tomorrow when you're not taking your mood out on the poor dough. You do the sprinkles. And make them colorful and happy, not dark and moody."

"Moody?" Frog said. "You moody, Mackenzie? How can anyone be moody looking at these little princesses?" He cooed at the babies like a pro. Suz stared down at him, astonished.

"Get up, Rodriguez. You're making me nervous," Suz said. "You're sounding uncomfortably fatherly."

Mackenzie smiled until she saw Daisy roaring up the drive on her motorcycle. The men jumped to their feet like a food truck had arrived and hustled outside—except for Frog. He stared at Suz, one brow cocked. Mackenzie held her breath.

"Go on," Suz said. "I know it's killing you, Rodriguez."

"What's killing me?"

Suz put the cookie dough down. "Look. I know they say a girl has to kiss a lot of frogs to find her prince, but I'm not looking for a prince, so you might as well exercise those hunk skills elsewhere."

Frog looked to Mackenzie, who couldn't move, didn't know what to say. After a minute, he shrugged and went out the door.

"What did you do that for?" Mackenzie demanded.

"He was dying to go see Easy Rider," Suz said flippantly.

"I don't think so," Mackenzie said. "Pretty sure you sent him away. Why?"

"Why do you keep pushing Justin away?" Suz slung some cookies into the oven.

"I don't." Mackenzie flicked a few sprinkles onto the cookies and wished Suz hadn't brought that up. "It's none of my business what Justin does with his time off. You, on the other hand, are definitely being courted. I'm sure of it."

"Oh, Rodriguez is just a ladies' man," Suz began, but the back door flew open and Daisy marched in, waving a fistful of papers.

"These are the signatures of all the people here who don't want the haunted house reopening," Daisy announced. "There's over five hundred, and for a town of two thousand, that's a quarter of our population."

"How many fake signatures on that petition?" Suz asked sweetly, snatching the papers from Daisy's hand.

"All real and verifiable. Not everybody thinks that haunted house did great things for this town. Folks are concerned about the traffic, the parking problems, the trash violations, the pollution, the increase in theft as strangers are drawn here." She smiled triumphantly. "Some of us want our quiet little town to stay quiet."

Suz studied the papers. "The first five names on here are just your usual band of rowdies, Daisy. Carson Dare, Dig Bailey, Clint Shanahan, Red Holmes and Gabriel Conyers. Nothing new to see. We'd expect them to back you."

"Keep reading," Daisy said, her tone challenging.

Mackenzie took half the papers from her sister to cast an eye over the names. "Monsieur Unmatchmaker?"

Daisy nodded, delighted to let a little air out of Mackenzie's happy balloon.

"But Cosette is with us," Mackenzie said. "She was at the meeting yesterday and voted for it."

"As you know, those two commonly play on opposite sides. It's what makes their marriage tick." Daisy admired her nails and sat down on a barstool without asking if she was welcome, which she wasn't. That wouldn't matter to Daisy.

Mackenzie's heart sank as she read over the names, realizing the signatures were legit and recognizing some of the people she'd never imagined might not be supportive of the Haunted H reopening.

Justin walked into the kitchen, and it was as if someone threw a switch in the room and shined a light on Daisy. "Hello, Justin," she said, crossing her legs to show off smooth skin ending in a sexy pair of white cowboy boots that went perfectly with her carnation-pink sundress.

Justin nodded. "Daisy. Suz. Mackenzie, have you got a second?"

Mackenzie handed the papers back to Suz. "Sure." She followed him out. "What's going on?"

"I just got a call from my brother, Jack. He says my father's in the hospital with a little summer cold that seems to be settling in his lungs. They're worried enough to call me. Dad's always been strong as an ox, but apparently he's asking for me. This time I feel I need to go."

"I'm so sorry! We'll be fine here. Don't worry about a thing."

He gazed down at her, so strong and handsome her heart beat harder. The first thought that came to her mind was, *What if he never comes back?*

That was silly. Of course he would.

"Are you leaving today?"

He nodded. "I think it's best. The guys are going to take me to the airport."

He was leaving his truck here—a thought Mackenzie found a little comforting. "Can I do anything besides be selfishly hopeful that everything will be fine with your father and that you'll come back?"

He smiled. Touched her cheek. "I can't make any promises."

"I know." What was she, three years old? She felt needy for even having said it. Justin had mentioned that his father wanted him to take over the family business. If something happened to his father, Justin would have to do what he had to do. "Of course you can't. What time is your flight?"

"I need to leave now." He waved toward the window; she saw Rodriguez loading a duffel bag into his truck. "I was able to catch a flight this afternoon."

It was happening too fast. She tried to think past the sudden realization that the weeks Justin had been at the ranch might be over, felt selfish for even thinking it when he was worried about his father. "Safe travels. I'll be thinking about your father. And you."

Justin nodded. "Thanks."

He looked like he wanted to say something else, but he turned and walked out instead. Mackenzie stood still, waving as they pulled away, Rodriguez driving, Squint and Sam in the back of the cab.

Just like that, Justin was gone.

Mackenzie went back inside. All four babies were wailing up a storm, and the look on Daisy's face was priceless. Suz ignored the whole scene, blithely rolling dough.

"I guess I'll go," Daisy said.

"Now that the guys are gone," Suz observed icily.

"Now that I've explained the situation about how BC really feels about your haunted house," Daisy said. "Not that I enjoy being the bearer of bad news. Goodness, those babies are *loud!*"

She shot out the door. Suz dropped her rolling pin and rushed to the babies. "What good girls you are to chase off the wicked witch! Let Aunt Suz kiss you and hug you darling little things!" She scooped up Heather and Hope, and Mackenzie grabbed Haven and Holly.

"Suz," Mackenzie said, trying not to smile, "did you use my daughters as weapons against Daisy?"

"Darn right!" She kissed the babies' heads as she

grabbed bottles of formula she'd been warming in a bowl of hot water. "Are you nursing?"

"Slowly weaning. Four is just about too much for me, and they seem to appreciate the speed of the bottle."

"That's a Hawthorne for you, expediency over everything." Mackenzie and Suz each grabbed bottles, testing them to see if the chill was off. The babies writhed, wailing unhappily.

"I didn't let them howl long," Suz said. "Just long enough to knock the self-righteous smirk off ol' Daiz's face and send her skittering out of here like a roach."

Mackenzie giggled in spite of herself. "A little mean."

"And effective. So," Suz said. "Rodriguez texted me that he was taking Justin to the airport. What gives?"

"Family emergency." It would do no good to worry about Justin; he was a big boy. Still, that was small comfort. "His dad's fallen ill."

"He'll be back," Suz said confidently. They settled the babies into the carriers on top of the kitchen table, sitting them up, each feeding two babies at a time. "Do you realize you're going to have to buy four prom gowns at a time? Save for four college educations?"

"They'll have to work to go to college, of course. But I'll help them all I can." Mackenzie smiled at her daughters. "It's kind of fun to imagine the future."

"Do you see Justin in that future?"

Mackenzie glanced at her sister. "I'm sort of on a day-to-day schedule in my life right now."

"Daisy noticed Justin didn't kiss you goodbye. She was watching, spying like she was in the CIA or something. It was awesome when the babies let it rip because I knew Daisy couldn't stand not being the center of attention." Suz giggled. "I was hoping one of them would have a nice pooey diaper to add to the general ruckus, because I just know Daisy's perfect little nose would have wrinkled up like an accordion." She looked pleased with the image.

"What difference does it make to Daisy if Justin kissed me or not? Why would he have, anyway?" Mackenzie wasn't going to admit that she'd been disappointed he hadn't kissed her, too.

Suz shrugged. "Easy, young ladies. You don't have to suck down the whole bottle at once." She took a napkin and dabbed at their chins. "Kind of figures he might want a little sugar for the road."

Mackenzie had certainly hoped so, and the fact that Daisy had noticed Justin hadn't kissed her was annoying. "You have my permission to tell Daisy and everyone else in BC that the sugar will be waiting right here for Justin whenever he gets back."

"I'll do it," Suz said, with a mysterious little smile. "You can bet I will."

Chapter 15

When Justin returned to Bridesmaids Creek two weeks later, he was greeted like a long-lost hero, a virtual rock star in a small town of folks who suddenly knew all about him and his business. And seemed to think he was getting married.

Cosette—Madame Matchmaker—beamed at him, waving him over from her booth in The Wedding Diner. "Justin! You're back!"

He went to join her, and she practically pulled him into her booth. "My flight got in about two hours ago. I took a taxi out here, thought I might pick up some goodies from Jane." It had been his intention to eat a hot meal, then head to the Hawthorne spread. If he ate now, he wouldn't be tempted to grab something from Mackenzie's kitchen. All of this had seemed like a good idea until he'd been stopped on the sidewalk by so many people inquiring after his father and his family and wondering if he was back for good. And letting him know how very glad they were that he was back.

It was quite suspicious, but it wasn't until Daisy had sidled up to him and said, "So I hear you're practically ready to propose to Mackenzie," that he realized something had gone terribly wrong while he was gone.

"So," Cosette said, her eyes twinkling. Justin steeled himself, and, sure enough, she didn't sugarcoat it. "Word is you'll not be needing my services."

He sighed. Accepted the cup of coffee Jane Chatham brought him with a nod, wasn't shocked at all when she pushed Cosette over in the booth and plopped down beside her, her eyes eager.

"Did something happen while I was gone?" Justin asked. If anybody knew what was going on, it was probably these two. "There seems to be a consensus of opinion that I'm looking for a bride."

Cosette grinned. "We did hear something of the sort."

Jane nodded. "Yes, we did. What can I get you to eat, Justin? You've been gone so long that I'll be happy to whip you up anything you want. I just know you're ready for some pot roast and mashed potatoes!"

He was getting the full treatment if Jane wasn't just going to put whatever she had in the kitchen in front of him. "That sounds wonderful. Thank you."

She made no move to leave the booth. He sighed.

"I don't know what happened, but I'm not getting married. Nor do I think the lady in question has any interest, anyway." He looked at them curiously. "Mind if I ask what got everyone all stirred up? I've been asked by about ten people when the wedding is just in the five minutes I was on the pavement outside."

Cosette grinned. "Suz told us all about it. She said Mackenzie can't wait for you to get home so she can give you lots of love and affection. That she misses you like a baby misses a tooth!"

Suz. It sort of made sense. "Suz is wrong. And I'm sure Mackenzie's going to give her what for when she hears what her sister's been sharing."

Jane and Cosette looked crushed. "You have no intentions at all?" Jane asked.

He wondered if he was still going to get the pot roast. Or anything at all to eat. "No intentions. I'm betting Mackenzie doesn't want me to have any intentions. Ladies, she's been pretty clear that ours is a professional relationship. I'm sure she's still not thrilled about her ex-husband and not ready to jump into another relationship." He wasn't any happier about it than they were, but he understood why Mackenzie wasn't looking for a new guy in her life.

Cosette and Jane looked so disturbed he knew he'd hit some kind of nerve.

"They weren't married very long," Jane said. "Tommy just did not turn out as expected."

"Yeah, we kind of misfired on that one." Cosette looked really down about it. "I look forward to the day we can erase that mistake from BC's books."

"Tommy was one of your deals? A Madame Matchmaker fix-up? Ty claimed he misfired."

Cosette and Jane's faces remained glum.

"Bridesmaids Creek is a family. One for all and all for one, or at least that's how most of us feel. Anyway," Cosette said, "never mind. Sorry for poking our noses where they weren't wanted, especially since we were really off-base. We don't usually embarrass ourselves this way."

Jane nodded. "We are the souls of discretion and genteel manners, usually. Sorry about that, Justin."

They vacated his booth like puffs of gentle wind. Justin sat alone with his coffee, which was getting cold, and his pride, which certainly was even colder and lonelier. Drumming his fingers on the tabletop, he wondered if the pot roast might ever arrive, figured it wouldn't. The ladies had clean forgotten about him now that he wasn't toting an engagement ring.

Which made him wonder if he should be.

Nah. Mackenzie didn't feel that way about him. She wasn't in love with him.

Was he in love with her?

Justin rubbed at the stubble that had grown during the past couple of weeks he'd been sitting by his father's side. He'd finally shaken off the pneumonia well enough to go home, got strong enough to tweak Justin about coming home to help with the ranch, run the family business. His brothers weren't really interested or suited. One was a fireman, another a big trader who at least kept the books but wasn't up for the running of a spread. Justin could appreciate that. A man either had the land in his soul or he didn't.

Justin did. But the land he felt strongly about was the land where Mackenzie and her babies were. Anywhere—it didn't matter. But he wanted to be with her, whether she ever felt anything for him or not.

He realized everyone in the diner was staring at him, curious, having already gotten the word from Jane and Cosette—however gossip was communicated here, ei-

ther by osmosis or by superfast BC grapevine, he didn't
know. Didn't matter. He could tell by the gawks and
sympathetic—sometimes disappointed—faces that he
wasn't the homecoming hero come to sweep their princess off her feet that they'd been hoping he was.

Still no pot roast, either, and he wasn't getting any.
Justin stood, nodded to the diners who suddenly weren't
staring, left a couple of dollars on the table for the cold
coffee and headed to the Hanging H.

Mackenzie hung up the phone and whirled to face
Suz. "Betty Harper just called! She said she heard a
rumor in town that Justin's proposing to me when he
gets into town, and that people seem to think the rumor
started with you!"

Suz's hair stuck up a bit wildly as one of the babies
pawed a tiny fist through it. "I didn't say anything about
a proposal, exactly. I just told a few people that you were
warm to Justin, warmer than you let on. And that you
couldn't wait for him to come back."

"Suz!" Mackenzie was horrified. "Someone will tell
Justin when he gets back—you know how BC is! In fact,
someone will probably congratulate him on our upcom-
ing wedding!" She gasped. "Or, worse, they might start
planning it!"

"That's probably already happening," Suz said. "You
know that BC believes in wedding preparedness. Keeps
the threat of elopements at bay. We're nothing if not a
man-friendly town, and weddings are celebrated like
ancient Roman feasts."

"You just can't do that," Mackenzie said. "You can't
stoke the gossip pot on purpose."

"But it's so much fun. And it was worth it to see the

look on Daisy's face. Oh, if you could have only seen it, Mackenzie. It was like watching a cake fall." Suz giggled, not sorry at all. "I believe in stretching the truth when necessary."

Mackenzie looked down at Holly, who somehow tugged a smile out of her no matter how upset she was with Suz at the moment. "It accomplished nothing. I'll be surprised if Justin even comes back to the Hanging H." She kissed her baby's head, then smiled at the other three. "I love these babies so much. It's hard to think about anything bad happening when I'm with them."

"What will you do, though, if Justin has to go back to Montana permanently?" Suz asked, her eyes round.

The sound of a motorcycle ripping up the drive stopped the practical answer Mackenzie had been about to make. The back door flew open.

"Ha! You think you're so smart," Daisy told the sisters. "You put out a rumor that Justin is taken, that he's even altar-bound. But funny thing," she said triumphantly. "He was in town today, and he specifically told Cosette and Jane that he has no intentions whatsoever of getting married. To you," she said to Mackenzie. She took a second to let that sink in. "Which means the field is wide, wide open, because if he's back, and you haven't even seen him yet, and the first place he went once he got back was into town, he's not too worried about returning to the Hanging H." She grinned. "Which also means that since he's been living here for a couple of months, and you've had him all to yourself, and apparently have made no impression whatsoever, you won't mind if I offer him a little bit of my own sugar," she said. She shot Suz's way, "I recall you saying something about your sister being all ready to sugar Justin up when he got back, but, obviously," she said, smiling at Mackenzie, "he's not too excited about *that* brand of sweet."

Suz looked like all the air had been taken out of her. Mackenzie shrugged and handed Daisy Holly. "Burp her, Daisy."

She bent down and picked up Haven from the play-pen, cooing at her.

"Is that all you have to say?" Daisy demanded. "'Burp her, Daisy?'" she mimicked. She patted the baby on the back, making a sour face when Holly did indeed burp. "Peeuw. She smells like day-old bread." She handed the baby over to Suz.

Mackenzie laughed and handed her Haven. "Try this one. Maybe she smells different."

"I am not here to burp your babies," Daisy said. Haven burped like a sailor before Daisy even really got a pat going, spitting up a little on her shoulder. "Okay, I get it. You were just hoping one of them would do that. Very funny."

"Not really." Suz got up to take Haven, and Mackenzie handed Daisy a cloth so she could clean her dress. "We just press everyone into action who comes into our home. All hands on deck, as they say."

"No, thank you," Daisy said, when Mackenzie tried to hand her Hope.

"You'll like this one. She's friendlier than the other two," Mackenzie said, and, to her surprise, Daisy took the baby.

"She is soft," Daisy said reluctantly, patting her back. "But back to Justin—"

Justin knocked and walked in the back door. Mackenzie thought he'd never looked so handsome—a fact that wasn't missed by Daisy as she twirled close to him with Hope.

"Welcome back, Justin," Daisy exclaimed. "And this little dumpling says welcome back, too!"

Justin smiled and took Hope from her. His gaze locked on Mackenzie, and she felt it right in her gut. Couldn't look away. Wished the two of them were alone in the kitchen so she could—

Then Daisy's words returned her to sanity. Clearly Mackenzie and Justin had been the subject of town gossip, and no doubt he felt awkward about it. "Hello, Justin," Mackenzie said. "It's good to see you."

"It's good to be back."

"Are you back for good?" Daisy asked, sidling nearer to him. "I sure hope so!"

"Depends on what the boss lady says." He flashed a smile at Mackenzie. Mackenzie smiled back, relaxing a little. Maybe Daisy was exaggerating. Maybe the gossip hadn't been on full boil in Bridesmaids Creek.

"You'll never believe what Daisy's father has talked me into," Justin said.

Mackenzie stiffened. "Robert Donovan?"

"Well, if it has anything to do with the Donovans, I'd recommend you steer clear," Suz said, sending a purposefully sweet smile Daisy's way.

"Hush, Suz, let Justin talk," Daisy said, and Mackenzie poured him a glass of iced tea and cut a slice of apple pie, which she put in front of him, taking Hope from him so he could eat. Their hands brushed as she took the baby, and, just for a second, it felt like he felt the same thing she did: a spark.

A very hot spark that was eager to flame to life.

"Robert Donovan says I need to do a run down Best

Man's Fork for charity," Justin said. "That's some kind of race thing, right?"

Mackenzie stared at Justin, recognizing at once where this was going. "It's a race."

"Yeah." He nodded. "And the winner gets to donate the prize to the charity of his choice. I thought that was a great idea."

Daisy grinned at Mackenzie, her eyes sly. "There's two prizes, you might say. We have a legend here in Bridesmaids Creek—"

"We have a few legends," Suz interrupted. "Most of them are really superstitions."

"Don't ruin it," Daisy said, wrapping an arm around Justin's. "Suz is a spoilsport. I'm so glad you took Dad up on his offer."

"You would be behind this," Mackenzie said.

"Hush, you," Daisy said. "Justin, did Dad tell you how the race works?"

"I and a bunch of other guys run down Best Man's Fork, which is some kind of magical road here." Justin sipped his tea, ate a bite of pie, then reached to take the baby back from Mackenzie. "It's winner take all, your father says. Donation of five thousand dollars to a charity and a secret prize of some sort."

"The 'some sort' is the kicker," Suz said. "If you pick the right side of the fork in Best Man's Fork, you win. You win because there's a woman waiting for you at the end—if you chose the right path—and you get the trophy, the prize and the woman. Supposedly, anyway."

Justin laughed. Met Mackenzie's eyes. "And if I don't pick the right side of the fork?"

"I'll be really sad," Daisy said. "I'm one of the

women chosen this year to give the award. So I hope you run fast and pick the path where I am."

Justin looked at Mackenzie. "Are you handing out the trophies, too?"

She shook her head. "I had my turn. Tommy won that year."

"Jeez." Justin glanced at the other women. "You girls are serious about this superstition thing."

The baby in his arms got a fistful of Daisy's hair and gave it a good jerk. "Ow!" she exclaimed, moving away after disentangling the tiny fingers from her hair. "Like mother, like daughter."

Mackenzie didn't look away from Justin. Shrugging, he took another bite of pie. "I'm not much for superstitions, as I've said before. But I'm willing to play for charity. Frog's going to run, too."

"Rodriguez is running?" Suz's voice rose an octave. "He can't!"

"Why not?" Justin glanced at Mackenzie, his brows raised. "He said he was planning to donate his charity bucks to the pet shelter in town. Said they do good work."

Mackenzie took the baby from him again. "Suz wasn't asked to be a presenter, either."

"Because she's just back from Africa," Daisy said quickly. "She wasn't here when the names were chosen."

"And you want all the men to yourself," Mackenzie said. "Which is totally understandable."

"Yeah, how else are you going to get one unless you rig the game," Suz said. She sighed and got up from the table. "You've been a cheater ever since we were in school, Daisy. You haven't learned a thing." She wandered out, and Mackenzie had a funny notion her sister was going to find Frog. She put the baby in the playpen, not able to meet Justin's eyes anymore.

"I guess I'll go," Daisy said. "I'll stop by to check on you later, Mackenzie."

Mackenzie raised a brow at this sudden show of concern. Daisy smiled at Justin, rubbed his arm and floated out the door.

When she was gone, Mackenzie said, "How's your father?"

"Better. He's going to be fine."

She ate him up with her eyes, wishing she weren't annoyed like all heck that he'd gotten roped into the Best Man's Fork run. Maybe Justin was right: all superstitions were silly.

Bridesmaids Creek lived on its fairy tales and legends. It was a great part of what brought tourists to the town. "It's nice of you to participate in the charity run, but are you needed back home?" She was almost afraid to hear the answer. She steeled herself to hear that his family needed him to return to Montana for good.

"I'm back permanently. Or for as long as you need me here."

Forever. Was that an option? She didn't dare speak it out loud. Darn Daisy had shaken her confidence with her tale that Justin had supposedly said he wasn't looking for a relationship. "You have to watch out for our small-town functions. They're all designed to get men to our town to settle down." Mackenzie smiled at Justin. "BC is a very man-friendly town—I'm sure you've heard by now. We have the Best Man's Fork run, the Bridesmaids Creek swim, which is guaranteed to bring every hopeful bride a husband in a matter of months, and a few other traditions we cherish."

Justin got up and crossed to her. "I have a tradition I cherish."

Mackenzie stared up at him, aware that he was standing very close to her, in her space. Wished he was closer. Mouth-on-hers close. "Oh?"

"Yeah. And this is it."

Chapter 16

Suddenly Justin's mouth was on hers, kissing her, tasting her as if he'd missed her almost as much as she'd missed him, which wasn't possible. Mackenzie leaned into him, wrapping her hands in his jacket, wishing she could crawl into his arms and tell him how much she'd thought about him, but she let her lips do the talking as she kissed him back.

"You have no idea how badly I wanted to do that," Justin said, drawing back. "I thought Daisy and Suz would never leave so I could."

He smelled like wood and something spicy, felt hot in her hands. Mackenzie's heart raced, shocked by the adrenaline of his unexpected kiss. "Kiss me again. Don't stop."

He smiled. "I plan to kiss you much more, no worries about that. But right now, I come bearing gifts for the girls."

She let him go, though she didn't want to, watching as he went out to his truck, then came back inside with four small stuffed animals. A pink giraffe, a white bunny, a pink-and-white-striped bear and a soft, cream-colored dog, all terry cloth and perfectly sized for the playpen or the babies' cribs. Mackenzie watched Justin "give" each baby her new toy, which entailed placing it beside them in the playpen. She got a little misty—she refused to call it teary—felt herself fall a bit more in love.

"Thank you," Mackenzie said.

"For what?" He glanced up at her but didn't stop showing the babies their new toys. Young as they were, they definitely seemed to know that something new was being introduced into their lives.

"The gifts." She took a deep breath. "And for coming back." That was the greatest gift of all.

He shook his head and smiled. "There was no question I'd be back."

Her heart jumped—there was no other word for it. Everything he was saying was so completely the opposite of what she'd heard from Daisy, which was so like her to spread doom and gloom designed to make you doubt yourself.

But Justin was in her kitchen, cozying up to her babies—to say nothing of the amazing kiss he'd given her—and Mackenzie decided it was time to say exactly what was on her mind. Leave no stone unturned.

"I'm glad you're back. I was worried about your dad—"

"Nah. He's strong as an ox." Justin took a seat on

a stool, shrugging. "Surprisingly, it was Dad who told me I should stay right here."

"Really?" She sat across from him, trying not to act like she was starved for another kiss, which she was.

"Yeah. Said I seemed happy. That my job agreed with me. Told him I had four little bosses and they kept me pretty busy."

Oh, God, that sounded good. Drew a smile from her. "The girls keep everyone busy."

"Daisy still causing trouble?"

So he'd noticed. "She goes from wanting to sue me to pretending to be my friend. When everything gets quiet with Daisy, I know a shoe is about to drop. It's all right. Daisy's got her group and her father, and the rest of us work around them."

"I heard about her petition."

"News does travel fast."

He nodded. "I've learned that about this town."

She felt a little warm, not quite a blush, but enough to wonder if he was teasing her about Suz's enthusiastic bragging about Justin and Mackenzie being a hot item. "Yes."

"I have an idea about Daisy."

"Don't worry about Daisy. She's always been this way." He had enough on his mind without having to worry about protecting her from a rival she completely understood.

"I'm not the slightest bit worried. So this fork-to-the-altar gig—"

"Best Man's Fork. It's a road that splits in two. You have to choose which path to take, sort of like Robert Frost's 'The Road Not Taken.'"

"And the gag is that a woman is waiting at the end of one lane, in this case Daisy."

She nodded. "This is what I hear."

"So you wait on the other lane. Make things interesting." He grinned. "Two rivals, two lanes, bachelors running wild for charity? That ought to liven things up for BC, right?"

Mackenzie smiled, aware that he was teasing. "That's the purpose of a manhunting scheme."

He winked at her, and Mackenzie couldn't help smiling back. He was just so darn sure of himself. "Who's in charge of this charity gig?"

"Cosette and Jane usually head it up."

"I'll tell them I want the rules changed to include you. School-yard rivals on the Fork." He got up to put his dishes in the sink. "Things will really get interesting if I should run down Daisy's side."

"Interesting, indeed."

"I have to go put up some feed I bought in town. I meant to get it before I left. Saw Ralph Chatham, by the way. Filled me in on the petition."

"I wasn't going to mention it. It's not important."

"It is if the Donovans are trying to drive a stake through your haunted house." He looked at her. "You wouldn't let them do that, would you?"

She shook her head.

"My guess is at least thirty percent of the nay votes on the petition were coerced."

The sting and hurt she'd felt at reading some of the names—her friends' names—on the petition began to melt away. "Why do you say that?"

"It was just something Mr. Chatham said. He'd received a visit from Donovan, as had Monsieur Matchmaker." Justin went to the door. "All of them received pressure from Donovan."

"Pressure?"

"You know Donovan owns a lot of this town. That's his deal, turn it into Donovan, Texas."

Mackenzie blinked. "How do you find all this out?"

"I talk to people." Justin grinned. "And I know that running a ranch like this isn't a game of bean bags. Small towns have their conspiracies and they pick sides. You have most on your side. Donovan has the money." Justin shrugged. "Money is a powerful tool."

"What a creep." She felt sorry for the people he'd leaned on, all in the name of taking over her ranch.

"Yeah, well, don't let him win. I've got my chips on you."

The back door opened, and Ty strode in.

"I thought I'd find you guys here," Ty said. "Heard you were back and—" He glanced down at the babies. "Is it my imagination or have they grown since I saw them last?"

"What's up, matchmaker?" Justin demanded.

"Matchmaker?" Ty looked confused until he saw Justin glance at Mackenzie. "Oh. I wasn't really playing matchmaker. Mackenzie needed help out here—you needed a job. I don't mess with Cosette's deal. That's bad juju."

"Sure," Justin said. "Why are you here?"

Ty glanced around the kitchen, and Mackenzie thought he looked a little wild-eyed, even for Ty. "I just heard in town that Cosette and her husband are getting a divorce!"

Mackenzie's jaw dropped. "That's not possible. You heard wrong. That's a mean rumor."

Ty sank onto a stool, dejected. "It's true. They're having financial problems. Donovan leaned on Philippe. Apparently Cosette didn't know that Philippe had gotten a lien on the store that he owns. It's bad, man." He looked at Justin desperately. "Without Madame Matchmaker and Monsieur Unmatchmaker, this town loses a lot of its magic. You may not believe in superstition, you can laugh all you like at our traditions and Jane's fortune-telling skills and Cosette's matchmaking games, but here we believe in stuff." His voice dropped, and Mackenzie could tell confident Ty was truly shaken. "This town runs on the power of positive thinking, man. You gotta do something!"

"I've got to do something?" Justin asked. "Like what?"

"I don't know. Help me think, for God's sake." Ty ran a hand through his short, bristly hair. "We have to put the magic back in BC or it's all over. No one comes to just another small town, a dot on the map, where there isn't any belief, wonder and magic."

Mackenzie patted Ty's shoulder, cut him a slice of pie and poured him some tea. "Poor Cosette. This is awful. For Philippe, too." She felt terrible.

"Hard times hit us all," Ty said, more low than she'd ever seen him.

"Are you sure they're filing?" Mackenzie asked, hoping this was just an overblown bit of gossip. Justin's gaze landed on her, and she saw that he looked as concerned as Ty.

"I got it from the courthouse. And then Jane Chatham. Not to mention Daisy." He practically growled the name. "Robert Donovan is going to buy up every inch of retail in our town. I hear he's planning on pressuring the planning and zoning committee to redraw the town square. And when that happens, we're lost. He'll open bars and God knows what else. We'll be nothing but *commercial,*" he said, alarmed.

"Take a deep breath. Eat your pie," Justin said. "Let us think."

"I feel awful for Cosette. And Philippe. It makes so much more sense that he signed Daisy's petition."

"And that's another thing." Ty waved his fork. "There's going to be no haunted house this year."

"What?" Mackenzie felt comforted when Justin put a hand over hers for a brief moment. "Why?"

"Apparently you have to have all kinds of new licenses for that. Everything you can imagine. Donovan's got this all figured out. He's prepared to tie up every single permit and license until the day the dinosaurs return. Lawyered up like mad."

Mackenzie shook her head. "He can't do that. One man can't ruin everyone's business."

"Donovan can. He just signed a major deal with a big chain of bars and liquor stores to bring their business here. You can bet there'll be strip clubs and—"

"Stop," Mackenzie said. "You're going to make yourself ill." She felt sick herself. "What can we do?"

"What can we do?" Ty asked rhetorically. "It's David against Goliath." He shook his head sadly. "When word gets out about all this, there really will be no magic left in Bridesmaids Creek, our little town that was built on fairy tales and wedding vows." He sighed deeply and hung his head. "It's going to take a miracle to keep our town from becoming a blot on the map instead of the shining star that it is."

Justin slid his arm around her shoulders and thumped

Ty on the back in commiseration. Magic and wonder, belief and superstition wouldn't last long in a town that would be overrun by commercialism in the not too distant future. Mackenzie left Justin's side and went to pick up Hope, who'd begun thrashing and letting out little cries, no doubt disturbed by Uncle Ty's dire tone. Justin picked up Haven, and Ty sighed as he got up to retrieve Heather. "Sorry, baby doll—you drew short straw," he told Holly, but Justin reached in and scooped her up, too. Ty muttered, "Oh, so that's how it's done," and rain started to fall outside, first a slight pitter-patter, then a full-blown rainstorm. Mackenzie told herself that rain brought beneficial gifts.

The thought raised her spirits.

"I'm going to kill him," Ty muttered with dark determination. "Donovan must *die*."

Chapter 17

"Whoa, buddy," Justin said. "It's not that bad. No one needs to die."

"I meant of natural causes," Ty said. "Soon."

"That's not the answer." Mackenzie looked at Justin, and he felt his heart pound. This was why he'd come back—Mackenzie and her daughters. "The answer is finding a way to beat the Donovans fair and square."

Spoken like the resilient fighter she was. Mackenzie had no idea what she was up against. But this was a woman who'd had four children with barely a complaint—he couldn't remember ever hearing her down and out about anything. She just kept rising to meet each challenge.

"Yeah, well, I came back here to win," Ty said. "I brought you here to help, not weenie out," he said to Justin. "You're a rebel, right? So get to rebelling here like you did on the rodeo circuit. By the way, how's the knee?"

Justin sank down on a stool. Mackenzie took the one next to him, cooing to the baby she held but still managing to press against his side, bulwarking him against Ty's idiocy.

It felt great.

"I saw the ortho guy while I was gone. The knee is good as new, for a twenty-seven-year-old rodeo rider, anyway."

"Well, I'd applaud and be happy that you can ride again, but you're not leaving here, and I'm not hitting the road to hunt up recruits. We're staying right here and helping Mackenzie and Suz beat the Donovans like a drum." Ty stabbed the counter with his finger, emphasizing his point.

"Ty, what exactly do you want Justin to do? How is he supposed to rebel? He's not from here," Mackenzie pointed out.

"Fair point. But sometimes an outsider's perspective is very helpful. Then again, Justin could become one of us," Ty said.

"And how would I do that?" Justin asked, instantly realizing he'd played right into Ty's harebrained game.

"Well, you'd marr—"

"No, he wouldn't." Mackenzie glared at Ty. "Look. I know about the matchmaking ad, Ty. And I know why you really sent Justin out here to help me. You claimed I needed help on the ranch, but you really wanted him to help me to the altar. Ty," she said, and Justin could practically feel her annoyance, "I've known you all my life, and I know your heart is in the right place, but please butt out."

Justin had gone still when he'd realized Ty's best suggestion was that he marry Mackenzie—but he was even more stunned that the idea didn't sound as ridiculous as it should. Shouldn't he be yelling at Ty, telling him marriage was the last thing he wanted?

Except it wasn't.

On the other hand, Mackenzie didn't sound all that warm to the idea—and who could blame her? Her ex had just tried to sue her for her ranch.

"Justin?" Ty said. "You've gotten awfully quiet over there."

Mackenzie didn't want to marry him. He could tell by the way she'd said it. Why did that feel like it cut him off somewhere around the knees?

Justin got up. "I'm fine," he said. He laid the babies gently back in the playpen, nodded to Mackenzie and Ty. "We'll get it figured out," he said. "I'll be back at work tomorrow," he told Mackenzie, and then he headed to the bunkhouse.

Justin regretted returning to the bunkhouse as soon as he opened the door. Frog, Sam and Squint were sitting around with several women, and one of those women was Suz, who sat in Squint's lap.

Which was all wrong on every level, because he knew darn well that if Suz had a thing going for anyone, it was the cowboy she called Rodriguez. He counted nine women and some men he didn't know. The fact that there were various stages of dress in the room indicated some kind of strip game was going on.

He reminded himself that Suz was very young—twenty-three—and she'd just gotten back from a Peace Corps tour in Africa, and he'd been a helluva lot wilder than she was when he was her age. "What the hell?" he demanded, his question directed to his three bunkmates.

"Join us," Sam said, and Justin shook his head.

"I don't think so." He looked at Suz. "What are you trying to do, kill these guys?"

She shrugged. "I didn't put this party together. I'm just livening it up."

At least she was fully dressed or he would have had to mess up his bunkmates big-time for stepping over the line with the boss's little sister. By the clearness of her eyes and the fact that her glass of wine had barely been touched, he figured Suz was a latecomer to the party. "All right, everybody out."

"Hey," Frog said, "we're developing our community relations."

"You dork." Justin jerked a thumb at the door. "Everybody out. If we want to get to know you, we'll do it with our clothes on."

The room vacated with no small amount of grumbling. When it was just his bunkmates and Suz left, Justin said, "We're going to plan how to help Mackenzie. You guys are not going to go rogue by making a play for the female population. And you are not going to encourage them in any of their hijinks," he said to Suz, "because your sister is up to her ass in alligators."

"Aye, aye, Cap'n sir," Suz shot back. "I was over here keeping these guys in line, by the way, not encouraging them."

She'd been keeping a careful eye on Rodriguez, if he had to bet. But whatever story she wanted to tell, Suz wasn't his problem. "Here's what I'm suggesting. This Best Man's Fork dog-and-pony show is something we need victims—I mean, participants—for. So you three are going to run with me." He waved at the three bunk-mates who had become his brotherhood, not unlike his rodeo brotherhood, except maybe a little less focused. A little less sane. He took a deep breath. "The four of us are going to do this."

Frog pulled his black T-shirt on. Justin figured he'd gotten there just in time, before more clothes were shed. Squint was only missing a belt, and Sam was missing his hat as he lounged in his chair like he'd been about to throw down a winning hand.

"You can't win," Sam said. "You have a gimp knee." He held up a hand as Justin was about to debate the point. "Speak whatever baloney you wish, and I heard all about you seeing your doc at home. Supposedly." Sam grimaced. "You didn't see a doctor because there wasn't time, and your knee isn't good enough for you to win. You know Daisy's going to put her band of rowdies up against you. You need us," he said, pointing to Frog and Squint, "to weight this in your favor."

Suz stared at him, her eyes huge. "Tag team? Relay? How are you going to do this if you can't run? The town blue hairs have their rules, and they're pretty tight."

Justin sat down and grabbed their cards to lay out a fork shape on the table. "Your sister will be here," he said, pointing to the ace of hearts.

"Daisy, you mean," Suz said.

"We're going to do this fun run a little differently. Mackenzie will be here, and Daisy will be here." He put the ace of clubs to indicate Daisy on the other fork. "The four of us will be here." He laid the four jacks at the beginning of the fork in the road.

Suz glanced at Rodriguez, clearly weighing whether

she wanted him running this race, where he might end up in Daisy's arms. Justin frowned.

"Explain this Best Man's Fork thing to me," he said. "I may not have the full significance."

"It's all about marriage," Suz said. "Every man who's made the run and chosen the proper path that leads to the woman has ended up married to her within thirty days."

"That's not possible," Justin said. The other three men stared at Suz, clearly calculating if making this run could be detrimental to their bachelorhood.

"It's a matter of town record. Go ask Jane Chatham for the book," Suz said. "She keeps a ledger of the date of each event in this town and what weddings may result from said event. She also keeps dates of divorces, in the back of the book, in order to discover if marriages stick or fail after BC's illustrious events."

"And?" Justin demanded, curious. Maybe he didn't want to get involved in something that had a high fail rate.

Suz smiled. "Scared?"

This woman very well could end up being his sister-in-law one day. Justin sighed, raising a hand at her teasing giggle. "Not scared. Looking to be informed. Information is power."

"Two percent."

Justin leaned back. "Two percent of these wedded couples didn't work out."

"Exactly. My sister. It is what it is." Suz shrugged. "They shouldn't have gotten married in the first place."

"Why?" Sam asked. "They had kids."

"Yeah, but Mackenzie was never in love with Tommy." She swept the fork of cards off the table, then shuffled the deck. "Tommy just wanted to marry the town's favorite daughter. Then he spooked because of the babies. No Best Man's Fork, no Bridesmaids Creek swim, can predict whether a man has a chicken side or not."

Justin frowned. Personally he thought the little girls were a huge bonus in his life. He loved those babies. When he'd been in Whitefish, he couldn't wait to get back to them and Mackenzie.

If this was the way things were done in Bridesmaids Creek, then he planned to win. "I don't have a chicken side."

"That I believe." Suz grinned at him. "It remains to be seen how fast you are. I can tell you right now that Daisy's going to be ticked when she finds out you've rigged the game with a fifty-fifty chance by putting Mackenzie in the other fork. Expect a formal protest. However, I'm willing to help you any way I can. Inside the rules, of course."

"Let me get this straight," Squint said. "I don't know why Daisy's using you for this event, because quite frankly, I'd be a more exciting candidate." He glared at Justin. "But if you're planning to secretly put Mackenzie on the other side of the game, I'd carry you on my back to get you over the finish line."

"I can run," Justin said. "Don't worry about me."

Sam looked at him doubtfully. "I guess we could make one of those chariot things. Like a litter or one of those Iditarod thingamabobs with the mush dogs." He grinned at Justin. "We'd drag you up to the finish line in record time."

"*Or,*" Frog said with great bravado, "we'll run the

race to the finish line just to secure the win, then double back and get Justin."

Justin laughed. "Double back and get me?"

"We won't let you down, bud," Frog said earnestly. "We won't let anyone else get your girl."

"Get my girl?" Justin's brow wrinkled. "That's not what this is all about. I'm trying to support Mackenzie. And Suz and the Hanging H. Bridesmaids Creek, in general." He raised a brow at Suz's giggle. "I'm protecting her against the Donovans."

"And what if you win the race and Mackenzie is in the fork you choose? Are you prepared for what happens in thirty days or less?" She gave him a Suz smirk. "I should warn you that some of the participants just went ahead and eloped that very night, as soon as the race was completed."

"Whoa," Frog said. "Maybe I don't want to run. What if I win Mackenzie?"

"No, no, no," Justin said. "We're a team. My team. You guys are just backup. You're just—"

"We're the guarantee," Sam said. "We get it. We just want to make sure you're not going to make us do the deed, too."

"What if I—we, the three of us—" Frog pointed to his buddies "—what if we choose the wrong fork?" His brows rose. "Daisy's fork?"

"That's just not going to happen," Justin said. "I have a sixth sense about these things."

"No, you don't," Suz said. "Even I know you don't believe in those things. You've said so a hundred times. In fact, this whole race, the only reason you're participating in it is that you believe it's a bunch of hokum."

"True," Justin conceded.

"It's just a charity event in which you're determined to beat out the Donovans," Suz said. "Which is all very noble except that my sister's heart is at stake. What will happen if you pick Daisy's lane? Just because you don't believe in the legend doesn't mean everybody else in Bridesmaids Creek doesn't. Very strange things happen on that road, and there's a reason those superstitions have come to pass. You've heard the saying, where's there's smoke, there's fire?" She studied Justin. "For every action, there's a reaction. It would be a bad reaction if you end up as Daisy's trophy."

"Won't happen."

"Because you think it's dumb. Because you don't believe," Suz argued. "In that case, I'll just take my sister's place."

"Hey!" Frog exclaimed. "Suz on one side, Daisy on the other side? Perforce the road not taken?" He looked distinctly uncomfortable. "In that case, I'll kneecap Justin."

Justin sighed, ignoring Frog's outburst. "That would work, Suz. You're a Hawthorne. Technically, you're single, a never-married bachelorette. It would work." He shook his head. "Anyway, it's not that I don't believe. I'm a participant, a bystander, new to this town. I don't have to embrace everything. I just play along."

Mackenzie walked in, and just the sight of her made Justin smile. "What are you guys doing?" she asked.

"Justin's trying to weasel," Suz said. "Who's watching the babies?"

"Jade and her mom came over," Mackenzie said, glancing around. "If you're going to play cards, you're welcome to do it at the house." She looked at Justin, and it felt like someone hit him with a bag of rocks.

He was in love with this woman.

"Are you being a weasel about something?" Mackenzie asked.

"I don't think so," he said. "We're trying to figure out how to win this race and stay inside the rules."

"He's sandbagging the race by having these three doofs run with him," Suz explained. "That way, he's inoculated from the whole wedding-in-thirty-days issue of the run, but he gets to be the big hero, too."

Mackenzie met Justin's gaze. "The way the Best Man's Fork run works is that one man makes a run to find a woman with whom he's truly in love. If he picks the right path and she's waiting at the end of the race for him, they're meant to be together. If he picks the road with no woman at the end, he might as well just keep on running."

Justin laughed. "I like my way better. The purpose is to win this thing, right? I don't want to win Daisy. So you're going to be on the other side. These three guys are going to run with me."

"On account of Justin's wonky leg," Suz explained. "Here's the thing he's not saying about this whole deal. Justin doesn't believe in the legend, but he wants to give it a trial run, you might say. Just in case it's true. But no one will ever know who is meant to be with you—or Daisy—because there'll be four runners. So basically it's just a charity run on a pretty day."

Mackenzie smiled. "Sounds fair to me."

Justin perked up. "Really?"

"Yeah. Let's do it Justin's way. No matter what happens, we win." She glanced at Justin. "Although you realize you're taking a terrible chance, Justin. You could end up married in thirty days. To Daisy. Fifty-fifty chance."

"Nope." He shook his head. "That's the good part about these goofs running with me. The curse will land on one of them. Probably Sam."

"Hey!" Squint sat up. "Who said it would be a curse?"

"I'm going up to the house to talk to Jade," Sam said. "She hasn't been around in a while, and I think she might have a little thing for me and is trying not to show it."

He departed. Justin glanced at Suz and Mackenzie. "Does she have a thing for Sam?"

"I doubt it very seriously." Suz stretched. "None of the four of you are long-timers here. Big *S*'s on your foreheads that stand for short-timers." She got up and whacked Frog lightly on the arm. "I'm going to be at that race. And if you run down the road where Daisy is, you might as well just keep on running, Rodriguez. Because you won't like what you get from Crazy Daisy."

She went out the door.

"Wow," Frog said. "Your sister scares me a little. In a good way. Pretty sure I like it."

Justin had had enough. He took Mackenzie's arm and pulled her outside, walking her away from the house. "Since it's about time to milk the cows—"

"We don't have dairy cows."

"Since it's about time to get up and drink our morning coffee," Justin said, "can you spare five minutes before you have to get back to the babies?"

"Maybe. Why?" Mackenzie asked.

"Mainly I want to make out with you." He pulled her into his arms, kissing her long and slow and deep. Sighed when she wrapped her arms around him, inhaled the sweet perfume of her hair and the softness of her skin.

"Suz says you're trying to rig the game your way," Mackenzie said.

"She's right. Every game has a better way to win it, you know. I'm not going to let the Donovans win."

"What's it to you?"

"What's it to me? I think BC's starting to weave its spell around me, that's what. And I happen to know a beautiful woman I feel like slaying dragons for."

"Very romantic." She cuddled up to him. She felt like part of his own body, his own breath. Justin closed his eyes, felt her trace his lips with her fingertips.

"So, listen. How does this end, when I win?" Justin asked.

Mackenzie smiled. "When you win, the Donovans slink off to figure out their next move. It's the never-ending chess game."

"I mean me and you. I try not to make too many moves on you, because of a thousand different reasons, not the least of which is you're the boss lady and everything else, although I think I'm past that. But how does this end?"

"Everything else?" She studied him. "What does that mean?"

"You've got the ex-husband trying to sue you, et cetera, et cetera, and being a general pain in the ass." Justin didn't stop himself when his hands somehow wandered down to her waist. "I guess I've figured you might not be interested in a—"

She kissed him. "Win the race. Then we'll find out how this ends."

Chapter 18

The day of the race dawned clear and beautiful; the sun warming everything in its path with rich, soft rays. Justin felt good about today. Really good.

It was a town-saving kind of day.

His knee felt great. In fact, he felt like a warrior of old, like he could ride bulls until the moon came up again.

"Hey, stud," Daisy said, flouncing past him when he came out of the bunkhouse.

Trouble was up, and she was wearing a smile. "Hello, Daisy," he said cautiously. "Isn't there a rule about how the runner and the prospective bride shouldn't see each other the day of the race?"

She shrugged one dainty shoulder, tossed her bronze locks. "Rules were made to be broken, weren't they? And you're a rebel, right? That's what they say around

the rodeo circuit, anyway." She went off, banged on
the kitchen door and was allowed entrance. Justin hung
back, deciding to delay his morning coffee and muf-
fin with the babies—and of course their sweet mother.

Nothing good could come of seeing the woman he
loved with the woman who intended to sabotage her
on the big day.

Daisy had no idea they were intending to slip Mackenzie into the opposite fork. A decoy, as it were.

History was about to be made in BC.

Justin checked his watch. Two hours before he gathered up his team, put on his running shoes and got ready
to prove everybody in Bridesmaids Creek wrong.

There was no such thing as a charmed and lucky
road.

No such thing as a creek with mystic powers.

All there was was hard work. Determination. And
a desire to win.

That was how you made magic.

"Good morning, Mackenzie," Daisy said with a smile
that somehow grated on Mackenzie's nerves right off
the bat. "How are the babies?"

"The girls are fine. They're just down for a nap."
Mackenzie glanced at the baby monitor to make sure
she'd switched it on. The girls had gotten into a routine
that was almost regular, no easy feat with four of them.
Somehow they seemed to have an intuition about each
other. When one was upset, they all got upset. Happiness seemed to settle over them as a general mood, as
well.

They'd come a long way.

"So today's the big race." Daisy looked at her. "It's

like being crowned the king and queen of homecoming, only this is for real."

Mackenzie looked at her. "Whatever." She went to wash up the baby bottles in the sink.

Daisy cocked her head. "You seem very unconcerned about Justin running the Best Man's Fork. I'm the prize, you know."

"Daisy, there isn't a magic spell on earth strong enough to get Justin anywhere near an altar that you're standing at."

Daisy laughed. "You're sure?"

"Positive." She checked the pound cake and the level on the tea, her mind on what she needed to leave behind for Jade and Betty's comfort. "Justin sees this as a charity function. The legend eludes him."

"That's because he's not from here. He doesn't understand how this town works."

"He's got a pretty fair idea." And he'd returned. Mackenzie smiled.

"You seem awfully confident."

"Look." Mackenzie turned to face Daisy just as Justin came in the back door. "Let me spell this out for you. You and your father and your gang can do anything you want to do to me, but you can't take the thing from me that I love most. You can't take my children, and you can't change who I am. You can talk about the man who died at our haunted house—"

"Was murdered," Daisy inserted.

"Never proven," Mackenzie snapped. "You can spread all the gossip and lies you want, and I'm still going to wake up every day being the same old Mackenzie Hawthorne my parents raised me to be. Which is more than you can take, because that's exactly what you're missing. Your spirit is damaged."

"Excuse me," Justin said. "I was going to grab a piece of that pound cake and maybe some coffee." He looked at Daisy. "Shame you picked me to be your runner. I'm really slow. Did anybody tell you they used to call me Turtle in high school?"

"What I heard," Daisy said, "is that you once ran a mile in under four minutes just to prove you could."

Mackenzie smiled at Justin. "I'll cut you some cake and get you some coffee. 'Bye, Daisy."

"I didn't come by just to talk," Daisy said. "I came by to let you know that there's going to be a tea after the race at The Wedding Diner. Held in our honor by Madame Matchmaker and Monsieur Unmatchmaker."

"I thought they were getting divorced," Mackenzie said.

"They are," Daisy said.

"Because your father ruined their marriage, the way the Donovans ruin everything."

"How is it our fault if Monsieur Unmatchmaker couldn't manage his finances?" Daisy asked. "Dad didn't have to loan him money."

"I'm sure he didn't." Mackenzie placed the cake and coffee in front of Justin.

To her absolute shock, he swept her into his lap, kissing her thoroughly.

"Wow," Mackenzie murmured.

"Um," Daisy said, "what the hell is that?"

"Collecting my prize early," Justin said.

Daisy's jaw dropped. "Are you two…an item?"

Mackenzie looked at Justin.

"Are we an item?" he asked.

"Do you want to be an item?" Mackenzie asked.

"Hey," Daisy said. "I want a different runner! You're out," she told Justin. "I'm going down right now to tell Jane Chatham and Cosette that I'm choosing a new guy to run the race."

She went out the door in a huff.

"Uh-oh. Look what you did," Mackenzie said.

"Couldn't help it." He kissed her again, this time longer.

"Guess you don't have to run today," Mackenzie said.

"Guess I don't."

"Which means I don't have to be waiting in the Fork to sabotage Daisy."

"It was such a great plan," Justin said. His hands stole up to her waist so he could tuck her closer against him.

"It was a great plan. But now that neither of us have to be at the race, we have time to do something else." Mackenzie touched his cheek, nibbled his lip, tried not to inhale him.

"Did you have something in mind?"

"I most certainly do."

"I was hoping you'd say that," Justin said.

Making love to Mackenzie was better than running a charity race for sure. It was sweet kisses and soft skin and gentle heat that grew into a fire he had no desire to control. Justin stared up at the ceiling while Mackenzie slept beside him, feeling satisfied for maybe the first time in his life.

All the old feelings of rebellion were gone. And they'd started to be erased in this house, with this woman, with her children.

Felt like the family he'd always wanted.

Not that he didn't love his family, but a man wanted his own—and this was the one he hoped to put down roots with.

If Mackenzie would have him.

She got up to dress, and he let his eyes roam wildly, drinking in every bit of smooth naked skin he could. Wondered if he could drag her back into bed before the babies awakened.

He heard a baby cry and banging at the back door at the same time. Time to get up.

"I'll get the baby," he said.

"Thanks." She kissed him and hurried down the hall.

There were excited voices coming from the kitchen. "Sounds like something fun is happening down there," he told the babies, who were gazing around, riled by Hope's crying, wondering if they should join the chorus. He picked Hope up, calmed her and then heard footsteps flying down the hall.

Mackenzie burst into the nursery. "Suz is in town and she's going to hobble Daisy for life because Daisy chose Frog—Rodriguez—to run in your place. Suz told Jade that Daisy will never walk in high heels again when she gets through with her."

Justin shook his head and resumed changing Hope's diaper. "Young lady, you have a firebrand of an aunt."

"I have to go into town." Mackenzie hurried off.

"Which means I need to go into town to keep your mother out of trouble. Would you girls like to go into town?"

"This is all my fault," he heard Mackenzie mutter.

"Your fault how?"

"Because I kissed you in front of Daisy. She decided to cut her losses."

"Hey!" Justin laughed. "I resent that. I kissed you."

"And I liked it," Mackenzie called from the other room. "But now my sister is going to turn Daisy into a pretzel."

He didn't doubt that at all. "But Frog and Suz don't have anything going on, do they?"

"No, but that won't stop Suz and Daisy. Daisy thought she was going to be homecoming queen, but Suz won. It's bad blood."

"Let's pack the girls up and let them watch their first Bridesmaids Creek brawl. Think we could make a legend about that?"

Mackenzie hurried into the nursery.

"I'll watch them," Jade called. "By the way, I can hear every word over the baby monitor. I feel a bit like a creeper. And I like the idea of a Bridesmaids Creek brawl."

"I don't want my little sister fighting over a man." Mackenzie looked at Justin. "I've got to stop her."

"That I agree with," Jade called. "People will just say that bad things happen at the Hawthorne place."

Mackenzie gasped. "She's right."

There was a lot at stake, even if he couldn't grasp the whole concept of the underlying currents. "Do we even know if Frog agreed to take my place?"

"He did," Jade said, coming into the room. "I hope you guys are decent. I didn't want to keep listening over the monitor. Feels so third wheel."

Mackenzie hugged her. "You're never third wheel. You're family."

"Go. Just hurry." Jade waved them on. "Your sister's been spring-loaded ever since Daisy started flirting with Frog. It's really weird, because I never saw Suz get giddy over a guy."

"That's true. This is serious." Mackenzie hugged Jade and grabbed Justin's hand. "You're sure you don't mind going with me?"

"Mind?" Justin smiled, feeling like a king with Mackenzie's hand in his. "I wouldn't miss it for the world."

Justin realized how serious Bridesmaids Creek was about their social events when he saw that at least half the town had shown up at Best Man's Fork, expecting a race of some type.

What they got instead was an all-out vigorous debate between Suz and Daisy, with Rodriguez clearly the focal point of the discussion. Somehow that got other ladies and gentlemen involved, and the next thing he knew, even Cosette and Philippe were standing on opposite sides of the road that branched off into the fork where the victims—or bachelors, depending on how one looked at it—went off on the adventure of a lifetime.

"The Road Not Taken," by Robert Frost. Deep stuff this town lived by.

And it got a little deeper when Suz jumped on Daisy and dragged her by her long dark hair to the ground.

"Oh, no!" Before he could stop her, Mackenzie jumped into the fray, and then it was on. He looked at Frog, whose boots seemed glued to the ground. A hundred people either yelled insults or rolled in the dirt, engaged in some kind of combat. The sheriff and his men watched from the sidelines, and Robert Donovan complained loudly to the sheriff about his daughter's handling at Suz's hands, despite the fact that Macken-zie was working as hard as she could to drag her off.

"Are you going to do something?" Justin asked Frog.

Rodriguez shrugged. "Personally, girl-on-girl con-flict is something a man probably wants to avoid. It's a no-win situation, or haven't you heard?"

"That's nice." Justin waded in, separated Suz and Daisy. "What the hell is wrong with you two?"

"I've wanted to tear you up for years," Suz said. "You just remember that, Daisy Donovan."

Daisy flounced off, straight to Frog.

Like a frog wanting out of a skillet, Frog took off. Squint and Sam looked at Justin.

"Are you going to help me separate the rest of these people?" Justin demanded.

"Not our battle," Squint said.

"Seems to be some kind of bad feelings in the gen-eral population around here," Sam said.

It wasn't his battle. Why did he feel so responsible?

Because he hadn't wanted to run. Hadn't believed in what the town believed in, what mattered to them—the legend that really covered up the last bits of hope they had that their town was going to survive.

It was falling apart.

Mackenzie ran to Suz. "Are you all right?"

Of course she was all right. Daisy was tough, but Suz was tougher. Daisy was sporting a fat lip and a scratch across a cheek, from what he could see at a distance, while Suz looked ready to go another round.

"I'm fine," Suz snapped. "It's just time someone taught Daisy Donovan a lesson, and her father, too."

That was all true. Even someone who was new to town could tell that the Donovans made consistent trouble for everyone. Even the haunted house might not ever rise from the ashes of the past.

Justin looked at the people scrabbling and arguing with each other all along the road—neighbors and friends who loved each other, when the Donovans weren't yanking everybody's chain and stealing their dreams—and took a deep breath.

"I'll run!" he yelled.

Chapter 19

Mackenzie gasped at Justin's pronouncement. Everyone within earshot quit arguing and battling, which made the rest of the people take a break to find out what was happening.

"You can't run," Mackenzie said. "You have a bad knee."

"It's fine."

No way was she allowing this to happen. If he thought for one second he was going to run with Daisy standing at the other end of Best Man's Fork, she was going to go all Suz on him. Well, not physically, of course, but definitely she was going to give him a piece of her mind.

"Not to me, it's not fine," Mackenzie said, glaring at him.

Now that someone else's annoyance was front and center, everybody grouped around to hear every word.

"I'll do the run," Justin said, holding her gaze with his, "if Mackenzie's at the end of the race."

Jane Chatham came to the front of the group, clearly in her official position as marshal and rules enforcer. "Typically it's a bachelorette who—"

"Mackenzie's single," Justin said.

"No, Justin," Mackenzie said. "If you pick the wrong road—"

"I know, I know, keep running because the charm's broken, and we won't get married in thirty days, and I might as well be cast out of society because I'll never marry." He grinned. "Did I sum it up?"

"Well, you're pretty close," Mackenzie said, "because I don't want to lose you this soon."

He grinned. "I have a feeling it'll be fine."

"It's supposed to be my run," Daisy complained loudly. "I ask for the right to put in a champion."

"A champion?" Cosette wrinkled her nose, checked the papers Jane held. "Is that in the rules?"

"I choose Carson Dare, Dig Bailey, Clint Shanahan, Red Holmes and Gabriel Conyers to run as my champions, as I'm obviously being thrown over here," Daisy announced loudly, and the entire crowd gasped.

Mackenzie glanced over at the five men in black jackets, boots and blue jeans. Of course the purpose of Daisy's plan was to keep Justin from winning. Any of those men could outrun Justin, even if he claimed his leg was whole now. "You just can't stand for anyone to be happy, can you, Daisy Donovan?"

"I'm very happy." Daisy smiled at her. "And since it's a charity race, I'll donate five thousand dollars to the charity of the winner's choice."

"Even the haunted house fund?" Justin demanded.

The crowd went totally silent.

"Sure. I don't care. One good cause is the same as another," Daisy said. "There won't ever be a haunted house, but I understand the Hawthorne ranch is underwater these days."

Mackenzie shook her head. "Actually, we're in a good place. Thanks."

"We'll see." She glanced at Suz. "Neither one of you makes any money. It can't go on forever."

Those were words straight from Robert Donovan's mouth. Justin smiled. "So, are we doing this thing or not?"

"Justin," Mackenzie said, "I really wish you wouldn't do this."

"You just go pick your side of the road." Justin winked at her. "I'll be right there."

"I don't get to pick," Mackenzie said a little desperately. "The sheriff takes the lady in his truck to the finish line. She draws a straw to determine which side she takes."

"It's okay." He kissed her. "I'll find you."

"I wish you wouldn't do this." What terrified her most was what Daisy's band of jacket-wearing rowdies would do once they got past the view of the people. The forks wound through forest and brush-lined trails. It was a five-mile run, with no shortcuts. The sheriff and Cosette and Jane had driven it several times to check the distance and condition of the road. "I don't like it."

Sam, Squint and Frog stepped up to the line. "We'll run with him," Sam said.

"We're a team," Frog said.

"Like to keep things even," Squint said, glaring at Daisy's gang.

"There's five of them and four of you," Suz said. "Are you just itching to get a beatdown?"

Frog grinned. "We kind of thought the fight was weighted toward our side."

"Very funny," Dig Bailey said.

"All right, then," Cosette said. "The rules have been agreed upon—the game begins. Everyone who wants to be at the finish line will pay the race fund five dollars, no charge for anyone under twelve years of age! Monsieur Unmatchmaker, will you please fire the starting gun?"

Philippe grinned at his wife. "I'm honored. Let's get ready to run!" he yelled, excited to be chosen.

"When's the last time one of these races was held?" Justin asked Mackenzie.

"When my ex ran it," Mackenzie said. "Although he didn't really run it so much as walk it. And he didn't get to the right lane."

"He quit," Suz interjected. "He had a blister on his heel. It wasn't a race so much as a walk."

Justin looked at Mackenzie. "So history is indeed being made today."

She grinned at him. "Actually, history is being made because there's never been a race like this one. The rules are completely changed."

"You just remember that there's never been a race like this one," Justin said, kissing her.

"How are you going to run in boots?"

He smiled. "You just get in the sheriff's truck. The people want a battle, and a battle they're going to get."

* * *

Justin wasn't stupid. He'd known when he and Mackenzie headed down here that there was going to be a race, and no man attended a race without a decent pair of running shoes. He'd tossed those in his truck, and he'd also tossed in a T-shirt.

"That's what you're running in?" Squint demanded, eyeing his jeans as the intrepid three pulled on extreme running gear. Their truck was parked beside his, providing perfect cover for their costume change.

"Yeah. I'm fine," Justin said.

Frog eyed him doubtfully. Reached over and lightly pounded his leg, scoffing in disgust. "You're still wearing that leg brace. Your leg isn't any better at all!"

"My leg is better," Justin said. "The doc said my knee would take a couple more weeks to fully heal the tear."

"That's just great," Sam said. "You can't run wearing a leg brace."

"I can run."

"Sure, Peg Leg." Frog's tone was total disgust. "You realize that if you take that brace off, your leg is frozen for a few days. You have to do therapy and crap to get the tendons and muscles and stuff back to normal. So you can't take that brace off because it won't do any good."

"I wasn't planning on taking it off," Justin said.

"Great," Squint said. "We're backing up Hopalong Cassidy. For five miles through forest and bush."

"Here's the deal," Frog said. "We've got your back. We're a team. So you run like hell and never look back, no matter what you hear behind you."

"What are you going to do?" Justin asked. They looked like they were getting ready for some kind of reconnaissance mission, all in black and camo. This was clearly just another mission to them.

"Just planning on keeping things honest," Sam said.

"We're quite familiar with the way nonbeneficial things can happen in competitive times."

"Remember," Squint said. "No looking back. Very critical to your success. You've heard about Lot's wife and the saltshaker?"

Justin forbore a sigh and eyed his stalwart companions. "I really appreciate you guys stepping up on my behalf."

"Nah," Frog said. "It's not about you. It's about the boss lady."

Justin smiled. "Yes, it is."

Mackenzie was nervous as she rode with the sheriff. Not nervous. Apprehensive.

Maybe Justin was right—maybe this whole legend thing was dumb.

Except it wasn't. Cosette, Jane and Jane's husband had been busy taking money for tickets. Most of the town had turned out, since this wasn't an event that happened often and no one wanted to be left out. It was good for the town, it was good for the people and hopefully it would be good for her and her family.

The amazing thing was that Justin had been game to do it.

"I think you like that cowboy," Sheriff Dennis said.

"I wouldn't do this if I didn't." Maybe that's why she was apprehensive—it really, really mattered to her which lane Justin chose.

"I guess we should have all known from how the race went down with Tommy that he was a mistake," Dennis said.

"It's hard for me to regret anything because of my daughters."

Sheriff Dennis smiled. "I'd feel the same way. By the way, I heard through the proverbial grapevine that Tommy was dumped. His little girlfriend went off to greener pastures."

Mackenzie shook her head. "Somehow it doesn't matter anymore."

"True love," Sheriff Dennis said happily, parking the truck near the end of the thick woods where the paths converged again. "You know, whoever dreamed this race up was a genius. We should hold one every six months just on principle."

"You know very well who thought it up," Mackenzie said. "Cosette, Philippe, Jane, her husband and you."

Sheriff Dennis laughed. "You have to build a town from something. This was as good as anything. And we started this thirty years ago. How would you know?"

"Because I remember my parents talking about it," Mackenzie said softly. "They always said they were going to try it out one day."

Sheriff Dennis patted her hand. "They'll be tickled that their daughter is getting to do it right this time." He pulled out two straws, then hid them in his beefy palms. "Pick. You either want the right side or the left side of the road. East or west, there can only be one." He extended his hands to Mackenzie. "Choose wisely, Mackenzie. I've always thought of you as a daughter. This time I want you to be happy."

Her hand hovered over his. "What made you dream up the idea of Best Man's Fork?"

"There's a best man at every wedding, isn't there?" He looked at her, his eyes twinkling. "The spotlight can't always be on the bride and groom. Guys want to get married more than you ladies think we do. And we want a big deal made of it, too!"

Mackenzie smiled. "That one." She tapped his left hand, and he opened it.

She stared at the straw in his hand. If she hadn't known better, she would have thought it sparkled. Twinkled.

"I'll be leaving you right here," Sheriff Dennis said. "Good luck, Mackenzie."

She got out. "Thanks."

"You know the drill. That right there is your path. In a few minutes, there'll be all kinds of people swarming the finish line, anxious to see if Justin chooses the right road. Have you got faith in your cowboy?"

She closed the truck door and waved goodbye. Set out for the lane she'd chosen. There was no need to answer Sheriff Dennis's rhetorical question; they both knew she did or she wouldn't be waiting here for him.

Sheriff Dennis drove away. Mackenzie pulled out her cell phone and called Jade.

"Hello?"

"How are the girls?"

"They're darling! Mom and I are having a blast. Where are you?"

"At the finish line."

"Already?" Jade gasped. "It's going to go very different this time, you know. This time it's going to be—"

"Oof," Mackenzie said as something knocked her to the ground. Her phone flew, shattering when it hit a rock.

"Daisy Donovan! What was that for?" Mackenzie sat up and glared at Daisy, who looked proud of her handiwork. "Do not make me kick your butt today!"

She jumped to her feet.

"I'm not missing out on my chance," Daisy said. "You've already had your turn. Now move."

"Move?" Mackenzie frowned. "I'm not going anywhere."

"Yes, you are. Either you get in that other lane, or I'm going to make you wish you had!"

Mackenzie raised a brow. "What are you doing?"

"I'm going to be right here when Justin arrives." Daisy pointed to the other lane. "Go."

"Why don't you go to that side?"

"Because I know this whole gig is a bunch of hooey. Either the sheriff told you which side to choose or you just called your position in to someone."

"I was checking on the babies," Mackenzie said, disgusted.

"And giving her a coded location so that she could call one of the three dunces to clue Justin in on which road to take." Daisy pointed again. "Go, or you'll regret making me lose my temper."

"Daisy, you're never going to learn. Has your scheming ever gotten you anything you wanted?"

"We'll know soon enough."

"Justin isn't going to marry you."

"He may not marry you, either. But at least I'll have the charmed legend on my side."

Mackenzie sighed. "You realize that's about as good as believing in Santa Claus."

"Which I do. He was a saint, thanks. You know, that's part of your problem, Mackenzie Hawthorne—you're not a romantic."

"And you are?" Mackenzie could feel her brows elevate involuntarily. "Daisy, this is dumb. If you want this lane so badly, you can have it."

"Good. Because I really didn't want to have to knock you out and hide you in the bushes."

There was no point in arguing with Daisy. She'd always wanted what everyone else had; nothing was going to change now. She was Suz's age, still young, but as tough as Suz could be, Daisy could be tougher. It was as if she missed a key part of her soul that most humans had that made them compassionate.

"I thought you had a thing for Frog," Mackenzie said.

"Just flirting, nothing serious," Daisy said. "Move along."

"Just flirting?" Poor Frog might have actually thought Daisy cared about him. "What about Squint? Are you just flirting with him, too?"

Something strange came over Daisy's face. "Don't talk to me about Squint. He thinks he's special."

"So he turned you down?"

"He did not turn me down." Daisy's gaze slid away. "He said he isn't available for anything resembling dating, a relationship or even friendship."

"Ouch." Mackenzie hadn't meant to say it, and once the word was out of her mouth, Daisy glowered at her.

"Get over there, and when Justin sweeps me off my feet, you accept your just desserts. You've had this coming to you for a long time." Daisy stalked around a rock, dusted it off and sat down. "Dad's going to make marrying me very lucrative for Justin."

"You live in a dream world where Daddy's money gets you what you want."

"And you live in a dream world where Daddy's money didn't. Get lost."

Mackenzie went to the other lane, a good thousand yards away, and decided she liked the way the sun dappled the trees and the light breeze touched the lane. There was a tall tree made for climbing, with a slab someone had hammered in it for a seat that rose just above the canopy. There also was a tree swing and a bench, so Mackenzie took the bench and made herself comfortable.

"What the hell are you doing?" Suz demanded, hidden by a clump of leafy bushes.

"I might ask you the same!"

"Don't look like you're talking to me," Suz instructed. "It would be frowned upon by the town busybodies. And Daisy is an epic tattletale." She looked at her sister with exasperation. "I heard the whole verbal squall. Why did you let Daisy push you around?"

"Because I don't care." Mackenzie scooted closer to the end of the bench so she could see Suz better. "She can do what she likes. It won't change my destiny."

"Well, that's serene of you. It was all I could do not to jump out of the bushes and perform major facial rearrangement on her. And your phone is totaled."

"I'll replace it. And I can handle Daisy. You've got to quit worrying. Back to why you're hanging out in the hedge?"

"Keeping Daisy kosher. I knew she'd pull something. I've known her ever since she came to BC, and she's always been a brat." Suz grinned. "Just happens to be I'm a bigger brat."

Suz was no brat. She was an angel with a good heart. "You're my darling sister, and I love you."

"Well, I wasn't going to let my big sister sit here on the biggest day of her life by herself," Suz said impishly. "I've got a good mind to go over there and do something to Daisy."

They both hesitated as the roar of vehicles heading up the road came to them.

"It's on," Suz said. "You've had your last five minutes to reflect on life as a single woman."

Mackenzie smiled. "It may not happen that way."

"Of course it will. Don't be silly. Daisy wouldn't have been so desperate to fight you for it if the legend hadn't come true every single time. Now you just sit there and think blissful thoughts. Your happy ending is on the way. By the way, this race is going to be a long one. You might want to get a nap in so you're fresh for your prince."

"Okay, I'll bite. What have you been up to?"

"Not me." Suz's face was the picture of innocence. "A little birdie told me Justin's knee is still in a soft cast. So he won't be tearing up the finish line to get to you." She grinned. "But he will."

"What are you talking about?" Mackenzie was alarmed. She hadn't seen anything on his leg. Not even when they'd made love.

"Just telling you what the birdies tell me." Suz grinned. "I think it's sweet."

She fell in love with Justin that much more, helplessly, happily in love. "Where are you going?" Mackenzie peered over the leaves that folded over where her sister's face had been.

Silence.

"Suz?"

But Suz was gone. Mackenzie smiled, thinking about how much she loved her sister. Nobody had helped her through her divorce and the ensuing bad times more than Suz.

She glanced over at Daisy to see what she was doing. No shock, she was combing her hair, primping in a mirror. Her long brown locks shone in the sun, her shapely, tanned legs daintily stretched in front of her in a skirt short enough to cause male heart failure.

While I'm wearing capri jeans, a sleeveless blouse and flat tennies, my hair in a ponytail.

It didn't matter. She'd held Justin in her arms. Even though he hadn't said the words, she knew he loved her.

She certainly was in love with him.

Mackenzie heard a squeal and commotion, and she glanced at Daisy again. Suz leaped on Daisy with a burlap bag, stuffing her in it before Ty carted her, struggling, to his truck bed and put her in it as if she were nothing more than a hay bale. He waved at Mackenzie; then he and Suz hopped in the truck and drove away.

Maybe it was cheating. Technically it was breaking the rules. Certainly she'd raised her sister to be more genteel and ladylike than to pin someone down and stuff them into a sack.

One day she'd return the favor for Suz. The very thought made her smile, and now that she was alone at the finish line of Best Man's Fork, Mackenzie suddenly felt very, very happy. In love.

As if this was the moment she'd been waiting for all her life.

Chapter 20

"Ready, set, go!" Cosette yelled and Philippe fired the starting gun, which brought a cheer from the crowd anxious to see Justin start the race.

He waved at everyone and took off at what he hoped was an impressive pace. His buddies had disappeared.

Which was fine with him. "I've got this," he muttered and headed to the fork. He didn't even hesitate; he already knew which way he was going.

He chose the left side of the fork, and a cheer went up from the crowd who'd gathered at the starting line. Justin couldn't say that this was something he'd ever imagined he'd be doing, but he was having a ton of fun. He felt like a warrior of some kind, a troubadour of old, going off to win his lady.

Which no doubt was exactly how Bridesmaids Creek intended a man to feel. Part of the fairy-tale charm and all that. Kind of silly, but if this was the way things were done here, he'd play along.

At the one-mile marker, the race monitor waved at him, offered him a water bottle, which Justin accepted, heading off without resting, determined to make a good showing.

At the one-and-a-half-mile marker—so designated by a giant heart-shaped sign posted on a tree—Justin was joined by the five doorknobs.

Daisy's gang set a pace behind him without saying a word. "More the merrier," he muttered and kept going.

They surrounded him at the two-mile marker, not touching him, but pacing along, in back and in front of him.

Annoying but not important. He had a job to do.

"Nice day, huh, fellows?" he said, just to be friendly, and then he ignored them as he tried to dismiss the fact that his knee was beginning to protest the treatment it was receiving.

Daisy's gang changed position, two on either side and one in the back. What the hell, maybe they figured they no longer needed a leader. He knew exactly where he was going, after all.

At the two-and-a-half-mile marker—another big heart-shaped sign—a commotion broke out behind him. Justin kept moving, not looking back, but his companions on either side of him did, and suddenly all hell broke loose.

Then silence.

"Don't look back, remember," he muttered and kept on going.

He ran alone after that, his thoughts busy with Mackenzie and the babies and how great it was going to feel when she told him yes. What man didn't think of the woman he loved telling him she wanted to be his wife?

He stopped dead in his tracks.

He'd *never* thought of it. Yet suddenly he couldn't *stop* thinking about it.

"Holy cow, there *is* something in the air around here." He glanced around, studying the thick foliage on either side of him. His shoes were dusty from the dirt road and his leg ached—he was far from his rodeo shape. The air was completely silent but for the occasional birdcall—mockingbird, for sure—and the sun beat down on him.

Some sixth sense or maybe even some of Bridesmaids Creek's enchantment pushed him into the woods. He crunched through tall grass and ground cover, beat back branches that rarely had experienced human contact until he got to the other road.

This was right. It was a rebel move, but he was playing a game with folks who were known to make the rules to suit themselves.

At the end of this road would be the woman of his dreams. That was how the legend went.

He ran like he'd never run before.

Justin nearly had heart failure when he saw the final race monitor a hundred yards from the finish line, because Mackenzie wasn't there. His spirits sank. He looked wildly past the monitor, barely heard the greeting offered to him and crossed the tape at the finish line, bent over to gasp for air.

He could not believe he'd picked the wrong road. He hung his head. What the hell—it was a dumb charity race. He'd made the town some money, felt like he was a newfound son they were trying to weave into the fabric of their town.

It would all work out. He'd still ask Mackenzie to marry him, and hopefully she would say yes.

She might be a little tangled up because of that business with her ex being a loser at the race and the legend not working out too well for her that first time, but he could get her past that. Somehow.

He'd just have to convince her how much he wanted to be with her and the girls, forever.

"Hi," he heard at his elbow, and Justin stood straight up. Stared into his gorgeous lady's eyes, felt the mysterious wonder of Bridesmaids Creek fill him, changing him forever.

"Mackenzie!" He swept her into his arms. "Will you marry me?"

She laughed, and it sounded like pure joy to him. "Yes! Yes, of course. I would love to be your wife."

"I'm sorry." Justin took a deep breath. "I meant to ask you more romantically with flowers, a ring, maybe some hot sex to convince you I'm the only man for you."

"That was all pretty romantic." She kissed him, and it *was* the happiest moment of his life. Justin held Mackenzie in his arms, hardly believing how perfect his world had suddenly become.

"You were supposed to be at the finish line, weren't you? I thought I'd taken the wrong road." He ate her up with his eyes, wondering if he could get her to a wedding ceremony fast enough to suit him.

"I had to get the girls." She smiled up at him, and he saw Jade and Betty with the stroller of babies waiting under a shady tree. "The babies wanted to see you win."

"I'm a dad," he said. "I'm going to be a father to four

beautiful little girls! I'm going to have four beautiful daughters and a gorgeous wife!" He laughed, hugging Mackenzie to him, his whole world opening up in a new way he'd waited his entire life to feel. Justin held Mackenzie, basking in the cheers from the townspeople who realized they were about to get their fondest wish, a wedding to attend.

"I love you, Mackenzie Hawthorne. The best thing that ever happened to me was the day Ty sent me to your ranch. I'm the luckiest man in the world."

Mackenzie laughed. "I love you, too," she said, "welcome home."

Justin grinned, reveling in the most magical, heavenly moment of his life. How had this happened to him? How had he gotten the woman of his dreams, and the family he'd always hoped he'd one day have? He looked at the smiling faces of the people around them, felt their joy as they shared this amazing moment with them. It didn't matter how the fairy tale had happened. All that mattered was Mackenzie and the daughters he loved with all his heart.

He was home at last.

Epilogue

"So what about the haunted house?" Ty asked Justin on a day that was so beautiful Justin didn't think he'd ever known a better one. Of course most of the beauty that was in his life now was thanks to Mackenzie and her babies. He grumbled, slightly nervous as Ty situated his jacket and tie, having never been a groom before, only the man running in the Best Man's Fork race just last week.

It had been worth everything he had to see the smile on Mackenzie's face when he'd chosen the right path.

He allowed Ty to stuff a pocket square in his jacket, a useless detail he felt was unnecessary for the casual wedding he and Mackenzie wanted, but Ty was a stickler for details. "Mackenzie says the haunted house is part of Bridesmaids Creek. Now that there's some confusion about whether folks really want it reopened or not—"

"Hogwash," Ty said. "That was just stuff Daisy stirred up."

True, but Justin had done his part, which was rescuing fair maidens, all five of them. Actually, they'd rescued him. Now he was going to enjoy life in their world. "Mackenzie says it's a battle she's going to let Suz handle at this point. She says if anyone can corral Daisy, it's Suz." Mackenzie had also said that her time would now be completely taken up by making love to him, and haunted houses would have to take a backseat to that.

Which made him very, very happy.

"I don't like it," Ty grumbled. "No one else has any good ideas on how to save BC. That was my best one."

"It's fine, old buddy. You did your part. You can relax now." He slapped Ty on the back. "I want to thank you for telling me about Mackenzie's fake dating ad, by the way. Madame Matchmaker better watch out for you, obviously."

Ty laughed, pleased with himself. "It wasn't fake. I just never let it go live. And that's the last thing you're dragging out of me. I can't give up all my trade secrets."

They went downstairs and made a path to the altar. Justin was amazed by how many people had arrived to see their wedding, but then he realized he shouldn't be—this was BC. Everybody was always going to be in everybody's business—which was something that no longer worried him.

"Now I just need my bride," Justin said, and on cue the three-piece orchestra of two violins and a harp began playing and the guests swiveled their heads to look for the bride.

Suz came down the aisle first, sassy in a short pink dress, unable to resist squashing Ty on the toe with her high heel before she took her place at the altar.

"What was that for?" Ty asked Justin.

"I think you're in the doghouse for not fixing her up, too." But Justin couldn't worry about his buddy right now, because Mackenzie came around the corner, escorted by Sheriff Dennis, and Justin's heart felt like it was going to explode with joy. The babies were wheeled in a white carriage hung with pretty pink-and-white bows to the edge of the altar so they could have a front-row seat, and a happy sigh went up from the guests.

Mackenzie stood beside him, a short veil gracing her midlength faint pink wedding gown, her smile all for him.

"You're beautiful," he said. "The happiest moment in my life was watching you and the babies come down that aisle." He took her hand and kissed it, and the guests sighed again. "I love you so much."

"I love you," Mackenzie said. "I do, and my girls do, too. We all do."

"Yeah," Suz whispered. "Welcome to our family."

Okay, so maybe most sisters-in-law wouldn't butt in, but it was Suz, and, frankly, he was delighted to hear that she thought he was a good thing for her sister. Mackenzie laughed and he smiled; the babies laid almost perfectly still in their pram, fussed over by Cosette and Jane, and Justin's life became a rodeo of a different kind. Bigger, better, happier.

Which was a completely happy ending for a rebel cowboy.

And if he thought he heard Ty mutter, "One down, three to go," he paid no attention to his buddy at all.

It was a most enchanted day in Bridesmaids Creek.

* * * * *

IF YOU ENJOYED THIS BOOK
WE THINK YOU WILL ALSO LOVE

HARLEQUIN
SPECIAL
EDITION

Believe in love. Overcome obstacles. Find happiness.

Relate to finding comfort and strength in the
support of loved ones and enjoy the journey
no matter what life throws your way.

6 NEW BOOKS AVAILABLE EVERY MONTH!

"I remember. I remember it all, Bethany."

Jeez. He hadn't meant for his voice to turn so serious, so reverent. But there was very little chance of hiding his real feelings when she was around.

"Me, too," she said.

For a few moments they ate in silence.

"Thanks for helping me here," she said. "You've done a lot of that since I've been back."

"Anytime. And I mean that."

"Ditto," she said.

He reached over and squeezed her hand but didn't let go. And suddenly he was looking—with that seriousness, with that reverence—into those green eyes that had also kept him up those nights when he couldn't stop thinking about her. They both leaned in at the same time, the kiss soft, tender, then with all the pent-up passion they'd clearly both been feeling these last days.

She pulled slightly away. "Uh-oh."

He let out a rough exhale, trying to pull himself together. "Right? You're leaving in a couple weeks. Maybe three tops. And I'm solely focused on being the best father I can be. So that's two really good reasons why we shouldn't kiss again." Except he leaned in again.

And so did she. This time there was nothing soft or tender about the kiss. Instead, it was pure passion. His hand wound in her silky brown hair, her hands on his face.

A puppy started barking, then another, then yet another. The three cockapoos.

"They're saving us from getting into trouble," Bethany said, glancing at the time on her phone. "Time for their potty break. They'll be interrupting us all night, so that should keep us in line."

He smiled. "We can get into a lot of trouble in between, though."

Don't miss
Home is Where the Hound Is *by Melissa Senate,*
available March 2022 wherever
Harlequin Special Edition books and ebooks are sold.

Harlequin.com

Love Harlequin romance?

DISCOVER.

Be the first to find out about promotions, news and exclusive content!

 Facebook.com/HarlequinBooks

Twitter.com/HarlequinBooks

Instagram.com/HarlequinBooks

Pinterest.com/HarlequinBooks

You Tube YouTube.com/HarlequinBooks

ReaderService.com

EXPLORE.

Sign up for the Harlequin e-newsletter and download a free book from any series at **TryHarlequin.com**

CONNECT.

Join our Harlequin community to share your thoughts and connect with other romance readers!
Facebook.com/groups/HarlequinConnection

HARLEQUIN

Heartfelt or thrilling, passionate or uplifting—Harlequin is more than just happily-ever-after.

With twelve different series to choose from and new books available every month, you are sure to find stories that will move you, uplift you, inspire and delight you.

SIGN UP FOR THE HARLEQUIN NEWSLETTER

Be the first to hear about great new reads and exciting offers!

Harlequin.com/newsletters